INK

& Intuition

F. A. SENG

2025 Staton House Paperback Edition.

Ink & Intuition. Copyright © 2025 by F. A. Seng

faseng-author.com

ISBN: 979-8-89496-367-9 (paperback)

ISBN: 979-8-89686-079-2 (hardcover)

ISBN: 979-8-89496-371-6 (ebook)

Originally Published in 2025 in the United States of America.

TO EVERYONE THAT'S TRIED TO PRAY
THE GAY AWAY.

This one's for you.

TRIGGER WARNING

This book contains explicit depictions and discussions of sexual assault, verbal and emotional abuse, including the emotional aftermath and the struggles of coping with trauma. It also explores themes of religious guilt, internalized shame surrounding homosexuality, and the conflict between personal identity and deeply ingrained beliefs. Additionally, the story includes mention of military death while deployed.

These topics are integral to the narrative and are handled with care, aiming to provide a realistic and empathetic portrayal of the complexities and pain associated with these experiences. However, they may be distressing or triggering for some readers.

Reader discretion is strongly advised. Please prioritize your mental and emotional well-being while engaging with this story. If you find these subjects overwhelming or upsetting, consider taking breaks or seeking support as needed.

Phoenix
Rising
Press

'INK & INTUITION' PLAYLIST:

1. 'Heart Attack - Rock Version' by Demi Lovato
2. 'imgonnagetyouback' by Taylor Swift
3. 'Too Sweet' by Hozier
4. 'THE DEATH OF PEACE OF MIND' by Bad Omens
5. 'Give Your Heart a Break - Rock Version' by Demi Lovato
6. 'I'm a Mess (with YUNGBLUD)' by Avril Lavigne
7. 'Misery Business' by Paramore
8. 'Euclid' by Sleep Token
9. 'The Great Escape' by BOYS LIKE GIRLS
10. 'That's What You Get' by Paramore
11. 'Just Pretend' by Bad Omens
12. 'Vacation' by Simple Plan
13. 'Fall for You' by Secondhand Serenade
14. 'Blank Space' by I Prevail
15. 'I Write Sins Not Tragedies' by Panic! at the Disco
16. 'I'm Not Okay (I Promise)' by My Chemical Romance
17. 'Addicted' by Simple Plan
18. 'My First Kiss (feat. Ke$ha)' by 3OH!3
19. '4 Ever 4 Me' by Demi Lovato

one

ALEX

March

I stand in the middle of the apartment, surveying the chaos of boxes and bags scattered across the floor. The place is mine now, and for the first time in a long while, I have the freedom to arrange things exactly the way I want. It feels strange, in a good way—like a fresh start. There are two rooms, one for me and one for my roommate and soon-to-be coworker, who has yet to arrive. But until then, I can do whatever I want with the space.

I start unpacking my books, placing them neatly on the shelves I dragged in earlier. The apartment is quiet, the kind of quiet that lets you think, lets you breathe. It's just me and my thoughts, the city humming faintly in the background through the open window. I'm not sure how to get used to living in Metro Heights.

I arrange my sketchbooks, place my favorite pencils in a jar on the small desk by the window, and try to make the place feel like home.

Just as I'm getting into the rhythm of setting things up, my phone rings, cutting through the peaceful silence. I glance at the screen—Mom. My stomach tightens. I know what's coming.

I sigh and answer. "Hey, Mom."

"Alex, have you gone to the local church yet?" she asks, her voice immediately slipping into that familiar tone of concern. No, *"How's the apartment?"* or *"How's the move?"* Just straight to the point: church.

I resist the urge to roll my eyes and keep my tone even. "No, Mom, I haven't had time yet. I've been busy getting the apartment in order. I just moved in, remember?"

There's a pause; I can feel her disappointment creeping through the line. "Alex, you need to make time. The Lord doesn't wait for anyone. You can't just ignore your faith because you're busy."

I feel my irritation rise. I've heard this speech a thousand times, and each time, it grates on me more. "I know, Mom, but I might not have time to go. I've got a lot going on. I'm starting my new job in two days and still trying to settle in here."

Her voice softens, but I can hear the steel underneath. "You have to make time, Alex. You can't just put off God. He's always watching, and He's given you so much. How can you even think about skipping church?"

I press my lips together, trying to keep the frustration from spilling out. "I'm not skipping, Mom. I just said I might not have time. I'll think about it, okay?"

But she's not letting up. "Think about it. Alex, how could you even say that? After everything the Lord has done for you, for our family? The world isn't just about work and your apartment. It's about your soul, your connection to God."

I rub the back of my neck, feeling the tension build. "Mom, I'm trying to get settled. I've got a lot on my plate right now. I'm not saying I won't go, okay? I just need some time to figure things out."

"But Alex—" she starts, her voice hitching again.

"Fine," I cut in, more sharply than I intended. I immediately regret it, but I can't help it. "Fine, I'll go to the church after I've settled into the apartment and after I start at my new job. Right now, I don't have time. I'm busy."

There's a moment of silence on the other end, and I can almost picture her sitting there, clutching the phone, her face etched with lines of worry. I hate that I have to speak to her like that, but her constant pressure is exhausting.

"Thank you, Alex," she says quietly, and I can tell she's trying to regain her composure. "Just... don't forget what's important."

"I won't," I mutter, already feeling the familiar combination of guilt and frustration bubbling up inside me. "I've got to go, Mom. I'll talk to you later."

Before she can say anything else, I hang up and toss the phone onto the bed. The room feels heavier now, the weight of the conversation lingering in the air. I stare down at the boxes I still need to unpack, but my motivation is gone.

It's always like this—her words sticking to me like glue, reminding me of the expectations I was raised with, the ones I'm still trying to break free from. I want to please her, to make her happy, but I also want to live my own life, free from the constant pressure to meet the standards of her faith.

I sit down on the edge of the bed, running a hand through my hair. I'm not even sure how I'm going to balance it all—the move, the new job, the church visits. It feels like I'm constantly being pulled in two directions, and no matter what I do, I'm disappointing someone.

I take a deep breath. "Alright, back to it," I mutter, more to convince myself than anything else. I pick up another stack of books, determined to make this place feel like my own, even if it takes a while to figure out what that really means.

I sit down on the couch and reach for my sketchbook, the worn cover familiar under my fingertips. Flipping it open, I

INK & *Intuition*

skim through the pages filled with rough sketches of buildings, statues, and other structures that have caught my eye. Each one is a glimpse into how I see the world—lines and shadows, angles and curves. I run my fingers along the lines and feel the roughness of the graphite, smelling the charcoal I use occasionally. Art has always been my escape, my way of processing everything around me.

I'm just starting to lose myself in the details of a Gothic Cathedral sketch when there's a sudden knock at the door. I snap the book shut, a little startled.

I look through the peephole, pushing my glasses up the bridge of my nose, and see a young man about my age with two large suitcases at his feet. He looks slightly out of breath, as if he's been rushing to get here. His neatly styled hair, and well-fitted button-down shirt paired with tailored slacks give him an air of effortless sophistication. A leather watch glints on his wrist, and his polished loafers look like they've never touched anything rougher than a carpeted floor. *It looks like my roommate finally showed up, and judging by his style, he's someone who probably doesn't think twice about splurging on the good stuff.*

"Hi," he says with a friendly smile as I open the door. "I'm Tommy Nguyen. You must be Alex Mitchell."

"Yeah," I reply, nodding. "I was beginning to wonder if you were ever going to show."

"Sorry about that," Tommy gives a light-hearted laugh, running a hand through his dark hair. "I missed my train and had to wait until the next day to catch another one. Got here as soon as I could."

"No worries," I say, stepping aside to let him in. "Let me help you with your luggage."

We carry his suitcases inside and set them down near the door.

"Thanks, man," Tommy says, looking around the apartment. "It's a nice place. I'm glad the company helped me find a roommate who would help me."

4

"It's the least I can do," I say with a small chuckle. He laughs, too. "Feel free to get yourself settled. I've got a few errands to run, so I'll be heading out for a bit."

"Sounds good," Tommy replies, already eyeing the empty room that will be his. "I'll start unpacking and putting things in order."

"Great. See you later, then." I grab my keys and wallet from the counter and head out the door.

As I step onto the street, I take a deep breath of the city air. This is it—my new life, my new home. The world feels full of possibilities, and I'm eager to see where it takes me.

As I stroll down the street, the sounds of the city buzz around me—cars honking, people chatting, and the distant hum of life moving at its usual pace. It's a different rhythm than what I'm used to, but I'm slowly getting the hang of it. The air is crisp, carrying a hint of smoke from the cars' exhausts.

A few blocks down, a brightly colored storefront catches my eye—a pet shop. The large windows display an array of animals, and my curiosity gets the better of me. I slow down, glancing inside.

Near the front, a bull terrier with its unmistakable, egg-shaped head and muscular build lounges lazily in its pen. Next to it is a massive and fluffy Saint Bernard that looks almost too big for the space it occupies. Then there's a Great Dane, towering above the rest, its sleek body moving gracefully as it paces back and forth. They're all impressive, and for a moment, I consider what it might be like to have a dog around—someone to keep me company in this new city.

As I lean in closer, my gaze shifts to something even more eye-catching—a massive Macaw perched on a stand just inside the shop. Its vibrant feathers—brilliant blues, reds, and yellows—are impossible to ignore. The bird tilts its head, seeming to notice me watching, and lets out a sharp squawk that makes me chuckle.

"Quite the character," I mutter to myself, entertained by the idea of having such a dramatic pet. But I tear myself away from the window, knowing I'm not ready for the responsibility of a pet just yet. Maybe one day, when I'm more settled.

Continuing down the street, I notice a group of men chatting near a small café. Figuring it can't hurt to get some local knowledge, I approach them and ask about the area. They are friendly enough, pointing out a few good places to eat, a park nearby that is great for jogging, and the best grocery store in the vicinity. They even mention a bakery that is famous for its fresh bread—a detail my carb-loving self files away for later.

Thanking them, I take their advice and check out the grocery store they recommended. As I walk through the automatic doors, the familiar scent of produce and baked goods greets me, comforting in its normalcy. I grab a basket and start down the aisles, mentally running through what I need for the week.

My thoughts drift to dinner as I pick up a box of pasta. Lasagna sounds like the perfect way to christen my new kitchen —a hearty, comforting dish that reminds me of home. I start gathering ingredients: ground beef, tomatoes, garlic, onions, and a block of mozzarella. I can already picture the layers of pasta, rich meat sauce, and gooey cheese baking in the oven, filling the apartment with warmth and deliciousness.

Lost in the idea of cooking, I add a few more items to the basket, thinking of the different ways I can tweak the recipe, maybe add a bit of spice or try a different cheese. By the time I reach the checkout, my basket is full, and I'm eager to get back and start cooking. It feels good to focus on something simple and tangible, something that feels like home in the middle of all this newness. My dad taught me this recipe once I was tall enough to reach the stove.

With the groceries balanced in my arms, I step out into the crisp air and start the walk back home, the anticipation of homey smells filling my chest with something close to contentment.

Turning the corner, I almost miss it—a small, unassuming shop nestled between a vintage clothing store and a tiny café. But what catches my eye isn't the shop's size or location; it's the poster plastered on the front window, practically begging for attention. The vivid colors almost jump out at me, a stark contrast to the muted tones of the buildings around it.

The poster is a chaotic masterpiece. Skulls with intricate details stare back at me, their hollow eyes somehow full of life. Next to them are skeletons in dynamic poses, almost as if they're dancing to some silent music. Flowers bloom in every corner of the design, their petals rendered with such precision that I can almost smell them. And then, unexpectedly, there's a unicorn—its mane flowing like a river of colors, a surreal addition to the otherwise dark and edgy theme.

Above it all, in bold, stylized letters is the name of the shop: "Eternal Ink."

The name stands out in my mind as I stand there like I've heard of it before. I can't help but be drawn to the different art styles on display; each tattoo tells a story about the skill and creativity that went into it. Some are traditional, with bold lines and simple shading, while others are more intricate, almost like paintings on skin. The contrast between the dark, gothic elements and the bursts of vibrant color fascinates me. There's something about the way it all comes together that feels alive as if the art is telling a story—a story I want to know more about.

I step closer to the window, my breath fogging the glass as I peer inside. The shop is dimly lit, but I can make out the sleek black chairs, the polished counters, and the walls lined with more designs. It's a small, intimate space, but there's an undeniable energy to it. It's the kind of place where art isn't just created but lived and breathed.

For a moment, I imagine what it would be like to walk in, sit in one of those chairs, and have one of those designs etched into my skin. A part of me—the part that has always admired tattoos from afar but never had the courage to get one—feels a tug of excitement. What would I choose? Something small, discreet? Or maybe something bold, like an intricate comic book character?

The thought lingers as I stand there, rooted to the spot. Eternal Ink. The name alone feels significant, like it promises something more than just a tattoo—something lasting, something that would stay with me even as the world around me changed.

I jog up the cobblestone path, grocery bags rustling in my arms. The cool March breeze nips at my neck as I fumble with my keys and shove the door open. Inside, Tommy is still unpacking a few boxes, but he's got headphones on, so I drop the bags on the counter, unpack the refrigerated items in record time, and glance out the sliding door of our balcony toward Eternal Ink in the distance. The shop's sign glows softly under the cloudy afternoon sky, pulling me back outside. I head out again, my steps quickening with anticipation.

two
CATO

I sit in my usual spot in the corner of the shop, the one that gives me the best view of the entire space. It's late, and the shop is closed for the night, but I find myself here more often than at home, especially when I have a commission piece I can't get out of my head. Tonight is no different. My sketchbook is tucked under my arm, and a pencil twirls absentmindedly between my fingers as I stare at the screen in front of me.

Google is a sea of possibilities, and I'm wading through image after image, article after article, searching for that perfect inspiration. The request is from a corporate lawyer—a guy who wants something that speaks to his profession but doesn't scream it. A tattoo that blends into his polished world yet still carries a personal, meaningful touch.

The tattoo shop is quiet, the hum of the computer the only sound breaking the silence. Eternal Ink isn't just a shop; it's an extension of me, a place where art lives and breathes, where each wall is a canvas, and every surface holds a story. The walls are covered in framed tattoo designs—some mine, others from guest artists I respect. Each one is a masterpiece in its own right, a testament to the creativity and skill that walks through these doors.

The floors are polished concrete, cool and smooth underfoot, with the occasional scuff mark from a chair or a heavy boot—a reminder that this is a working space, not a gallery. The chairs, sleek and black, are adjustable and worn in just the right places from years of use. The counters are cluttered with ink bottles, machines, gloves, and paper towels—everything meticulously organized yet still giving off that lived-in feel.

I look around, taking in the details, as I often do when I need to clear my mind. The dim lighting casts soft shadows, highlighting the metallic glint of the tools on the counter and the faint gleam of the inks in their bottles. The scent of disinfectant lingers in the air, mixed with the faint, familiar smell of leather from the chairs.

Turning my attention back to the screen, I scroll through images of scales, gavels, and Lady Justice statues. *Too obvious.* The lawyer doesn't want something cliché; he wants something that resonates on a deeper level. I think about what the law means—balance, justice, the weight of decisions, the fine line between right and wrong. These are the concepts I need to translate into art.

I start sketching, the pencil gliding over the paper with ease. A set of scales, but not the typical ones you see in courtrooms—these are abstract, almost geometric, with one side slightly heavier than the other, a subtle nod to the complexity of justice. I add a gavel, but instead of making it the centerpiece, I blend it into the background, almost like a shadow. It's not meant to stand out but to be an integral part of the whole—a silent enforcer.

As I sketch, I lose myself in the process. The world outside the shop fades away, and it's just me, the pencil, and the paper. This is why I love what I do—the ability to take an idea or a concept and turn it into something tangible, something permanent. A tattoo isn't just ink on skin; it's a story, a statement, a piece of the person who wears it.

I stop, lift the pencil, and lean back in my chair to study the design. It's not finished yet, but I can see it taking shape. It has the balance I'm looking for—the subtlety that will appeal to someone in the corporate world while still conveying depth and meaning.

I glance at the clock on the wall—a minimalist design with no numbers, just sleek lines marking the hours. It's getting late, but I'm not ready to stop. This is the part of the process I love most—the quiet, the focus, the sense that I'm on the brink of creating something unique. I lean forward again, the pencil back in my hand, ready to dive into the next phase of the design.

I notice him the moment he stops outside the shop—a young man, maybe in his twenties, standing in front of the window, staring at the designs with curiosity and hesitation. It's a look I've seen countless times before. He's probably wondering what it would be like to walk inside, to sit in one of the chairs, to let the needle etch something permanent onto his skin. I can't help but smile.

When they stand there like that, most people are on the edge of a decision. They either get discouraged, worried about the pain or what others might say, or they take that first step inside. The designs on display are meant to inspire and provoke thought, but they also serve as a filter. Not everyone has the courage to walk through those doors.

Watching him, I can't help but think back to when I was fifteen. The memory is as clear as if it happened yesterday.

I'm standing in front of the only tattoo shop in our small Michigan town, my heart pounding in my chest. Tattoos aren't as widely accepted as they are now, especially in a place like this. But I've been fascinated by them for as long as I can remember—by the stories they tell, by the art of it all. It feels like a calling, something I need to be a part of.

I'm nervous, but there's a fire in me that won't be extinguished. The shop is a small, unassuming place, the kind you could walk past a hundred times without really noticing. The owner, a grizzled old man with more ink on his body than I've ever seen in my life, notices me lingering outside and steps out. Instead of giving me the usual "get lost, kid" look, he surprises me by inviting me in for a coffee. I don't hesitate. This is my chance.

We sit in the back, surrounded by the buzz of tattoo machines and the sharp, clean scent of antiseptic. He talks to me about art, about life, about the permanence of the choices we make. I hang on to every word, soaking in the wisdom he seems to pour so effortlessly into the air. By the time we're done, my mind is made up. I don't just want a tattoo—I need one. It feels like a rite of passage, a way to mark the start of my journey into the world of art.

When I finally get it done—a simple design, nothing too flashy—I feel like I've crossed a threshold. I'm no longer just another 18-year-old in a small town. I'm marked, different, and defined by something meaningful. But the aftermath? That's a whole other story.

At school, I become the talk of the halls. Some of my classmates think it's cool; others whisper behind my back. But the real storm hits at home.

My parents, especially my father, are furious. They don't understand why I would do something so "stupid," as they call it. They think I've ruined my chances of getting a respectable job, of being taken seriously. The arguments last for days, voices rising and echoing through the house. It's clear I've crossed a line that I can't uncross.

Even in the chaos, I don't regret it. That tattoo is a symbol of my passion, of the path I'm determined to take—no matter what anyone else thinks.

As I watch the young man outside Eternal Ink, I notice his dirty blonde hair, slightly disheveled, catching the fading light of the evening. His green eyes flicker with hesitation, scanning the shop as if searching for a sign. His pale skin seems to glow faintly under the streetlights, giving him an almost ethereal quality. I wonder if he's at that same crossroads—if he's ready to step into a world that might not always be easy but is undoubtedly rewarding. I hope he finds the courage to come back tomorrow, to make that choice for himself, just as I did all those years ago.

F. A. SENG

My phone buzzes on the table, pulling me away from the intricate sketch I've been working on. The number on the screen is familiar—a client I've been corresponding with for a while. I can sense this is more than just another tattoo for him; it's something deeply personal. Setting my pencil down, I answer.

"Eternal Ink, this is Cato."

"Hi, Cato," comes the voice from the other end, laced with a nervous energy I've heard before. "It's Ronny, and I've been thinking about that design we discussed—the river flowing down my forearms, with the islands scattered around."

I lean back in my chair, letting my gaze drift over the sketches taped to the walls of my shop. I've spent hours working on that concept, trying to capture the aesthetic and meaning behind it. "Yeah, I remember. You mentioned those islands were meant to cover up scars, right? From your childhood?"

There's a pause, a heavy silence that speaks volumes. "Yeah," he finally says, his voice softer now. "I don't really talk about it much, but those scars... they're not just physical, you know? They're reminders of what I went through. I've always wanted to hide them, to make them disappear."

I nod, even though he can't see me. His story isn't new to me, but it's no less heartbreaking. Tattoos are often more than just ink on the skin; they're shields, symbols of resilience, or, sometimes, a way to rewrite the past. I sit up, an idea forming in my mind that feels right. "What if we didn't hide them?"

There's a sharp intake of breath on the other end. "What do you mean?"

"What if we make those scars part of the story?" I suggest, leaning forward in my chair, my fingers tracing the edge of my sketchbook. "We could turn the scars into more prominent islands, almost like landmarks. And then, imagine a ship navigating through these islands. The river wouldn't just flow; it would tell a story—your story. Not one of a victim who had to hide his pain, but of a survivor who navigated through it, who came out stronger on the other side."

INK & *Intuition*

The silence that follows is thick, filled with the weight of unspoken thoughts. I can feel him processing, considering the idea.

"You think that would work?" he asks, his voice almost tentative, as if he's afraid to hope.

"I know it would," I say, a quiet conviction threading through my words. "We can turn those wounds into something powerful, something that speaks to your strength. It's not about hiding where you've been; it's about showing how far you've come."

There's another pause, but this time, it feels different. Lighter, somehow.

"I like that," he finally says, and I can hear a shift in his tone, a trace of relief. "I really like that. Let's do it."

"Glad to hear it," I reply, already making notes in my sketchbook. "We'll schedule the session for two weeks from now. That'll give me time to refine the design and make sure it's exactly what you're envisioning."

"Two weeks… that sounds good," he agrees, a mix of anticipation and nerves coloring his words. "Thanks, Cato. This… this means a lot."

"It's what I'm here for," I say with a small smile as I hang up the phone.

I barely have time to set the phone down before the bell above the door chimes. Clearly, I forgot to lock the door. I look up to see the young man who had been lingering outside earlier finally stepping inside. He stands there, looking around with wide eyes, like he's absorbing every detail, trying to summon the courage to take the plunge.

Leaning back in my chair, I let a knowing smile tug at the corner of my mouth. I remember that feeling all too well— the mix of fear and excitement, the sense of standing on the edge of something big. Hell, I felt it myself years ago when I was just a kid staring at the only tattoo shop in Everest, Michigan, wondering if I had the guts to go through with it.

14

I set aside my sketchbook and offer him a warm smile. Making a good first impression is important; it sets the tone for what I hope will be a positive experience.

"Hey there," I greet him, extending a hand. "Welcome to Eternal Ink. I'm Cato. What can I do for you today?"

The man hesitates for a moment, then introduces himself. "I'm Alex. Actually, I'm not entirely sure if I want a tattoo right now. I just… wanted to come in and learn more about them."

I nod, sensing his hesitation. Deciding to get a tattoo is a big step; it's natural to want to explore your options before making a commitment. "Sure thing, Alex. Why don't we start with you telling me a bit about yourself? It might help narrow down what you're looking for—or at least give us a starting point."

Alex seems to appreciate the approach and begins to open up. "Well, I just moved to Metro Heights recently, and I'm trying to explore new things. I grew up in a really religious town, and tattoos were kind of… taboo there. I never really had the chance to think about getting one until now."

I listen intently, nodding as he speaks. His story is similar to my own. Many people who grew up in conservative environments find themselves drawn to tattoos later in life, often as a form of self-expression or rebellion. "I get that. Moving to a new place can open up a lot of new possibilities. Tattoos… they're definitely a way to explore who you are and what you stand for."

Alex looks a bit uneasy as he rolls up his sleeve, revealing a small tattoo of a cross on his hand. "This is the only tattoo I have. I got it when I was eighteen. It's… kind of a reminder of my past, I guess. I'm a bit embarrassed about it, honestly."

I take a closer look, keeping my expression neutral. "Hey, don't be embarrassed. Tattoos are deeply personal, and everyone's journey with them is different. Whether it's a small cross or a full sleeve, it's part of your story. I don't judge anyone for their choices."

15

Alex's shoulders relax a bit at my words. "Thanks, Cato. I appreciate that. I'm still not sure what kind of tattoo I want. I was hoping you could help me figure it out."

I smile, feeling a sense of enthusiasm for the task ahead. "Absolutely. Let's start with what you're drawn to. Do you have any ideas or themes in mind? Or maybe something you've always wanted to express but haven't found the right way to do it yet?"

Alex seems to think for a moment, then shakes his head. "I'm not really sure. I've looked at a lot of designs, but nothing's really clicked yet."

As Alex walks over to the consultation area, I pull out a chair and gesture for him to sit. "Go ahead and make yourself comfortable. I'll grab my sketch book, and we can start brainstorming some ideas."

Alex settles into the chair, his posture relaxed, except his eyes are betraying a hint of nervous excitement. I retrieve my well-worn sketchbook from my desk—a crucial tool for sketching initial concepts and jotting down client ideas. Flipping it open to a fresh page, I gesture for Alex to begin. "So, Alex, let's dive into what kind of tattoo you're thinking about. You mentioned earlier that you're from a conservative town. Is that something you'd like to incorporate, or are you looking for something else?"

Alex looks thoughtful. "Actually, I've been really into traveling and exploring new places. It's something I've always wanted to do, and I keep dreaming about traveling the world one day."

"That's a great theme," I say, starting to jot down a few notes. "Traveling can be such a rich source of inspiration for tattoos. It sounds like you might want something that reflects that passion. Do you have any specific symbols or imagery in mind related to travel?"

He hesitates, then shrugs slightly. "Not exactly. This is all pretty new to me."

I nod, my mind already racing with design possibilities. "A compass and a globe are both excellent choices. They symbolize direction, exploration, and adventure—perfect for someone who's passionate about travel. Let's start with the compass. It's a classic symbol that can be both intricate and meaningful."

Flipping to a blank page, I sketch a rough outline of a compass. "The compass can be designed in many styles, from ornate and detailed to simple and modern. It's all about what resonates with you. Do you envision it as a centerpiece or something that complements other elements?"

Alex leans in, examining the sketch. "I think I'd like it to be more of a central piece. Maybe on my forearm, so it's visible and reminds me of my goal every day."

"Got it," I say, making a few more notes. "A central piece on your forearm will definitely make a statement. Now, about the globe—do you want it to be a full globe or something more stylized?"

Alex thinks for a moment. "I'm thinking a smaller globe might work better, maybe integrated with the compass. It could be a bit stylized, but still recognizable."

I hold his wrist and make a small circle with my finger on his forearm. "This could be the center of the compass." I trace a line from the circle to his wrist, noticing a faint flush of color in his cheeks.

Turning back to the sketch, I draw a smaller globe, positioning it next to the compass in the design. "I can see how combining the two would work really well. The globe could look like it's part of the compass, creating a cohesive look. We can add details like latitude and longitude lines to give it a bit more texture and depth."

Alex's eyes light up. "That sounds awesome. I like the idea of the globe being a part of the compass. It's like the compass is guiding me to explore the world."

"Exactly," I say, nodding in agreement. "It's a powerful representation of your journey and aspirations. We can also play with the details, like adding a few subtle elements that reflect your personal style. Maybe some fine line work or shading to enhance the design."

As I continue sketching, I explain the different design options: "We could go for a traditional-style tattoo with intricate detailing or something more modern with clean lines and minimalistic features. The globe can be detailed or abstract, depending on how you want it to fit with the compass."

Alex seems to enjoy the process. "I think I'd like a mix of both—detailed enough to be interesting but still clean and modern."

"Great choice," I say, finalizing the sketch. "We'll make sure the design balances detail with a modern aesthetic. Once we have the final design, I'll be able to make any adjustments you want before we start the tattooing process."

Alex nods, looking pleased with the progress. "This is really coming together. Thanks for helping me figure this out."

"No problem," I reply with a smile. "It's my job to help bring your vision to life. I'm excited to work on this with you. We'll schedule a time to go over the final design and get everything set up."

As Alex stands up to leave, he glances at the sketch with a satisfied grin. "I can't wait to see how it turns out. Thanks again, Cato."

"Anytime," I say, shaking his hand. "Here's my card. Shoot me a text or give me a call so I have your number, and we can finalize the details. Have a great day, Alex."

He smiles, a hint of excitement lighting up his face as he heads out the door. I watch him leave, feeling the familiar satisfaction of helping someone begin a journey toward self-expression. Tattoos are never just designs on skin—they're pieces of people's lives, dreams, and memories made visible.

As the door closes behind him, I sit back down, glancing at the sketches on my desk. The lawyer's tattoo concept waits patiently on the page while Alex's idea of a compass and globe stirs in my mind, reminding me of the endless ways art can shape and define our stories. I pick up my pencil again, ready to dive back into my work, a smile tugging at the corners of my mouth.

F. A. SENG

Tomorrow brings new clients and new ideas, but for tonight, it's just me, my sketches, and the stillness of the shop—a sanctuary for creation where ink and paper blend with imagination to bring stories to life.

three

ALEX

After I leave the tattoo shop, I walk back to my place, feeling a strange mix of excitement and anxiety. The sketches of the compass and globe are still fresh in my mind, and I can't help but trace the outline of the design in the air with my fingers. Even though it was brief and professional, Cato's touch rests on my skin—warm and purposeful. I lie down on the bed, staring at the ceiling, trying to shake off the lingering sensation.

The apartment is quiet. Tommy is out running errands or meeting friends, or whatever it is he does. I'm alone with my thoughts, and those thoughts soon turn back to my mother. Just as I'm beginning to drift into contemplation, my phone buzzes on the bedside table. I pick it up, seeing my mother's name flashing on the screen.

"Hi, Mom," I answer, trying to keep my voice upbeat.

"Alex, sweetie," she says, her voice laced with concern. "How's everything going? Have you found a good church to attend like we discussed earlier?"

I sigh internally, rolling my eyes even though she can't see me. "Yeah, I've actually just got back from checking out a few churches around here," I lie. "I'm planning to start going next Sunday."

"That's good to hear," she replies, though there's a hint of hesitation. "I'm really glad you're making an effort. The city can be a dangerous place, full of temptations and vices. You need to be careful and stay grounded."

A knot forms in my stomach. I don't want to get into another long conversation about the city's supposed dangers. "I understand. I'll be careful. I just think it's important to find my own path and, you know, experience things for myself."

"Oh, Alex," she says, her voice rising slightly. "It's not just about experiencing things; it's about staying away from the bad influences. You remember what happened to people in the city we've heard about on the news. You don't want to fall into that kind of lifestyle."

I feel my irritation rising but try to keep my voice calm. "Mom, I'm aware of the risks. I'm doing my best to stay on the right path. It's not like I'm going to get dragged into anything I don't want to be a part of."

"There's always a danger of that," she insists, almost pleading. "I know you think you're strong and independent, but it's easy to get caught up in things you didn't expect. The city can be very overwhelming."

"I get it, really," I say, trying to suppress the frustration in my voice. "I'll start going to church, like I said. I'll make sure to stay true to my values."

"Promise me you'll be careful," she says, her tone softer now but still earnest. "And don't forget your father and I are always here for you, even if we can't be there physically."

"I promise," I reply, though I feel a pang of guilt for the irritation I'd felt. "I appreciate your concern, Mom. I've got to get going now, though. There's some stuff I need to take care of."

"Alright, dear," she says, sounding a bit resigned. "Let us know how everything goes. We miss you."

"I will," I assure her. "I'll talk to you soon. Bye."

As I hang up the call, I feel relief, but I also feel some lingering frustration. My mother's incessant worry is understandable, but it always feels like a cloud hanging over my independence. I turn my attention back to the room, trying to focus on more immediate things. Tommy's absence has left me with plenty of time to think, but now I just want to relax and maybe get some work done.

* * *

As the final slide disappears from the screen, my new boss, Amelia Noor, rings out in a crisp and clear voice, signaling the end of the day. "So, guys, this is it for today," she announces, her tone as efficient as her demeanor.

It's my first day, and while I feel like I've been under a microscope, I also can't shake the subtle sense of accomplishment. Surviving day one is no small feat.

I turn to Tommy, who has been seated next to me throughout the presentation. His expression is full of exhaustion with a hint of amusement. "Man, I was so bored, I thought I was going to fall asleep," he mutters, his voice barely above a whisper but with enough exaggeration to make me chuckle.

"Yeah, I get it," I reply, unable to suppress a grin. The presentation has been dry—necessary, but dry. Tommy's playful complaint is the perfect way to cut through the lingering tension.

Just as I'm about to say something else, I hear my name being called. "Alex?"

I freeze, my smile fading as I turn to see Amelia standing a few feet away. My heart skips a beat. Has she overheard us? The thought of her catching Tommy's joke—and my reaction—sends a cold sweat trickling down my spine. My mind races, trying to recall exactly what we said, but it's too late to second-guess.

I quickly straighten up and walk over to her, attempting to mask my nervousness with a professional smile. "Yes, Miss Noor?" I greet her, trying to keep my voice steady.

Amelia's expression remains neutral, her gaze sharp as she studies me for a moment. "I've read your resume and some of your previous work," she begins, her tone serious but not unkind. "I have great expectations from you, Alex."

A wave of relief washes over me, easing the tension in my shoulders. I even feel a small swell of pride at her words. For a brief moment, I'm convinced I was about to get reprimanded. Instead, I'm receiving a rare compliment.

"Thank you," I manage to say, my voice more confident now. "I'll do my best not to disappoint you."

She nods, her expression softening just a fraction. "Good. We have some new projects coming up, but we'll discuss those tomorrow. For now, you should get settled in."

I nod in agreement, feeling both relieved and eager to prove myself. "I'm looking forward to it," I reply, genuinely excited about the opportunities ahead.

With that, Amelia gives me a curt nod and turns to head back to her office.

"Hey, so I heard back from my tattoo artist, Cato, last night so I'm heading back to Eternal Ink today to meet with him again," I say to Tommy over the divider of our desks. "I probably won't be home until late."

Tommy's head pops up over the barrier, his eyes wide and mouth slightly open.

"You good, dude?" I chuckle.

"Did you just say… Cato?" Tommy asks, like he's trying to confirm he didn't mishear.

"Yeah… Cato something," I admit, scratching the back of my neck. "I can't remember his last name. He works at Eternal Ink."

"Shut the hell up!" Tommy nearly yells, ducking into my cubicle. We're both suddenly aware of the curious stares around us.

"Dude, keep it down," I mutter.

"Do you have any idea who that is?" Tommy says, slapping my arm. "That's Cato Sinclair—one of the best tattoo artists in the world. How on earth did you get a meeting with him?"

INK & *Intuition*

I blink, finally connecting the dots. Eternal Ink had been mentioned more than once on *Ink Masters*—and so had Cato. No wonder the name sounded so familiar.

"Hello? Earth to Alex." Tommy waves a hand in front of my face, snapping me out of my thoughts.

I bat his hand away, laughing. "I literally just walked in. We're only brainstorming ideas right now; no appointment or anything yet."

Tommy shakes his head, grinning like I've just told him I casually ran into a celebrity. "You better let me meet him sometime, man. That guy's a legend."

I laugh, trying to play it cool despite Tommy's enthusiasm.

That evening, I find myself standing outside Eternal Ink again, the shop's neon sign casting a warm glow over the sidewalk. It's been on my mind all day—the idea of getting a tattoo, something meaningful, something that speaks to who I am or maybe who I want to be.

Pushing open the door, I'm greeted by the chime of the bell and the low hum of *"THE DEATH OF PEACE OF MIND" by Bad Omens* playing in the background. The scent of ink and antiseptic fills the air, mingling with the soft sounds of needles buzzing and quiet conversations. Cato is at his station, sketching something intricate, but when he sees me, he sets down his pencil and gives me a nod.

"Alex! I'm glad you could make it," he says with a small smile, wiping his hands on a rag before turning to face me fully. His brown hair is slightly tousled, falling just above his blue eyes, which are kind and inviting. Tattoos cover his arms and peek out from the collar of his shirt, a vibrant tapestry of ink that adds to his rugged charm. A hint of stubble frames his jaw, giving him a casual, effortless appeal.

"Hey, I've been thinking a lot about what we talked about," I say, trying to keep the nervousness out of my voice. I spent hours the previous night sketching out ideas, my mind racing with possibilities. "I have some ideas I wanted to share with you."

24

"Let's see 'em," Cato says, pulling out a chair for me and motioning for me to sit. He grabs his sketchbook and a few pencils, ready to start translating thoughts into designs.

I carefully pull out my own sketchbook from my bag, feeling both excitement and trepidation. I haven't shown my drawings to many people, especially not someone as talented as Cato. But he seems genuinely interested, and that's enough to push the hesitation aside.

I flip open the book, revealing the first drawing. It's a detailed compass, its points sharp and precise, with intricate lines radiating from the center. Around the compass, I've drawn the outline of a globe, the continents shaded delicately within the circles of latitude and longitude.

"This is the main idea," I explain, tracing the lines with my finger. "I want the compass to represent the direction and the journey I'm on. The globe— that's for my love of travel. I've always wanted to see the world, and I thought this could be a way to remind myself of that dream."

Cato leans in, studying the sketch closely. His expression is thoughtful, and he nods as he takes it in. "These are really good," he says, his voice carrying a note of admiration. "You've got a real eye for detail."

A sense of joy spreads through me at his words. "Thanks," I say, feeling a bit more at ease. "I wasn't sure if it was too ambitious or not."

"Not at all," Cato replies, flipping through a few pages in his own sketchbook. "In fact, it gives us a great jumping point. We can work with these elements and build something unique. Maybe we could play with the idea of the compass—make it look a little aged like it's been used for years, guiding you through uncharted territories."

I nod, liking the sound of that. "Yeah, that sounds perfect. I want it to feel personal like it's been a part of me all along."

Cato continues to flip through my sketches, pausing on a design I drew of a small ship sailing across the ocean, its sails full of wind. "What about this?" he asks, tapping the page. "We could incorporate the ship, maybe have it sailing across the globe, with the compass as its guide. It could represent your journey—both where you've been and where you're headed."

The idea resonates immediately. "I really like that idea," I say, a smile spreading across my face. "It ties everything together."

Cato grins back, his enthusiasm contagious. "I think we've got something here," he says, reaching for a pencil. "Let's sketch it out, see how it all fits together."

He leans back slightly, his gaze drifting over the sketches I've spread on the counter. There's respect in his expression, but something deeper, too—maybe thoughtfulness or a shared understanding of the personal meaning behind the design. He looks up at me with that intense focus he always seems to have.

"You know," he says, his voice calm and measured, "if you're looking for something that ties into your faith, why not add a small cross somewhere in the design? It could be subtle, but it would blend your beliefs with your love for art."

The suggestion catches me off guard, and a knot forms in my stomach. My mind flashes to my family, the stern looks and heavy silence that would inevitably follow if they saw me with another tattoo—especially one so visible, so tied to the faith that has always felt more like an obligation than a choice.

I must make a face without realizing it because Cato immediately picks up on my hesitation. He raises a hand, almost as if to retract the idea, his expression softening. "No pressure," he says quickly, his tone gentle. "I can see that might not be what you're looking for."

I nod, relieved he doesn't press the issue. I don't want to reject the idea outright, but I'm not ready to have a symbol that would constantly remind me of the parts of my life I'm trying to navigate away from. I'm carving out a space to be myself without the constant worry of living up to others' expectations.

Sensing the shift in my mood, Cato smoothly changes the subject. He begins discussing the different techniques he learned during his tattoo training, explaining the intricacies of line work, shading, and color blending. He speaks with an infectious passion, his hands moving animatedly as he describes the process of creating a design from scratch, how each stroke of the needle is like a brushstroke on a canvas.

I find myself relaxing and getting lost in the details of what he says. I am fascinated by the technical aspects of tattooing—the precision required and the way an artist can bring a simple sketch to life on someone's skin. Cato's smooth voice draws me in as he explains the differences between traditional and modern styles, the challenges of working with different skin tones, and how he's developed his own unique style over the years.

We start talking about our favorite art styles. I tell him about my love for clean, minimalist designs—sharp lines, simple shapes, and geometric patterns. Cato nods thoughtfully, sharing his appreciation for those styles but also expressing his love for more intricate, detailed work—floral patterns, abstract designs, and how he enjoys playing with contrasts to create something truly unique.

"Every piece tells a story," he says, his eyes lighting up as he speaks. "It's not just about what looks good on the surface. It's about the meaning behind it and the emotions it evokes. That's what makes tattooing an art form, not just a craft."

His words resonate with me. I've always seen art as a way to express what can't be put into words, and hearing him talk about tattooing, in the same way, makes me feel a connection—a shared understanding of what it means to create something meaningful, something that could impact someone's life.

As we talk, I realize I'm thinking more about getting another tattoo—not just as art on my skin but as a symbol of the journey I'm on and the changes I'm making in my life. Cato seems to understand that without me needing to say it out loud. He's patient, listening carefully to my thoughts and offering insights without pushing his own ideas on me.

"Take a look at this," Cato smiles, turning his sketch toward me. "I added more detail to the globe and shaded some of the land masses."

"Cato," I pause, trying to think of how to put my thoughts into words. "This is amazing. This is better than I could've envisioned. How did you do this all with just a pencil?"

"Thanks," Cato laughs, scratching the back of his neck. "If you think I'm good with a pencil, just wait til you see what I can do with my gun."

By the time we wrap up our conversation, a warm sense of joy fills me, a feeling I hadn't expected. I'm not just thinking about getting a tattoo—I'm thinking about what it could represent, how it could be a part of the story I'm writing for myself. For the first time in a long while, I feel like I'm on the right path, like I'm finally starting to take control of my own narrative.

four
CATO

The doorbell rings, pulling me out of my focus on the laptop screen. I glance up, half-expecting to see Alex's face peeking through the doorway. Just the thought of him walking in makes my heart skip a beat. I've been thinking about our conversation more than I should, wondering if he has any ideas he might bring in today and what new sketches he might show me. But as the door swings open, my momentary excitement fades.

It's not Alex.

"Marcus," I greet, trying to mask the disappointment in my voice as I see the familiar figure of Marcus Ashford standing in the doorway. "Come on in, straight to the chair."

Marcus gives a brief nod, his expression as stoic as ever. He's a regular here, a bouncer at one of the local bars, with a body that looks like it's been carved out of stone. He makes his way to the chair with the kind of ease that comes from knowing the routine all too well. As he pulls off his shirt, I take in the sight of his back—a broad, muscular canvas already adorned with ink.

The crow and skull tattoo we've been working on dominates his shoulder blades. The crow's wings are spread wide, the feathers etched in stark black lines that contrast against the pale expanse of his skin. Beneath the crow, the skull grins in a macabre, twisted smile, its details sharp and precise. The lines of the tattoo flow seamlessly with the contours of Marcus's muscles, almost as if the design was always on him like he was born with it.

I place the stencil and pick up the tattoo gun, the weight settling in my hand as I begin to work. The buzz of the needle fills the room, a sound that always brings a certain calm with it. As I trace the lines of the tattoo, I can't help but let my mind wander back to Alex.

Will he come in later? Will he decide on that compass design, or will he surprise me with something new? I push the thoughts aside, focusing on the task at hand. Marcus is a man of few words, but his tattoos tell stories—stories of battles fought, both inside and out. The crow and skull are just another chapter.

As I work, I can feel the tension in Marcus's muscles ease. His body relaxes under the sensation of the needle. The tattoo is nearly complete, and the final touches bring it to life on his skin.

The doorbell rings again, breaking the steady rhythm of my work. I glance up from the intricate shading I'm doing on Marcus's tattoo, expecting just another walk-in or maybe Demi coming back early from her break, but when my eyes land on the door, there he is—Alex.

He stands there, hesitant but smiling. For a moment, the tension I didn't realize I was holding in my shoulders eases. I nod toward the chair by the wall, a silent invitation, and Alex quickly takes a seat, clutching his sketchbook like it's a lifeline.

I return to my work, the hum of the tattoo gun filling the space between us. Marcus, under the needle, barely flinching as I finish the final details. The crow's wings need just a bit more

30

depth, a touch more shadow to make them seem as if they're about to lift off his back and take flight. I lose myself in the precision of it; each stroke of the needle is a practiced movement that has become second nature over the years.

I'm acutely aware of Alex's presence. I can feel his eyes on me, and the thought of him watching makes me hyperconscious of every motion. Not that it makes me nervous, just more of a heightened awareness, like I want to do my best work with him in the room, even if he's just there to observe.

Fifteen minutes later, I lean back, assessing the final product. The crow and skull now look even more dynamic, the shadows giving the impression of movement as if the crow is about to swoop down on its prey. I wipe down Marcus's back, admiring how the ink aligns perfectly with the flow of his muscles.

"We're done," I say, my voice cutting through the soft whirl of the machine winding down. "Go ahead and check it out."

Marcus walks over to the mirror, and a small smile pulls at the corner of his lips, his standard sign of approval.

"Give me a call when you want to book your next session." I nod.

Marcus nods in his usual silent agreement and stands to examine the work in the mirror. I remove my gloves, toss them in the bin, and wipe my hands clean before finally turning my attention to Alex.

When I look over, I see him hunched over his sketchbook, completely absorbed. As I approach, I realize he isn't just doodling—he's sketching me. More specifically, he's sketching me as I work on Marcus, capturing the intensity of the moment, the way my hands move with precision over the client's skin.

"You've got a good eye," I say, breaking the silence between us. Alex looks up, a bit startled, but when he sees I'm genuinely impressed, a small smile tugs at the corners of his mouth.

31

"I, uh, just thought I'd draw while I waited," he replies, a bit sheepishly.

I nod, studying the lines he's put to paper. It's a rough sketch, sure, except there's a certain energy in it that I recognize —like he isn't just drawing what he sees but what he feels in the room, too.

"I can tell," I say, pointing to the way he's captured how I'd leaned in close, my eyes focused on the needle's path. "You've got a way of getting the movement right, the way things flow together. It's impressive."

Alex looks down at his sketch, then back at me, his cheeks flushing slightly under the praise. "Thanks," he mutters, clearly not used to getting compliments on his work.

I smile, nodding toward the empty chair at my station. "Ready to talk about that tattoo?"

As Alex settles into the chair, I can't resist lightening the mood with a joke. "You know," I say with a playful grin, "why don't you just get my face tattooed on your arm? That way, you'll never forget your favorite tattoo artist."

Alex's laughter fills the room, a warm sound that immediately eases the slight tension in the air. "I'm not sure if that would be a good idea," he replies, still chuckling. "But it would definitely be unique."

We share a laugh, the sound blending with the shop's ambient noise. It's a good moment—a simple connection over humor that feels natural and easy. Then, the conversation shifts, taking on a more serious tone as Alex pulls out his sketchbook. The mood changes from light-hearted banter to something more focused.

He opens the sketchbook to a page that shows a detailed drawing of a globe with a compass orbiting around it. The design is intricate, with delicate lines and thoughtful details that reveal just how much care he's put into it. It's not just a doodle; it's something he's clearly thought about, something that means something to him.

"This is what I was thinking," Alex says, his tone more serious. "A rustic globe with clean compass lines."

I study the sketch, appreciating how the compass guides the globe, almost like it's leading a journey. It's a strong, personal concept, though he hasn't said so yet.

"This is solid," I say, tracing the lines with my eyes.

Alex nods thoughtfully. "I think it could work."

"Tattoos are more than images; they're stories," I say. "How does this feel to you? It needs to resonate every time you see it."

He looks down at the sketch, his fingers tracing the lines he's drawn. "I guess I'm still figuring that out," he admits, his voice quiet. "I know I want something that represents this part of my life, but I'm not sure exactly how."

I lean back in my chair, considering his words. "That's okay," I tell him. "We don't have to rush this. Sometimes, the best designs come from letting things sit for a while, letting the idea evolve naturally. We can explore different styles, different interpretations, and see what feels right."

Alex looks up at me, his eyes filled with gratitude, even if there is some uncertainty. "I really appreciate that," he says. "This is important to me, and I want to get it right."

"Tattoos are a lifelong commitment," I say, my tone more serious now. "You can't always just get something on a whim or out of spite. It has to mean something, something you'll still be proud of when you're sixty." I let my words settle, watching as Alex absorbs the weight of what I'm saying. "Hang on a second," I add, standing up from my chair. "I'll be right back."

"Where are you going?" Alex questions.

"I was gonna go make some coffee," I say, nodding toward the kitchen. "Want some?"

Alex looks up, a faint smile tugging at his lips. "Yeah, sure. Thanks."

I head toward the small kitchen at the back of the shop, the normal creak of the floorboards under my boots giving way to the soft hum of the espresso machine. Making coffee for a client when things get serious has become something of a ritual. It's grounding, a way to bring us both back to earth.

INK & *Intuition*

As I wait for the machine to finish, I glance through the slight gap in the door. Alex sits there, still as a statue, his eyes wandering over the walls adorned with flash art and framed photographs of completed work. He's smiling—a subtle, almost childlike smile that suggests he's somewhere between admiration and contemplation. He's looking at those tattoos as if he's trying to absorb them, to understand the stories they tell.

A small flutter spreads in my chest. There's something about Alex, something in the way he carries himself, that makes me want to help him figure this out. He's at a crossroads; I can tell. Hell, I've been there myself more times than I can count. Maybe that's why I feel this pull to guide him through it.

As the coffee finishes brewing, I pour it into two mugs, watching the steam rise and curl in the air. I push the door open with my shoulder, careful not to spill a drop, and walk back to where Alex sits. He looks up as I approach, that smile still lingering on his lips, but now there's something else in his eyes —appreciation, maybe.

"Here you go," I say, handing him a cup. Our fingers brush for the briefest moment as he takes it, and I feel a spark, something almost electric, pass between us. I pull my hand back, trying not to read too much into it, but the feeling stays, hanging in the air between us.

"Thanks," Alex says, his voice soft. He takes a sip, the heat of the coffee seeming to relax him further. I watch as he glances around the shop again, his eyes tracing the lines of the tattoos on the walls, the designs that have become as much a part of this place as the ink that's seeped into the floors and counters over the years.

"This place is incredible," he says, almost to himself. "Every piece has its own story, its own life."

I nod, leaning back against the counter, my own cup cradled in my hands. "Yeah, that's the thing about tattoos," I reply. "They're more than just art. They're a part of you. And every time you look at them, you're reminded of where you've been, what you've survived, and who you are now. It's a commitment, but it's also a declaration."

He takes in my words, his expression thoughtful as if he's trying to match the gravity of what I'm saying with the decision he's about to make. There's a long silence, but it's not uncomfortable. It's the kind of silence that comes when two people are really connecting, really understanding each other on a deeper level.

"So, what do you think?" I ask finally, breaking the quiet. "Are you ready to make that kind of commitment?"

Alex looks down at his coffee, then back up at me, his eyes steady and serious. "I think I am," he says, but there's still a note of uncertainty, something that tells me he's not completely there yet.

I give him a reassuring smile, one that says it's okay to take his time. "Good," I say. "Remember, this isn't something you need to rush into. We'll take our time; make sure it's exactly what you want."

He nods, taking another sip of coffee, and I can see that some of the tension has left his shoulders. He's more at ease now, more open to the idea of waiting, of letting the right design come to him naturally.

After a moment, I feel a natural curiosity about Alex and want to understand him better. "So, what do your parents do?" I ask, leaning in slightly, hoping to bridge the gap between us.

Alex looks down into his coffee cup for a moment as if the answer is written in the steam rising from it. When he finally looks up, there's a trace of weariness in his eyes, a kind of resignation that speaks of deep-seated struggles. "My parents… they're good people. Really good people. My dad runs a small auto repair shop, and my mom helps out. They're hardworking and caring."

I nod, listening intently. "Sounds like they're salt-of-the-earth folks."

Alex smiles faintly, but there's a hint of sadness too. "Yeah, they are. They'll do anything for you, but… it was always so suffocating. Everything was regimented, so controlled. It was like living in a bubble where anything outside their beliefs was wrong or dangerous."

I can see the conflict in his eyes, the way he struggles to reconcile his love for his parents with the constraints they imposed. "How do you cope with that?" I ask, genuinely interested.

Alex shrugs, the gesture carrying years of frustration and adaptation. "I've managed somehow. I followed their rules and tried to fit in, but it was like… I was always on the outside looking in. When I went to college, it was like a breath of fresh air. I could finally be myself, but even now, there's this constant pressure, like I'm living in two worlds at once."

His words paint a picture of a divided life, of walking a tightrope between personal freedom and familial expectations. I can see the strain in his shoulders and the way he tries to hold it all together. "That sounds incredibly tough," I say, my voice softening. "Living under that kind of pressure, trying to meet expectations while also finding your own path—it's not easy."

Alex nods, his gaze fixed on his coffee cup again. "It's like there's this constant internal conflict. I want to honor their beliefs and respect them, but I also need to live my life on my own terms. It's a balancing act that I'm still figuring out."

I take a moment to process what he's shared, feeling a deep sense of empathy. "I can imagine how challenging that must be," I say, trying to offer some solace. "But remember, finding your own path doesn't mean you're betraying them. It's about being true to yourself while still honoring where you come from."

Alex looks up, and there's a flicker of gratitude in his eyes. "Thanks. It helps to talk about it."

I smile, feeling the connection between us deepen. "Anytime. I'm here to listen, and if there's anything I can do to help, whether it's with tattoos or just talking things through, you've got it."

Alex rises from his seat, his fingers brushing absently against the edge of the counter as if grounding himself one last time. He pulls his jacket tighter around him, the weight of the conversation still lingering in the air between us. "Thanks again," he says, his voice quieter now, more reflective. There's a brief pause, his eyes meeting mine with a softness that speaks volumes. "I'll think about what you said."

With that, he offers a small smile before turning toward the door, the sound of the bell above marking his departure. As he steps out into the evening, I watch through the glass, hoping that, for him, this was the start of something lighter.

five
ALEX

I rub the sleep out of my eyes and let out a long yawn as I replay yesterday's conversation with Cato in my mind. The conversation was surprisingly eye-opening. Cato has this way of making me realize that the constraints I've grown up with don't have to define me. It's like he's handed me a permission slip to explore who I am beyond the limits imposed by my upbringing. I feel a sense of clarity I haven't had before, but there's also a hint of unease as I grapple with this new perspective.

Just as I'm sinking into these thoughts, my phone buzzes insistently on the bedside table. I glance at the screen, seeing that it's my mother calling. I hesitate, hoping she'll take the hint and let me be. But the phone is relentless—soon enough, the screen lights up with a barrage of messages from her.

I can't ignore her any longer, so I decide to read her texts.

Mom:

> Alex, where have you been? I've been trying to reach you!

I can hear her voice in my head and picture her tapping her foot while sitting in her chair.

Me:

> I've been busy. I had some things to take care of.

Mom:

> Busy with what? Have you been to the church like you promised?

Me:

> Yes, Mom, I went. It was fine. Nothing special.

I feel bad for lying, but I moved away so I could live my own life, not the life everyone else wants for me.

Mom:

> What do you mean 'nothing special'? The church is a sacred place. I hope you took it seriously. There's a lot of temptation in the city. You need to stay grounded.

I feel a pang of irritation rise in my chest before responding.

Me:

INK & *Intuition*

> I went, I'm okay. I really need to get to work now.

Mom:

> Well, just make sure you're staying on the right path, and don't let the city's views get to you.

Me:

> I'll keep that in mind. I'll call later this week. Gotta go now.

Before she can say anything more, I toss my phone back onto the bed next to me. The well-known mix of irritation and guilt swirls in my chest, a feeling that seems to accompany every conversation with her. I try to shake it off and refocus on the positive changes I'm contemplating. Cato has given me a lot to think about, and I don't want to let my mother's incessant reminders pull me back into the constraints I'm trying to break free from.

* * *

Dragging myself out of bed, I start planning my next steps. It's the Saturday after my first week at work. The excitement from this week's conversation with Cato is still reeling through me, but practicality demands my attention. I want to keep moving forward with my tattoo plans, and that means getting groceries and, more importantly, paying a visit to a church. It's a necessary task to keep my mother off my back—she seems to have an uncanny ability to sniff out any deviation from her expectations.

I glance around my room, spotting the old notebook I've used for years to track groceries. It's a habit from childhood, a small vestige of simpler times when grocery shopping was part of my weekly routine. Even now, I find comfort in keeping lists.

I grab the notebook from the desk and flip to a fresh page. I write out the heading: "Grocery List." My handwriting, though a bit rushed, is neat and legible. I jot down the essentials —bread, milk, vegetables—anything I need to keep my kitchen stocked. I pause, thinking about how I could use this list to help me start fresh. Maybe it isn't just about getting food; it's about creating a new routine for myself, one that aligns with this newfound sense of freedom.

Thoughts of Cato's shop pop into my head again, and I remember the taste of the coffee he gave me. I've been thinking about getting some for myself, too, so I scribble "coffee" and "coffee maker" onto the list, feeling a small, satisfied smile tug at my lips.

* * *

Walking down the grocery store aisle, my eyes dart between my list and the neatly arranged shelves. It's a mundane task, but I find a certain rhythm in it, a sense of normalcy I welcome after the whirlwind of recent events. I'm so focused on checking off items from my list—milk, bread, eggs—that I almost don't notice the tall figure a few paces ahead of me.

It's Marcus, the guy with the crow and skull tattoo I'd seen at the shop. His presence is oddly familiar, yet the setting feels completely out of context. I hesitate, feeling a jolt of recognition. We'd seen each other in a much different setting, and here, in the fluorescent-lit grocery store, it felt almost surreal.

As I approach, Marcus catches my eye. He raises his hand and gives a friendly nod, his lips curving into a smile. I return the gesture, feeling a bit awkward, though his easy demeanor puts me more at ease.

"Marcus Ashford," he says, extending his hand for a shake. I'm a bit taken aback by the unexpected greeting but quickly recover. I grasp his hand, noting the firm grip. "Alex Mitchell," I reply, trying to match his relaxed tone.

Marcus's smile widens. "I've seen you around at Eternal Ink. You're the guy with the sketches, right?" His recognition catches me off guard, and I nod. "Yeah, that's me."

He continues, "I had a call with Cato last night. He mentioned a customer had made a really nice sketch of him. I'm guessing that was you?" There's a hint of curiosity in his voice, with honest interest.

I feel a small flush of pride at the mention of my sketches. "Yeah, that would be me. I've always had a habit of sketching things that catch my eye or inspire me. I guess it's just a way of holding onto those moments, you know?"

Marcus nods appreciatively. "Cato showed me your sketches. He thought they were pretty impressive. It's cool to see someone with an eye for detail like that. It's always nice to see art from a different perspective."

I chuckle, feeling a bit shy. I must've left some of my loose drawings behind. "Thanks. I've always been into drawing and sketching. It's kind of my way of processing things, I suppose. And seeing your tattoo in person—it was pretty inspiring."

Marcus's expression turns thoughtful. "I get that. There's something about seeing a piece of art that's been brought to life. It's different from just seeing it on paper. Anyway, it's nice to meet you outside the shop."

"Yeah, same here," I say, feeling more at ease. "I guess the grocery store is a bit of a change of scenery compared to Eternal Ink."

We talk about mundane things, but my curiosity gets the better of me. "Why the crow and skull?" I ask, unable to hold back. The tattoo has fascinated me since I first saw it. I wonder if there's a story behind it.

Marcus lets out a chuckle, and I see the weight of his past in his eyes. "Well, that's a story," he begins, his voice carrying a hint of nostalgia. "Before I started working as a bouncer, I was in the army. I spent some time in places that weren't exactly; how should I put it… pleasant."

He pauses, gathering his thoughts. "One thing I noticed during those deployments was that the people who were careless or didn't take things seriously always ended up being watched by crows. It's a bit grim, but where we were, those birds were often around bodies left behind, pecking at them."

I listen, spellbound, as Marcus speaks. The imagery is vivid and haunting; I understand why such an experience would leave a mark. "So, the tattoo...?"

"It's a reminder," Marcus says, his voice steady and thoughtful. "A reminder to never forget what I need to do and where I stand in this world. It's a way of keeping myself grounded and aware of the reality around me. Every time I look at it, I'm reminded of my duty and the importance of staying focused."

I'm mesmerized by his story. The tattoo isn't just ink on skin; it's a symbol of survival and remembrance, a tangible connection to Marcus's past experiences. It gives me a new perspective on the meaning behind tattoos and how they can encapsulate personal journeys and reflections.

"Good running into you, Alex," Marcus says, glancing at his watch. "I'm sure we'll meet again, probably at the shop."

"Yeah, definitely," I reply, feeling a large amount of admiration and respect. "Thanks for sharing your story."

* * *

As I walk toward the tattoo shop, a surge of anticipation fills me. I'm eager to discuss my tattoo ideas with Cato and see where we can take them. The bell chimes as I push the door open, but the shop seems empty, to my disappointment. I'm about to call out when I hear his voice coming from the kitchen.

"Church," Cato says, his tone light. "There is one customer who will be going to church."

I stop in my tracks, suddenly self-conscious. It feels like my private conversation with Cato is being dissected behind that kitchen door. I can't quite make out the other person's reply at first, but the tone is unmistakable.

"Really? Why?" the voice asks.

"I don't know," Cato replies. "Maybe strict parents."

I can almost hear the smile in Cato's voice, and then the other person's mocking tone follows, "Or maybe a bit too much god-loving."

Cato chuckles lightly, and that's when I feel a pang of hurt. It's not just that he's talking about church; it's the fact that I seem to be the subject of their conversation, maybe even their amusement. My heart sinks as I realize that something deeply personal to me might be little more than a casual joke for them.

A wave of embarrassment washes over me, accompanied by a sudden sense of disconnection. I'd trusted Cato and confided in him about my conservative upbringing, my struggles with identity, and my efforts to reconcile those parts of myself. Now, hearing him casually discuss something so private makes me feel exposed and vulnerable like my inner conflicts are just another topic of small talk.

I don't want to intrude further, and I don't want to make a scene. So I turn on my heel and walk out of the shop, my steps feeling heavier with each one. The chime of the door rings out louder than usual, echoing in my mind as I leave, carrying with it an unexpected sense of finality. I try to shake off the feeling, but it lingers, sinking deeper the farther I go. Even if Cato hadn't meant to hurt me, the sting of feeling misunderstood—judged, even—is all too real.

As I continue down the street, I replay the words in my head, trying to make sense of it. I'd opened up, hoping for empathy and understanding. Instead, it feels as though my concerns were brushed aside and trivialized. I know Cato might not have meant it the way it came across, but the hurt is still fresh, and it's hard to ignore.

I stuff my hands in my pockets, walking faster as if putting distance between myself and the shop might ease the weight of it all. But with every step, my thoughts keep circling back to what happened. This was supposed to be my way of moving forward, of stepping into something new. Now, I'm not so sure.

A block or two down, I pull out my phone, tempted to call Tommy or anyone who could help me sort through the mess of emotions swirling around inside me, but I hesitate, unsure of what to say or where to start. How do I explain this strange sense of betrayal, this sudden loss of the confidence I'd felt just hours ago?

Taking a deep breath, I tell myself to slow down. This is just one moment, one misunderstanding—maybe one that deserves a second chance to talk things through with Cato when I'm ready. For now, all I want is a quiet space to clear my head and let the sting of it fade.

INK & *Intuition*

Six

CATO

As I lean against the counter in the back kitchen, the familiar sound of the bell chiming at the entrance barely registers. I'm mid-conversation with Demi, who's lounging at the small table by the window, sipping her coffee.

"Church," I say, glancing over my shoulder with a raised eyebrow. "There's this one customer who's been talking about going to church."

Demi, always the inquisitive one, looks up from her cup, smirking through her blue and purple hair. "Really? Why? Don't tell me they're trying to save your soul, Cato."

I chuckle softly, leaning back on the counter. "Nah, I think it's more of a personal thing. Probably strict parents or something. You know how it is."

Her smirk turns teasing, her eyes lighting up with mischief. "Or maybe a little too much God-loving," she says with a dramatic eye roll. "What a burden, huh?"

I laugh at her tone but stop, realizing I don't want this to sound like we're making fun of anyone's beliefs—especially not Alex's.. I shake my head, looking at her seriously.

"Still," I say, "it's up to the person to decide what they want, Demi. Just because someone's more into faith or church doesn't mean we should judge. You shouldn't laugh at someone just because they believe in something you don't."

She leans back, feigning offense and pressing a hand to her chest. "Oh, aren't you the goody two-shoes, dear Cato? Next, you'll be preaching about kindness and compassion."

I smile, my tone light but honest. "No preaching here, Demi. Just saying—it's a personal choice. You never know what someone's dealing with, right? Might be important to them in ways we don't get."

Demi shrugs, sipping her coffee with an amused look. "Maybe. But you're way too nice sometimes. You ever get tired of being so understanding?"

I chuckle, wiping my hands on a rag. "It's called balance. Be nice when it's deserved, but don't let people walk all over you."

She raises an eyebrow, clearly entertained. "And here I thought you were all ink and muscle. Turns out you've got a heart in there somewhere."

I roll my eyes, tossing the rag onto the counter with a smirk. "Maybe I do."

Just then, I remember the bell's chime and realize someone's probably waiting out front. I glance toward the door leading back to the shop, hoping it's Alex.

"I should probably go greet whoever's out there," I say, pushing off the counter and heading toward the door.

"Go get 'em, tiger," Demi calls after me, her tone dripping with playful mockery. I can feel her eyes on me as I walk out, half expecting another jab.

But as I step into the front of the shop, my smile fades. The front door is gently swinging closed, and the space is empty.

I look around, frowning slightly. "Huh," I mutter under my breath, scratching the back of my neck. There's no sign of anyone—no footsteps, no lingering presence. It's like they came in and immediately walked right back out.

I stand there for a moment, scanning the empty room one more time.

* * *

I stand at the gates of what can only be described as a modern-day castle. Calling it a mansion doesn't do it justice—the place looms over the landscape with towering stone walls, immaculate gardens, and sprawling courtyards. The sheer grandeur of it all is almost overwhelming, but I've been in my fair share of impressive homes. Still, this one's in a league of its own.

As I step inside, a man in a pristine white tuxedo greets me. His appearance is flawless, and he looks at me like I'm the final piece in some well-curated event.

"It's a privilege that an artist like you could give me some of your time," he says, his voice smooth and formal like it's a well-practiced line.

I nod, giving him a polite smile. "Always a pleasure to help with my services."

His smile widens as he gestures for me to follow. The small entourage behind him—helpers, a few people clad in black who I assume are bodyguards—barely move as we pass them and head deeper into the mansion. My eyes take in the surroundings: hallways lined with expensive artwork and chandeliers hanging from high ceilings. This isn't just wealth; it's opulence.

Eventually, we reach a large set of wooden double doors, which, with a silent push, open into a grand salon. The air is thick with the scent of expensive oils and perfumes. At the center of the room, surrounded by plush furniture and marble floors, is a large massage table. A man lies stretched out on it, and women massage his shoulders and back.

"Mr. Sinclair has arrived, sir," the man in the tuxedo announces.

The man on the table turns his head, a grin spreading across his face when his eyes meet mine. He gestures for the women to leave, waving them off as he slowly sits up. As they depart, their hands slick with oil, I get a full view of him—Mr. Ramirez, the man who brought me here. His reputation precedes him. Here, though, I'm just another artist commissioned for his services.

"Good afternoon, Mr. Ramirez," I greet him, keeping it professional.

Ramirez chuckles, getting up from the table and grabbing a towel to wipe off the oil. "No need to be so formal, Cato. We've known each other long enough. Call me Carlos."

"I absolutely cannot do that, Mr. Ramirez," I reply, polite but firm. Boundaries are important, especially with clients like him.

He grins, clearly amused by my insistence. "You're always so respectful. I like it." He nods toward the table. "Shall we continue?"

"Absolutely," I say, setting my equipment down and preparing my tools.

The man in the tuxedo gives a small bow and leaves, the room falling into silence save for the soft crackle of the fireplace in the corner. Ramirez turns around, revealing the unfinished tattoo of a tiger's head on his back. It's bold, intricate, and fierce —much like the man himself. I've been working on it for the past few sessions, and today, we're set to finish.

As I prep the tattoo gun, Ramirez glances over his shoulder. "You know, I've had some of the finest tattoo artists from all over the world, but none of them have the touch you do."

I smile slightly. "I appreciate that, Mr. Ramirez. I take pride in my work. Every piece tells a story."

He settles back onto the table, crossing his arms beneath his chin. "Ah, stories. This one's special to me. You know why I chose the tiger, don't you?"

I nod as I clean the area, running a hand over the detailed outline. "You mentioned it's a symbol of strength. Fierce and untouchable, like you."

He chuckles softly, the sound low and rumbling. "That's part of it, yes. It's more than just strength. The tiger is solitary, always watching, always moving silently until it strikes. That's me, Cato. That's my life." His tone shifts, the lightness fading slightly. "Always watching. Always prepared."

I glance at him briefly before focusing on the tattoo. It's a sentiment I understand. Even in my line of work, I have to be constantly vigilant—aware of the people around me, my clients, and the unspoken pressures. But Ramirez's world is darker; filled with power games, I want no part of.

"You don't have to explain yourself to me," I say, the hum of the tattoo gun filling the air. "Your tattoo already says enough."

He lets out another chuckle, softer this time. "I like that about you, Cato. You don't pry, don't ask unnecessary questions."

I fall into the rhythm of my craft, my focus grounding me as I work on the shading. The buzz of the needle is a fond comfort.

Ramirez breaks the silence eventually, his tone more intense. "You know, I respect you, Cato. You've built something for yourself, something powerful. People come to you because they want a piece of that power."

I look up from the tattoo, meeting his gaze. "I'm just an artist, Mr. Ramirez. I don't have the kind of power you're talking about."

He shakes his head slowly. "You're wrong. Your art—it gives people identity. It gives them a story. You have more influence than you realize; I mean, you're the top tattoo artist in the world."

I don't respond, focusing on the final touches. To me, tattooing is about connection, about expressing something personal, not about fame or money. Ramirez, on the other hand, sees everything through the lens of control and dominance.

I wipe the excess ink from his back, revealing the completed tiger. "It's done," I say, stepping back.

He walks over to the mirror, a satisfied grin spreading across his face. "Magnificent," he murmurs. "You've outdone yourself, Cato."

"Glad you like it," I reply, packing up my equipment. As much as I appreciate his praise, I'm ready to leave. Ramirez's world is one I've never quite understood, and even though I respect the man, something about him keeps me on edge.

He turns to face me, eyes sharp but appreciative. "It's not just the tattoo—it's the way you handle yourself, Cato. You've got a touch that not everyone has."

I offer a polite smile. "Just doing my job, Mr. Ramirez."

He claps a heavy hand on my shoulder, his grin widening. "Don't be so modest, Cato. You're an artist and a damn good one."

The intensity in his gaze makes the room feel a bit smaller, and I'm grateful when he lets go. I finish packing up, giving him a nod. "I'll see you when you're ready for your next tattoo, Mr. Ramirez."

"Looking forward to it, Cato."

* * *

I sit in the shop, phone resting heavily in my hand, staring at the screen as if it might suddenly light up with a message from Alex. I've sent him multiple texts over the past few days—short, casual ones.

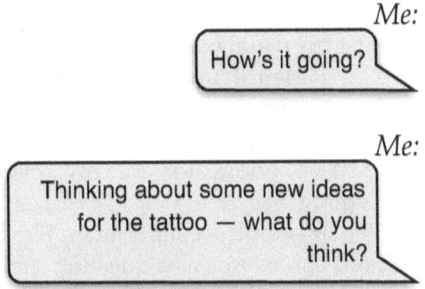

Me:

How's it going?

Me:

Thinking about some new ideas for the tattoo — what do you think?

Unfortunately, there's been nothing. Not a single reply. The longer the silence stretches, the more it gnaws at me. Just as

51

I'm about to send another message, the door creaks open. I look up, and there he is—Alex. Relief washes over me, but it's short-lived.

"Alex," I greet, trying to keep steadiness in my voice, hoping to dissolve whatever strange tension seems to linger. "Good to see you."

His response is flat. Cold, almost. "Hey," he mutters, not even looking me in the eye as he steps into the shop. His movements are hurried like he doesn't want to be here any longer than necessary.

A knot forms in my stomach. "Everything okay?" I ask, gauging his mood.

"Yeah, sure," he says, but there's no conviction behind it. He avoids my gaze, eyes flitting around the room instead. Then he adds, "Let's just get started. I've got to head to work soon."

The abruptness, the businesslike tone—it throws me. It's like the Alex I've come to know, the thoughtful, open guy, has vanished. This feels... robotic.

"Sure," I say slowly, watching as he sits down and pulls out his sketchbook. There's no small talk, no playful banter like we used to have. He doesn't even look at me when he hands me the book; he just keeps his eyes down.

I take the sketchbook, flipping it open, but the drawings inside... aren't like his usual work. They're rough, rushed, and lacking the care and detail I've come to expect from him. The lines are harsh and jagged in places. The composition feels off, lacking his usual balance and thoughtfulness.

I glance up, keeping my voice neutral. "These look... different. Were you in a rush when you did these?"

Alex shrugs, still avoiding my eyes. "I just want to get it done. I've got a lot on my plate right now. Work, life—everything."

His tone's a sharp edge like he's trying to push me away before I can even ask a question. Irritation flickers up inside me. He's treating this—us—like a task to tick off his list. This is his tattoo, something deeply personal, not just an errand to rush through.

"Alex," I say, keeping my tone calm, "I think maybe we should slow down for a second. I get that you're busy, but this... this is permanent. We can't just rush through it."

His eyes flash as he finally looks at me. "Why? Why do we need to slow down? Because you think I'm too much of a religious freak to focus on a tattoo right now?"

The sarcasm in his voice feels like a slap to the face. I blink, taken aback, trying to understand where that even came from. Does he think I'm judging him? Does he think I'm looking down on him because of his faith?

"Wait, what?" I say, genuinely confused. "Alex, where is this coming from? I never said anything like that—"

"You don't have to say it," he snaps, cutting me off. "It's obvious, isn't it? I'm the guy with an overbearing religious family. I'm the guy who can't get his life together. I'm the guy who's too wrapped up in my own shit to even respond to your texts. So, yeah, let's just get the tattoo done, okay? I don't need a lecture."

I stare at him, the feelings of frustration and hurt building up inside. How did we get here? Just a few weeks ago, we were connecting and understanding each other. Now, it's like he's deliberately pushing me away.

I let out a slow breath, keeping my voice even. "Alex, I'm not judging you. I've never judged you. But this—this tattoo —means something to you. I just think maybe right now isn't the right time."

He scoffs, rolling his eyes. "Right. So, what, you think I need time away? Some spiritual retreat or something? You think I'm not in the right headspace, is that it?"

"I think you're going through something," I say carefully, "and maybe it's affecting the way you're looking at this. The sketches, Alex, they're not like your usual work. They're rushed like you're trying to get it over with instead of enjoying the process."

He stiffens, jaw clenched. For a moment, he says nothing, and the tension between us thickens. I want to reach out, to pull him back from whatever dark place he's retreating to, but I don't know how.

After a long silence, Alex abruptly stands, grabbing his bag. "I don't have time for this right now," he mutters, voice cold. "I need to get to work."

I stand there, helpless, as he heads for the door. "Alex, wait—"

The door swings shut behind him with a dull thud, leaving me alone in the empty shop, staring at the spot where he'd been. The room feels heavy, like all the life and energy had been sucked out of it the moment Alex left. I sit down slowly, still holding the sketchbook in my hands. My thumb traces over one of the rough lines, the jagged edge a stark contrast to the smooth, detailed sketches Alex usually makes. Something was wrong—really wrong.

* * *

I lie on my bed, staring up at the ceiling, feeling the weight of the day pressing down on me. Bailey, my golden retriever, is curled up next to me, his head resting on my chest. His soft, warm body offers comfort I didn't realize I needed, but even his familiar presence isn't enough to shake the unease sitting heavy in my chest.

Bailey's been shedding a lot lately, leaving fur all over the bed. I probably should at least train him to stay off the furniture, but I don't have the heart to. He's more than just a dog to me—he's family. His soft breathing is a reminder of the only consistency I have.

I absently run my fingers through his fur, my mind elsewhere, replaying the events of the day repeatedly. Alex. Something was really off with him today, and I can't wrap my head around it. I've seen it all. People come in grumpy, distracted, sometimes downright angry, but this? This isn't just any client. Alex's distance, the way he snapped at me, how his words came out so bitterly—it's hitting me harder than I care to admit.

Why does it matter so much? Why is it messing with my head like this? I've handled grumpy clients before, but none of them have ever gotten under my skin like this.

Bailey lets out a little huff and shifts his weight against me, probably sensing my restless thoughts. I sigh and scratch his head again, feeling the softness of his fur under my fingers. "Guess it's just you and me tonight, huh, boy?"

Bailey responds by snuggling closer, and I let myself sink into the comfort of his presence, even as my mind continues to spiral with thoughts of Alex. What the hell is going on with him?

seven

ALEX

April

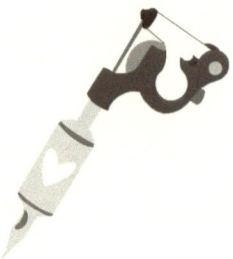

I sit at my desk, trying to focus on the graphic design project in front of me. The task isn't anything too complicated—just a logo redesign for a small company—but my mind is miles away.

I haven't stopped thinking about Cato since our last conversation last week. I'm constantly replaying every word, every look, wondering if I pushed too far, if I've ruined everything between us.

The lines on the iPad start blurring, and my fingers hover over the keyboard, unsure of what to do next.

The sharp ring of my office phone snaps me out of my thoughts. I glance at the caller ID, my heart skipping a beat when I see Amelia Noor's name—my boss. Great.

I take a breath and answer. "Hello?"

"Alex," she says, her voice calm but with a firm edge. "Could you come to my office for a moment?"

"Uh, yeah. Sure." I hang up, feeling my stomach tighten. Amelia isn't the type to call people in for a casual chat. I save my work, even though I haven't done much, and stand up, adjusting my shirt. The walk to her office feels longer than usual, and I run through the possibilities in my head—could it be something about my recent projects? Has she noticed I've been distracted? Damn. I should've been paying more attention.

I knock lightly on her door.

"Come in," she calls from the other side.

I push the door open, stepping into the bright, sleek space of her office. Amelia sits behind her large desk, her hands clasped in front of her. Looking up at me with sharp, no-nonsense eyes, she gestures toward the chair opposite her.

"Have a seat, Alex."

I sit down, trying not to look too stiff. The atmosphere in the room is professional, but there's something about it that makes me feel like a kid being called into the principal's office. I force a smile, hoping to lighten the mood, but she doesn't return it.

"Alex, I wanted to talk to you about your focus at work," she begins, her tone direct but not harsh. "You've been doing well here, and I know you've got the talent to succeed, but lately... something's been off."

My heart sinks. She's noticed. Of course she has. I try to keep my face neutral, but inside, I'm scrambling for an explanation.

"I, uh... I didn't realize it was that noticeable," I say, rubbing the back of my neck awkwardly. "I've just had a lot on my mind lately. But I'm still getting everything done—"

"That's not the point," she interrupts gently but firmly. "I can see that you're trying, but your work isn't reflecting the level of focus and creativity that I know you're capable of. You've been distracted. And while I understand that things

INK & *Intuition*

happen outside of work, I need you to keep your head in the game when you're here."

I nod, feeling embarrassment and frustration with myself. "I know, I'm sorry. I'll do better."

Amelia leans back slightly, crossing her arms. She's not angry, but there's a clear seriousness in her expression. "I'm not asking for an apology, Alex. I just want you to be honest with yourself. If something's going on—if something's pulling your attention away—address it. Don't let it fester."

Her words hit harder than I expect, and I shift uncomfortably in the chair. She's right. I've been letting things fester—my conflicted feelings about Cato, the pressure from my mom, and the weight of everything crashing down on me all at once. It's like trying to juggle too many things, and I'm dropping the ball at work because of it.

"I appreciate you telling me, Amelia," I say, my voice quieter now. "I've just… I've been dealing with some personal stuff, but I'll make sure it doesn't affect my work anymore."

Amelia nods, her expression softening a bit. "I'm not here to pry into your personal life, Alex. Everyone goes through things, and I get that. But this is your career, and you've got a lot of potential. I don't want to see you lose focus now when you're just starting to build something solid here."

I swallow hard, feeling the weight of her words. She's not wrong. This job—it's supposed to be my fresh start, the place where I can build something for myself without all the baggage from my past dragging me down. And yet here I am, letting everything bleed into it. I have to get a grip.

"I understand," I say, my voice firmer now. "I won't let it happen again. I'll stay focused."

She smiles just a little, and it feels like a small victory. "Good. I know you can do it, Alex. You've shown me your talent. Just don't lose sight of what's important, both here and outside of work. Balance is key."

I nod again, grateful she's not being harder on me. "Thanks, Amelia. I'll make sure I'm back on track."

She gives me a short nod, picking up a pen and glancing back at her computer. "Alright then. Go ahead and finish up your project for the day, and if you need to talk, my door's open. Just... stay focused, okay?"

"I will," I say, standing up. "I appreciate it."

* * *

I wander aimlessly through the city, the noise of the streets swirling around me, but none of it really sinks in. My head feels clouded, like I'm walking through a fog, everything slightly out of focus. I have my new sketchbook tucked under my arm; I haven't had the nerve to go get my other one from Cato. I'm just hoping that drawing might help clear my mind—even if just for a few moments.

I don't have a specific destination in mind, but eventually, I find myself at a park. It's the kind of place where everything seems to stand still, no matter how fast the world spins around it. The benches are mostly empty, save for the occasional person passing by, and a few pigeons peck at crumbs left behind by someone who probably had a better day than I'm having.

I sit down on a worn, wooden bench where the paint is chipped from years of use and let out a long breath. The weight on my chest doesn't go away, though. It just sits there, heavy and unmoving.

"Alright, Alex," I mutter to myself, flipping open my sketchbook. "Let's try this again."

I glance around, my eyes settling on a nearby building just outside the park's edge. It's nothing special—just a standard city building, a few windows and some bricks. I figure it'll be simple enough to draw. Something to focus on. Something to help me forget, even if just for a few minutes.

I pick up my pencil and start drawing, but the lines come out shaky. The building looks blurred on the page as if my hand is translating the mess in my mind onto the paper. I pause, staring down at the page, frustrated. I can't even draw a straight line. The building is supposed to be simple, but nothing about it looks clear.

"Come on," I mutter under my breath, gripping the pencil a little tighter. "Just… get it right."

I try again, my pencil scratching across the page, but every time I look down, the lines are wrong. Too wavy. Too loose. Too… off. I groan, running a hand through my hair and staring at the half-finished mess in front of me.

The pigeons waddle closer, probably hoping I have food. I watch them for a moment, their heads bobbing back and forth as they peck at the last remnants of some discarded crackers. I let out a humorless chuckle. "At least you guys know what you're doing."

One of the pigeons tilts its head at me, then goes back to pecking at the crumbs. I sigh and flip to a new page in my sketchbook, trying to start over. Maybe a tree this time. There are plenty of those around. I look up at the oak tree standing a few feet away, its branches swaying slightly in the breeze.

"Alright, tree," I say quietly, more to myself than to the tree. "You're sturdy, you've got roots, you're not going anywhere. Help me out here."

I sketch the outline of the trunk, but once again, the lines aren't smooth. They waver, not like the branches of a tree in the wind, but like my hand can't find its balance. I clench my jaw, feeling the frustration build again.

"Why can't I get this right?" I say, my voice louder this time, though no one is around to hear me. "It's a damn tree. It should be easy."

The tree doesn't respond, of course. It just stands there, strong and steady, like it always has been. Unbothered by anything. I wish I could be like that. Strong. Unbothered. Instead, I feel like every little gust of wind is constantly blowing me off course. Everything feels out of balance.

I stare down at my sketchbook again, at the jagged lines that don't make any sense. It's like they mirror my thoughts—unfocused, all over the place. The building, the tree, none of it looks like what it's supposed to. Just like my life doesn't feel like what it's supposed to.

"What the hell am I even doing?" I mumble, flipping the pencil between my fingers. "Why can't I just... figure it out? Why can't I get anything right?"

The pigeons are still hovering around me, their little beady eyes watching, probably disappointed I don't have food. I look at them and sigh. "I don't have crackers, guys. Just a sketchbook full of shit."

I set the pencil down, resting my head in my hands. My mind is a mess; no matter what I do, I can't clear it. I can't get Cato out of my head—the look on his face when I left the shop, his calm voice telling me we should take some time away from working on the tattoo. Like I can just stop thinking about everything for a minute. Like my mind would suddenly let me breathe.

"I wish it were that easy," I mutter to myself, leaning back on the bench. The tree branches overhead sway gently, and I find myself talking to it again. "How do you do it? How do you just stand there, solid, while everything else keeps moving around you?"

The tree, like the pigeons, offers no answer. I scoff at myself, shaking my head. I'm talking to trees now. *Great. Real productive, Alex.*

I pick up my sketchbook again, flipping through the pages of half-finished drawings. Each one feels incomplete and rushed. Like I've been trying to get something down on paper, but the meaning never quite sticks.

As I'm sitting there, still staring up at the tree branches overhead, I hear the soft shuffle of footsteps approaching. I glance to my left and see an older woman, maybe in her '70s or '80s, making her way toward the bench. She has a kind, weathered face that looks like it's lived through a lot but still holds kindness. Her gray hair is tied back in a loose bun, and she has a walking stick, though she doesn't seem to rely on it too much.

I shift a little, making space on the bench, figuring she'll probably sit for a while and enjoy the quiet like I am. But to my surprise, she doesn't just sit down. She looks at me—really looks at me—and smiles.

"You look like you've got the weight of the world on your shoulders, young man," she says, her voice soft.

I blink, taken aback by her directness. "Uh, yeah, I guess you could say that."

Without asking, she sits down next to me, her walking stick resting against the bench. "You know, I always come to this park when I feel like I need to clear my head. The trees, the birds… they help, don't they?"

I manage a small smile, though it doesn't quite reach my eyes. "Yeah, I guess. The pigeons are pretty relentless, though."

She chuckles, her laughter like a soft breeze. "Oh, don't mind them. They're just doing what pigeons do—always looking for their next meal, never thinking about much else. You should take a lesson from them."

I raise an eyebrow, curious. "A lesson from pigeons?"

She nods, her eyes twinkling with a bit of mischief. "They don't get wrapped up in worries like we do. They're simple creatures. Sometimes, we humans like to complicate everything, don't we?"

I can't argue with that. "Yeah, I guess we do."

There's a brief pause before she looks at me again, more seriously this time. "What's got you looking so lost? You're not from Texas, are you? I can hear it in your voice."

I hesitate. For some reason, it feels easier to talk to this stranger than it does to anyone else in my life right now. Maybe it's because she doesn't know me. Maybe because she doesn't expect anything. "Yeah, I just moved here all the way from Minnesota, and everything's kind of a mess right now. I feel like I'm out of control, like no matter what I do, I can't get anything right. Even my drawings are all over the place."

She tilts her head, considering my words carefully. "Life tends to feel like that sometimes. But let me tell you something, dear—it's not always about getting things 'right.' Sometimes, it's just about getting through."

I glance at her, curious. "You sound like you've been through your fair share of things."

She lets out a deep, nostalgic sigh, a smile tugging at the corners of her lips. "Oh, I've lived through enough, believe me, but my husband? Now, he was a man who really knew how to handle chaos."

I look at her, intrigued. "What do you mean?"

Her eyes sparkle with amusement. "My husband, God bless his soul, fought in two wars. A soldier through and through. You know, he could assemble and disassemble a gun in 45 seconds flat. Never seen anyone do it faster. He was trained for combat, for structure, for discipline. You'd think he had it all figured out, right?"

I nod, imagining the kind of man she's describing. Strong, capable—like someone who had life all under control.

She leans closer, her voice dropping to a conspiratorial whisper. "But God help him if he had to fold a sheet."

I blink, confused for a second before the absurdity of it hits me. "Wait, what?"

She grins, clearly enjoying herself now. "I kid you not! The man could handle weapons like a machine, but every time I asked him to fold the laundry—especially the fitted sheets—he looked like a lost puppy. Couldn't for the life of him figure it out. He'd wrestle with those sheets like he was in a battle, cursing under his breath the whole time. It was the most ridiculous thing."

I find myself laughing, a real laugh, one that loosens some of the knots in my chest. "Seriously? A soldier who couldn't fold a sheet?"

She nods, laughing along with me. "Oh, yes. It was quite the sight. He'd come back from missions, looking sharp as ever, but then he'd stand there, holding a fitted sheet, completely defeated. I used to tease him about it all the time."

I shake my head, still smiling. "That's... kind of amazing, actually. You wouldn't think someone like that would struggle with something so simple."

She smiles warmly, leaning back on the bench. "That's just it, though. No matter how put together someone seems, there's always something that throws them off. Even the strongest people have their weak spots. My husband could face war, but God forbid I asked him to do anything domestic."

Her words settle over me, the humor giving way to something deeper. She's right. Even the most capable people have things they can't quite master. Here I am, sitting here beating myself up over not having everything together, but maybe that's okay. Maybe not having everything in perfect order isn't the end of the world.

"You know," I say slowly, "that makes a lot of sense. I guess I've been trying too hard to figure it all out, and it's just... not working."

The old woman looks at me kindly, her eyes softening. "That's because life isn't always meant to be figured out. Sometimes, you just have to let it be messy. Let yourself be messy. Eventually, things have a way of falling into place."

I let her words sink in, feeling the weight on my shoulders ease a little. "Thank you," I say quietly, genuinely. "I think I needed to hear that."

She smiles again, patting my hand gently. "Of course, dear. We all need a little reminder that it's okay not to be perfect."

We sit in comfortable silence for a few moments, the breeze rustling through the leaves above us, the pigeons still pecking at crumbs by our feet. For the first time in days, I feel a little lighter, a little less tangled up in my own thoughts.

After a while, the old woman slowly stands up, leaning on her walking stick. "Well, I should get going. Remember, Alex," she says, surprising me by using my name, "even soldiers have trouble folding sheets."

I grin. "I'll keep that in mind."

She winks at me before turning to leave, her footsteps soft and measured as she makes her way down the path. I watch her go, feeling like maybe, just maybe, things aren't as hopeless as they seemed when I first sat down.

F. A. SENG

As I look down at my sketchbook, I don't feel the same pressure to make the lines perfect. Instead, I just let my hand move freely, sketching the pigeons, the trees, the feeling of the moment. It's not perfect, but it feels honest.

And for now, that's all I need.

eight
ALEX

I wander back toward my apartment, and all I can think about is Eternal Ink. I hadn't planned on walking by it, but my feet seemed to have a mind of their own, pulling me in that direction. Before I know it, here I am—standing right across from the shop, staring at the familiar sign.

My heart gives a little tug, and I shift on my feet, feeling torn. Part of me wants to walk in, to see him, to talk about what's going. But the other part—the part that's tired, confused, and full of doubt—tells me to keep moving. The last time I was here, things got weird. I'd snapped at him, and now it feels like there's this wall between us. I'm not even sure if it's one I can break down.

I take a few steps toward the door, hand half-raised to push it open. But then I stop. What would I even say? I have no idea how to explain the mess in my head, how to tell Cato what I'm feeling. Hell, I'm not even sure I understand it myself.

I stuff my hands into my pockets, exhaling slowly, and turn away from the shop. Not today.

The walk back to my apartment is quieter, the noise of the city fading into the background as I try to clear my thoughts. By the time I push open the door to my place, I feel drained—physically, mentally, emotionally. I just want to collapse into bed and forget everything for a while.

As I walk in, I spot Tommy on the couch, his legs stretched out, a bag of chips in his lap as he scrolls through his phone. He looks up when he sees me, raising an eyebrow.

"Hey, man. You look like you've been hit by a truck," he says, his usual sarcasm laced with a hint of concern.

I flop down on the couch next to him, letting out a groan. "Feels like it."

He tosses the bag of chips onto the coffee table and turns to face me. "What's going on with you? You've been acting weird for days."

I rub my face, not sure where to start. "It's just... everything. Cato, work, my mom, my head—it's all a mess."

Tommy raises an eyebrow, leaning back against the couch. "Well, that's vague. Care to elaborate?"

I sigh, slumping further into the cushions. "I don't know. I don't even know how to explain it. I've been all over the place, and I feel like I've just... pushed Cato away. I can't stop thinking about him, but I don't even know how to talk to him anymore."

Tommy snorts. "You're making this more complicated than it needs to be."

I shoot him a look. "Really? I'm pretty sure it's already complicated."

He waves a hand dismissively. "Dude, it's only complicated because you're making it that way. Just tell him how you feel."

I blink at him like it's that easy. "Tell him? Just like that?"

"Yeah, just like that," Tommy says as if it's the most obvious thing in the world. "You're over here stressing yourself out, and for what? He's not a mind reader, man. He's probably just as confused as you are."

I run a hand through my hair, feeling the weight of Tommy's words settle over me. "It's not that simple, Tommy. What if... I don't even know what I feel. I just—I'm upset with what he said about me behind my back."

Tommy tilts his head, studying me for a second. "Okay, first of all, it's obvious that you like him. Like, even an idiot could see that." He pauses, smirking. "And second, if you're scared, that's all the more reason to talk to him. You're going to let fear stop you from figuring out something that could be great?"

I roll my eyes. "I don't know him well enough to like him like that. I mean, yeah, maybe I have a small crush on him, but that's it. And I'm not scared; I'm just mad."

"You are scared, or you would be talking to him right now," Tommy says.

I frown, picking at the edge of the couch cushion. "I don't even know if he feels the same way."

Tommy rolls his eyes dramatically. "Oh, come on. The guy's been texting you non-stop, and from what you've told me, he's been nothing but patient with you. Trust me, he feels something. You don't act like that around someone you don't care about."

I think about the texts. Cato has been reaching out, and I've ignored most of them, too scared to deal with the conversation that might follow. What if Tommy's right? What if Cato is just as confused as I am?

"Okay," I say slowly, turning the idea over in my head. "But what do I even say?"

Tommy shrugs. "The truth. Tell him what you just told me. That you've been a mess, but also that you don't appreciate hearing him talk about you the way he was and that you can't stop thinking about him."

I scoff. "Yeah, sure. That'll go over well. 'Hey, Cato, I've been avoiding you because I have a crush on you, and you were talking about me being religious behind my back. Cool, right?'"

Tommy grins. "Exactly."

I give him a look, but part of me knows he isn't wrong. I have to talk to Cato. I can't keep avoiding him, can't keep pretending like I don't care when the truth is, I care more than I know how to handle.

Tommy stands up, stretching his arms above his head. "Look, man. You're going to drive yourself insane if you keep playing this game of back-and-forth. Just be honest with him. It's better than doing nothing and wondering what could've been."

I sigh, standing up as well, feeling a little less heavy than when I first walked in. "Yeah, maybe you're right."

Tommy claps me on the shoulder. "Of course I'm right. Now go talk to him before you dig yourself into a deeper hole."

I nod, grabbing my phone from the table, the familiar knot of anxiety twisting in my gut. I don't know what I'm going to say or how the conversation will go, but Tommy's right. I can't keep running from this.

nine

CATO

I'm sitting on the couch in my penthouse, staring at the half-finished sketch in front of me. The lines are there, sure, but they don't mean much. I've been trying to focus, trying to throw myself into my work to distract myself from all the noise in my head, but nothing is sticking. Alex hasn't left my mind since that awkward conversation at the shop. His sarcastic comments about church, the frustration in his voice… it wasn't just a bad day for him; it felt like something deeper, something we hadn't figured out yet.

I sigh, leaning back into the couch. Bailey lies at my feet, his head resting on his paws, completely unaware of the storm swirling around in my brain. I reach down to scratch behind his ears, hoping the small comfort will ground me. Nothing is making sense right now.

* * *

I arrive at Eternal Ink around 11 a.m. The usual email checking, appointment verification, and the constant pacing back and forth all seem very tedious today. I lean back in my chair, staring at the tattoo sketches on the wall, trying to distract myself from the mess in my head.

I need to get out of here for a bit.

I stand up, stretching my back, and the first thought that pops into my mind is coffee. I need caffeine if I'm going to make it through the rest of the day. And there's only one place I want to go—Emma's Café.

Emma's place is a few blocks away, a little hole-in-the-wall café that I've been going to for years. Emma always has something comforting to say, and her coffee is hands down the best in the city. Plus, the quiet, relaxed atmosphere is exactly what I need after dealing with that last client. A walk and some fresh air sound good, too.

First, I need to check in with Demi. I pull out my phone and dial her number. It rings a couple of times before she picks up.

"Hey, Cato," Demi's voice is upbeat as always. "You still alive in there? Or has the shop driven you mad yet?"

I chuckle lightly, rubbing my temple. "Barely hanging on, Demi. I just dealt with the weirdest client. She came in with this wild tattoo idea—like, intricate, detailed—but then she tried to turn it into something else, you know?"

Demi laughs on the other end, clearly amused. "Oh, let me guess. She was trying to seduce the famous Cato Sinclair into giving her more than just a tattoo, huh?"

I roll my eyes, even though she can't see me. "Pretty much. I shut it down, but God, it was uncomfortable. She didn't know when to quit."

"Some people, man," Demi says with a sigh. "It's like they forget you're a tattoo artist, not some celebrity they can hit on."

"Yeah, well, she figured it out eventually." I grab my jacket from the back of the chair, already planning my escape. "Anyway, I'm thinking about taking a break and heading over to Emma's Café for a coffee. I need to clear my head before I finish up the day's appointments."

"Good idea," she says. "You sound like you need it. Speaking of which, you've got a pretty packed schedule today. I can move a couple of appointments around if you need more time."

I think about it for a moment as I shrug into my jacket. "How's the rest of the day looking?"

Demi clicks her tongue as she looks over the schedule. "You've got a consultation with Jordan at three, then two smaller sessions at four and five. I can shift one of those to tomorrow if you want a longer break."

I glance out the shop window at the late morning light filtering through. A long walk sounds good. I need to shake off this weird energy and get my head straight before diving back into work. Besides, I'm not in the mood to rush through the rest of the day, especially not after the morning I've had.

"Yeah," I say, nodding to myself. "Push the four o'clock to tomorrow. I'll take the time slot after Jordan's consultation for a walk. Clear my head a bit."

"Got it," she says, typing away. "You're all set then. Enjoy your coffee, and try not to let any more strange clients come in and ruin your day."

I laugh, feeling a little lighter just talking to her. "I'll do my best. Thanks, Demi."

"No problem, boss," she says, her tone playful. "Go get that caffeine fix."

I hang up the phone, feeling a little more grounded. Demi always has a way of keeping things running smoothly, and right now, I'm grateful for that. I lock up the shop, pull the sign on the door to "Back Soon", and head out into the street.

I pass by the pet shop on the corner, its window full of adorable puppies and kittens tumbling over each other. I slow down, glancing through the glass. Maybe it's time to get Bailey a little company. The thought makes me chuckle to myself, imagining Bailey's reaction to a new dog—especially a brother. A new friend for Bailey, huh?

The more I think about it, the more the idea doesn't seem half-bad. Bailey has been my only companion for a while, and

F. A. SENG

I've been so busy with the shop and everything else that maybe he needs some extra company. It could be good for both of us.

With that thought in mind, I find myself walking into the shop. The bell above the door jingles as I step inside, and the familiar scent of fresh pet food, hay, and a little bit of puppy mischief hits me instantly. The place is packed with cages and kennels, each one filled with small, playful animals. A few dogs bark from the back, and a couple of curious kittens meow from a display near the front.

As I enter, a woman behind the counter looks up. She smiles warmly and waves me over. "Hey there! Are you looking for something for your dog today?"

I smile back and walk over to her. "Yeah, something like that. I was actually thinking about getting a second dog. Bailey's been with me for years, and I think it might be time for him to have a friend."

Her eyes light up at that. "Oh, that's exciting! What kind of dog is Bailey?"

I smile, leaning against the counter. "He's a Golden Retriever and honestly the best dog I've ever had. He's super calm and well-behaved, but I think he's ready for some company. Maybe a female this time, so he doesn't feel like the only one running the show."

The thought makes me chuckle again. I imagine Bailey's reaction to sharing the space with someone else. He'd probably be jealous for about a week, then get over it.

The woman smiles, clearly enjoying the idea. "Well, you've come to the right place. We have a few beautiful dogs here, both males and females, and they're all super friendly. What kind of personality are you looking for? Another retriever like Bailey, or are you thinking of mixing it up?"

I think for a second, glancing over at the kennels. A few different dogs wag their tails, their eyes bright with excitement. "I'm open to mixing it up. It doesn't have to be another retriever. Just someone who gets along with him. He's pretty chill, so as long as the dog isn't too hyper, I think we'll be fine."

She nods, stepping out from behind the counter. "Follow me. I'll show you a few options. We've got a couple of retrievers, but we also have some smaller breeds if you want something different."

I follow her to the back of the shop, where the kennels are set up. There are all kinds of dogs—retrievers, labradors, and even a few smaller breeds like terriers and cocker spaniels. One of the golden retrievers immediately catches my eye—a beautiful female with soft, caramel-colored fur. She's calm, sitting near the back of the kennel, her eyes focused on me, curious but not overly excited.

"She's gorgeous," I say, pointing to the retriever. "What's her story?"

The woman smiles. "She's about two years old. She came from a good home, but her previous owner couldn't keep her anymore due to personal reasons. She's very gentle and really sweet, and she'd get along great with another calm dog like Bailey."

I crouch down, looking through the bars at the retriever. She tilts her head slightly, then slowly stands up and walks over to me, pressing her nose through the bars to sniff my hand.

"She's perfect," I say softly, smiling at the dog as she wags her tail lightly. "Bailey would love her."

The woman leans against the kennel, watching us with a smile. "You want to take her for a walk, see how she does?"

I stand up, feeling a mix of excitement and hesitation. "Honestly, I'm tempted, but I think I should think about it first. Bailey's pretty territorial, and I want to make sure I'm ready for the commitment of adding another dog."

She nods, understanding. "Totally fair. It's a big decision, and it's good that you're thinking it through. I can hold her for a few days if you want to take some time to decide. She's not going anywhere."

I give her a grateful smile. "Thanks, I appreciate that. Let me give it some thought. I'll check in with you soon."

"Absolutely," she says, leading me back toward the front of the shop. "Take your time. We're here whenever you're ready."

I wave goodbye, stepping back out into the street, the idea still bouncing around in my head. A companion for Bailey. Maybe that isn't such a bad idea after all. But I'll have to be sure. Adding another dog is a big deal, and right now, with everything else going on—Alex, the overseas clients, the shop—I don't want to make a decision I'm not ready for.

As I walk away from the shop, I chuckle to myself. "A girlfriend for Bailey, huh? I'll have to talk to him about that one."

* * *

The door of Emma's Café swings open, and the familiar scent of fresh coffee and baked goods hits me like a warm hug. Today, it isn't as quiet and calm as usual. The place is bustling—every table is filled with people chatting, sipping their drinks, and taking refuge from the busy city outside. It's a lot more crowded than I expected for this time of day. I scan the room, hoping to find a corner where I can sit down and enjoy a moment of peace.

A waitress, a young woman with short blonde hair, approaches me with an apologetic smile. "Hey there! We're kind of packed today. There's only one table left, and it's at the back," she says, pointing toward the far end of the café.

I give her a small nod. "That's fine. I'll take it."

"Great! What can I get you today?" she asks, pulling out her notepad.

"Just the usual. Black coffee, strong," I reply, already feeling the need for caffeine kicking in after the morning I've had.

"Coming right up," she says, scribbling down the order. "I'll bring it to you in a minute."

I make my way through the café, weaving between the tables and the occasional bursts of laughter from groups of friends catching up. The last table is tucked away in the back corner, offering a little bit of privacy. But as I get closer, my steps slow.

Alex is sitting at the table, which she said was empty. He must've just found a seat without going to the counter.

INK & *Intuition*

My heart does a quick, unexpected flip in my chest, and I hesitate for a second. Of all the tables, of all the cafés in the city, I have to run into him here. He hasn't seen me yet—he's hunched over, sketching something in a new sketchbook, completely absorbed in whatever he's drawing. This reminds me, I need to return the other one that he left at the shop. His brow is furrowed in concentration, and he keeps brushing a lock of blonde hair out of his eyes, not noticing the people moving around him.

I consider walking out, but that idea feels stupid. We can't keep dancing around each other like this, avoiding conversations that we clearly need to have. So, instead, I take a deep breath and walk over to the table.

As soon as I say "Hey," the tension between us is palpable. Alex looks up from his sketchbook, his green eyes widening with surprise and something else I can't quite place. His lips part slightly, and for a second, it feels like he doesn't know what to say either.

"Oh. Hey," he finally says, his voice sounding a little stiff like he's caught off guard but trying to play it cool.

There's a moment of silence. Not the comfortable kind we used to have, but the kind where you can feel all the unspoken words hanging in the air, thick and heavy. Great. This isn't going to be easy. I can already tell.

I pull out the chair across from him and sit down, trying to act casual, though I can feel the tension in every inch of my body. He sets his pencil down and closes his sketchbook slowly like he's putting up a barrier between us, something to hide behind.

We sit quietly for a few minutes, pretending to look anywhere but at each other. The waitress returns with my coffee, and I mutter a quick "Thanks" as she places it in front of me. She smiles politely, but I can tell she senses the awkwardness. I take a sip of the coffee, letting its warmth ground me a little.

"So, uh, how's work going?" I ask, breaking the silence, my voice sounding more casual than I feel. It's a safe question, but the way Alex stiffens at it tells me it isn't exactly what he wants to talk about.

"Busy," Alex replies, his voice clipped. "Nothing new."

I nod, trying to keep the conversation going. "That's good. Busy means good, right?"

Alex just shrugs, his eyes shifting back to his coffee cup. "Yeah, I guess. Busy's good."

More silence. This isn't how I want it to be. We used to be able to talk so easily when he came into the shop, but now, everything feels forced, like we're both tiptoeing around some invisible line, afraid to cross it.

I drum my fingers on the edge of the table, searching for something else to say. Before I can think of anything, Alex looks up, his expression more serious than before.

"What do you think about religious people?" he asks suddenly, his voice low, almost cautious.

The question catches me off guard. I blink, staring at him for a moment. "What do you mean?"

"You know," he says, shifting uncomfortably in his seat, "people who are, like, really into religion. What do you think about them?"

I can hear the edge in his voice, and I know where this is coming from. That comment he made at the shop, the one about being a religious freak, is still weighing on him.

I sigh, choosing my words carefully. "Honestly? I don't judge people based on their beliefs. I think everyone's entitled to believe what they want. As long as they're not hurting anyone, I don't really care."

Alex stares at me for a moment, his jaw tightening. "Yeah, well, not everyone sees it that way."

I frown, leaning forward a little. "Alex, what are you talking about?"

"I walked into the shop a while back to show you some things, and I overheard you talking with someone and laughing about 'church' and 'being god loving,'" Alex says, his voice laced with hurt.

INK & *Intuition*

"Alex, again, what are you…" I start, but then I remember that day. Someone had come into the shop and left before I could get out there. "That was you who left."

Alex nods, "Yeah, I heard everything."

I swallow hard, realizing that what I said hurt Alex. "I never meant to make you feel judged. If that's what you think, I'm sorry. I wasn't trying to say anything bad about your beliefs or your upbringing. I even told Demi that we shouldn't judge people for being who they are."

His eyes flick to mine, a mix of frustration and something else—something deeper. "It's not that, Cato. It's just… I've been dealing with a lot of stuff. My family, how I was raised, trying to figure out what I believe and what I don't. Then I heard you make that comment about church—"

I hold up a hand, cutting him off gently. "Wait. Hold on. If I said something that upset you, I'm really sorry. I didn't mean to. I wasn't mocking you or your faith, I swear. It was just… bad timing or something. But I never meant for you to feel like I was making fun of you."

He looks away, adjusting his glasses as his fingers fidget with the edge of his coffee cup. "I guess I just… I don't know. I've been trying to balance everything—my family, what they expect, what I actually want for myself—and sometimes it feels like no matter what I do, I'm not enough."

His words hit me hard, and suddenly, all the tension between us makes sense. It isn't just about me or the shop. It's about everything he's carrying.

"Alex, I get it," I say softly. "I mean, I can't say I know exactly what you're going through, but I understand feeling torn between what people expect of you and what you really want for yourself. That's not easy to figure out."

He lets out a long breath, his shoulders relaxing just a little. "Yeah, well, it sucks."

I chuckle lightly. "Yeah, it does. But listen, if I ever say something that rubs you the wrong way, just call me out on it, okay? I'd rather you tell me straight up than let it build up like this."

78

He nods slowly, his eyes meeting mine again. "I didn't mean to snap at you. That day at the shop... I don't know, I just —"

"It's okay," I say, cutting him off gently. "We both had stuff going on. But I don't want you to feel like you can't talk to me, you know? I'm not here to judge you or tell you how to live your life."

Alex is quiet for a moment, processing my words. Finally, he lets out a soft chuckle, shaking his head. "I guess I overreacted, huh?"

I smile, relieved to see him loosening up a little. "Maybe a little, but I probably should've been more careful with my words."

He takes a deep breath, leaning back in his chair. "I just... I've been carrying a lot of stuff around, and sometimes I don't even realize it until it spills over."

"I get it," I say, nodding. "And I'm here, okay? You don't have to figure it all out by yourself."

We sit there for a moment, the tension between us finally lifting. It isn't perfect, and there's still a lot we need to talk about, but it feels like we're on the same page again. The waitress comes back with refills, and we thank her, and it feels less awkward.

"So," I say, breaking the silence, "how about we hit the reset button?"

Alex looks at me, a small smile tugging at the corner of his lips. "Yeah. Let's do that."

ten

ALEX

I push open the door to Eternal Ink, balancing two large pizzas in my hands. The chime of the bell announces my arrival, and I'm greeted by the sight of Cato at the front desk, hunched over a large sketchbook. Demi perches nearby on a stool, scrolling through her phone and sipping what I assume is one of her ever-present energy drinks.

"Hey, guys! I come bearing gifts," I announce with a grin, holding up the pizza boxes.

Cato looks up from his work, a smile spreading across his face. "Alex! Perfect timing, I was just starting to get hungry."

Demi's eyes light up as she slides off her stool. "Is that what I think it is?" she asks, practically bouncing over to me.

I chuckle, setting the pizzas down on the worktable. "Yep, I thought I'd bring over some lunch. One pepperoni, one-half veggie, half cheese. Wasn't sure what everyone liked."

"You're officially my new favorite person," Demi declares, already opening one of the boxes and grabbing a slice of the veggie pizza.

Cato puts down his pencil and rolls his chair over to join us. "This is great, Alex. Thanks for thinking of us."

I shrug, feeling gratified by their enthusiasm. "It's the least I could do. You guys have been awesome, putting up with my chaoticness lately."

"Hey, we get it," Cato says, reaching for a slice of pepperoni. "Moving to a new city, starting a new job – it's a lot to handle. We're just glad you're here now."

I sit down on the stool next to Cato, grabbing a slice for myself. "Me too. I've got to say, outside of my roommate Tommy, you guys are pretty much my only friends in the city."

Demi, mouth full of pizza, gives me a thumbs up. "Well, now you're stuck with us. Anyone who brings pizza automatically gets friend status."

We all laugh, and I feel a sense of belonging wash over me. The easy banter and shared meal create a comfortable atmosphere, worlds away from the tension I'd been worried about earlier.

"So, Cato," I say, nodding towards his sketchbook. "What were you working on when I came in? Anything exciting?"

Cato's eyes light up. "Oh man, wait till you see this. I've been playing around with some new designs that I think you're going to love."

As Cato starts showing me his latest sketches and Demi chimes in with her opinions, I can't help but smile. This is exactly what I needed—good food, great company, and the promise of amazing art. The worries I had about fitting in and balancing my new life seem to melt away in the pleasant atmosphere of Eternal Ink.

As we sit around the counter, laughing and eating pizza, I start to feel like things are finally normalizing. It's the first time in days that I'm not carrying the weight of everything I've been bottling up. Cato stands up and stretches after finishing his slice, giving his dog a little pat on the head as he moves toward the back of the shop.

"I'm going to make some coffee," he says, glancing at me with a small smile. "You want some?"

I nod. "Yeah, coffee sounds great."

Demi raises her hand, still grinning. "You know I'm always down for coffee."

Cato chuckles as he walks toward the kitchen in the back of the shop, leaving Demi and me alone at the counter. The second he's out of earshot, the atmosphere shifts just a little. Demi's smile fades slightly, and she looks over at me, her expression more serious than before.

She puts down her half-eaten slice of pizza and clears her throat. "Hey, Alex," she starts, her voice soft, "before Cato gets back, I just wanted to say something."

I raise an eyebrow, leaning back in my chair. "Yeah?"

Demi hesitates for a moment, like she's gathering her thoughts. Then she sighs, running a hand through her short hair. "Cato told me you overheard our conversation, and I wanted to apologize for the stuff I said before... you know, when we were talking about the whole church thing and everything. I didn't mean to be disrespectful. I know I can be a little... blunt sometimes, and I just want you to know I didn't mean anything by it."

I blink, surprised. I hadn't expected her to bring this up, but the fact that she does means a lot. I shift in my seat, shaking my head. "It's okay, Demi. Really. Cato told me everything. He explained that you didn't mean any harm by it."

She exhales, looking relieved. "I'm glad he did. I just felt like I needed to say it myself. He told me you've got a lot going on with your family and... well, everything. And I don't want to make it harder for you."

I look at her, appreciating the fact that she's willing to own up to it. I can tell Demi isn't the type to apologize easily. "It's fine. I get it. You were just joking around, and I probably overreacted a little. I was carrying a lot of baggage, and it wasn't fair for me to react the way I did."

Demi smiles a little, her eyes softening. "Your reaction is justified. We just want to make sure you're okay. Cato especially. He's been… worried."

I nod, glancing toward the kitchen, where I hear the faint clink of mugs and the sound of coffee brewing. "Yeah, I know. I've been kind of a mess lately, and he's been… more patient than I probably deserve."

Demi chuckles quietly. "Cato's good like that. He doesn't give up on people easily. You should've seen him when we first opened the shop. There were days when everything was falling apart, but he just kept going, no matter what."

I smile at that, imagining Cato dealing with the chaos of running a tattoo shop. "Yeah, I can see that in him."

Demi leans forward, resting her elbows on the table. "I know things between you two are… complicated. But whatever happens, just know that I'm here for you too. I know we don't really know each other, but any friend of Cato's is a friend of mine. And I'm not trying to step on your beliefs or anything like that. I just want to make sure you're not carrying all this stuff alone."

I look at her, feeling a lightness settle in my chest. It isn't just Cato who cares—Demi does, too. And in this moment, I realize how much I appreciate having them both in my life.

"Thanks, Demi," I say quietly, giving her a small smile. "That means a lot. And honestly, I'm glad you're around. You seem really cool, even when I've been… less than cool."

She waves her hand, brushing off the compliment with a grin. "Nah, you've been fine. Besides, no one's perfect. We've all got our stuff. Hell, you should've seen me when I first started working here—I was a total nightmare."

I laugh at that, feeling the tension between us dissolve completely. "I'll take your word for it."

The awkwardness from earlier is gone, replaced by a sense of understanding. Demi has always been the type to tell it like it is, but now I see that she genuinely cares beneath all that bluntness.

As Cato comes back from the kitchen with mugs of coffee, I can feel the shift in the room. The earlier laughter with Demi has dissipated, and even though we're all trying to act normal, the air feels thick—like there's something more beneath the surface that no one wants to address.

He hands me the mug, and I mumble a quiet "Thanks," taking a sip of the hot coffee. It's strong, just the way I like it, but even that doesn't do much to ease the knot in my stomach. There's still so much left unsaid between us.

Demi, ever the one to pick up on tension, glances between the two of us. She lets out a small sigh and stands up, smoothing down her shirt. "Well," she says, breaking the silence, "I've got an appointment in a bit, so I'm going to head out. You boys can handle the rest, right?"

Cato glances up at her, surprised. "You sure? You didn't finish your coffee."

She waves him off, flashing a quick grin. "It's fine. I'll grab some on the way. Besides, you two probably need some time to talk, anyway."

I glance at Cato, who's staring into his coffee like it holds all the answers to the universe. Demi shoots me a knowing look and gives me a small wink before she grabs her bag and heads for the door.

"See you later, guys," she says as she walks out, the bell jingling as the door swings shut behind her.

Then it's just us. Cato and I. Alone. The silence that follows is heavy, almost oppressive, and I can feel my palms start to sweat around the mug I'm holding. The ticking of the wall clock is the only sound in the room, and I can tell that Cato is just as uncomfortable as I am.

He clears his throat, shifting in his seat. "So, uh…" he starts, his voice a little strained. "Maybe we should go over to the table. You can show me those sketches you've been working on for the tattoo."

I nod, more out of reflex than anything else. "Yeah, sure. That sounds good."

We both stand up at the same time, moving toward his worktable at the back of the shop. As I turn to follow him, something happens that catches me completely off guard. Without thinking, Cato reaches out and grabs my hand.

It's instinctive, I can tell. Just a brief touch, like he doesn't even realize he's doing it. But the warmth of his fingers against mine sends a sudden jolt through my entire body, freezing me in place. My heart races, and I can't stop the way my breath catches in my throat.

For a split second, we stand there like that—his hand lightly holding mine. It feels right but also confusing. Then, as if realizing what he's done, Cato quickly retracts his hand, his eyes widening with an apologetic expression.

"Shit—sorry," he mutters, looking flustered. "I didn't mean to—"

I shake my head quickly, trying to brush it off even though my heart is still racing. "No, it's okay. Really. It's fine."

Cato opens his mouth to say something else but then just closes it, rubbing the back of his neck awkwardly. "Let's, uh, let's head to the table."

We both move over to the worktable, sitting side by side. My hands are still a little shaky, but I try to focus on the task at hand—the tattoo. This is supposed to be about the tattoo, not whatever confusing feelings are swirling between us.

I pull out my sketchbook, flipping through the pages until I find the rough designs I've been working on. They're not perfect, not by a long shot, but they're the first ideas that came to mind when I thought about getting something done by Cato.

"So," I say, sliding the sketchbook over to him. The book lies open, the design staring back at me like a window to a world that's just within reach. The globe on the page glows in shades of deep blue and lush green, its continents are bold against the swirls of the ocean. A compass stretches through the center, its sharp lines slicing across the globe as if guiding it. Near the equator, a tiny brown sailboat tilts forward as if it's caught a gust of wind, edging closer to a place I can almost feel. The boat points upward, just shy of the midpoint—a reminder of how close I am to where I want to be.

Cato doesn't say anything at first, but I can sense his empathy. He knows what it's like to feel pulled in different directions, torn between who you are and who others want you to be.

"Alex," he says softly, "this is amazing."

Heat spreads through my chest at Cato's words; his sapphire eyes meeting mine only makes me more nervous.

"I'm glad you think so," I murmur. I look away quickly, feeling a flush creep up my neck as his gaze lingers on me.

As he leans in to study the drawing in more detail, our arms brush against each other, causing my heart to pound faster than ever before.

"Cato," I whisper, my voice cracking with nerves. "I feel like I should tell you something."

Cato swallows hard and focuses all of his attention on me. "What is it?"

I exhale and force myself to speak, "I think I li—"

Before I can finish, my phone begins to ring, cutting off the little confidence I had. I look down to see Tommy calling, but he hangs up the call before I can answer. I glance at the clock and realize how much time has flown by. "Weird..." I say, looking up at Cato. "Tommy just called and instantly hung up."

"Must've been a butt-dial," Cato shrugs.

He's probably right. And now I've lost my nerve, chickening out on telling him that I like him.

After about another hour or so, Cato looks up at the clock and yawns. "It's getting late."

I nod, suddenly aware of the time. "Yeah, you're right. I should probably get going. Tommy might be wondering where I am."

We both move toward the door, the air between us feeling more relaxed and familiar than before, yet something still left unsaid. As we reach the door, Cato pauses for a moment, his hand hovering over the handle, his eyes meeting mine.

"So... I guess I'll see you soon?" he asks, his voice soft.

I give him a small smile. "Yeah, definitely. We'll keep working on the finer details when I come in next."

He smiles that easy, warm smile that always makes things feel better, even when they're complicated. "Have a good night, Alex."

"You too," I say, and then, without thinking, I add, "Thanks for today. It was good… really good."

He nods again, his eyes lingering on mine for just a second longer than usual. "Anytime."

I turn and step out of the shop into the cool night air, the door closing behind me. I can't help but feel a mix of contentment and lingering anticipation. The words I couldn't quite say still hang in the air, waiting for another moment, another chance.

My mind is still back there with Cato—replaying the last hour, the conversations, the touches, the moment that I almost told him that I like him.

As I walk through the busy streets, I can't help but notice a few couples passing by, holding hands, some laughing, others wrapped up in their own little world. Out of the corner of my eye, I even catch a glimpse of a couple stealing a quick kiss under the streetlights, and it stirs something in me. *That could be us.*

I shake the thought away, quickening my pace. *Get a grip, Alex. You're reading too much into everything,* I tell myself, trying to clear my head as I make my way back to the apartment.

When I reach my building, it's quiet, and the lights in the hallway are dim as usual. I open the door to my apartment and immediately notice that Tommy isn't home. His shoes are gone, and the place is empty. Probably out late again, I think.

I toss my bag onto the couch and make my way to my room, collapsing onto the bed with a heavy sigh.

I stretch my arm out above me, staring at my hand—his hand. I can still feel it, like the feeling has imprinted itself on my skin. My fingers twitch slightly, remembering the brief moment of contact, the instinctive way we reached for each other without thinking.

INK & *Intuition*

Before I can stop myself, I bring my hand closer to my lips, almost as if I can still feel Cato there. My heart races, and I don't know why I'm doing it—why this simple touch has stuck with me so much. It's not like this is the first time we've been close, but it's the first time he grabbed my hand. More real.

Suddenly, the door to my room swings open, and I nearly jump out of my skin, quickly dropping my hand to my side. Shit.

Tommy walks in, looking as carefree as ever, his eyes immediately landing on me sprawled out on the bed. He raises an eyebrow. "Hey man, you look... different. Like better. What's going on?"

I sit up, feeling my face flush. Is it that obvious? I rub the back of my neck, trying to play it cool. "What do you mean?"

Tommy shrugs, leaning against the doorframe of my room and crossing his arms. "I don't know. You just look... lighter. Like something finally clicked or something. Did you see Cato today?"

I pause for a second, trying to figure out how much I want to tell him. He's just walked in and already has me figured out. "Yeah, I went to Eternal Ink earlier."

Tommy smirks, clearly intrigued. "Ah, so that's why you look like you've got something on your mind. How'd it go? You two finally talk things out?"

I hesitate but then nod. "Yeah, we talked... not as much as we have been, but we're getting back to normal. I mean, we didn't do anything crazy, but it felt good. We worked on the tattoo design and... I don't know, man, something just feels different."

"Different, how?" Tommy asks, stepping further into the room and plopping down on the chair near my desk.

I sigh, leaning back against the wall. "It's hard to explain. I mean, things are still kind of awkward, but not in a bad way. It's like we're both waiting for something to happen, but neither of us knows how to make the first move."

Tommy raises an eyebrow, looking amused. "So, let me get this straight—you're both into each other, you've spent the whole day together, and you're still waiting for something to happen?"

I roll my eyes, grabbing a pillow and tossing it at him. "It's not that simple, Tommy. I don't know if he's into me, but I almost let it slip that I like him."

Tommy catches the pillow and grins. "Yeah, well, maybe it's time to let it come out, not slip, but say it with your chest. You're overthinking it."

"Maybe," I mutter, glancing down at my hand again. The tingling is still there.

Tommy leans forward, his expression softening just a bit. "Look, Alex, whatever it is between you two, don't let it get away just because you're scared. If today felt different, maybe that's a good thing. Maybe it means you're both ready to stop tiptoeing around it."

I look at him, the words sinking deeper than I'm ready to admit. Maybe he's right. Maybe we're both waiting for the other person to make the first move.

"Yeah," I say quietly.

Tommy grins, standing up and heading for the kitchen. "Alright, well, I'm going to grab a snack. You, my friend, need to stop staring at your hand like it holds all the answers and start thinking about what you actually want."

I chuckle, shaking my head as he walks out of the room. What do I want? That's the question, isn't it?

eleven

CATO

I sit at my worktable, flipping through some sketches, but my focus is barely on the designs in front of me. Alex has been on my mind since yesterday—the way we talked, that brief moment when I instinctively held his hand… the way he left with the words 'he liked me' hovering in the air but not said. *Why did I let him leave?*

I glance up to see Demi at the counter, tapping away in the appointment book, probably organizing the chaos that is our daily schedule.

"Hey, Demi," I call, still half-distracted. "How many clients do we have booked for today?"

She doesn't look up from her iPad, her voice all business as usual. "Four clients this afternoon. Three more in the evening." She pauses, glancing at me over the top of her glasses. "Oh, and we've had some requests for home visits too. But I put those on hold for now."

I raise an eyebrow at that. Home visits are rare, but they usually come with a hefty payout. "Home visits, huh? Why'd you put them on hold?"

Demi finally looks up, giving me a knowing smirk. "Because you've been busy, Cato. And I figured you'd want to be in the shop today instead of running around the city with all the stuff you've got on your mind."

I lean back, running a hand through my hair. She's not wrong. My head's been all over the place, and I haven't even thought about anything outside the shop. "Good call. Let's keep them on hold for now."

She nods, tapping her pen on the desk before continuing. "First clients should be here in the next twenty minutes or so. Thought you'd want to know so you don't disappear on me."

I give her a small smile, trying to refocus. "Got it. I'll be ready."

No matter how hard I try to concentrate, my eyes keep drifting to the front door, as if I'm waiting for something—or someone.

Demi, ever observant, catches the movement and raises an eyebrow, her lips quirking into a teasing grin. "You know... Alex doesn't have an appointment today."

I roll my eyes, but I can't help the smile tugging at my lips. "Who says I was thinking about Alex?"

Demi laughs, shaking her head. "You also didn't deny it either. It's written all over your face, dude. You've been distracted ever since you guys talked yesterday."

I don't bother denying it. There's no point. Demi knows me better than I'd like to admit sometimes. "Yeah, maybe I've been thinking about him. We had a good talk yesterday... I don't know. If I'm being honest, it sounded like he was about to tell me he liked me."

Demi raises an eyebrow, her grin widening. "About to? How was he about to say that?"

I shrug, trying to keep my cool even though thoughts of Alex have my head spinning. "It sounded like he was about to say, 'I like you,' but he got a phone call, and then he left."

She nods, her expression softening a little. "And you didn't say it back or try to have him repeat it?"

I nod in agreement. "Maybe you're right, but I just didn't want to push him."

Demi smiles gently. "I get it, but honestly, I don't think you would push him if he was about to say it."

I smile, appreciating her reassurance. "You're probably right, but I need to clear my head before the first client arrives. I'm going to head out for a bit."

Demi gives me a curious look, crossing her arms. "Where are you going?"

I stand up, grabbing my jacket from the back of the chair. "I'm just gonna pop out and grab a coffee really quick. I'll be back before the first appointment."

* * *

I'm only gone for 10 minutes before I'm back at the shop.

"Enjoy your coffee?" Demi asks, leaning back in her chair, arms crossed.

I nod, trying to shake off the restlessness lingering in my chest. "Yeah, it was nice to get out for a bit."

"Good, because your first client just got here," she says, pointing her thumb toward the waiting area. "Brace yourself."

I raise an eyebrow. "Brace myself? What do you mean?"

Demi rolls her eyes, a smirk playing at the corner of her lips. "Let's just say… this one's a bit of a handful. Rich kid who thinks he knows everything but really just wants something flashy. Doesn't give a crap about the art or the meaning behind it, which we both know isn't your style."

"Fuck," I sigh. Just what I need—some spoiled kid who wants a tattoo to impress his friends. Rubbing the back of my neck, I feel the tension creeping in. "Alright, let's get this over with."

I head over to the waiting area, where a kid—who couldn't be older than 22—is lounging on one of the chairs.

F. A. SENG

Dressed in designer clothes and every part of him screaming money, he has a perfectly styled head of hair and a smug expression, like he owns the place. As soon as he sees me, he stands up, looking me up and down like he's sizing me up.

"You're the artist, right?" he asks, his tone casual but carrying an air of arrogance.

I nod, keeping my voice neutral. "Yeah, I'm Cato. You must be the one with the appointment."

"Yep, that's me," he says, smirking as he shoves his hands into his pockets. "I want a tattoo on my arm. Something big. I don't really care what it is; just make sure it looks cool."

I stare at him for a second, trying to process what he just said. "You don't care what the tattoo is?"

He shrugs, waving a hand like it's no big deal. "Nah. I just want something that'll get people talking. You know, something to show off at parties. Maybe a skull or a dragon or something. Whatever's trendy."

I take a deep breath, trying to keep my cool. This isn't about the money; it's about the principle of the craft, and being who I am, I don't need the money. "Look, man, tattoos are permanent. You don't want to throw something on your body without thinking it through."

He rolls his eyes, clearly unimpressed. "Yeah, yeah, I know. But that's your job, right? Just make it look good, and I'll pay whatever. I've got cash. I don't care about the price."

I clench my jaw, feeling irritation bubble up. "It's not about the price. It's about making sure you're getting something you actually want, something that means something to you. Tattoos aren't just decoration."

The kid just shrugs his smirk still firmly in place. "I don't care about all that deep stuff, man. I just want something that looks badass. You're the best artist around, right? So do your thing."

I stare at him, my patience thinning fast. I've dealt with clients like this before, and every time, it leaves a sour taste in my mouth. This isn't what tattooing is about.

"Let me ask you something," I say, crossing my arms. "Why do you want a tattoo in the first place?"

He blinks, looking confused by the question. "Uh, because they're cool?"

I shake my head, feeling the exhaustion creeping in. "No, I mean, why do you want it on your body? It's going to be there forever. You'll look at it every day. Don't you want it to mean something?"

He looks at me like I'm speaking another language. "Dude, I just want to look cool. Who cares what it means? It's not like I'm gonna be staring at it all day."

And there it is. The exact attitude I can't stand. The kind of client who doesn't respect the craft doesn't get what tattoos are really about. I can already feel my energy draining just talking to him.

I take a steadying breath, trying to decide if this is even worth it. Then I make up my mind. "Look," I say, keeping my tone firm but polite, "I'm not the artist for you."

The kid blinks, clearly caught off guard. "What?"

"I'm not going to do a tattoo just for the sake of showing off," I continue, crossing my arms. "If you don't care about the design, if you don't care about the meaning behind it, then I'm not the right artist for you. There are plenty of places where you can go if you just want something trendy. But that's not how I work."

His smirk fades, replaced by confusion and growing annoyance. "Wait, are you serious? I'm offering to pay you whatever you want."

I shake my head. "It's not about the money; it's about the art. I'm not going to put something on your skin that you'll regret later just because it 'looks cool' for now. That's not what I do."

The kid stares at me for a long moment, trying to process the fact that I'm turning him down. Then, with a huff, he shoves his hands into his pockets, glaring at me. "Fine. Whatever, man. I'll find someone else."

"Good luck," I say, turning away and heading back to my worktable. I don't watch him leave, but the frustrated stomp of his expensive shoes and the jingle of the bell above the door tell me he's gone.

I let out a long breath, rubbing my temples. God, that was exhausting. I've barely been back in the shop for ten minutes, and I already feel like I need another break.

Demi looks up from the counter, eyebrow raised. "Let me guess—some rich kid with no idea what he actually wanted?"

"Exactly," I mutter, collapsing back into my chair. "He didn't give a shit about the tattoo. Just wanted something flashy to show off at parties."

She smirks, clearly amused. "Bet you handled it well, though. You always do."

I snort. "Yeah, well, I basically told him to fuck off."

Demi laughs. "Good. The kid didn't deserve your time anyway."

I lean back in my chair, staring at the ceiling. "I swear, clients like that make me question why I'm even doing this sometimes."

Demi rolls her eyes. "Oh, come on, Cato. You know why you do this. Because of the people who actually get it. The ones who care about the art, about the meaning. Not everyone's a spoiled brat."

"Yeah," I sigh, closing my eyes for a moment. "You're right. It's just... days like this make it hard to remember that."

Demi nods, her smirk softening. "Well, you'll bounce back. You always do."

I give her a tired smile. "Let's hope so."

* * *

I walk down the familiar path at the park, past the benches and trees, and my mind drifts to Alex. We had a decent conversation yesterday, and I can't stop thinking about how things feel... different between us. There's this tension, but not the bad kind—the kind that feels like something is just waiting to surface.

Without thinking too much, I pull out my phone and dial Alex's number. It rings a couple of times before he answers.

"Hey, Cato," he says, his voice casual.

"Hey," I reply, feeling more relaxed just hearing him. "Are you free right now?"

There's a pause, the sound of some shuffling on his end, before he responds. "Yeah, actually, I just got out of a meeting. I'm free for the rest of the day. What's up?"

I smile, glad he's up for it. "I'm at the park. Thought maybe we could hang out, take a walk or something."

Alex's voice brightens. "Sounds good. I'm only a few minutes away. I'll meet you there."

"Great. See you in a bit."

I hang up, sit back on the bench, and wait. Just the thought of seeing Alex lifts my mood, and the stress from that rich kid client starts to fade. Before long, I spot Alex heading toward me, a slight grin on his face as he approaches.

"Hey," he greets, a little out of breath from his quick walk. "How's your morning been? By the looks of it, you need a little break."

I stand up, giving him a small smile. "Yeah, perfect timing. Figured we could walk and talk for a bit."

Alex nods, and without another word, we start down the path together. The park is quieter now, with only a few people scattered around, most of them absorbed in their own worlds. It's nice—a calm space away from the usual hustle.

For a few minutes, we walk in silence—the kind that doesn't need to be filled with pointless chatter. I glance over and catch him looking at the trees, his face relaxed.

"So, how was the meeting?" I ask, breaking the quiet.

He shrugs, slipping his hands into his pockets. "It was fine. Mostly just project stuff for work. You know, the usual boring stuff."

I chuckle. "Sounds about right. Still, better than dealing with spoiled rich kids who want tattoos for no reason."

Alex raises an eyebrow, a smirk tugging at his lips. "Sounds like you had an interesting morning."

I groan. "Yeah, let's just say I had to kick a client out of the shop. The kid didn't care about the art—they just wanted something to show off. It was exhausting."

Alex laughs softly. "Bet that went well."

I shrug. "Eh, he didn't take it too well, but I'm not about to do a tattoo that doesn't mean anything. You know how I am."

"Yeah," Alex nods. "That's why you're the best, though. You care."

We keep walking, the conversation flowing easily. It feels good—natural—like things are finally falling into place between us. As we round a corner near the edge of the park, my phone buzzes in my pocket. I glance at the screen.

I sigh and answer, "Hey, Demi. What's up?"

"Hey, Cato," her voice comes through the line. "Just giving you a heads-up—the next client's here, she arrived early. I told her you might be a little bit as you stepped out, but I thought you'd want to know."

I glance at Alex, feeling a pang of disappointment. Just when things were getting good. "Thanks for the heads-up," I say to Demi. "I'll head back now."

"No problem. See you soon," she says, hanging up.

I slip my phone back into my pocket and turn to Alex, offering an apologetic smile. "Looks like I have to get back to the shop. My appointment showed up a little early."

Alex's face falls slightly, but he nods, understanding. "Yeah, no worries. Work calls."

I hesitate for a second, then ask, "What about later? Anything fun happening later for you?"

Alex bites his lip, glancing away before meeting my eyes again. "Not really. I'm gonna head back home and just relax for a little bit. What about you, do you have clients?"

I nod, rubbing the back of my neck. "Yeah, I've got a few appointments this evening. It's gonna be a busy night."

He looks a little disappointed, but he quickly recovers, nodding. "Aw, damn."

I cock an eyebrow, looking at him with interest. "Why? Did you have something in mind?"

Alex blushes slightly. "I mean, not really. I just thought if we were both free, we could hang out together?"

I smile a bit. "Oh, I'm sorry. Maybe later this week, we can catch up and grab a drink or something? I think I'm free Wednesday night?"

Alex's eyes brighten, and he nods. "Yeah, that sounds great."

"Great," I say, feeling a sense of relief settle over me. "It'll be good to hang out without having to rush off."

Alex grins, his green eyes shining in the soft afternoon light. "Yeah, Wednesday then."

We stand there for a moment, neither of us really wanting to leave but knowing we have to. I give him a small smile, then gesture toward the park's exit. "I'll walk you out."

He smiles back, and we head toward the park gate together. Once we reach the entrance, we linger for a second, like neither of us really wants to say goodbye.

"I'll see you Wednesday," Alex says, giving me a gentle-eyed stare that makes something stir in my chest.

"Yeah," I reply, my voice a little quieter than usual. "Wednesday."

With that, we finally part ways. As I walk back toward the shop, I can't help but feel happier. The middle of the week can't come soon enough.

twelve
ALEX

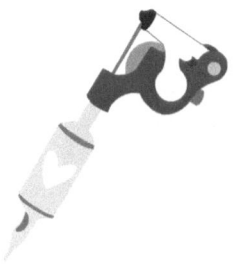

I can't remember the last time I felt this good like my feet barely touch the ground. The whole evening has been playing through my mind ever since I left the park and waved goodbye to Cato. We've made plans to see each other tomorrow, and I can already feel the excitement building. Finally, a chance to spend time together without interruptions.

With Tommy out for the night, the apartment is all mine, and I plan to enjoy every minute of it. I throw myself back onto the bed, grinning like an idiot, barely able to keep from laughing. I can't help it—I'm absolutely giddy. Maybe things with Cato are starting to fall into place.

I flop around on the bed, jittery with excitement. Eventually, the energy takes over. I jump up, turn on *"Too Sweet" by Hozier*, and let the sound fill the room as I dance around like a maniac. I don't care how ridiculous I look; it feels amazing to let loose.

INK & *Intuition*

The beat thumps in my ears as I twirl around the room, humming and swaying like I actually know what I'm doing. I'm mid-spin when I hear a knock at the door. I pause, catching my breath. "Tommy?" I call, because I wasn't expecting him to be home so soon.

The knocking comes again, and I sigh, dragging myself over to the door. Leave it to Tommy to return just as I'm in the middle of a bedroom rock concert. I open the door with an easy grin, ready to make a joke about his timing while also reminding him to remember his key, but instead of Tommy, there's a girl standing in the doorway.

She's around my age, with medium-length blonde hair framing her face and warm brown eyes that hold a hint of surprise as she takes in the sight of me. She's carrying a backpack over one shoulder and has a small suitcase at her feet.

"Uh, hi?" I say, momentarily thrown off.

She gives me an embarrassed smile, glancing down at a piece of paper in her hand. "Hi! I'm so sorry to bother you... is this apartment 203?"

I shake my head, trying to process the situation. "Nope, this is 201, 203's just down the hall—you take a left, and it's the first door."

Her face flushes a little. "Oh, great! Thank you. I swear, I must've read this paper three times and still managed to get it wrong." She laughs lightly, her cheeks pink.

I chuckle, shrugging. "Hey, it happens. This building's like a maze anyway. You'd be surprised how many people knock on the wrong door."

I chuckle, shutting the door as she disappears around the corner. Well, that was... random. Shaking my head, I turn back to my room, laughing softly to myself. I can't even make it through one evening of dancing like an idiot without someone catching me.

Once I'm back in my room, I crank the music up a little louder, feeling even more energized. "*Keep dancing,*" she'd said, and who am I to argue? With the entire apartment to myself, I'm free to dance like nobody's watching—because nobody is.

Grinning, I throw myself back into the beat, spinning around the room, humming along, and letting every worry, every stray thought, fade away.

Later on, I'm lying on my bed, scrolling through my phone, trying not to count the hours until I get to see Cato again. We left things open after yesterday's walk in the park, and I don't want to push it, but the excitement fluttering in my stomach hasn't faded one bit. Just when I'm about to settle into a show to distract myself, my phone buzzes with a new message.

I glance down, and as soon as I see Cato's name on the screen, my heart does this ridiculous little flip. *God, Alex, pull it together.*

Cato:

> Hey, my last client cancelled for the day and there's someone here at the shop I'd like you to meet. Any chance you might wanna come by?

I blink at the text, reading it over again just to make sure I haven't misread. My fingers hover over the screen, my heart beating faster than it has any right to.

I type back a quick reply.

Me:

> Who is it?

Cato:

> It's a surprise.

Me:

> Well, I don't usually like surprises, but since it's you, I guess it's fine lol. I'll be there soon.

As soon as I hit send, a new wave of nerves washes over me. I can feel the butterflies swirling in my stomach.

"Alright, deep breaths, Alex," I mutter to myself, standing up and glancing around the room. "It's just a visit and a random stranger. Nothing to freak out about."

I pace around, trying to shake off the nerves, but the more I think about it, the more excited I feel. Cato and I haven't had real uninterrupted time like this in… well, ever. I take a quick look in the mirror, trying to tame my hair a bit. "Okay, no big deal. Just going to a tattoo shop to hang out and meet one of his friends. Not a date. Definitely not a date."

But I know that I'm lying to myself. I straighten my shirt, adjust my jeans, and then give myself one last look in the mirror before grabbing my phone and keys.

* * *

I push open the door to Eternal Ink, feeling the positive energy that always hits when I step into Cato's world. But today, something feels different. There's an extra person in the shop—a tall, broad-shouldered man, probably in his late forties, with a head as bald and smooth as polished marble. Well, not completely smooth; a massive, intricately detailed spider tattoo crawls across his scalp, its legs stretching down toward his temples. His entire presence fills the room, and I feel a slight twinge of nerves as his piercing gaze lands on me.

Cato looks up as I walk in, his face breaking into a warm smile. "Hey. Perfect timing."

I return his smile, glancing between him and the man. "Hey. Glad I could make it."

Cato nods, gesturing for me to come closer. Demi is also there, perched at the edge of the counter. Her usual smirk is replaced by a more subdued expression as she watches the man beside her.

"Alex," Cato says, motioning to the man, "this is Richmond Greece." There's both admiration and respect in his eyes. "Richmond's… well, he's the one who taught me most of what I know about tattooing."

I nod, trying to hide my surprise. This intense guy with the spider tattoo is Cato's mentor? I wouldn't have guessed it, but it makes sense, seeing the serious look in Cato's eyes.

Richmond's gaze shifts to me. For a second, I feel pinned in place under his stare. But then he surprises me by smiling—a small, almost gentle smile that eases his rugged features.

"Nice to meet you, Alex," Richmond says, his voice much softer than I expected. "You're the one keeping Cato on his toes, huh?"

I chuckle nervously, rubbing the back of my neck. "I don't know about that, but yeah, I guess I'm around here a lot."

Richmond's smile widens just a little, and he turns back to Cato. "You've got good taste in friends, kid. This one seems genuine."

Cato nods, looking at me with a fondness I can't quite place. "Yeah, he's definitely one of a kind."

I feel a blush creeping up my neck, but I try to play it cool. "So, you're the one who taught Cato everything he knows?"

Richmond shakes his head, his tone humble yet firm. "No, not everything. Cato had the skills from the start. I only taught him the basics—the technical parts, how to handle the gun, shading techniques." He glances at Cato with a smirk. "He always had the eye. The kid could see the detail better than half the artists twice his age."

Cato laughs quietly, shaking his head. "Richmond's giving himself too little credit. I'd probably still be floundering around if it weren't for him. He taught me how to respect the craft, how to connect with a client, and how to make every tattoo mean something."

Richmond shrugs, his fingers absently tracing the edge of his coffee cup. "Told you, Cato—you had it in you already. I just showed you how to use it."

I look between the two of them, noticing the easy way they talk and the respect clear in their words. "How long have you guys known each other?"

Cato tilts his head, thinking back. "Let's see... what, ten years now?"

Richmond nods, chuckling. "Ten years, give or take. Found this guy barely out of art school, and he already had a waiting list of clients for his sketches alone. I remember thinking, 'Who the hell is this kid who thinks he can skip the line?'"

Demi snorts from her corner, finally speaking up. "Oh, that sounds like Cato, alright. Always acting like he's one step ahead of everyone else."

Cato rolls his eyes, but his smile is warm. "Hey, I was just eager to learn. Richmond saw something in me, thankfully. Otherwise, I'd probably still be just a kid with a sketchbook."

Richmond shakes his head, his expression softening as he looks at Cato. "Nah, you had it from the start, kid. You would've found your way, with or without me."

I take a seat with Cato, Demi, and Richmond, feeling more at ease now that the initial introductions are out of the way. Richmond might look intimidating with that spider tattoo across his head, but his easy smile and calm demeanor quickly change his intense aura. He leans back, his arms crossed, giving me a curious look as I sit down.

"So, Alex," Richmond starts, a smirk tugging at the corner of his mouth, "I've gotta know—what brings a guy like you into a place like this?"

I chuckle, shrugging a bit. "Honestly? Pure curiosity at first. I'd just moved to the city and happened to walk by Eternal Ink one day. I thought about getting a tattoo, but... it was more of a pipe dream than anything serious."

Demi laughs, shaking her head. "Yeah, and yet here you are, practically a regular these days. What changed?"

I glance at Cato, who's watching me with a small, knowing smile. "I guess... Cato changed that. I told myself I'd just come in to ask about designs, but the more I saw his work, the more I realized this wasn't just any tattoo shop. Cato made it feel like... like there was real meaning behind every piece he created. Well, that made me want to get one, too."

Richmond raises an eyebrow, looking impressed. "That so? Sounds like Cato's got himself a dedicated client, huh?"

I chuckle, nodding. "Yeah, you could say that. I think I've been here more often than not lately. We've been working on a design for a while now."

Richmond leans forward, intrigued. "So, what's the design? What did you two cook up?"

I glance at Cato, who nods, giving me the go-ahead to share. "We've been working on a compass design," I say, feeling a mix of excitement and nerves. "Originally, it was for my love of travel, and it still kind of is, but I think it's grown since we started the design. Now, this tattoo symbolizes... finding my way. I've done a lot of growing since moving out here and figuring out who I am, so it felt like the right fit. Cato added some amazing details to it. I don't think I'd have come up with anything this good on my own."

Richmond's eyes light up, and he nods approvingly. "A compass, huh? Now, that's a tattoo with some real purpose behind it. Sounds like you're putting a lot of thought into it, which is more than most people can say."

I laugh, rubbing the back of my neck. "Yeah, well, I had some help in that department. Cato's pretty good at making sure his clients get something that actually means something."

Cato shrugs, pretending to look modest but unable to hide the proud glint in his eye. "It's the best part of the job, to be honest. There's something satisfying about helping someone put their story on their skin."

Demi grins. "And it's been entertaining watching Alex come in and out of the shop, adjusting the design with you every other day. The poor guy's been obsessing over it."

I roll my eyes, feeling a bit embarrassed. "Hey, when you're putting something on your body for the rest of your life, it's worth obsessing over."

Richmond laughs, nodding. "I get it. Trust me, I've seen people make the mistake of rushing into it, then coming back asking for cover-ups. You're doing it right, kid. Besides, you couldn't be in better hands."

I glance at Cato, my heart skipping a beat at Richmond's words. "Yeah... I'm pretty lucky to have found the best."

Cato chuckles, his eyes flicking to me with embarrassment. "Don't give me too much credit. You came in with some great ideas of your own. The compass and the meaning behind it—that's all you, Alex."

I shrug, feeling a flutter in my chest as I meet his eyes. "Maybe, but you made it come to life. And, well... I wouldn't trust anyone else to do it."

Richmond watches us with an amused smile, leaning back in his chair. "Looks like you two make a solid team. That's something rare to find—an artist and a client who really connect."

Cato gives a small nod, looking back at Richmond. "I owe a lot of that to you, Richmond. You always told me it wasn't just about the ink but the people and the stories. Alex here reminded me of that."

Demi grins, clearly enjoying the banter. "Yeah, Alex has practically become part of the Eternal Ink family at this point."

I chuckle, and a feeling of gratitude spreads through me. "Well, I couldn't ask for a better group of people to walk me through this. You guys have made the whole thing... I don't know. It's like getting a tattoo and making friends at the same time."

Richmond raises his coffee cup in a mock toast. "Here's to meaningful tattoos and good people, then."

I smile, raising an imaginary glass back at him. "I'll drink to that."

* * *

I walk back toward the apartment, my mind racing with thoughts from the evening. Sitting around the table with Cato, Demi, and Richmond felt more like home than I've felt in ages. I'm smiling to myself, replaying some of the jokes and easy conversation, when I almost walk straight into someone coming from the opposite direction.

"Oh, sorry—" I start, then freeze as I recognize her.

Amelia. She's the last person I expect to see on my way home, but she stands there, smiling at me with her usual calm, assured expression.

"Alex!" she greets, her eyes lighting up. "Small world, huh?"

I chuckle, nodding. "Yeah, it really is. What brings you out here?"

She shrugs, gesturing to the street behind her. "Just finishing up some errands, thought I'd grab a late-night coffee before heading home. How about you?"

"Same here, actually. Just came from the tattoo shop, working on some design ideas."

Her eyebrows lift, interest flickering across her face. "The famous tattoo project, huh? Is it coming along?"

I chuckle, scratching the back of my neck, realizing I must've told her about my new tattoo endeavor. "Yeah, we're getting there," I say, feeling that recurring joy bubble up. "It's been a process, but I think we're onto something really good."

Amelia's smile softens, her curiosity evident. "Well, if you're free, would you like to grab a coffee with me? I've been wanting to hear more about your tattoo adventure."

I nod, a bit surprised but eager. "Sure! I'd love that."

We walk to a cozy little café I've passed a few times but never tried. Inside, it's inviting, filled with the scent of coffee beans and freshly baked pastries. We order—her a black coffee, me a cappuccino—and find a table by the window.

As we settle in, Amelia takes a sip of her coffee and gives me a knowing smile. "Tell me, what inspired you to finally get this tattoo?"

"Well, it's a bit of a long story. Moving to the city, I guess I felt like I was starting fresh. I'd always wanted a tattoo, but back home, that wasn't exactly… encouraged. Here, it just felt like the right time, you know?"

She nods thoughtfully. "I get it. New places have a way of pushing us out of our comfort zones. So, what are you getting?"

I go over the design that Cato and I have been working on.

Amelia raises an eyebrow, clearly intrigued. "A compass. I like that. Feels symbolic, especially for someone just starting out in a new city." She pauses, her eyes scanning my face with curiosity. "Cato's been helping you, you say?"

"Yeah," I reply, smiling as I think of him. "He's... well, he's amazing at what he does. It's been a lot of back-and-forth to get the design just right, but I wouldn't trust anyone else with it."

She smiles knowingly. "Is he *just* your tattoo artist?"

I feel my face warm and laugh, brushing it off. "I mean, we're friends too. I guess we've gotten close through all this. He really makes you think about the meaning behind everything, makes the whole experience... personal."

Amelia nods, a glint of amusement in her eyes. "Well, that sounds like quite the bond. I have to say, I'm a little jealous. My only tattoo was a very quick decision. Didn't put nearly as much thought into them."

I laugh, genuinely enjoying the easy conversation. "Well, maybe you'll come by Eternal Ink sometime, and Cato can convince you to get another one with more meaning."

She shakes her head, smiling. "Oh, I think one is enough for me, thank you very much. But I'll take your word for it." She takes another sip of her coffee, glancing around the café with a content expression. "It's nice, though, seeing you enjoying the city. It suits you."

"Thanks," I say, feeling the kindness in her words. "Honestly, a lot of the thanks should be to you. You've made work way easier than I expected."

Amelia waves a hand dismissively though she's smiling. "Oh, please. You're a natural, Alex. We're lucky to have you." She glances at her watch, her smile turning a bit regretful. "Speaking of work, I should probably get going. I've got some early meetings tomorrow."

"Yeah, of course," I say, finishing off my coffee. "Thanks for inviting me. It was nice to talk outside of the office."

She smiles warmly, standing up and grabbing her bag. "It was. We should do this again sometime."

"Definitely," I reply, genuinely meaning it.

thirteen

CATO

I'm in the middle of organizing my workspace when my phone buzzes. Glancing at the screen, I see Richmond's name appear unexpectedly. Richmond rarely calls unless something big is on his mind, so I pick up right away, curious.

"Hey, Richmond," I say, tucking the phone between my shoulder and ear as I continue straightening my tools. "What's up?"

"Cato!" His voice comes through with a gruff I haven't heard in a while, and I can almost picture his broad smile on the other end. "I forgot to tell you yesterday, but I've finally made up my mind. I'm opening the gallery."

I freeze, letting his words sink in. Richmond's art gallery —the one he's talked about for years but never quite committed to. "Richmond, that's incredible," I say, feeling a rush of happiness for him. "So it's official?"

"It's official." He sounds almost giddy, a rare tone for him. "Got the venue, date's set, invitations going out this week.

Figured it was about time I stopped talking about it and just made it happen, you know?"

"Absolutely." I lean back against the front desk, grinning. Richmond is as talented an artist as he is a mentor, and the world deserves to see his work displayed. "I can't wait to see it. Let me know if you need help setting up."

"I might take you up on that," he laughs. "But listen, the reason I'm calling is... well, I wanted to make sure you'd come. It'd mean a lot to me if you were there."

"Wouldn't miss it for the world, Richmond," I say, meaning every word. "I'll be there."

"Good, good," he says, sounding relieved. Then, his tone shifts with a hint of amusement. "And hey, Cato—bring that kid Alex with you."

I blink, caught a little off guard. "Alex?"

"Yeah," he says, like it's the most obvious thing in the world. "That boy's got a spark. And I can tell he's already important to you. Besides, he's got an eye for art, even if he doesn't fully realize it yet."

A smile tugs at the corners of my mouth. Richmond really picks up on things, doesn't he? I try to keep my tone neutral, though I can feel a little spark of anticipation building in my chest. "Yeah, I think he'd love it. I'll ask him if he's up for it."

"Good. I think he could benefit from seeing the gallery, seeing what's possible when you follow your passion," Richmond says, a thoughtful edge to his voice. "And Cato... I can tell he's got a place in your world, whether you've figured that out yet or not."

I feel my face warm at his words, grateful he can't see the grin spreading across my face. "Yeah, he's... he's important," I admit, my voice softer than I intended.

Richmond chuckles. "You don't have to explain yourself to me, kid. Just bring him along. I think it'll be good for both of you."

I nod, even though he can't see me. "I'll let him know. Thanks for inviting us, Richmond. And congratulations on making this happen. It's going to be amazing."

"Thank you, Cato. Couldn't have gotten here without folks like you keeping me on the right path." He pauses, then adds, "See you soon."

* * *

I lean against the counter in the shop, drumming my fingers as I dial Alex's number. Richmond's gallery opening is coming together quickly, and I want to make sure Alex is available before proceeding with the plans. The phone rings a couple of times before he picks up.

"Hey, Cato," Alex's voice comes through, slightly muffled. "What's up?"

"Hey, Alex. Just wondering if you're free anytime soon?"

There's a pause on the other end, followed by a quick rustling sound. "I'm at work right now, actually. I'll be free in about three hours—does that work?"

"Yeah, sure," I say, leaning back against the wall with a grin. "Just give me a call when you're done. Nothing urgent, but I wanted to ask you something."

"Alright, sounds good," he replies, sounding a little curious but not pressing further. "I'll call you as soon as I'm out."

"Perfect. Talk soon," I say, hanging up.

With that settled, I get back to the task at hand—figuring out a gift for Richmond's gallery opening—something personal but meaningful. Richmond isn't the kind of guy to go for anything flashy; he values thoughtfulness over cost every time. Maybe a custom frame for one of his pieces? I start jotting down ideas, mentally listing places to pick up a card with an elegant, classic design that would suit him.

Just as I'm getting into brainstorming, my phone rings again. I instinctively glance down, expecting it to be another client, but when I see Alex's name, I freeze for a second. I thought he had meetings.

I pick up quickly, a bit surprised. "Alex? Everything okay?"

There's a short pause, and then his familiar voice comes through, sounding more curious than anything. "Yeah, all good. I just... couldn't help wondering why you called earlier."

I chuckle, settling back into my chair. "Impatient, huh?"

He laughs. "Maybe a little. I mean, you don't usually call me in the middle of the day just to check in."

"Fair point," I say, shaking my head with a grin. "So, here's the deal—I just got an invitation to Richmond's gallery opening. He's finally launching his own art gallery after all these years, and he specifically told me to bring you along. Thought I'd check if you're up for it."

I can practically hear him thinking it over on the other end. "Richmond's opening a gallery? That's awesome!"

"Yeah!" I say, smiling even though he can't see it. "The gallery's kind of a big deal for him. He's been talking about it for years, but this is the first time he's actually made it happen."

"Wow," Alex says, sounding impressed. "I didn't realize it was such a big deal. That's amazing."

"It really is," I say, feeling the pride in my voice. "He thinks you'd enjoy it, and honestly, I think you would too. It's going to be a pretty interesting crowd, lots of artists, collectors... a good experience."

There's a pause, and then Alex's voice comes through, a little hesitant but excited. "When is it?"

"This Friday," I tell him, mentally calculating the days. "Four days from now."

He doesn't even hesitate. "I'm in. I'd love to come."

I feel a small thrill run through me at his response, though I keep my tone casual. "Great. I'll pick you up around six, then. It'll give us time to grab something to eat beforehand if you're up for it."

"Sounds perfect," Alex replies, and I can practically hear the smile in his voice. "I'll make sure my schedule's clear. This... this actually sounds like a lot of fun."

I smile, feeling that familiar warmth settle over me. "It will be. Richmond's gallery... well, it's going to be an incredible night."

"Alright," he says, genuinely enthusiastic. "Thanks for inviting me, Cato. I'm looking forward to it."

"Same here," I reply softly. "I'll see you later."

* * *

I grab my phone and dial Alex's number. The faint hum of the city comes through as he picks up.

"Hey, Cato!" he says, his voice bright. "I just got out of my last meeting. What's up?"

"Hey, Alex," I reply, leaning back and feeling a grin spread across my face. "Just checking in—how was work today?"

"Not bad, actually," he says. "It's been pretty manageable lately. I've been able to compile everything ahead of time, so I'm actually a little ahead of my deadlines."

"Sounds like you've got it all under control," I say, truly impressed.

He chuckles. "Yeah, for once. Makes things a little easier."

I pause for a moment, and then, feeling a spark of an idea, I ask, "So, are you still up for hanging out tonight?"

There's a beat of curiosity on the other end. "Sure. What would you like to do?"

"Well," I start, trying to sound casual, "I've been trying to figure out the perfect gift for Richmond's gallery opening, but… I could use a second opinion. Think you might want to join me in finding the perfect gift?"

"Oh," he replies, sounding pleased. "Yeah, I'd love to. Where were you thinking?"

"How about Vista Valley Mall? It's got a good mix of stores, and they usually have some unique stuff. We could meet there, say, in half an hour?"

"Perfect," he says without hesitation. "See you there."

* * *

I arrive at Vista Valley first, leaning against one of the entrance pillars and scanning the crowd. When Alex shows up, he's all smiles, and the slight chill in the evening air does nothing to dampen his energy.

"Hey!" he greets, looking relaxed as he strolls up.

"Hey," I reply, giving him a quick nod. "Ready to dive into the maze of gift hunting?"

He laughs. "Bring it on. I'm the best gift finder."

"Oh, really?" I laugh.

Alex nudges me with his elbow playfully. "You laugh now, but you'll see."

We step inside, and the mall buzzes with energy—people milling around, bright lights, and stores on every side. I glance at Alex, feeling a strange comfort having him here for this. Richmond's important to me, and it means something to have Alex helping me pick out this gift.

"So," he says, hands in his pockets as he glances around, "what do you think Richmond would like? Something classic or something a bit... bold?"

I consider it, tapping my chin thoughtfully. "Honestly, I think he'd appreciate something that speaks to his style—meaningful but understated. He's not big on flashy."

Alex nods. "Alright, understated but meaningful. I like it. How about we start over there?" He gestures toward a small store specializing in vintage collectibles and art pieces.

We wander over, browsing through vintage record players and vinyls, antique clocks, and small sculptures. Alex picks up a small, intricately forged metal skeleton key, running his fingers over it.

"This one's pretty unique," he says, showing it to me. "Kind of fits the theme of his gallery, doesn't it? Opening himself to a new branch of the art world and all."

I examine it, nodding. "It's definitely got some character. But I feel like we need something... I don't know, a bit more personal."

Alex nods, setting the key back. "Fair point. We'll keep looking."

We continue walking through the mall, peeking into a few more stores, each offering an assortment of art, books, and trinkets. After a while, we find ourselves in front of a small, locally owned art gallery tucked into a corner of the plaza.

"How about here?" Alex suggests, his eyes lighting up. "A small gallery like this might have something unique."

"Worth a shot," I agree, and we step inside.

The gallery is quiet, the walls lined with paintings, sketches, and sculptures, each piece carrying its own sense of story and emotion. We walk slowly, examining each artwork, occasionally pointing out ones we like. Then, in one corner of the gallery, a particular painting catches Alex's eye.

"Cato, look at this," he says, gesturing toward a medium-sized painting hanging slightly off to the side. It's an abstract piece, with dark, swirling colors that blend into soft, warm tones. It feels like a mix of mystery and hope—just the kind of complexity Richmond would appreciate.

I step closer, studying it. "This... actually, this feels perfect. It's different, but it's got this depth to it. Richmond would love this."

Alex grins, clearly pleased. "Yeah, it kind of pulls you in, doesn't it? Like there's a story in there you have to find."

I nod, genuinely appreciating his insight. "Exactly. Good eye, Alex."

"Oh shit, wait." Alex pauses, looking pale.

"What is it?" I look at him and then notice that he's pointing at the price tag.

"Um, Cato. It's $10,000." Alex whispers.

"Okay, and?" I chuckle.

"And?" Alex looks confused. "That's expensive."

"Not really," I shrug. "Alex, don't worry. I've got it."

"Well, can I at least help cover the cost?" Alex asks, pulling out his wallet. His face shows a look of apprehension.

"Absolutely not," I snap. "You're not helping me pay for this. I've got it."

I can tell he's uncomfortable, but he asks, "Are you sure?"

"Of course, this one's on me."

We call over the gallery assistant and arrange the purchase. As they wrap it up, I turn to Alex with a smile.

"Thanks for this, really. I couldn't have picked something like this on my own."

He shrugs, looking a little embarrassed. "No problem. Honestly, this was a lot of fun. I don't usually get to help people with things like this."

"Well, you were right though, you've got a knack for it," I say, giving him a grin. "I think Richmond's going to love it."

fourteen
CATO

May

The gallery pulsates with life when we arrive, filled with the steady hum of people mingling, admiring the artwork, and exchanging appreciative nods. I glance over at Alex as we enter; he's taking it all in, his eyes wide with awe. He looks a bit starstruck, especially when I catch him glancing around at some familiar faces in the crowd. It's not just art enthusiasts here tonight but some of the industry's biggest names. I can tell he's impressed—and maybe a little intimidated.

"Whoa," Alex murmurs under his breath. "I didn't realize this would be such a… high-profile crowd. I think I just spotted my CEO." He gives a short laugh, looking at me with a bit of disbelief.

I chuckle, nudging him. "Welcome to Richmond's world. He's got connections everywhere. Didn't expect your CEO to be here, huh?"

"Not even a little," Alex replies, shaking his head. "But I'm glad we're here. It's incredible to see so many people coming together for something like this."

Just then, Richmond appears, weaving his way through the crowd with the ease of someone well accustomed to commanding attention. His eyes light up as he spots us, and he strides over, extending his hand with a warm smile.

"Cato! Alex! Glad you both could make it," Richmond greets us, shaking our hands. "It means a lot to have you here tonight."

"Wouldn't have missed it for anything," I say, smiling. "Congratulations, Richmond. This place—it's everything you've been working toward."

Richmond's eyes soften, and a grateful smile crosses his face. "Thanks, Cato. And Alex," he says, turning to him, "thank you for helping with the gift. I heard you had a hand in picking it out."

Alex's face brightens with pride. "Yeah, Cato wanted to find something that fit your style."

"Alex picked it out. It's from the both of us. We hope you like it."

Richmond chuckles, glancing at the wrapped painting we hand him. "I'm sure I will. This whole night's been... a long time coming. And having friends here, people who understand —well, that's the real gift."

"Couldn't agree more," I say.

Richmond claps a hand on my shoulder. "Alright, you two, enjoy the art and the company. Plenty of new pieces here that might surprise you." With a final nod, he excuses himself to greet a couple nearby who are eyeing a large sculpture with fascination.

With Richmond off in the crowd, Alex and I start moving through the gallery, both of us caught up in the sheer beauty and depth of the pieces on display. Paintings line the walls in vibrant splashes of color and muted tones; each one layered with texture and emotion. Intricately crafted sculptures stand on pedestals under careful lighting, casting shadows across the floor.

We stop at one painting—an abstract piece with soft blues, oranges, and grays blending together in a wave-like motion.

"I love this one," Alex says, tilting his head as he studies the brushstrokes. "There's something calming about it... but also a sense of movement. It's like the colors are alive."

I smile, nodding. "Exactly. That's the kind of art I'm drawn to. Something that feels like it's breathing like it's got a pulse. Richmond always says that the best pieces are the ones that feel like they could step off the canvas."

Alex's eyes brighten, and he glances at me with a newfound understanding. "You know, that's how I feel about the design of my tattoo."

My heart does a little flip at his words. "Art's meant to reflect life; life is always changing and evolving. Every line, every color... it's like a heartbeat."

We continue down the gallery, stopping at a sculpture—a figure crafted from twisted metal and glass, with bold red and black accents glinting in the light.

Alex studies it for a long moment, his brow furrowing. "This one... it feels intense, almost unsettling. But there's something enchanting about it like it's holding onto a hidden story."

I nod, admiring his eye for detail. "It's raw, isn't it? Art doesn't always have to be comforting. Sometimes it's about facing something uncomfortable, something that maybe we don't want to see."

Alex glances at me, a hint of awe in his gaze. "You really get it, don't you? I've always felt like art was... well, something to admire, but I never realized how much depth was in each piece until I met you."

We continue, weaving through the rooms, stopping at each piece that catches our attention. The more we talk, the more we discover how similar our perspectives are. We both love how art captures emotions, telling stories without words. There's a quiet understanding between us, a sense that we're seeing these pieces not just through our own eyes but through each other's as well.

Eventually, we stop in front of another painting—a soft, earthy piece with subtle greens and browns depicting a misty forest at dawn.

"This one," Alex says, his voice barely above a whisper, "it reminds me of where I grew up. Those quiet mornings when the world feels... endless."

I look at him, seeing the way his eyes soften, and feel a strange pang of recognition. "It's peaceful. Nostalgic, almost."

He nods, turning to me with a small smile. "I think... sometimes we look for art that reminds us of pieces of ourselves. Memories, moments we want to hold onto."

"Maybe that's why you and I both connect with Richmond's work," I say quietly. "He's always encouraged me to find that, to go deeper than the surface."

Alex looks at me, his gaze warm and steady. "You do that already, Cato. It's in everything you make. Every line and every stroke. It's what drew me to your work in the first place."

Silence settles between us, the noise of the crowd fading into the background. For a moment, it's just us, standing in the midst of a room filled with stories, both spoken and unspoken.

I take a deep breath, breaking the silence but keeping my tone soft. "This whole night... I just— I'm having a lot of fun with you, Alex."

He smiles in return. "I am, too."

We've been moving through the gallery for a while now; Alex and I caught up in quiet conversations about each piece, the depth of colors, and the inspiration behind the works. I don't even realize when my hand drifts to his, and suddenly we're standing there, fingers laced together as if it's the most natural thing in the world. There's a mutual understanding between us, and everything feels... right. I glance at him from the corner of my eye, noting the way his expression relaxes as he takes in each painting and sculpture, seeing it all through fresh eyes.

As we stand admiring a large, abstract sculpture, I notice Richmond approaching us. He looks like he's about to say something, but his eyes flick to our hands, and he gives a subtle, knowing smile. Without interrupting, he turns and melts back into the crowd, leaving us alone.

I smile to myself, feeling a sense of gratitude. Richmond has always had a knack for knowing when to give space, especially when something important is unfolding.

Alex breaks the silence, pulling me back to the present. "This sculpture," he says, studying the piece—a complex structure of swirling metal and glass, both sharp and soft at once. "How does Richmond manage to make things like this… and then switch back to painting? Isn't that hard?"

The question catches me off guard, and before I know it, a laugh escapes. Alex looks up, clearly puzzled.

"What? Why are you laughing?" He furrows his brow, a small smile tugging at his lips. "Is it that funny?"

I shake my head, still grinning. "No, no, it's just… take a closer look at the artist's name."

Alex squints at the small plaque beside the sculpture, tilting his head. "Why would reading Richmond's name make any difference?"

I chuckle, nudging him slightly. "Just read it."

With an exaggerated sigh, Alex leans closer, and his eyes widen as he takes in the name. "Jean Buena?" He straightens, looking back at me with a baffled expression. "I thought… I assumed all of this was Richmond's work."

I can't help but laugh again, shaking my head. "Nope. This isn't a solo exhibition. It's actually a group exhibit— Richmond organized it with pieces from some of his artist friends, people he's collaborated with over the years."

Alex's face lights up with realization and surprise. "Oh… wow, I had no idea! I thought it was all him."

I smile, leaning against the wall beside us. "It's a common misconception, especially when one artist organizes a gallery, but exhibitions like this are usually a mix of works from multiple artists who share similar styles or themes. Richmond's always been a huge advocate for collaborative art. He wanted to showcase not just his work but the talents of other artists he respects."

Alex nods, his face thoughtful. "So it's almost like... like he's giving us a window into his world, the people and art that inspire him."

"Exactly," I say, feeling a rush of appreciation for Richmond's vision. "That's what makes this exhibit special. Each piece here isn't just about Richmond—it's about the friendships, the collaborations, and the shared passion for art. It's not just a collection; it's like... a story of his journey."

He looks around the gallery, his gaze lingering on each piece with newfound understanding. "I guess I've never thought about it that way. The idea that an exhibition isn't just art for art's sake, but it's a reflection of all the people who made it possible."

I nod, squeezing his hand a little. "And that's why artists like Richmond love it. It's about sharing stories, perspectives, and—like you said—bringing people into their world."

Alex glances at me, his eyes mellowing as he takes in my words. "You really know how to see the bigger picture, don't you?"

I shrug, smiling. "Maybe. But I think you're starting to see it, too."

* * *

As we step out of the gallery, the cool night air hits us, a refreshing change after the warm hum of voices inside. Alex is grinning; his face lit up with that particular excitement only art seems to bring out in people. I match his smile, feeling the same high from the night. We've spent hours inside, but it feels like minutes.

We start down the sidewalk, the city lights casting a glow over the streets. I glance at Alex, who's still looking thoughtful, hands in his pockets as he walks beside me.

"That was... something else," he says, shaking his head slightly. "I don't think I've ever seen so many different styles in one place. Every piece had its own voice, you know?"

I nod, shoving my hands into my jacket pockets. "That's what makes a good exhibition. Each piece stands on its own, but together, they create something bigger. Richmond knew what he was doing, bringing in so many styles to tell a story."

He nods, eyes alight with curiosity. "And I loved how some of the artists used traditional techniques, like oil painting, while others went all out with digital art or mixed media. It's amazing how something like a sculpture and a digital painting can coexist like that."

"That's the beauty of it," I agree. "Art doesn't follow rules. You can throw together things you wouldn't expect to work, and suddenly, it becomes something incredible."

He looks at me, brow furrowing with interest. "Who's your favorite artist, Cato?"

I pause, thinking it over. "It's hard to say. There are so many, and each one brings something unique. But if I had to pick, I'd say... Viktor Drexler. His work has this timeless quality like every line was crafted with purpose. His art feels alive to me, and that's what I always try to capture in my own work."

Alex nods, eyes lighting up. "Drexler, huh? I can see that in your work, actually—the detailed line work, the elegance of it. I would've pegged you as more of a Surrealism fan, though."

I chuckle, nudging him. "You're not wrong. I'm a big fan of surrealism, too. It challenges the viewer to look beyond the obvious to question reality. But there's something about Art Nouveau, about how it takes everyday life and elevates it into something beautiful, that just resonates with me."

Alex grins, clearly enjoying the conversation. "I get that. I think... I'm still figuring out what styles speak to me. I mean, I love realism—the way artists can capture every tiny detail, like in a photograph. But at the same time, I can't help but be drawn to abstract art. The way it lets your mind interpret whatever you want from it."

I raise an eyebrow, intrigued. "Abstract, huh? I wouldn't have guessed that about you."

He shrugs, smiling. "Yeah, I guess it's surprising. There's something freeing about it like the artist gives you permission to feel whatever you want. No rules, no clear meaning... it's all up to the viewer."

I nod, feeling a new sense of admiration for him. "I get that. Abstract is all about letting go, isn't it? Just... feeling, without overthinking. And that's powerful. Takes a lot of courage to create something without a clear message and just let people interpret it."

He looks at me, his expression softening. "You're right. It's like... trusting people to find their own meaning in it. There's something vulnerable about that, something brave."

We keep walking, the conversation flowing effortlessly. We talk about artists from all over the world—Arlo's rebellious street art, Naomi Finch's raw, emotional self-portraits, and Xavier Kinross's expressive brushstrokes. I see the awe in Alex's eyes as he talks about them.

"Van Gogh," he says, his voice quieter now. "There's something tragic about his work, but also... hopeful. Like he was pouring everything he had onto the canvas, even when the world didn't see him."

I nod, feeling the weight of his words. "Yeah. Kinross's art has a kind of raw honesty. He didn't paint to impress anyone; he painted because he needed to. That's what makes his work so timeless. It's real, unfiltered."

We walk in silence for a moment, both of us lost in thought. Then Alex looks over at me, a small smile on his lips. "You know, tonight made me realize something."

"Oh?" I ask, raising an eyebrow.

He nods, gaze steady. "I think... I want to start creating again. More than just sketching, but painting—whatever it is. I want to find that part of myself that I lost somewhere along the way."

A warm feeling spreads through me as I look at him. "Alex, that's incredible. You should. Art's always been there for you, waiting. You just have to let yourself dive back in."

He smiles, looking a little shy but determined. "Thanks, Cato. I feel like… tonight gave me permission to take that first step."

I squeeze his shoulder, feeling a surge of pride. "You don't need anyone's permission, Alex. You just need to trust yourself. I'll be here, cheering you on every step of the way."

He grins, his eyes bright. "I'm glad. It… it means a lot to me."

We reach his building, but neither of us seems in a hurry to say goodbye. The night feels special, like a turning point. And as we stand there, under the dim streetlight, I realize I can't remember the last time I felt this close to someone, this understood.

"So," I say, breaking the comfortable silence, "next time we go to an art exhibit, I expect to see one of your pieces on the wall."

He laughs, rolling his eyes. "One step at a time, Cato. But… who knows? Maybe one day."

I grin. "I'll be there, first in line to buy it."

He shakes his head, but his smile is genuine. "Goodnight, Cato. And… thanks for tonight. It was unforgettable."

"Goodnight, Alex," I say softly, watching as he disappears into the building, leaving me standing there with a smile that I know won't fade anytime soon.

fifteen
CATO

Later that night, I settle onto the couch, still feeling the rush of the evening as I scroll Instagram. My phone buzzes on the coffee table. Excitedly, I glance at the screen, hoping it's Alex. When I look down and notice it isn't and see an unknown number, I frown slightly.

Curious, I open the message, and the words on the screen make me freeze.

Unknown Number:

> Hey, Cato. I'm in town. We should catch up.

I stare at the text, unease creeping up in a way that it always does. Derek. It's been a while since I've heard from him, but the tone—short and assuming, like he expects me to drop everything just because he's around. There's no question of whether I want to meet; he just assumes I'll say yes, like he's somehow entitled to my time.

I take a slow breath, my thumb hovering over the keyboard as a flood of memories stir.

Then another text pops up.

Unknown Number:

> Come on, Cato. Don't leave me hanging.

I scoff, shaking my head. Throughout our entire relationship, he always put himself first, the way he acted like he was somehow above everyone else—it overshadowed any decent memories we shared.

Another message arrives before I even have a chance to respond.

Unknown Number:

> I'm free tomorrow afternoon. Let's meet at our old spot. I'll see you at 2.

I clench my jaw, feeling a wave of irritation at his arrogance. Our old spot, as if I'd want to go back there.

Taking a deep breath, I type out a short reply.

Me:

> Hey, Derek. Tomorrow's not going to work.

I hit send, hoping he'll take the hint. But almost instantly, another text appears.

Unknown Number:

> Cato. Don't play hard to get. You always liked our little reunions.

Anger bubbles up now, his words stirring that resentment I used to feel. Playing hard to get? Does he really think this is a game?

I type again, no longer concerned about being polite.

Me:

> Derek, I'm not interested in 'reuniting' just because you're in town. Things are done between us. I have nothing left to say.

The silence on the other end stretches, and I can almost feel his irritation through it. Then, predictably, his reply arrives.

Unknown Number:

> Cato, you were never one to pretend you're better than anyone. This new attitude doesn't suit you.

I take a deep breath, forcing myself to stay calm. He always knew how to twist things, make it seem like I'm the unreasonable one, like setting boundaries is somehow beneath me.

Me:

> I'm not pretending. I just have other things that matter to me now. So if you're looking for someone to waste the afternoon with, I'm not your guy.

129

There's a long pause, and I assume he's given up, however, he hasn't. When he replies, his response is surprisingly short.

Unknown Number:

> Fine. But don't act like I'm the one who ruined things between us. I only ever wanted the best for you, Cato.

I clench my jaw, taking a slow breath before replying. I can feel the weight of his words pressing down, that sense of guilt he always knew how to evoke, even when he was in the wrong.

Me:

> If you really wanted the best for me, Derek, you would have respected what I needed back then. And you'd respect it now. Take care.

No response this time, and I watch the screen, half-expecting another guilt-tripping reply. But it stays silent.

Setting my phone down, I lean back on the couch as the emotions gradually settle. Derek always had a way of pulling me back into that old version of myself—the one who couldn't say no, who would bend just to keep the peace. Not this time.

As I sit there, my thoughts drift back to tonight: the gallery, Alex, and the feeling of being around someone I could actually see myself with. For the first time in a long time, I feel like I'm finally moving forward, building something better and I won't let Derek pull me back.

F. A. SENG

The memories of Derek hit sharp and sudden, and as much as I hate to admit it, his text pulls me right back to when we first met. I'm 22, wide-eyed and fresh in the city, eager to explore, to break free from the solitude of my small art studio and feel the pulse of something new.

It's my first time at the bar, and the smell of stale beer with the low hum of laughter filling the dimly lit room. The bartender barely glances at me, but I order a drink anyway, feeling slightly out of place but determined to blend in. That's when I notice Derek—tall, with that confident swagger, leaning casually against the bar as if he owns the place. He catches me watching, and before I know it, he's striding over, a mischievous smirk on his face.

"You look a little... lost," he says, his voice cutting through the music as he sizes me up, eyes sharp but amused.

I try to shrug it off, gripping my drink a little tighter. "Nah, just... new here. Thought I'd check out the place."

Derek grins, raising an eyebrow. "First time at a bar, or first time in the city?"

"Both, actually," I admit, laughing a bit. "Just moved here a few months ago."

"Well, let me be the first to give you a proper welcome, then," he says, leaning closer and clinking his glass against mine. "My name's Derek. What's your's?"

"Cato," I reply, feeling that initial spark of nervousness meeting someone who seems so... bold.

"So, Cato," he continues, eyes gleaming with mischief, "since it's your first time here, we have to make it memorable. How about a little contest?"

"A contest?" I ask, surprised but intrigued.

He smirks, lifting his drink. "Yeah. Simple. We drink, one after another, until one of us can't handle it anymore."

I laugh, rolling my eyes. "And what's the prize?"

He taps his chin, pretending to think it over. "How about... if you win, I'll buy you another round. And if I win... you have to come back here next Friday."

I eye him, curiosity bubbling up. "And how do you know I actually show up?"

He grins, leaning back. "Guess I just have to trust you, won't I?"

Chuckling, I give in. "Alright, Derek. You're on."

We clink glasses and throw back the first drink. The burn of the alcohol hits hard, but I shake it off, determined not to look like a lightweight. Derek raises an eyebrow, clearly impressed.

"Not bad, city newbie," he teases, already refilling our glasses.

We keep going, each round loosening the tension a bit more, laughter coming easier. Derek launches into stories—about the ridiculous people he's met at this very bar, about his escapades around the city, each tale more exaggerated than the last.

"So, Cato," he slurs slightly, raising his glass with a sly grin, "what brings you to the big city? Running from something, or are you chasing a dream?"

"Chasing a dream," I admit, smiling. "I'm an artist. Thought this place would be... I don't know, inspiring?"

"An artist, huh?" He leans in, interest flashing in his eyes. "What kind of art?"

"Tattoos, mostly. But I dabble in everything." I take another sip, watching as his eyes light up. "I'm hoping to open my own shop one day."

Derek lets out a low whistle. "Ambitious. I like it."

"What about you?" I ask, curious now. "What do you do?"

He shrugs, a hint of cockiness in his smile. "I work here and there, mostly finance. But that's just the day job. Nighttime, though? This city's my playground." He leans in, eyes dancing with something electric. "And tonight, so are you."

I feel my face warm, grinning despite myself. It's new for me, this kind of bold flirting. "Is that so?"

"Absolutely." He gives me a smirk, finishing off his drink and clinking his glass down on the table. "Now, you gonna keep up with me, or are you ready to admit defeat?"

I laugh, shaking my head. "Not a chance. You're not getting rid of me that easily."

We keep going, drink after drink, until the room blurs around the edges, our laughter blending with the noise of the bar. Somewhere between the fourth and fifth round, I know I'm done, but I don't want *to give him the satisfaction, so I push through, laughing even as my vision sways.*

At some point, Derek leans in, his face inches from mine. "You've got guts, Cato. I respect that."

"Likewise," I manage to slur back, feeling the warmth of his presence, the slight sway of his breath on my cheek.

Then he's leaning closer, voice low. "Next Friday, then? Win or lose, I'm still buying you that drink."

I nod, the thrill in my chest going beyond the alcohol. "It's a date."

Thinking back to those two years with Derek is like walking through a maze of memories, each turn darker than the last. It starts out so promising, so exhilarating. I'm young, naive, flattered by his attention. He seems to know exactly what he wants and I'm drawn to his confidence, his charm. But gradually, that charm twists into control and pain.

We've been planning this night for weeks. We've gone to dinner, taken a long romantic walk in the park, and after the movie, we're going back to his place. So I'm finding it hard to focus on the movie because I am so nervous. I hope Derek doesn't notice. Before I know it, the credits are rolling up the screen. I look around; everyone is leaving the theater.

"Are you ready?" Derek asks.

"Um, sure," I reply. As we leave the theater, he takes my hand, and we walk to the car together. Derek has always been very romantic. He always opens my door and pulls out my chair. So he opens my door.

"So what do you want to do now?" Derek asks. I look at him and shrug my shoulders.

"Do you want to go to my place now?" says Derek. I just nod. He smiles, and I get into the passenger seat. He goes around, gets into the driver's side, and starts the car. We leave the parking lot and go to his place.

Soon we pull up in his driveway, and we get out of the car. While we're walking towards the door, he fumbles with the keys and opens the door.

"There you go," he says. I enter the house first, and he follows. He closes the door and looks at me.

INK & *Intuition*

"Do you want anything to drink?" he asks.

I just shake my head, trying not to show how nervous I am. He walks over to me, looks me in the eyes, and gives me the deepest kiss I've ever had in my life. My heart starts pounding in my chest. He takes my hand and puts it on the very noticeable bulge in his pants. I've been with him almost six months, and I've never seen his cock once. But touching it now, it feels huge. Now I'm even more apprehensive. He slowly pulls his lips away from mine.

"Come on." He says, leading me to his bedroom.

When he opens the door, there is a king-size bed with condoms and a tube of lube on the nightstand. He closes the door. I turn to him to see him taking off his shirt and tossing it on the floor. He takes my hand and places it on his bulging crotch again.

"You feel that? That's all for you," he says to me.

My hand starts to shake with the second thoughts going through my head. I had no idea that I would be this nervous. He starts unbuckling my pants, and the next thing I know, my pants and boxers are around my ankles.

"Step out of them."

I do as he says, taking my hand from his crotch as he grabs my cock. I gasp when his hand touches. He shoves his tongue into my mouth and kisses me hard while he jacks my cock. I'm as hard as a rock in seconds. He puts his free hand on my ass and caresses it.

"Take off your shirt," he says. I freeze and look at him.

"Wait, Derek," I say to him.

He stops and looks at me.

"I don't think I'm ready for this. I want to stop."

At first, he just looks at me confused, but then something in his face changes. He just shakes his head.

"No, we're not going to stop now," he tells me. He takes the bottom of my shirt and pulls it over my head, tightening it around my wrists. I start to struggle with him.

He pushes me flat on my back to the bed.

"Don't move," he says. I freeze, not knowing what to do. Derek pulls off his pants and underwear in one move. His cock pops out, standing at attention, already leaking precum. I look at it; it's 9 inches at least and a lot of girth. He kicks his pants to the side and

134

climbs on the bed, forcing his knee between my legs. My legs open automatically.

"Please, Derek, I love you. I don't want to do this tonight. I'm not ready. Can we just slow down a little?" I try to get up, but he pushes me back to the bed. He looks down at me. When I look into his eyes, he looks like a different person. Not the Derek that I love.

"I'm not taking you home until..."

I cut him off. "You don't have to. I'll call someone to pick me up," I tell him. He shakes his head.

"No, you're not going home until I get what I've earned over these past months," Derek says.

"Derek, please..."

Suddenly, I feel a hard smack across my face.

"Shut up," he yells. My body tenses as he reaches over to the nightstand and picks up the lube.

I try to push him off of me, but he is too strong. He drops the lube on the floor.

"Shit. Fuck it. I'll do you dry." He loops his arms under my knees and pushes my knees to my chest. I've never been fucked before, let alone dry.

"Derek, no, please," I beg him. I push against him. He slaps my cheek again and again and again. He continues until my body falls still.

"Don't fight me. You won't win."

He's right. He's much bigger and much stronger.

"Stop, please, Derek, please don't do this."

Not listening to me, he aims his huge cock at my un-lubed entrance. I feel him touching my ass with his dick, coated in precum, in circles. He starts to shove himself in me. The pain shoots through my body, sending pain throughout.

"Ahh! No! Stop!" I scream.

He grabs my hips and forces his cock all the way into me to the hilt. I scream so loud and so hard that all the air from my lungs is spent.

"You like this cock, don't you, Seth?"

Seth. His ex before me. I can't breathe. Tears well up in my eyes. The pain is too much. He pulls out, leaving the head in, and forces

135

it all the way back in. I finally take a deep breath. It feels like my ass is being shredded by broken glass.

"Derek, ahh, please slow down." He ignores me and keeps up the same rhythm. I can't believe he is doing this to me.

He fucks me with no lube, no condom, and no time to adjust. He bites my shoulder as he fucks my ass raw. There's nothing I can do except let him finish. I close my eyes and hope that my ass and the rest of my body will go numb. But it doesn't. It is just constant pain for over an hour. He grabs my hair and makes me look him in the eyes.

"Tell me to fuck you," he commands.

I don't want to, but what other choice do I have? "Fuck me," I cry, the tears are a constant flow.

"Tell me again," he commands.

"Please fuck me, Derek." He thrusts his cock into me about a dozen more times. I just lay there, trying to fight the pain. I feel something warm running from my ass. I know it has to be blood. Derek starts to fuck me harder and faster.

"Oh fuck." Suddenly, I can feel him come inside of me.

After a few thrusts, he lets his cock fall out and lies on top of me for a few minutes to catch his breath. He rolls off of me. I wipe the tears from my face. My legs are shaking from the shock of pain. He reaches into the nightstand, pulls out some money, and throws it at me.

"Here, you can call a cab and go home now."

After that happened, Derek just got even more… shitty. I remember him coming to my tattoo shop, arms crossed as he looks over my sketches, pointing out what he thinks will "sell better" or telling me which designs are "a waste of time."

"Cato," he sighs in that patronizing way, "you're so talented. But you need to be realistic. Forget these side projects and focus on what people actually want. You can't just tattoo whatever you like."

Sometimes, I try to argue. "I want to create art that means something, Derek. That's the whole point of my shop."

He shakes his head, rolling his eyes like I'm a child who doesn't understand. "See, this is exactly why I need to help you. You don't get the real world, Cato. Let me guide you, okay?"

At first, I thought he was trying to help. I thought I saw potential in me, that he genuinely wanted me to succeed.

But as time went on, his "advice" turned to orders, his "guidance" more like suffocation.

I come home from the shop late, exhausted but pleased with the work I've done. I've spent hours on a new piece, something I've sketched from my own ideas. But as soon as I walk in, Derek's waiting, arms crossed, expression icy.

"You're late," he says flatly.

I blink, my stomach dropping. "Yeah, I... lost track of time. I was working on a new design."

He raises an eyebrow, tone laced with sarcasm. "Another one of those 'creative' projects of yours? When are you going to realize those don't pay the bills?"

My face heats up with frustration, but I try to keep my voice steady. "Derek, it's my work. I love what I do, and if I don't try new things —"

"Enough," he snaps, cutting me off. "You're being selfish. You have a real shot at success, and you're throwing it away on these ridiculous whims."

This becomes a pattern. Derek belittles my work, my choices, even my friends. He insists on knowing where I am at all times, and I find myself constantly defending every decision, every moment I spend outside his sight.

One evening, I plan to meet some friends for dinner. It's a small group, people I haven't seen in ages. But as I'm getting ready to leave, Derek blocks the door, his expression cold and calculating.

"You're not going," he says, crossing his arms.

I stare at him, feeling a mix of shock and anger. "What? Derek, they're just friends. I've known them for years —"

"They're a distraction, Cato," he says, his tone dripping with condescension. "You don't need people like that in your life. You have me. Isn't that enough?"

I feel trapped, like a caged bird, my freedom slipping further with each passing day. The more I try to reason with him, the more he twists my words, making me feel like I'm the one in the wrong, like I'm somehow failing him by wanting a life of my own.

The breaking point comes on a night that should be a celebration.

I've just completed a piece I'm proud of—something that feels true to my style, to my vision. I'm thrilled, ready to show it off, but Derek takes one look at it and scoffs.

"This?" he says, smirking. "This is what you wasted your time on? No wonder you're struggling, Cato. No one's going to pay for... whatever this is."

I feel something snap inside me, a rush of anger I can no longer contain. "You know what, Derek?" I say, my voice shaking. "I'm done. I'm tired of you putting down my work, my friends, my life. This isn't... this isn't what I want."

He stares at me, eyes narrowing. "Oh, so you're the victim now? Poor Cato, always misunderstood, always the little artist dreaming his dreams. You think you can make it without me?"

I take a deep breath, steadying myself. "I don't think—I know I can. And I don't need you controlling my every move."

His face twists in anger, and he takes a step closer, voice cold. "You're making a big mistake. You'll come crawling back, Cato. People like you don't survive without someone to keep them in line."

"Maybe," I reply, voice barely above a whisper, "but I'd rather fail on my own terms than succeed on yours."

The breakup is messy, full of arguments, accusations, and scenes that leave me drained and humiliated. He shows up at my shop, yells at me in front of clients, calls me repeatedly, leaving messages that veer between threats and apologies.

"Cato, pick up the damn phone. You can't ignore me forever."

"I was only ever looking out for you. You think anyone else will care like I did?"

The messages go on, each one leaving me more shaken. But I refuse to answer, to give him the satisfaction of a response. Instead, I pour myself into my work, each tattoo a small step toward reclaiming my life.

And eventually, he stops calling.

sixteen
ALEX

I walk into Eternal Ink the following Monday. Seeing Cato has become something I genuinely look forward to, but today… something feels off the moment I step inside.

He's at the front desk, as usual, hovering over his iPad, studying something intently. When he looks up and sees me, he gives me a nod, but his smile seems off. It's a little stiff, like he's distracted. Normally, Cato's smile has this certain type of energy to it, like he's actually glad to see me, but today? It feels… off.

"Hey, Alex," he says, his voice low, almost distant.

I smile back, but I can feel the tension hanging in the air. "Hey, Cato. Ready to get started?"

He nods and moves quickly toward his station, avoiding eye contact. "Yeah, let's get right into it."

I follow him to the chair, but the usual easy banter between us is missing. Normally, we'd chat about the design, crack a few jokes, and fall into this natural rhythm. Not today

139

though. There's none of that. He barely says a word as he sets up, and I can't shake the feeling that something's wrong.

I sit down, trying to focus on the work, but after a few minutes of silence, it starts to get to me. Why is he so distant? Cato's never been like this with me before, and the more I think about it, the more it gnaws at me.

Finally, I clear my throat, trying to keep my tone casual. "So… you free later today? Thought maybe we could grab a coffee or something."

Cato hesitates, not looking up from his work. "I don't know, Alex. Might not have time."

That hits me harder than I expect, and I feel worry tighten in my chest. Something is definitely off.

I lean forward slightly, trying to catch his eye. "What about a quick coffee? I thought it'd be nice to chat for a little bit."

He still doesn't look up, his hands moving over the tools, adjusting them. "I'm not sure, I'll think about it."

I stare at him for a moment, frustration mingling with concern. He's not giving me a real answer, just dodging, like he doesn't want to face whatever is bothering him. And it's not like Cato to shut me out.

Taking a deep breath, I decide to push just a little more. "Cato, what's going on? You've been quiet since I walked in, and now you're dodging coffee? If something's bothering you, just… talk to me."

He finally looks up, his blue eyes meeting mine, but it looks as if he's about to cry at any moment. He sighs, rubbing the back of his neck. "It's nothing, Alex. Just… stuff I'm dealing with. Personal stuff."

I tilt my head, not buying it. "Okay, but you don't have to deal with it alone, you know? I'm here. And I get it if you don't want to talk about it right now, but maybe getting out of the shop for a bit would help clear your head."

He hesitates again, biting his lip like he's debating whether to say something or not. After a long moment, he finally nods, though it seems reluctant. "Okay. Coffee. Just for a little while."

I smile, relieved that he's at least agreeing. "Just coffee and who knows? A change of scenery might actually help."

* * *

We settle into a cozy corner of the café, our coffees steaming in front of us. I watch as Cato takes a sip of his black coffee, his movements slow. His face still seems a bit clouded, but I can tell he's making an effort to be present, to push aside whatever's weighing him down.

Taking a deep breath, I feel a bit of anticipation bubbling up. Maybe this is a chance to lighten the mood, to focus on something positive.

"You know," I begin, leaning forward a bit, "I've been thinking a lot about the gallery last week. It was amazing, honestly."

Cato's eyes shift to me, a faint but genuine smile tugging at the corner of his lips. "I'm glad you liked it."

"I really did." I say, feeling my enthusiasm growing as I speak. "The variety of styles, the boldness of the artists, the way each piece felt like a glimpse into someone's soul. It was really nice to be around some like-minded people."

Cato nods, his gaze softening a bit. "Well then I'm really glad that I invited you and that you came."

I grin, feeling a bit more confident. "Being there made me think about something I've always wanted to do but never really admitted out loud."

He raises an eyebrow, a hint of curiosity in his eyes. "What's that?"

I hesitate for a moment, feeling a bit vulnerable, but then I decide to just go for it. "I'd love to have a personal gallery someday. My own art, my own creations, all in one place. I want to share my work with people, to have them see the things I see, to feel the emotions I try to put into my sketches."

Cato's expression shifts, becoming more intent, more focused. He leans forward slightly, his eyes locked on mine. "Really? You've thought about having your own gallery?"

I nod, feeling a rush of excitement. "Yeah. I mean, I know it's probably a long way off, and I have a lot of work to do, but… just being at Richmond's gallery made me feel like it's possible. Like maybe one day, I could actually make it happen."

His gaze relaxes even more, and a small, warm smile appears on his face. "Alex, that's incredible. I didn't know you had that dream."

I shrug, feeling a bit shy under his intense gaze. "It's something I've kept to myself for a while. I guess I didn't think it was realistic. But seeing all those artists, seeing how their work was celebrated… it just made me realize that maybe I should stop holding back."

Cato nods thoughtfully, still smiling. "You absolutely should. You're talented, Alex. I mean it. I've seen your sketches, and I can tell there's a lot of you in your work and it's real. You shouldn't be afraid to show it."

His words send a tenderness through me, a sense of validation I hadn't expected. "Thanks, Cato. I really mean that."

He shakes his head slightly, his eyes never leaving mine. "It's the truth, Alex. You've got potential. More importantly, you have passion. That's what makes a good artist—someone who isn't afraid to pour themselves into their work."

I feel a swell of emotion, and I try to keep my voice steady. "I think what really hit me at the gallery was seeing how each piece had a story. I want that for my own work. I want people to look at my art and feel something, even if it's just a small connection."

Cato's smile widens a bit, his expression filled with a kind of quiet pride. "They will, Alex. You have a unique perspective, a way of seeing things that's all your own. That's what will make your gallery special when it happens."

"When it happens?" I repeat, surprised by his confidence.

He nods firmly. "Yes, when. Not if. You've already got the drive, and now you just need to trust yourself. I believe you can make it happen."

I feel a rush of gratitude, my heart swelling at his words. "You really think so?"

"I do," he says simply, his voice steady. "And if you ever need help with it—planning, promoting, anything—I'm here. Just say the word."

I smile, feeling a new feeling of desire spread through me, not just from his words but from the sincerity behind them. "Thank you, Cato. I don't think I'd even be considering this if it weren't for you and all the encouragement you've given me."

He shrugs, but his smile remains. "I'm just glad you're thinking about it, Alex. The world deserves to see your art."

* * *.

After we finish our coffee, I sense he's still carrying that heaviness with him, and I'm not quite ready to end our time together, not with everything that feels left unsaid.

"Hey," I say, trying to keep things light, "how about we go for a walk? It's still early, and the weather's nice."

Cato hesitates, his gaze shifting as if he's looking for a reason to say no. "I don't know, Alex. I should probably get back."

I nod, careful not to push too hard, but I'm not about to let him close himself off, either. "I get it. But maybe a walk could help clear your head? No pressure, just fresh air and a change of scenery."

He glances at me, his expression relaxing just a bit. "Alright," he says with a reluctant smile. "Just a short one."

We step outside, and the late afternoon light casts a golden glow over the street. We walk side by side, our steps in sync, and although we're quiet at first, the silence feels weighted. I keep sneaking glances at him, trying to read his face, to understand what's really bothering him.

Finally, I can't hold back any longer. "Cato... is something wrong? You've been kind of distant today."

He doesn't respond immediately, his eyes fixed on the ground in front of us. I can tell he's debating whether or not to let me in. Just as he seems like he might respond, his phone buzzes in his pocket. He checks the screen, his jaw tightening slightly as he reads the message.

"Everything okay?" I ask, concern settling in my chest.

Cato hesitates, then slips the phone back into his pocket without responding. I notice the tension in his posture, his whole demeanor tightening again.

"Cato," I say, stopping and turning to face him. "Something's clearly bothering you, and I don't want to push, but... I care about you. You don't have to go through this alone."

He sighs heavily, finally meeting my gaze. "It's my ex, Derek," he says quietly, his voice barely above a whisper.

"Oh, I'm assuming things didn't end well?" I ask, my voice cautious. "Is he wanting something from you now?"

Cato nods, his shoulders slumping slightly. "No, they didn't end well. He texted me out of the blue a couple of days ago, saying he wants to meet up. It's like he thinks he can just walk back into my life like nothing happened."

Frustration flares up inside me, a protective anger on his behalf. "What does he want?"

Cato shakes his head, his face etched with weariness. "No idea and I have no interest in finding out. He's always been this controlling and arrogant prick. He thinks he can just show up, and I'll fall back into the same pattern."

I reach out, gently placing a hand on his arm. "Cato, you don't owe him anything. You're not obligated to meet him or even respond to his messages."

He looks at me, and I see the hurt in his eyes, pain that runs deeper than words. "Derek was... he was my first serious relationship. But it wasn't just bad—it was toxic. He controlled everything. My work, my friends, even where I went. I felt trapped, like I couldn't breathe without his permission."

My chest tightens as I listen, feeling a surge of sympathy and protectiveness. "That sounds horrible, Cato. No one deserves to go through that."

He nods slowly, his gaze distant. "It was. I nearly lost everything because of him—my art, my shop, even myself. He was... abusive, Alex. Not physically, but emotionally. He tore me down little by little, until I didn't recognize myself."

I feel a deep ache inside as I take in his words. "I'm so sorry. I can't imagine how hard that must have been."

He takes a shaky breath, his voice hoarse. "It took me years to rebuild myself after him. To even think about dating again. And now, here he is, trying to wedge his way back in, as if nothing happened."

I step closer, making sure he can see the sincerity in my eyes. "You've come so far, Cato. You've built something incredible, and you've found yourself again. Don't let him take that away from you."

He looks down, his voice softer. "I know. But part of me is still scared, Alex. Scared that he'll find a way to break me again."

Hearing this, I feel a pang of sadness for him. "You're not the same person you were back then. You're stronger now, and you have people who care about you—people who won't let you fall back into that darkness."

He glances up, a faint glimmer of hope in his eyes. "You really think I can keep him away? That I can stay strong?"

I nod firmly. "I know you can, Cato. And I'll be here to help you, however I can. You're not alone in this."

He lets out a sigh, but it sounds a little lighter this time, less burdened. "Thanks, Alex. It means a lot, having someone who listens, who actually understands."

I give his arm a gentle squeeze. "Always. If you ever feel overwhelmed, remember—you don't have to face it alone. You've got me, and you've got people who care about you. We're here."

A small smile tugs at his lips, the first real one I've seen all day. "I appreciate it, Alex. More than you know."

We stand there, the world moving around us, but for a moment, it feels like it's just the two of us. The hurt in his gaze seems to ease, replaced by kindness, by trust.

"Let's keep walking," he says calmly, his voice more relaxed.

I smile back, nodding. "Yeah. Let's keep walking."

seventeen
CATO

June

We settle into Demi's cozy apartment, a mug of coffee warming my hands. The space feels just like her—small but bursting with personality. Minimalist décor, a few bold paintings on the walls, and shelves lined with tattoo design books and art supplies. It's cozy and inviting, with a vibe that makes it easy to relax and feel at home.

Demi sits cross-legged on the floor in front of me, her iPad open in front of her and a notebook by her side. Her hair's pulled up in a messy bun, and she's unusually focused as she scrolls through the calendar on her screen.

"Alright, Cato," she says, her voice a blend of business and her usual laid-back tone. "Next week's looking pretty wild. We'll need to be smart about it."

I lean forward, glancing at her screen from the couch. "Yeah, I figured as much. Who's first on the list?"

She clicks on the first name, reading through her notes. "Monday, we start with Mr. Henderson. He wants a full back piece—dragons, flames, the whole works. I've been trying to get him to finalize the design for weeks, but he keeps tweaking the details."

I laugh, shaking my head. "Classic Henderson. We'll have to pin him down this time."

Demi rolls her eyes a bit. "Right? I swear, his indecision could make a statue fidget. But he's usually good once we start. I've blocked out most of the morning for him."

"Good call," I say, taking a sip of coffee. "I'll be sure to bring extra patience."

She laughs, nudging my leg with her elbow. "You and I both. After that, we've got Jessica Ortiz for a sleeve—florals mixed with geometric patterns."

I tilt my head thoughtfully. "I remember her. She was clear about wanting something bold but elegant."

"Thank god, too," Demi says, flipping through her notes. "She seems solid and knows what she wants, which is always refreshing."

I smile. "Definitely makes things easier."

She smirks, her eyes sparkling with mischief. "Speaking of clients with visions, Mr. Patel is back on Tuesday afternoon. Remember him? The 'spiritual journey' guy?"

I laugh. "Oh, I remember. He kept quoting Rumi during the entire session. Hard to tell if he was more into the tattoo or giving us a poetry reading."

"Exactly," she says, grinning. "Now he wants to add a 'third eye awakening' element to it. I've booked him for a longer session since you know he's going to be chatting the whole time."

I shake my head, still smiling. "I might need more than just coffee after that. Maybe a strong drink."

"Deal," she says with a laugh. "We'll get through it together."

She scrolls down the list, her expression turning more serious. "Then we've got Mr. Ramirez for final touches on his tiger piece. You okay handling that one?"

I hesitate for a moment, remembering how intense the last session was with Ramirez. He's tough—quiet but always insistent on perfection. "Yeah, I can handle it. Ramirez knows what he wants and isn't shy about saying it. A challenge, but doable."

Demi nods, a flicker of concern in her eyes. "He's particular, but you're the best person to finish that piece. He trusts you."

I give her a small smile, grateful for the vote of confidence. "Thanks, Demi. I'll make sure it's exactly what he wants."

We keep going through the list, talking about clients like Alice, who wants a watercolor-style bird on her wrist, and Peter, coming in for his first tattoo—a simple anchor on his forearm.

Demi leans back, stretching her arms. "You know, for as chaotic as it gets, I wouldn't trade this for anything. Working with you, dealing with all these characters—it's worth it."

I feel a warmth spread through me at her words. "Same here, Demi. It can be crazy, but it's our kind of crazy."

She smiles, her eyes lightening. "And we do crazy like it's no one else's business."

I raise my coffee mug in a mock toast. "To the chaos. And to us handling it like pros."

She clinks her mug against mine, laughing. "To the chaos."

ALEX

I'm hunched over my desk, eyes glued to the screen as I tweak the latest design for a gaming company's logo. It's been a long process, but I'm finally getting somewhere. The logo needs to be bold yet sleek, edgy but not too overwhelming—a balance that's proving to be a real challenge.

Next to me, Tommy leans over, examining the draft with his usual honest feedback.

"Dude, that's coming together really well," he says, nodding approvingly. "But maybe make that line a bit sharper? You know, more like a sword than a stick."

I chuckle, making the adjustment. "Good call. It's supposed to be a warrior-themed game, after all. The sword has to look intimidating."

"Exactly," Tommy agrees, leaning back in his chair, still watching the screen. "I like how the colors pop now. It's got that 'in-your-face' vibe they're going for."

"Glad you think so," I say, feeling a bit of pride. "It's been a struggle to get the right balance, but I think this version might actually work."

We both stare at the design for a moment, and I feel a sense of accomplishment settling in. There's still work to be done, but this feels like progress. As I save the file, I catch Tommy looking at me with a mischievous grin—the kind that usually means he's about to ask for something.

"What's that look for?" I ask, raising an eyebrow.

He rubs the back of his neck, still grinning. "Well, there's this little thing I need to ask you."

I turn in my chair, intrigued. "Okay, shoot. What's up?"

Tommy hesitates for a second, then looks me straight in the eye, blinking exaggeratedly. "So, here's the deal—I was hoping my girlfriend could come over tonight. You know, just for a bit of time together."

I smirk, already sensing where this is going. "Oh, really? And how does that involve me?"

Tommy leans in, lowering his voice as if he's sharing a secret. "Well, I was kind of hoping you could, you know… give us some private time. Maybe disappear for a few hours? Just tonight?"

I laugh, shaking my head. "Wow, you're really pulling out the big guns, huh? Even the puppy dog eyes?"

Tommy clasps his hands together, looking as pathetic as he can manage. "Come on, man! It's been a while since we had some time alone, and she really wants to hang out without a third wheel around."

I sigh dramatically, leaning back in my chair. "Fine, fine. But you owe me one, big time."

He grins, a bit too quickly. "Absolutely. I'll buy you dinner, cover your coffee for a week, whatever it takes. Just this one time, okay?"

I roll my eyes, unable to hide my smile. "Alright, I'll clear out for the evening. But when.. I mean if, I ever bring someone home, you have to clear out for me. Deal?"

Tommy laughs, slapping my shoulder playfully. "Deal. And you're the best, you know that?"

"Yeah, yeah," I say, waving him off. "Just make sure you don't do anything that'll get us kicked out of the apartment."

"No promises," he jokes, winking. "Seriously, thanks, Alex. I owe you."

"You better," I reply, turning back to my screen. "Now, let me finish this logo before you kick me out of my own apartment."

He chuckles, getting up from his chair. "Fair enough. Thanks again, man."

* * *

CATO

It's close to 7 PM on Friday, and I'm standing in front of the Grand Premier Theatre, leaning against one of the old brick columns. The evening air is crisp, and the glow of the streetlights mixes with the neon from the theater's marquee, casting a slightly surreal light over everything. I adjust my black jacket—my usual goth-inspired look, complete with a worn band tee underneath. It's my comfort zone, my armor.

Alex had texted me asking if I was free tonight, which I could've sworn my calendar was booked for this evening, but right as he texted me, Demi had let me know that my last few clients had all canceled, which never happens. So when I said I was free Alex was quick to respond.

Alex:

> Great. Then it's a date. I'll see you at 7 o'clock tonight.

So here I am. Standing outside of the theatre waiting for Alex.

A few minutes later, I spot him walking toward me, and *holy fuck* he looks good. He's dressed in a pristine white blazer, a sky-blue shirt underneath, and light gray trousers that almost seem out of place in this part of town. But somehow, it works, like he's a pop of color against a monochrome backdrop.

"Hey!" I call out, giving him a wave.

He hurries over, a slight smile on his face. "Hey, Cato. Glad you could make it."

I nod, taking in his outfit with an amused smile. "Wow, you're looking sharp tonight. What's the occasion? Job interview after this?"

Alex laughs, glancing down at his clothes as if noticing how dressed up he is. "Not exactly. Just figured I'd try to look decent. And, well, I had to escape the apartment for a bit."

I raise an eyebrow, intrigued. "Oh? What's with the sudden need for an escape?"

He grins, looking a bit sheepish. "Tommy actually. He asked for some alone time with his girlfriend—the kind of 'alone time' where a roommate is definitely not welcome."

I burst out laughing, shaking my head. "Ah, young love. Kids these days and their urgent 'alone time.'" I tease, still chuckling. "Can't say I blame him, though. Privacy is a rare commodity with roommates."

Alex nudges me with a smirk. "You're not that much older. Are you calling me a kid, too?"

I look him up and down, noting the sharpness of his outfit. "I'm ten years older than you," I laugh. "But you're definitely stepping up your game. Though, I have to admit, I never thought I'd see you in a white blazer."

He laughs, looking a little relieved. "Yeah, figured I'd try something new. Not exactly your style, I know."

151

INK & *Intuition*

"True," I agree, glancing down at my own outfit. "But that's what makes this interesting, right? A little contrast."

Alex nods, his eyes bright. "I think so. So, what's the plan for the evening, Mr. punk-rocker?"

I scratch my head, glancing at the theater's marquee. "Honestly? I wasn't sure what you had in mind. Thought maybe we'd catch a movie here, or we could just grab dinner somewhere close. Your call."

He thinks about it, his face lighting up as an idea clicks. "I mean, I could eat."

I chuckle, appreciating his spontaneity. "Sounds like a plan."

He laughs, looking more relaxed. "Alright, then. There's a great Chinese place a block down. They have amazing dumplings."

"Lead the way," I say, gesturing down the street. "I'm always up for dumplings."

We start walking, our conversation flowing naturally, the initial awkwardness melting away.

"So," I ask, trying to keep things light, "how's work going? Still stuck on that gaming logo?"

Alex nods, a bit of frustration flashing in his eyes. "Yeah, it's been… a process. I think I'm getting there. It's just hard to balance creativity with what the client wants."

"Tell me about it," I reply with a knowing sigh. "It's the same with tattoos. Some clients want the moon, but they only have the budget for a paper star."

Alex laughs, shaking his head. "I can imagine. It must be tough to hold back your own ideas sometimes."

"Yeah," I agree. "But it's part of the process. Sometimes you compromise, but other times, you find ways to sneak in your own touch. It's a dance, really."

Alex looks thoughtful. "I get that. I guess it's like finding a balance between what's expected and what feels right to you as an artist."

I nod, feeling that familiar sense of understanding between us.

"I'm not even tired yet, Any chance you'd want to see a movie after all?" I ask as we pay the bill for our dumplings.

Alex smiles at the thought. "I'd love to."

* * *

The neon lights of the Grand Premier Theatre flicker above us as we step up to the ticket booth and glance at the options. The place is packed, and most of the shows are completely sold out except for one—a romantic film called *The Last First Date*. I chuckle, glancing over at Alex. "Romance, huh? Not exactly what I expected for tonight."

He laughs, looking a bit embarrassed. "Yeah, not the typical choice, I guess. But hey, it's the only one available. Besides, it could be good."

I raise an eyebrow, teasing him a bit. "You think so? You don't exactly strike me as a romance movie kind of guy."

He shrugs, grinning. "There's a first time for everything, right? Besides, maybe it'll be good."

"Fair enough," I say, handing over the cash to the cashier. "Two for *The Last First Date*, please."

* * *

We find our seats near the back, settling in as the lights dim and the opening credits roll. I shift slightly, trying to get comfortable in the plush, red theater chair, but I can't help glancing sideways at Alex. He's watching the screen intently, his face illuminated by the flickering light, and there's this odd sense of anticipation in the air.

As the movie unfolds, it becomes clear that it's centered around two protagonists with a complicated, slow-burn kind of romance. They're polar opposites, drawn together by some inexplicable force but held back by misunderstandings, circumstances, and their own fears.

Alex leans closer, his glasses catching the faint flicker of the screen's light as he whispers, "You think they'll actually get together by the end?"

I smirk, turning my head toward him, our faces just inches apart in the dim light. "In a romance movie? I'd say the odds are in their favor."

153

He chuckles, shaking his head. "Yeah, but it feels so… real. Like, they're not just being dramatic for the sake of it."

I nod, keeping my voice low. "That's what makes it good, I guess. When you can feel the tension, the longing, even when they're not saying much."

We keep watching, whispering back and forth as the characters share stolen glances and lingering touches. It's both cheesy and compelling, and I can't help but get caught up in the atmosphere.

"Do you think they'll kiss in this scene?" Alex asks quietly during one particularly intense moment.

I squint at the screen, watching the protagonists move closer. "Probably not. It's too soon. They'll pull away at the last second."

Sure enough, they do. We both laugh softly, our shoulders brushing against each other. I feel the heat of the contact, and before I know it, our hands have drifted closer, fingers lightly brushing. The simple touch sends a jolt through me, and instinctively, I lace my fingers with Alex's.

He glances down at our hands, then up at me, his eyes wide but curious. "Cato…"

I try to play it off, but the words come out softer than I intend. "Sorry, I—"

But he shakes his head, a small smile playing at the corner of his lips. "No, it's okay."

We continue holding hands, nerves spreading through me in a way I haven't felt in a long time. The movie's still rolling, but my focus has shifted entirely. It's less about what's happening on the screen and more about what's happening between us.

I reach for the popcorn, and as I turn, I find my face just inches from Alex's. The proximity is unexpected, and I freeze, our eyes locking in the dim light. There's a moment of silence, and time seems to stretch endlessly with every detail heightened —the rise and fall of Alex's breath, the faint scent of his cologne, the anticipation building between us.

Neither of us says a word, and before I realize what I'm doing, I lean in slightly, closing the small gap between us. He doesn't pull away, instead, he meets me halfway, his lips firm yet pliant against mine.

The kiss is tentative at first, almost as if we're testing the waters. Then, something shifts, and it deepens, becoming more urgent, more real. I feel a rush of emotions—relief, desire, and a strange sense of inevitability. My hand moves instinctively to the back of his neck, pulling him closer.

Alex responds with the same intensity, his hand gripping mine tighter as he leans into the kiss. It's as if all the tension, all the unspoken feelings between us, are finally finding their voice. The rest of the world fades away—the movie, the other people in the theater—all of it becomes background noise.

When we finally pull back, we're both a little breathless, our foreheads resting against each other. I open my eyes, finding Alex's gaze still on me, a mix of surprise and something deeper in his eyes.

"Wow," he whispers, his voice barely audible.

"Yeah," I agree, a bit dazed. "That... wasn't what I expected tonight."

He laughs softly, his breath against my skin. "Me neither. But I'm not complaining."

I grin, feeling a strange, almost giddy sensation wash over me. "Neither am I."

We sit there for a few more moments, our fingers still interlocked, letting the reality of what just happened sink in.

INK & *Intuition*

eighteen
ALEX

I sit at my desk, surrounded by papers, design drafts, and my trusty tablet. I've just started sketching concepts for a new project—a branding overhaul for a sports apparel company. It's one of those big projects that could really help me grow in the field. I'm too consumed by the thought of my first kiss with Cato, even though I should be working on conceptualizing the corporate logo, when my phone buzzes.

It's a message from Amelia, my manager.

Amelia:

> Come to my office when you have a minute.

I frown, wondering what it could be about. Saving my work, I quickly make my way down the hall, my heart picking up speed. Amelia is usually direct, and she doesn't call people into her office for small talk.

I knock on her door, feeling a bit anxious. "You wanted to see me?"

Amelia looks up from her desk, her usual composed expression replaced with a small smile. "Yes, Alex. Come in, take a seat."

I sit down, still trying to read her face. "Is everything okay?"

Her smile widens, and there's a hint of excitement in her eyes. "More than okay, actually. I have some good news for you."

My heart leaps, but I try to keep my voice steady. "Oh? What's the news?"

Amelia leans forward, folding her hands on the desk. "You've been selected by the client for an on-site project starting in the new year. They loved your initial concepts and want you to work with them directly. It's a big opportunity, Alex."

I stare at her in disbelief. "Wait, seriously? They want me to work on-site with them?"

She nods, her smile turning into a grin. "Yes, they do. It's not just a temporary assignment either. It's a six-month engagement, with the possibility of it extending based on your performance."

I blink, trying to process it all. "Wow, I... I don't know what to say. This is huge."

"It is," she agrees. "Not only will you get the chance to work closely with their creative team, but there will also be a significant increase in your salary."

I feel a rush of pride, but there's a hint of nervousness mixed in. "That's amazing, Amelia. I mean, I never expected this to happen so quickly."

She leans back, her expression turning a bit more serious. "You deserve it, Alex. You've been working hard for the ninety days that you've been here, and the clients noticed. It's not just about the money or the title. They're also providing better accommodations. You'll be staying in one of their corporate apartments, which should be a nice upgrade from your current place."

I try to imagine it—better pay, better living conditions, and a chance to work on-site with a major client. It all feels surreal. "This is… unbelievable. I can't thank you enough for this opportunity, Amelia."

She shakes her head. "Don't thank me, Alex. You earned this. The client specifically mentioned how impressed they were with your creativity and attention to detail. They want someone who can bring fresh ideas to the table, and that's you."

I smile, feeling a swell of pride. "It means a lot to hear that. I've always wanted to work more closely with clients, to really understand their vision."

Amelia's expression softens. "I know you have. This could be a game-changer for your career, Alex. It'll give you exposure to bigger projects and allow you to build stronger connections in the industry."

I nod, already feeling the gears turning in my head. "Where exactly is the site?"

"So it's quite a ways away. The company would pay for you to relocate to Seattle," she explains. "The company is setting up a new headquarters, and they want you to be part of the team that establishes their brand presence from the ground up."

"Wow," I say again, still trying to absorb everything. "Seattle?"

Amelia laughs. "Yes, Seattle. Now, you don't need to make a decision now, but we do need an answer soon. I have a feeling you're going to do great if you go."

I take a deep breath, feeling a tinge of anxiousness. "I appreciate this, Amelia. I'll really consider this. I'm just not sure about uprooting my life after just moving here, even if it's temporary."

"I get it, Alex. I know you'll consider all your options," she says confidently. "Now, go back and finish your current project. You've got a lot to think about, but we'll be with you every step of the way. The HR team will reach out to you with more details about the move and logistics."

"Thank you, Amelia," I say sincerely. "This is really a dream come true."

She nods, her smile genuine. "You've worked for it, Alex. Just keep that focus, and remember to enjoy the journey."

I stand up, feeling adrenaline and gratitude. "I will. And again, thank you. I won't forget this."

As I leave her office and walk back to my desk, I feel like I'm walking on air. This is it—the opportunity I've been waiting for, a chance to prove myself and take a huge step forward in my career. I can't wait to tell Tommy, however, I don't know how I'm going to tell the news with Cato.

* * *

I sit in my room, staring at the glowing screen of my laptop, Amelia's words from the meeting still fresh in my mind. This opportunity is incredible—better pay, a corporate apartment, and six months working directly on-site with the client. Everything I've been working toward, right?

Despite the incredible opportunity, there's this gnawing feeling in my gut, a weight making the whole thing feel a little less straightforward. Cato's face flashes through my mind, and I can't help but feel a pang of uncertainty.

I sigh, closing the laptop and leaning back in my chair. I need to talk this out, to hear a different perspective.

"Tommy!" I call, hoping he's around. A moment later, I hear his familiar footsteps coming down the hall, and he appears at my door, a curious look on his face.

"What's up, man? You look like you've seen a ghost," he says, stepping into my room.

I motion for him to sit on the bed, feeling a swirl of frustration and confusion. "It's not a ghost. It's a job offer."

Tommy raises an eyebrow, settling onto the bed. "A job offer? That's good news, right? You've been waiting for something like this."

I nod, running a hand through my hair. "Yeah, it is. It's a huge opportunity. The client wants me to work on-site for six months, maybe longer. It comes with a raise, a better place to stay—basically everything I've been aiming for."

Tommy's eyes widen, a grin spreading across his face. "Dude, that's amazing! So, what's the problem?"

I bite my lip, feeling the conflict rise inside me. "The problem is... I'd have to leave here, at least for a while. And... I'd have to leave Cato too."

Tommy's expression softens, and he leans forward. "Ah, I see. So it's not just about the job, huh?"

I nod slowly. "Exactly. Cato and I have finally started getting close, especially after that kiss we had on Friday. Things are just starting to feel... right. Now, I'd have to step away from all of it. It feels like I'm being forced to choose between my career and my personal life."

Tommy quickly holds up a hand as if to stop the conversation. "I'm sorry, how are you just going to skate over the fact that you and Cato fucking kissed?!"

I sigh and roll my eyes. "My God, Tommy." I laugh. "It's not a huge deal."

"Ooo, you *like* him," Tommy taunts, making kissy faces.

"Shut up!" I laugh, throwing a scrap piece of paper at his face.

Tommy laughs, and then is quiet for a moment before giving a small, understanding smile. "Seriously though, Alex, I get it. This is a tough call. But you've worked hard to get to this point. You deserve this opportunity."

I look down, feeling the weight of his words. "I know I do. But I feel like I'd be abandoning something important here. Cato's been through a lot, and I don't want to let him down."

Tommy leans back, crossing his arms thoughtfully. "Look, man, I'm not going to tell you what to do. These kinds of opportunities come and go, but they're also rare. You can't ignore how important this could be for your career."

I nod, but the uncertainty lingers. "I know, but Cato's... he's not someone I can just walk away from. Not when I feel the way I do about him, and I don't want to lose that."

Tommy sighs, his voice gentle. "I get that, Alex. And I know how much he means to you. But you have to think about what's best for you, too. You have to decide if this opportunity is worth taking a step away, even if it's just temporary."

I lean forward, feeling torn. "What if I take this job and lose everything I've built with him? What if he thinks I'm choosing my career over him?"

Tommy shakes his head. "If Cato really cares about you, he'll understand why you need to do this. He might not like it, sure, but he'll get it. And if it's meant to be, you two can work it out, even with the distance."

I sigh, my voice barely above a whisper. "I just don't want to lose him."

Tommy puts a reassuring hand on my shoulder. "You're not going to lose him, Alex. Not if you're honest about how you feel and why you're making this choice. You've got to trust that the bond you have is strong enough to handle this."

I look at him, feeling a bit more grounded by his words. "You really think it's possible? To have both?"

He smiles, giving me a supportive nod. "I do. But make the decision based on what you want, not just what you're afraid of losing. Talk to Cato. Tell him everything. You'll know what to do after that."

I take a deep breath, feeling the clarity slowly return. "You're right. I have to talk to him."

* * *

My heart pounds as I dial Cato's number, my fingers trembling slightly, anxiety pooling in my stomach. This conversation isn't going to be easy. I take a deep breath, trying to steady myself as the phone rings.

"Hey, handsome," he answers, his voice inviting. "What's up?"

I clear my throat, working to sound more composed than I feel. "Hey. Are you free right now? I was hoping we could meet up."

"Sure," he replies without hesitation. "I'm actually at the park near the shop, just taking a break. You want to come here?"

"Yeah," I respond quickly. "I'll be there in a few minutes."

161

INK & *Intuition*

As I hang up, I feel the weight of what I'm about to say settling over me.

* * *

The walk to the park feels longer than usual, my mind racing with some fear. I want to share the good news with Cato, but I'm terrified of what comes next—the part where I'll have to tell him about the move. When I finally spot him sitting on a bench under a large oak tree, his back to me, he looks relaxed, lost in thought with his tattooed arms resting on the back of the bench.

As I approach, he turns, a smile breaking across his face. "Hey, there you are!"

"Hey," I manage, returning his smile but feeling my heart still thudding in my chest. I sit beside him, gripping my hands to steady myself. "Thanks for meeting me like this."

He nods, his curiosity showing. "Of course. What's on your mind? When you called, it sounded like something was bothering you."

I take a deep breath, deciding to start with the good part first. "Well, I have some news. It's... big news, actually."

His eyes light up, his smile widening. "Oh? What is it?"

"I got a promotion," I say, letting the enthusiasm slip into my voice as I say the words out loud. "The client I've been working with wants me to join their team on-site. It's a huge opportunity—better pay, a better place to stay, everything."

His grin broadens, full of pride. "That's amazing, babe! I knew you had it in you. Congratulations!"

His excitement gives me a moment of relief, and I smile, feeling his support. "Thanks. It's really like a dream come true."

He nods, still smiling. "I'm really proud of you. You've worked hard for this. You deserve it."

Hearing his words stirs something bittersweet in me, knowing what I have to say next. I look down, my fingers fidgeting. "There's more to it, though."

The shift in my tone dims his smile slightly. "What is it?"

162

I draw a breath, trying to find the words. "The job... it's not here. I'd have to move... to Seattle, at least for six months, maybe longer if things go well."

Cato's face falls, the happiness slowly draining from his eyes as he looks away, staring at the ground. The silence between us thickens, and I can feel the distance forming, even though we're side by side.

"Cato?" I ask quietly, breaking the silence. "What do you think?"

After a moment, he speaks, his voice measured but distant, almost hurt. "I think... it's a great opportunity, Alex. You should go for it if it's what you want."

His words sting more for what they don't say than for what they do. "What about us?" I press gently. "I mean, I'm really starting to feel connected to you, and if I just leave? It feels like... like I'm walking away from someone I really care about."

He turns to look at me, his blue eyes conflicted. Sadness lingers there, with a resignation I hadn't expected. "Alex, you need to do what's best for you. This is your career, your future. I don't want to hold you back."

A lump forms in my throat. "It's not just about my career. I care about you, Cato. I don't want to leave you behind."

He nods, but his gaze remains steady, his voice hollow. "I know. And I care about you, too, Alex. But sometimes, you have to make tough choices. You can't build your life around someone else's expectations—not even mine."

I swallow hard, his words settling heavily in my chest. "I get that, but it feels like I'm choosing between two things that matter to me."

Cato's expression softens, a flicker of pain crossing his face. "I get it, Alex. I really do. But you've worked so hard for this, and I don't want to be the reason you let it go. You deserve to see where this opportunity can take you. Regardless of what happens, I care about you and we can make whatever work. "

I search for the right words, something to close the distance I feel growing between us. "So... you think I should just go?"

He sighs, his voice a little gentler now. "I think you need to make the decision based on what feels right for you. I won't stand in your way, but I also won't pretend it's easy for me to let you go."

Tears prick the back of my eyes, but I blink them away, trying to hold myself together. "I don't want to lose what we have, Cato. But I also don't want to miss this chance."

His look turns bittersweet, his voice barely above a whisper. "I know. And I hope, no matter what happens, we can still find a way to stay connected. But you need to go and see what's out there for you. I'll be here, figuring things out on my own."

I reach for his hand, squeezing it gently. "I wish things were easier."

He squeezes back, his voice soft. "Me too, Alex. But no important decisions are ever easy to make."

We sit in silence, absorbing the intensity of the moment. It's not the ending I'd hoped for, but it feels like a necessary step toward something unknown yet maybe essential for both of us.

* * *

I close the door behind me, the seriousness of the conversation with Cato still heavy on my chest. As I step into my apartment, I try to shake off the lingering emotions, but they cling to me, making the space feel oddly empty.

I collapse onto the couch, staring up at the ceiling. I know I need to share the news with my mom—she's always been one of the few people who celebrates my achievements, no matter what. Maybe hearing her excitement will make the opportunity feel a bit more real, more... positive.

I pull out my phone and dial her number, my thumb hesitating for a moment before pressing *Call*. The line rings a few times, and then I hear her familiar, cheerful voice on the other end.

"Alex, my sweet boy! How are you?" she asks, her voice full of energy.

"Hey, Mom," I say, trying to muster some enthusiasm. "I'm okay. I actually have some news I wanted to share."

164

F. A. SENG

Her tone immediately shifts to one of anticipation. "News? Oh, tell me, tell me! What's happening?"

I can't help but smile a little at her elation. "I got a promotion at work, Mom. A big one. The client wants me to work with them on-site for a while."

There's a brief moment of silence, and then I hear her let out a gasp. "Oh, Alex! That's wonderful news! Thank the Lord! Thank the Lord!"

I wince slightly at her immediate reaction, but I know it's just her way. "Yeah, it's a pretty big deal, Mom. I'll be working directly with the client, and there's a good pay raise too."

She lets out a delighted laugh, and I can almost see her beaming on the other end of the line. "Oh, Alex, I'm so proud of you! This is all God's plan, you know. I've been praying for you every day, and look how He's answered!"

I nod, even though she can't see me. "I know, Mom. I'm grateful for the opportunity."

But she's already caught up in her own excitement, her voice full of devotion. "It's just like I always say, Alex—trust in the Lord, and He will guide you. See how He's paved the way for you? This is all His doing."

I feel a slight irritation creeping up, not because of her faith but because of how she seems to attribute every success to something beyond my own hard work. "Yeah, Mom, I know. But I've also put a lot of effort into this, you know? It's not all just… divine intervention."

She pauses, her tone still gentle but a bit more insistent. "Of course, my dear. But you must always remember to thank Him first. He's the one who gives you the strength to achieve these things. You couldn't have done it alone."

I close my eyes, taking a deep breath to keep my frustration in check. "I get that, Mom. I do. But sometimes, it feels like you forget how much I've worked to get here."

"Alex," she says, her voice now having concern and patience, "I know you've worked hard. But it's the Lord who opens the doors for you. You have to see that."

165

A wave of exhaustion washes over me, both from the day and from this predictable conversation. "I know, Mom. I know you believe that. Maybe we can just... leave it at that for tonight? It's been a long day, and I'm really tired."

Her voice is laced with love. "Of course, dear. I didn't mean to upset you. I'm just so grateful to God for all the blessings you've received."

"I know, Mom," I say quietly, trying to sound reassuring. "I really appreciate your prayers. I'm just... tired. I should probably get to bed now."

She sighs, sounding slightly disappointed but understanding. "Alright, Alex. Rest well, and remember that I'm always here for you. I'll keep praying for you, okay?"

"Okay, Mom," I reply, feeling a mix of gratitude and weariness. "Thanks. Goodnight."

"Goodnight, Alex. I love you."

"I love you too, Mom," I say quietly before ending the call.

nineteen

CATO

The hum of the tattoo machine is rhythmic, a sound that always brings me comfort. I'm in the middle of working on a detailed back piece, the needle moving smoothly over the client's skin, when the chime of the door echoes through the shop.

I glance up briefly, spotting Demi entering with her usual energy. She's carrying a stack of papers and a sketchbook, a clear sign that we have more designs to go over. She gives me a quick nod before setting the papers down on the counter, waiting patiently for me to finish up.

"All right, just hold still a bit longer," I say to my client, focusing back on the design. "We're almost done here."

After a few more minutes of shading and detailing, I wipe down the area, feeling satisfied with how it's turned out. "There you go, man. Take a look in the mirror and let me know what you think."

The client gets up, checking out the work with a big grin. "Looks amazing, Cato. Exactly what I had in mind."

"Glad you like it," I say, smiling. "Just follow the aftercare instructions, and it should heal up nicely."

Once he pays and heads out, I turn to Demi, who's already flipping through her sketchbook. "So, what's on the agenda today?" I ask, wiping down my station.

She raises an eyebrow, looking both excited and a little mischievous. "We've got some interesting requests, actually. A couple of new designs came in this morning, and they're pretty unusual. Thought you'd want to see them."

I step closer, my curiosity piqued. "Unusual, huh? Let's see what we've got."

She spreads the sketches out on the counter, her eyes glinting with enthusiasm. The first one is a sunset, but not the typical vibrant, serene kind. This one has a darker edge—muted colors, almost eerie, with jagged rays that look more like cracks in the sky.

"This one's supposed to be a 'dark sunset,'" Demi explains. "The client wants it to have a more gothic vibe. I was thinking maybe adding some shadowy silhouettes of barren trees in the foreground. What do you think?"

I lean over, studying the design. "Yeah, that could work. The trees would add a nice contrast, make the sunset feel more ominous. Maybe even add some bats flying in the distance? Just to play up the gothic element."

Demi grins, nodding. "I like that idea. It'll give the whole piece more depth."

She then points to the second design, which shows a cloud with crows flying out of it. The crows are small and scattered, as if they're emerging from the cloud itself.

"The client for this one is going for a 'haunted skies' theme," Demi says, sounding intrigued. "They want it to be a blend of realism and surrealism, with the crows representing something darker—like a storm brewing inside."

I raise my eyebrows, already picturing ways to bring that concept to life. "We could add a few wispy tendrils of cloud around the crows, like they're dragging the mist with them. Maybe even make one of the crows larger, more detailed, to create a focal point."

Demi's eyes light up at the suggestion. "Yes! What if we make that larger crow have an eerie glow around its eyes? Not too obvious, just a faint glow to add a sense of something supernatural."

I grin, feeling the creative spark between us. "I love it. Adds a layer of mystery, like there's something lurking just beyond the clouds."

She chuckles, her excitement infectious. "You always have a knack for making things darker. But that's exactly what the client wants, so we're right on track."

I nod, feeling a sense of satisfaction as we brainstorm. "Yeah, it's always fun to push the boundaries a bit. Gothic art has a lot of room for interpretation, and clients who are into it are usually open to more experimental designs."

Demi leans back, crossing her arms with a smirk. "Speaking of experimental, I was thinking we could start incorporating more gothic elements into our overall portfolio. We've got a good mix already, but there's a growing demand for darker, more surreal pieces."

I scratch my chin thoughtfully. "I've noticed that too. People are getting more interested in tattoos that tell a darker story, rather than just looking pretty. It's like they want something that reflects their inner struggles, not just their surface interests."

"Exactly," she says, her tone serious. "And I think we're really good at that. We don't just give people tattoos; we give them a story, something they can connect with on a deeper level."

I smile at her passion, feeling a sense of camaraderie. "Yeah, that's always been the goal, hasn't it?"

She nods, a hint of pride in her eyes. "That's why we make a good team, Cato. You get the art, but you also get the people behind it."

I glance back at the sketches, feeling a rush of inspiration. "All right, let's finalize these designs, and then we can show them to the clients. I think they'll love the added gothic touch."

"Sounds like a plan," Demi says with a satisfied smile. "Oh, and by the way—don't forget you've got a consultation with another client in an hour. He's asking for a full sleeve with gothic architecture."

I can't help but laugh. "Gothic architecture? Now that's my kind of challenge."

Demi chuckles, gathering up the sketches. "I figured you'd say that. Now, let's get to work. The darkness awaits."

* * *

I sit at my worktable, completely absorbed in the final lines of a new sketch when the door chime rings. Expecting another walk-in or maybe Demi with coffee, I glance up—and my heart drops. Standing in the doorway, wearing a confident smirk and a maroon leather jacket, is Derek. The sight of him brings a flood of old emotions—anger, unease, and that familiar tension I thought I'd left behind.

"Hey, Cato," he says smoothly, stepping further into the shop.

I straighten, forcing myself to keep calm. "Derek. What are you doing here?"

He approaches slowly, his eyes taking in the room before finally locking onto mine. "I needed to see you. We need to talk."

I sigh, feeling my shoulders tighten. "We've had all the talks we needed, Derek. We're done."

He shakes his head, his expression serious. "No, we're not done, Cato. Not by a long shot. I want to make things right between us."

A bitter laugh escapes me. "Make things right? After everything you put me through? You really think that's possible?"

He steps closer, his tone lightening, though his presence feels more intense. "I know I messed up. I was controlling, manipulative… I get it. But I've changed, Cato. I swear. I've had time to think, to reflect on how I treated you, and I want another chance."

His words sink into the room, heavy and unshakable, and I can't tell if there's real sincerity behind them or if it's just another one of his tactics. I take a step back, keeping some distance. "Derek, it's too late for that. I've moved on. You should too."

He doesn't back down; instead, he steps closer, invading my space, his voice insistent. "Please, Cato. I'm not the same person I was before. I know I hurt you, but I still care about you —more than you realize. I want to fix things between us."

The old, toxic pull—the nostalgia and resentment—tugs at me. I clench my fists, trying to keep my voice steady. "You can't just show up at my fucking tattoo shop and expect everything to be okay, Derek. You can't erase what you did."

He reaches out, placing a hand gently on my arm. "I know I can't erase it, but I can try to make it better. We had something real once, and I believe we can have it again. Just give me a chance."

The closeness is suffocating, a reminder of the same cycle I fought so hard to escape. Just as I'm about to push him away, the door chimes again. I turn, and there stands Alex, his expression a mix of surprise and confusion.

"Cato?" Alex says, his voice hesitant as he takes in the scene—Derek standing too close, his hand still on my arm.

I quickly pull back, stepping away from Derek's touch. "Alex... this is Derek."

Alex's eyes widen slightly, and his voice drops, uncertain. "Derek? As in... your ex?"

I nod, feeling the awkwardness grow. "Yeah. He just... showed up."

Derek's smirk returns, laced with arrogance. "I'm here to make things right, Alex. Cato and I have history, and I think we deserve another shot."

I shoot Derek a warning look, but Alex's face is already clouded with confusion and hurt. "I... I didn't know you two were still... hanging out."

"Alex, it's not what it looks like," I say quickly, stepping toward him. "Derek just showed up, unannounced. I didn't ask for this."

But the damage is already done. Alex's gaze flickers between me and Derek, disbelief and pain in his eyes. "I... I should go."

"Alex, wait," I call, reaching out, but he's already moving toward the door.

He pauses briefly, looking back at me with a vulnerability that cuts deep. "I thought things were different now, Cato."

Before I can respond, he turns and walks out, the door chime ringing in his wake, leaving a silence that feels unbearable.

Derek lets out a low chuckle, satisfaction glinting in his eyes. "Looks like your new boy toy can't handle a little competition."

The weight of his hand on my arm lingers like a bruise, a reminder of a past I've fought to move beyond. He steps closer, his grip tightening as I feel the swell of fear with a bit of helplessness, but I push it back with everything I have.

Taking a deep breath, I pull my arm away, forcing myself to sound calm. "Derek, I told you, it's over. I don't want you here, and I don't want you in my life. Now, get the fuck out of here!"

Derek's face shifts from surprise to something darker, anger flashing in his eyes. He doesn't back off. Instead, he grabs my wrist, His words slip through a tight jaw; low and forceful. "Cato, you're making a mistake. You know what we had—no one else will ever understand you like I did. You have to rethink this."

My heart races, that old, suffocating fear wrapping around me. My body tenses, every instinct telling me to submit, to wait until it's over. Why does breaking free feel so impossible?

"I don't want this," I manage to say, my voice barely steady. "You don't get to control me anymore."

He leans in, his voice a menacing whisper. "Are you sure about that? Because it looks like you're still scared of me, Cato. You're still that same weak kid."

The words sting, hitting deep, and for a moment, I feel myself shrinking, old trauma tightening around me. Just then, the door bursts open, and Demi strides in, her eyes immediately locking onto us. She takes in the scene—Derek's grip on my wrist, my pale face—and her expression sharpens.

"Hey!" she snaps, her voice cutting through the tension like a blade. "Get your hands off him, now."

Derek barely glances at her, his grip still firm on me. "This isn't your business, lady."

Demi steps closer, her voice low and unyielding. "You better believe it's my business. Let go of him, or I'm calling the cops right now."

Derek's eyes flicker with anger, but he releases me, stepping back with a scowl. "Fine," he says, voice cold. "This isn't over, Cato. Think about what you're giving up."

I take a shaky step back, catching my breath. "I've already thought about it, Derek. It's over."

He scoffs, lingering one last time before turning toward the door. "You'll regret this."

As he leaves, relief and lingering fear washes over me. My wrist still stings, but the sharper pain is the reminder of everything I've fought to leave behind.

Demi is beside me in an instant, her voice gentle but filled with concern. "Cato, are you okay?"

I nod, though my heart still pounds. "Yeah, I just… need a minute."

Her eyes are full of worry. "You sure? That guy seems next level crazy, Cato. I've never seen you look like that before."

I take a steadying breath, rubbing my wrist. "It's just… old stuff coming back up. I'll be fine. I just need some time. I also need to figure out how I'm going to explain all of this to Alex."

Demi places a reassuring hand on my shoulder. "Take all the time you need. Remember, you're not alone in this."

I manage a weak smile, grateful. "Thanks, Demi."

She nods firmly. "And if he ever shows up here again, you tell me. We're not letting him drag you back into that darkness."

I watch as she heads to the front of the shop, giving me space, and as the weight of Derek's visit settles, I take in a breath, grateful for the support and ready to rebuild the strength he tried to take from me.

ALEX

I storm down the dimly lit street, my mind racing and my chest tight. The image of Derek's hand gripping Cato's arm burns in my memory, making my stomach churn. Cato had looked trapped, submissive—a side of him I've never seen before, one that makes me realize just how deep his past wounds run.

A part of me thinks I hear a girl's voice.

Maybe I overreacted. I should've stayed with Cato and not left him.

The air is cold, and I pull my jacket tighter, trying to push away the unsettling thoughts. Why was Derek there? What did he want from Cato? I feel anger and helplessness, wishing I could've done something to intervene, to protect Cato from whatever pain Derek stirred up.

My phone buzzes in my pocket, interrupting my thoughts. I take it out and see Demi's name on the screen. I hesitate before answering, my voice tense. "Hey, Demi."

"Alex," she says urgently, her tone full of concern. "I yelled your name when I saw you leaving the tattoo shop. Listen, Cato told me what happened and I thought you should know—Derek's gone. I got him out, but Cato's not doing well. He's... shaken up."

My grip on the phone tightens. "Is he okay? Did Derek hurt him?"

"No, not physically," Demi replies quickly. "Emotionally? Yes, absolutely. It was like seeing a ghost for him.

174

He's in shock, Alex. I tried getting him to talk, but he's just sitting there, staring at the wall. He really need someone right now."

Her words hit me hard, the worry I've been trying to suppress flaring up. "Do you think I should come back?"

She pauses, as if carefully choosing her words. "I think he needs you, Alex."

I feel a surge of emotions—guilt for having walked away, anger at Derek, and a strong urge to be there for Cato. But doubt creeps in. Will he even want to see me? After everything that just happened, will my presence help or make things worse?

I stop walking, standing under a streetlamp, weighing my options. The moment I left the shop replays in my mind, Cato's face filled with confusion and pain. I shouldn't have left, not when he needed someone.

"Alright," I say finally, determination settling in my voice. "I'm coming back. Tell him I'll be there soon."

"Thank you, Alex," Demi says, relief evident. "Just... be gentle with him, okay? He's not himself right now."

"I will," I promise, already turning around and heading back toward the shop. "I'll be there in a few minutes."

twenty

ALEX

My heart races as I reach the entrance of Eternal Ink. I pull on the door and notice it's locked. They must've locked up early after Derek left. I immediately spot Demi near the counter, her expression full of worry and relief when she approaches the door to let me in.

"Alex, good, you're here," she says, her voice barely above a whisper.

I nod, my chest tightening as I catch sight of Cato in the back room. He sits on a stool, shoulders slumped, head bowed, like the weight of everything has become too much.

"How is he?" I ask quietly.

Demi sighs, glancing back toward Cato. "Not great. He hasn't said anything really since that prick left. I tried to talk to him, but he's pretty shaken up right now."

A wave of urgency crashes over me—a desperate need to reach him, to pierce through the shadows that have consumed

176

him. "Let me try," I say, with determination and a little vulnerability.

Demi nods slowly. "He's all yours, Alex. I think you're the only one who can reach him right now."

With a final squeeze on my shoulder, she turns and heads toward the front door, giving us space. I take a deep breath, gathering my thoughts before stepping into the back room.

Cato is still, head bowed, hands hanging loosely in his lap. I approach him slowly, not wanting to startle him.

"Babe," I say softly, sitting down beside him on the small bench.

He doesn't look up, but I see his shoulders tense slightly. I can't tell if he's trying to keep himself together or just holding back tears. Either way, seeing him like this breaks my heart.

I try again, my voice gentle. "Cato, it's me. I'm here."

Finally, he lifts his head, his blue eyes filled with a sadness that cuts deep. His voice is hoarse, barely a whisper. "Why did you come back?"

A lump forms in my throat, and my words come out more emotional than I intend. "Because I shouldn't have left in the first place. Not after I saw him here."

He lets out a shaky sigh, running a hand through his hair. "I didn't want you to see that, Alex. I don't want you to see me like... this."

I reach out, gently placing a hand on his arm. "Hey, it's okay to be vulnerable. It's okay to feel hurt. You don't have to hide it from me."

His eyes fill with tears, and he quickly looks away, trying to keep his composure. "It's just... seeing Derek again, feeling his grip on me—it brought everything back. I thought I'd buried it all, but it's still there, lurking in the corners."

I squeeze his arm lightly, offering comfort. "I understand. I really do. But you don't have to face this alone anymore. I'm here for you, no matter how messy it gets."

He shakes his head, his voice breaking. "I don't want to drag you into my mess, Alex. You don't deserve that."

Frustration bubbles up within me, sharp and unrelenting—not at him, but at the situation that's put him here. "It's not about what I deserve, Cato. It's about being there for someone I care about. I want to help, even if it's just by sitting here with you."

His gaze shifts, the vulnerability more visible now. "You really mean that, don't you?"

I nod, my voice firm but filled with emotion. "Yes, I do. I care about you, Cato. And I hate seeing you hurt like this."

He looks down, his voice almost a whisper. "I'm scared, Alex. I'm scared that I'll never be free of him, that he'll always have this hold over me."

A pang strikes my chest, hearing the raw fear in his voice. "You've already come so far, Cato. You've built this amazing life for yourself, and you've shown so much strength. Derek's presence doesn't change who you are now."

He nods slowly, a tear escaping down his cheek. "I want to believe that. I really do. But right now, it just feels like I'm back in that dark place, and I don't know how to get out."

I can't hold back any longer. I lean closer, wrapping my arms around him in a gentle, protective hug. "I'm right here, and I'm not going anywhere."

He stiffens for a moment, then slowly relaxes, leaning into the embrace. His head rests against my shoulder, and I feel him tremble slightly.

After a long moment, Cato pulls away from the hug, and we sit quietly, our knees almost touching. His eyes are puffy, the pain still present, but with a curious blend of tenderness and strength in them now. It's as though he's teetering on the edge of vulnerability, waiting to let the words out.

"Cato," I begin, breaking the silence. "I know it's hard, but if you want to talk about it… about what happened between you and Derek, I'm here to listen. You don't have to hold back."

He lets out a shaky sigh, his gaze dropping to the floor. For a moment, I'm not sure if he'll open up, but then he looks back at me, his eyes filled with a haunted expression I haven't seen before.

"Alright," he says, his voice low and filled with hesitation, but I also see determination. "I'll tell you. It's not pretty, though."

I lean in a bit, trying to offer some encouragement. "I'm not looking for pretty, Cato. I just want to understand. I want to know what you went through."

He nods slowly, then takes a deep breath, as if gathering the strength to revisit the past. "I met Derek when I was 22, just a few years into my career as a tattoo artist. Back then, I was still figuring things out, still trying to make a name for myself. Derek was... charismatic. Confident in a way I wasn't. He had this magnetic pull that made me feel excited and terrified."

I can hear the strain in his voice, as if he's reliving those early days all over again. "At first, it was good. He was attentive, passionate, and he made me feel special, like I was the center of his world. I thought I'd found something that could last."

I nod, keeping my voice steady. "Sounds like it started off as a dream."

Cato's face twists into a bitter smile. "Yeah, it felt like a dream. But it doesn't take long to turn into a nightmare. Derek had this need to control everything—what I did, who I talked to, even how I dressed. It starts with small things, like insisting on what we ate or where we went out. But it escalated quickly."

He pauses, his voice trembling slightly. "He'd criticize my designs, say they weren't good enough, or that I was wasting my time on clients who didn't matter. At first, I thought he was just being honest, trying to help me improve. Then I realized he wasn't trying to make me better—he was trying to make me dependent on him."

Anger surges in me on Cato's behalf. "That's awful, Cato. I can't believe someone would do that to you."

He nods, his eyes filled with a mix of pain and regret. "It got worse over time. Derek started showing up at the shop unexpectedly, he would make a scene if I was working late or talking to a client he didn't like. It was suffocating, but I was too afraid to leave. I thought I needed him, that I couldn't make it without him."

His voice breaks, and I see the raw emotion behind his words. "He made me believe that I was nothing without him. He'd say things like, 'You wouldn't survive on your own,' or, 'I'm the only one who truly understands you.' And the worst part? I believed him. I started doubting my own worth."

I reach out, placing a hand on his arm. "Cato, I'm so sorry. No one deserves to be treated like that."

He looks at me, his eyes showing gratitude but also a lingering sadness. "Thank you, Alex. It has taken me years to realize that. I feel like I'm trapped in this cycle of thinking I need to prove myself to him, to win his approval. I stopped creating art for myself and started doing it just to make him happy."

I can see the weight of those years in his eyes, the exhaustion from trying to meet someone else's expectations. "How did it end?" I ask gently.

Cato lets out a bitter laugh, shaking his head. "Messily. Very messy. One night, we had a huge fight. He hated my work and was never truly proud of me. He was nasty, throwing things, calling me names, telling me how worthless I was. It was like everything he'd held back came spilling out in this uncontrollable rage."

He pauses, his voice barely above a whisper. "That night, I finally snapped. I realized that I couldn't do it anymore, that I was losing myself completely. I told him I was leaving, and he laughed in my face, said that I'd come crawling back. But I didn't. I packed my shit and left, even though I didn't have anywhere to go."

A lump forms in my throat, imagining how hard it must be for him to walk away from something so toxic yet so familiar. "You're brave, Cato. You saved yourself, even when it was hard."

He looks at me, his eyes showing relief and lingering guilt. "It didn't feel brave at the time. It felt like I was giving up. I spent months in a haze, doubting myself, wondering if I made the right choice."

I squeeze his arm gently, offering comfort. "You did make the right choice, Cato. You chose yourself, your own sanity, and your own happiness. You didn't give up, Cato. He gave you up."

He nods, a small smile finally breaking through. "I know that now. But seeing Derek today—it brings it all back, all the doubts, all the fear. I never thought I'd have to face him again, and I don't know how to handle it."

I lean in, my voice sincere. "You don't have to handle it alone, Cato. Not anymore. I'm here, and I want to help, in whatever way I can."

He reaches out, taking my hand, the gesture both tentative and hopeful. "Thank you, Alex. I didn't think I'd ever find someone who could understand… or even try to."

I squeeze his hand back, feeling the connection between us grow stronger. "I don't just want to try, Cato. I want to be here for you, no matter what."

We sit there in silence for a moment, holding each other's gaze. The past isn't erased, the wounds aren't fully healed, but in this moment, a fresh energy lingers between us, full of potential to grow something authentic and meaningful.

There is something that stands out in my mind since hearing part of his story. I hesitate for a second, then decide to just go for it. "Cato, can I ask you something?"

He looks up, curiosity and vulnerability in his eyes. "Of course, Alex. You can ask me anything."

I take a deep breath, my voice a bit shaky. "Are you… okay with me being here? I mean, does it make you uncomfortable that I've been coming around so much? I don't want to impose, especially after everything you've been through."

His eyes change gently, and he seems to relax a bit, as if the lingering tension between us is finally easing. "No, Alex," he says quietly. "It doesn't make me uncomfortable at all. In fact, it's the opposite."

I feel a flicker of hope, but I need more clarity. "The opposite? What do you mean?"

He looks down for a moment, gathering his thoughts, then meets my gaze with steady intensity. "I mean that I've liked having you around. More than liked it, actually. You make me feel things I haven't felt in a long time, things I didn't think I would ever feel again."

My heart speeds up, the weight of his words sinking in. "Are you saying that you're…"

He nods slowly, his voice low but sincere. "Yes, Alex. I'm saying that my feelings for you have shifted into something more. It's unexpected, to be honest. I wasn't looking for it, but then you came into my life, and everything started to shift."

I feel a warmth spreading through my chest, a large amount of relief. "Cato, I… I feel the same way."

He smiles, a bit shyly, as if he's not used to expressing these kinds of emotions. "I know I've been guarded, maybe even distant at times. It's just that, after everything with Derek, I'm not sure if I can open myself up to someone again. But you've shown me a different kind of closeness—one that's not suffocating, one that feels genuine and safe."

His words make my heart swell, and I find myself smiling widely. "Cato, I never want to push you or make you feel trapped. I just want to be here, to be someone you can count on. I've felt something between us too. And it's been hard to hold back, especially knowing how I feel about you."

He looks relieved, as if a weight is lifted from his chest. "I'm afraid that if I tell you how I feel, it will scare you off. That maybe you'll see me as too damaged, too complicated to be with."

I shake my head firmly, reaching out to take his hand again. "Cato, you're not too damaged for me. You're a survivor, and I'd rather be with someone who's honest about their past than someone who pretends they're perfect. We all have scars, and yours don't make me want to run. They make me want to stay."

He exhales slowly, his eyes shining with multiple emotions—relief, gratitude, maybe even happiness. "You have no idea how much that means to me, Alex. You brought something good into my life, something I didn't think was possible after everything."

I squeeze his hand, feeling the energy of his skin against mine. "And you do the same for me, Cato. You make me realize what it feels like to truly care about someone, to want to be there for them no matter what."

We hear a soft shuffle near the door. We both turn to see Demi standing there, holding a tray with two steaming cups of coffee. Her eyes widen slightly when she sees us holding hands, a soft smile forming on her lips.

"Oh," she says awkwardly, clearly not wanting to intrude. "I was just bringing you guys some coffee, but... it looks like you're having a moment."

Cato chuckles, a bit of color rising to his cheeks. "Thanks, Demi. Appreciate it, but maybe we'll have it later."

Demi grins, giving me a knowing look before turning back to Cato. "Alright, I'm gonna head out, I'll leave these on the counter. I'll also be sure to lock the door on my way out."

She winks, then quietly steps back and leaves the shop, leaving us alone again.

Cato turns back to me, his smile soft but genuine. "So... where do we go from here, Alex?"

For a moment, the world seems to stand still. Cato's eyes are locked onto mine, and I can feel the air between us shifting—charged, electric, full of possibility. There's something in his gaze that's more than just relief; it's longing, the kind that makes my heart race and my breath hitch.

His hand is still warm in mine, and I find myself leaning in, drawn by an invisible force I can't resist any longer. "Cato," I whisper, my voice barely audible, "I really want to kiss you right now."

His breath hitches, and I see a spark in his eyes—one that mirrors the one I feel inside me. "Then do it," he says, his voice low, inviting, filled with an urgency that matches my own.

I don't need any more encouragement. I close the distance between us, my lips pressing against his with tenderness and hunger. His lips are inviting and even more delicate than I remember, and the moment our mouths meet, it's like a dam breaking, all the pent-up emotions pouring out at

183

once. The kiss deepens, and our mouths move in sync, the kiss growing more fervent, more demanding.

His hands move to the back of my neck, fingers tangling in my hair, pulling me closer. I feel a shiver run down my spine, my own hands instinctively wrapping around his waist, feeling the firmness of his body under my touch. It's intoxicating, the way his body presses against mine, the heat of the moment enveloping us both.

"Alex," he murmurs against my lips, his voice hoarse and filled with need. "I've wanted this for so long."

My heart surges at his words, and I pull him even closer, our kiss turning desperate. I can't get enough of him—his taste, his touch, the way he makes me feel so alive. "Me too," I whisper back, my lips barely leaving his. "God, me too."

Before I know it, we're on our feet and stumbling backward, still kissing, bumping into the edge of the tattoo chair. We laugh breathlessly, the laughter quickly fading into another heated kiss, our hands exploring each other with an urgency that feels unstoppable. His fingers trace the line of my jaw, then slide down to my chest, making my skin tingle with anticipation.

I press him gently against the back wall, my hands sliding under his shirt, feeling the rigid muscles on his abdomen. His breath hitches, a soft gasp escaping his lips as my fingers brush over his tattoos. "Alex," he breathes, his voice filled with desire, but a hint of vulnerability is there.

I pause, looking into his eyes, searching for any sign of hesitation. "Is this okay?" I ask, my voice low but earnest.

He nods, his gaze intense and full of want. "Yes," he says firmly, pulling me closer. "More than okay."

That's all I need to hear. We stumble toward the small couch in the corner of the shop, our lips never breaking contact. I can feel the passion building between us, an intensity that's both exhilarating and overwhelming. We collapse onto the couch, our bodies tangled together, the soft leather creaking beneath us.

His hands roam over my back, my shoulders, his touch sending sparks through me. I respond with the same fervor—my lips trailing down his neck, tasting the salt of his skin. His head tilts back slightly, giving me more access, a soft moan escaping his throat. It's like a fever, consuming us both, the world outside fading into a blur as we lose ourselves in each other.

We kiss again, harder this time, our breaths mingling, our bodies pressing closer until there's barely any space left between us. I can feel his heartbeat against mine, fast and erratic, matching the rhythm of my own. "You have no idea how much I've wanted this," I whisper between kisses, my voice filled with raw honesty.

His response is immediate, his hands gripping my shirt as if he couldn't bear the thought of letting go. "Then don't stop," he whispers back, his words sending a jolt of desire through me. "Please, don't stop."

We don't. We keep kissing, our touches becoming more intimate. I feel his fingers slip under my shirt, tracing patterns on my skin, and I do the same, exploring every inch of him that I can reach. It's chaotic but it feels right.

At some point, the intensity wanes, our kisses slowing, becoming more tender. We pull back slightly, our foreheads resting against each other's, our breaths mingling in the small space between us. "Cato," I murmur, my voice filled with emotion. "This feels... real."

He nods, his eyes filled with a gentleness that makes my heart ache in the best way. "It is real, Alex," he says quietly, his fingers delicately caressing my cheek. "It's very real."

Exhaustion begins to settle in, the adrenaline of the moment giving way to a comforting fatigue. We shift on the couch, finding a better position, my head resting on his chest, his arms wrapped around me. It isn't a perfect setup, but it's enough —more than enough.

I feel my eyes grow heavy, the assurance of his embrace lulling me into a sense of peace I haven't felt in a long time. "I could get used to this," I mumble sleepily, my voice barely audible.

His hand gently strokes my hair, his touch soothing. "Me too," he whispers, his voice quiet but filled with certainty.

185

And just like that, we drift off, our bodies intertwined, the shop silent except for the sound of our breathing. I fall asleep with a sense of belonging, knowing that whatever happens next, this is real—this is us, together.

twenty-one
ALEX

I close the door behind me, feeling several emotions as I drop my keys onto the table. Yesterday had been intense—from seeing how Cato was around Derek to spending time with Cato after. Before I can fully process everything, my phone buzzes. It's Amelia, my boss.

Taking a deep breath, I answer the call. "Hello, Amelia."

"Alex, I'm glad I caught you," Amelia's voice comes through, sounding thrilled. "I've got some news about the promotion."

My heart races. "Oh? What's up?"

"Well, it seems they want you pretty badly," she chuckles. "They've made an offer to let you take the promotion remotely, while only traveling to Seattle for a couple of days each month. You wouldn't have to leave after all."

I'm stunned into silence for a moment. "Wait, really? They'd let me stay here?"

"Yes, really," Amelia confirms. "They were impressed with your work and are willing to be flexible. So, what do you think? This could be a great opportunity without the need to uproot your life."

I take a moment to process this new information, anticipation building within me. "Wow, that's... that's amazing, Amelia. I want to take it."

"Excellent!" Amelia says, her voice filled with pride. "I'll let them know right away. Congratulations, Alex. You've earned this."

After hanging up, I sit down, my mind reeling from this new development. The promotion without having to leave—it seems like the perfect solution. I realize I need to share this news with my mom and Cato.

I pull out my phone again and scroll through my contacts until I find "Mom." My finger hovers over the call button for a moment before I press it. The line rings a couple of times before her voice comes through.

"Alex, dear! How are you?" she asks warmly.

"I'm great, Mom. I've got some exciting news about the promotion," I reply, unable to keep the enthusiasm out of my voice.

"Oh? What's the news?" she asks, her interest piqued.

I take a deep breath. "Well, they've offered to let me take the promotion remotely. I wouldn't have to move, and... I've decided to accept it."

There's a moment of excited silence before she responds. "Alex, that's wonderful news! I'm so proud of you. This is exactly what you've been working towards."

I smile, feeling a wave of relief and happiness. "Thanks, Mom. It feels like the best of both worlds. I get to advance my career and stay in a place where I've built a life."

"I'm so happy for you, dear," she says, her voice filled with pride. "You deserve this. And I'm glad you don't have to leave behind the connections you've made there. Clearly, the Lord is showing you all of his blessings."

We chat for a few more minutes about the details of the promotion before hanging up. I'm left with a sense of anticipation for what's to come.

The next call is to Cato, and I hit the call button without hesitation. The phone barely rings once before he picks up.

"Hey, Alex!" Cato's voice is filled with enthusiasm, making me smile immediately. "What's up?"

"Hey," I say, my voice filled with thrilled anxiety. "I've got some news."

"Oh?" he asks, the anticipation clear. "What's the news?"

I take a deep breath. "They offered me the promotion to work remotely, and... I've decided to take it. I'm staying here, but with a new position."

There's a pause on the other end, and when Cato speaks again, his voice is a mosaic of feelings. "Wow, Alex. That's... that's great news. Congratulations."

I can sense a hint of uncertainty in his voice. "Thanks, Cato. I'm really excited about it. It means I can advance my career without having to leave everything behind."

"I'm happy for you, Alex," he says, his voice reassuring. "You deserve this opportunity. And I'm glad you get to stay here too."

I feel relief wash over me. "Thanks, Cato. Your support means a lot to me. I was hoping you'd be happy about this."

"Of course I am," he says, sounding more enthusiastic now. "This is a big deal for you. We should celebrate!"

I laugh, feeling the tension dissipate. "I'd love that. Want to get together tonight?"

"Absolutely," Cato agrees. "Come over, and we'll figure out how to properly toast to your success."

As I hang up, I feel content. The promotion is a big step forward, and knowing that I can pursue it while staying close to Cato and the life I've built here feels like the best possible outcome. I'm looking forward to seeing what the future holds, both professionally and personally.

INK & *Intuition*

twenty-two
CATO

Bailey and I stand by the floor-to-ceiling windows of my penthouse, watching the city skyline begin to light up as the sun sets. The twinkling lights below never fail to amaze me, but tonight, my attention is elsewhere. I'm waiting for Alex.

The idea of inviting him over is spontaneous, yet it feels like the right move. I want him to see more of my world, the part I don't often share with others. The intercom rings, signaling he's arrived downstairs.

I press the intercom button. "Hey, handsome. Glad you could make it."

Watching the elevator panel, I see the light indicating the ascent from the ground floor. As it climbs, a bit of nervousness stirs inside me. What will Alex think of my place? It's a part of me, a big part, and letting him in means letting him see more of who I really am.

The elevator doors slide open with a soft ding, and there he is. Alex steps out, looking a bit dazed from the long ride, his eyes wide as he takes in the expansive view of the penthouse.

"Hey," I say, smiling as I step forward to greet him. "Welcome to my place."

"Hey," he responds, still looking around in awe. "Holy shit, Cato... this is incredible."

A small sense of pride rises as I watch him take it all in. The open living area is filled with sleek, dark wood furniture, tasteful deep green art pieces on the obsidian, textured walls, and a massive window that offers a panoramic view of Metro Heights.

"Thanks. It's home, for better or worse," I say, trying to sound casual.

He walks slowly toward the window, his eyes fixed on the city lights below. "The view is... breathtaking. I can't believe you get to see this every day."

I join him by the window, looking out at the twinkling city lights. "Yeah, it's one of the things I love about this place. No matter how chaotic things get, the view always reminds me to take a step back."

Alex turns to face me, his eyes still filled with awe. "I've never been in a place like this before. It's like something out of a movie."

I laugh quietly, feeling a bit shy despite the grandeur of the setting. "It can feel that way sometimes. Honestly, it's just... home. A big one, sure, but still a place where I can unwind and be myself."

He nods, his gaze softening as he looks around. "I can definitely see why you love it here."

His words fill me with comfort, and I motion toward the living area. "Come on, let me give you the tour."

He follows as I lead him through the open-floor plan, pointing out the different areas. "This is the living room, obviously. Over there's the kitchen—state-of-the-art appliances, but I barely use them. I'm more of a takeout guy."

Alex chuckles, glancing at the kitchen's sleek, stainless-steel design. "I can't imagine you cooking a gourmet meal here."

"Hey, I can make a mean grilled cheese," I joke, earning a laugh from him.

We continue through the minimalist dining area, which opens onto a large balcony. "This is one of my favorite spots," I say, sliding open the glass door.

Alex steps out onto the balcony, the cool night breeze ruffling his hair. He leans against the railing, looking out at the city below. "I can see why. It's peaceful up here, above all the noise."

I stand next to him, feeling the wind on my face. "It is. Sometimes, I just come out here and sit for hours, just thinking or sketching. It helps clear my mind."

He turns to look at me, his eyes filled with curiosity. "Do you ever get lonely up here? I mean, it's so big, and it's just you and Bailey."

The question catches me off guard, and I feel a pang of honesty rise to the surface. "Sometimes," I admit. "It can get pretty quiet, especially at night. But I guess we've gotten used to it. It's been a long time since I've shared a place with someone."

His expression lightens, and he steps closer, his voice gentle. "Well, I'm here now."

In his voice, there's an authenticity that resonates, making my chest tighten with emotion. I reach out, hesitating for just a moment before taking his hand. "Yeah, you are. And it feels… right, having you here."

He squeezes my hand, a small smile on his lips. "I'm glad you invited me, Cato. I really love spending time with you."

I smile back, feeling an urge to be closer to him. "I'm glad you came, Alex. I wanted to show you more of my life, not just the tattoo shop."

He nods, his gaze sincere. "I want to know all of you, Cato. The shop, the penthouse, everything."

His words stir something deep within me, and before I know it, I'm leaning in, my lips finding his in a slow, lingering kiss. He responds immediately, his hands resting gently on my waist, pulling me closer.

The kiss deepens, the moment charged with tenderness and desire. I feel his fingers trace the back of my neck, sending shivers down my spine. I tighten my hold on him, savoring the comforting sensation of his body against mine.

When we finally pull back, we're both a little breathless. I rest my forehead against his, a smile tugging at my lips. "I've wanted to do that since you walked in."

He chuckles softly, his breath warm against my skin. "I've wanted you to do that since I last saw you."

For a few more breaths, we remain together, the muted gleam of the city lights casting us in their amber glow. It's one of those moments that feels both surreal and incredibly real, like a scene from a dream I never want to end.

"Come inside," I whisper, leading him back into the penthouse. "Let's make some coffee, and I'll show you the rest of the place."

As we step back into the golden hue of the penthouse lights, I feel a strange, comforting sense of anticipation. The space is filled with paintings, sculptures, and artifacts I've collected over the years—each piece telling its own story. Art has always been a kind of solace for me, but tonight, sharing it with Alex feels more significant.

We pause in front of a wall lined with framed canvases, each piece carefully lit to reveal its details. Alex's eyes dart from one painting to another, his curiosity clear in his expression.

"You've got quite the collection here," Alex says, tilting his head and giving the paintings on my walls an approving nod. "I recognize some of these artists. Not to brag, but I did once take an art history class as an elective."

"Oh, so we've got an art connoisseur in the house?" I tease, crossing my arms and leaning casually against the wall. "Should I be worried you're about to critique my taste?"

He flashes a grin. "Maybe. Let's see what you've got first." He steps closer to the centerpiece of the wall—a vivid mix of greens and blues, bold strokes that practically leap off the

193

canvas—and squints like he's auditioning to be the next Sherlock Holmes. "This one... wait a second. Is this a Vanguard acquisition?"

I raise an eyebrow, impressed. "Good eye. It's a Vivienne Morcant piece—one of her lesser-known works from the early '80s."

He nods slowly, his brow furrowing in concentration like he's this close to unlocking the meaning of life. "Ah, yes, of course. Vivienne Morcant. So, uh... how much did it set you back?" His casual tone doesn't quite mask his curiosity.

I let out a soft chuckle, trying to downplay it. "About $506,000."

His head snaps toward me so fast I'm worried he'll sprain something. "Half a million dollars? On one painting?"

"Technically $506,000," I say with a shrug. "But who's counting?"

"Apparently *you*," he quips, his expression hovering between awe and mild horror. "Seriously, though, what's it like to spend that much money and not immediately throw up?"

I laugh, because fair. "I mean, sure, it's a lot. But it's not just about the money—it's about the story behind it, the emotion. This piece... it spoke to me. The way it captures the chaos of nature and the rawness of human emotion? It felt like it was meant to be mine."

Alex looks back at the painting, his features softening. "Okay, I get that. Art isn't about the price tag—it's about what it makes you feel. Like when I bought a knock-off Banksy print for $20 in college and swore it 'spoke to my soul.'"

"Exactly," I say, ignoring the Banksy bit. "And that's what makes it worth it."

I gesture to another painting nearby, a bold abstract piece with thick, textured strokes in fiery reds and golds. "This one's got an even crazier story. It was a gift from a client."

"A gift?" Alex echoes, turning to me like I've just told him I was given a yacht as a freebie. "From who? The Queen of England?"

"Close," I say with a smirk. "An eccentric millionaire who loved the back piece I tattooed on him. After I finished, he handed me this painting as a thank-you. Turns out it's a Gerhard Richter."

Alex's eyes go wide, and I can almost hear his brain short-circuiting. "Wait... the Gerhard Richter? Like, museum-level famous? Sell-your-soul-to-the-devil famous?"

"Yep," I say, grinning. "And it's worth about $2.6 million."

Alex blinks at me, his mouth opening and closing like he's trying to form words but can't quite get there. "Two point six... million... just... given to you?"

"Pretty much," I say with a shrug, trying to look casual but failing. "Not everyday someone hands you a multi-million-dollar painting as a tip, right?"

"Right," Alex says faintly, as though he's imagining himself fainting right now. "If someone gave me something worth that much, I think I'd just combust on the spot. Like, spontaneously burst into flames. Poof."

"Same," I admit, laughing. "I think I actually blacked out for a second when he handed it to me. One minute, I'm handing him an invoice for a tattoo, and the next, I'm standing there holding more money in art than I ever thought I'd see in my lifetime."

Alex shakes his head, still processing. "Your life is like one of those movies where a struggling artist suddenly becomes rich and famous, except you skipped the 'struggling' part and went straight to this." He gestures at the penthouse, the paintings, and me like I'm the final puzzle piece.

I laugh, because he's not completely wrong. "It wasn't all smooth sailing. But yeah, sometimes I look around and think, 'How the hell did this happen?'"

Alex's gaze eases as he looks back at the painting, then at me. "Honestly, Cato, you've built an amazing life. It's not just the art or the penthouse—it's everything. You've worked for this, and it shows."

I blink at him, caught off guard by the sincerity in his voice. For all the jokes and wide-eyed reactions, there's something deeper there, something that makes my chest feel a little tighter.

"Thanks, Alex," I say, my voice quieter than before. "That means a lot."

He grins again, the moment not lost on him. "No problem. Just don't forget me when you're buying your next half-a-million-dollar painting, okay?"

I laugh, shaking my head. "I could never."

As Alex walks along the walls, his eyes darting from painting to painting with awe, I can't help but watch him. There's something about the way he takes it all in—like a kid wandering through a candy store for the first time. Having him here, in my space, makes the penthouse feel less like an echo chamber of expensive stuff and more like… home.

Then he stops. Dead in his tracks. His head tilts, his brows furrow, and his gaze fixed on a small frame tucked between two of the more dramatic, look-at-me pieces. Just like that, my heart starts doing this embarrassing little tap dance in my chest because I know exactly what he's looking at.

"Wait… is this…?" he whispers, leaning closer, his hand almost instinctively reaching toward the glass as if he can't quite believe it's real.

I step closer, a smile tugging at my lips. "Yeah, it's yours, Alex."

His eyes widen, and he turns to me so fast I'm worried he might get whiplash. "Mine? Cato, you framed it? And hung it up? Here? With these?" He waves vaguely at the museum-worthy masterpieces surrounding it, as though the paintings might suddenly rear up and protest.

"Of course, I did," I say, trying to sound casual, even though I'm already fighting the blush creeping up my neck. "The moment you showed it to me—and then left it behind like some kind of art-forgetting maniac—I knew it was special. Not just because it's your sketch, but because of what it represents. Your story, your journey, and… well, the connection we've built. It belongs here, with everything else that matters to me."

For a second, he just stares at me, blinking like I've just handed him a winning lottery ticket and told him he's also been elected mayor of the city. "I… I can't believe it," he finally says, turning back to the frame, his voice barely above a whisper. "It's just a rough sketch. It's nowhere near the level of, like… any of this."

I step closer until we're practically shoulder-to-shoulder. "Alex, it's not about the level. It's about the meaning. This sketch means more to me than a lot of the art here. It's raw, it's real, and it came from you. That's what makes it a masterpiece."

His head snaps back to me, and suddenly his eyes are a little shinier than they were a moment ago. "Cato, I… I don't even know what to say. I never thought you'd care about something like this. I mean, you're… you." He gestures vaguely at me, as though "you" encapsulates my entire personality, penthouse, and questionable taste in wine.

I reach out, gently cupping his face, my thumb brushing against his cheekbone in what I hope is a reassuring way and not a weird way. "You're more than just an artist to me, Alex. You've become… incredibly important in my life. Framing that sketch wasn't just about the art—it was about honoring the impact you've had on me."

His cheeks flush, and he leans into my hand slightly. His smile is completely unguarded. "I never imagined my work would be appreciated like this, especially by someone like you."

I raise an eyebrow, a grin tugging at the corners of my lips. "Someone like me? What's that supposed to mean? Devastatingly handsome, wildly successful, and modest?"

He lets out a laugh—smooth, mellow, and maybe a little bit emotional. "Yes, and humble, too. And the kind of person who frames a terrible sketch and makes it feel like the Mona Lisa."

I smile, feeling tenderness and pride swell in my chest. "It's not just about appreciating the work, Alex. It's about appreciating you. I wanted you to know that what you create—

what you share—matters to me. It's not just art on a wall. It's a part of who you are, and I want that part of you here, with me."

He laughs again, a little more choked up this time, his eyes brimming with something I can only describe as pure joy. "I can't believe you did this. It's… it's one of the nicest things anyone's ever done for me."

I lean in, my voice low and sincere. "You deserve it, Alex. You deserve to be celebrated, just like the artists whose work hangs here."

He smiles at me, and for a moment, the world feels like it's shrunk to just the two of us, standing in this penthouse surrounded by a collection of art that suddenly feels a lot less important than the person standing in front of me.

* * *

I grab the chilled bottle of champagne from the mini-fridge in the kitchen, a grin tugging at my lips as I head back to the living room. Alex is lounging on the couch, his face lit up with that quiet joy that makes everything feel a little brighter. Tonight isn't just about the champagne or the cupcakes or even the absurdly comfortable couch—it's about celebrating us. And honestly? I've never been so ready to pop a bottle in my life.

I hold up the champagne like it's a trophy. "Ready for some bubbles?"

Alex's eyes light up, his smile widening. "Absolutely. Champagne and cupcakes? You really know how to spoil a guy."

I peel the foil off dramatically, playing up the suspense, and work the cork loose. With a satisfying pop, the cork flies off, and champagne froths over the edge, spilling onto my hand.

"Now that is how you open a bottle," Alex says, laughing and clapping like I've just performed some kind of magic trick.

"What can I say? I've got skills," I tease, grabbing a couple of glasses and pouring us both a healthy amount. I hand him a glass, and he clinks it gently against mine.

"To us," he says, his voice velvety but brimming with care.

"To us," I echo, feeling a little thrill at how right those words sound. We both sip, the fizz tickling my nose and leaving a tender brilliance as it goes down.

I gesture to the tray of cupcakes I'd carefully selected earlier from the bakery. "And of course, I couldn't let tonight happen without these bad boys. We deserve something sweet to go with the champagne."

Alex's eyes widen, and he gives me the kind of delighted grin that makes my heart do an embarrassing flip. "Who are you, and how did I get so lucky?"

"I'm the lucky one," I say with a smile.

We settle onto the couch, sipping champagne and nibbling on cupcakes while the city lights cast a tone of amber through the windows. The atmosphere is cozy and electric at the same time, like we're in our own little world where nothing bad can touch us.

Alex leans forward, still laughing, his champagne glass dangling from his fingers. "Alright, I have to ask—how many tattoos do you even have? Because every time I think I've spotted the last one, another sneaks up on me."

I smirk, swirling the remaining champagne in my glass. "Last time I counted? Eighty-seven."

Alex's jaw drops, his eyes wide with incredulous delight. "Eighty-seven? Are you serious? That's not just a collection—it's an empire!"

I chuckle, leaning back. "What can I say? I've got stories to tell, and ink's how I like to tell 'em."

He shakes his head in amazement. "Alright, you've got to share—give me some highlights. What's the story behind the skull on your neck? It's kind of intimidating."

I instinctively touch the ink on the side of my neck, my fingers brushing over it lightly. "The skull? That one's a reminder. Life's short. Don't take anything for granted. I got it after my first art gallery show. A weird way to celebrate, I know, but it felt right."

He nods slowly, taking it in. "Okay, I can see that. What about the cat? I mean, you're obviously a dog person—because, you know, Bailey."

I grin, scratching the back of my neck. "Yeah, well, cats are independent. They do what they want, when they want. I liked that. Got it after my breakup with Derek—kind of a promise to myself to stay true to me."

Alex studies me for a beat, his expression softening. "That's… actually really cool. And a little poetic."

I laugh, trying to brush off the sudden heat in my cheeks. "Don't get used to me being deep. Most of my tattoos are just for fun, but are still a part of me and things I enjoy."

"Like what?" he presses, his curiosity unrelenting.

"Oh, you know," I say, grinning. "The slice of pizza on my ankle. That one's for my eternal devotion to carbs."

Alex snorts, shaking his head. "Eighty-seven tattoos, and you've got pizza permanently inked on you. I love it."

"Eight-seven, last I counted," I tease, pointing at him mock-seriously. "And hey, pizza is sacred."

He raises his glass with a wink. "To pizza. And tattoos. And to you being way cooler than I thought."

I roll my eyes, but the smile tugging at my lips won't quit. "I'll drink to that."

Eventually, the cupcakes are gone, the champagne glasses are nearly empty, and we're leaning back on the couch, the city lights painting the room in flickering hues. I glance over at Alex, his face glowing with happiness, and feel a rush of something so big it takes my breath away.

"You know," I say softly, setting my glass on the table, "I didn't think I'd ever feel this kind of joy again. But here we are."

Alex looks at me, his expression tender, his voice equally quiet. "I feel the same way. You've brought something back into my life I didn't even realize I'd lost."

I reach out, taking his hand in mine. Our fingers interlock, and the gesture feels as natural as breathing. "I guess we're both surprising each other, then."

He leans in a little closer, his smile genuine. "Yeah, I guess we are."

And in that moment, surrounded by laughter, stories, and the pleasantness of shared champagne, I know for certain: this isn't just a celebration. It's the beginning of something bigger than either of us expected.

twenty-three

ALEX

July

It's a bright Saturday morning, and I find myself standing at the base of Mountain Trail Park, adjusting the straps of my backpack and tingling with nervous energy. Demi has organized a group hike, and I'm here with Cato and a handful of Demi's friends, none of whom I've met before. It feels a bit like a test—of both endurance and social skills. Like one of those escape rooms, except instead of solving puzzles to get out, you're navigating small talk and pretending you're not mentally calculating how long you can stand before needing a breather.

Demi bounces over, brimming with energy. "Alright, everyone! We're all set, right? Got your water, snacks, and, most importantly, your positive vibes?"

I chuckle, appreciating her enthusiasm. "Got all three," I reply, giving her a thumbs-up.

Cato is beside me, securing his own backpack. He shoots me a playful grin. "Ready to tackle the wild, babe?"

I smirk back, feeling a wave of competitive energy. "Oh, I'm more than ready. Question is, are you?"

He laughs, the sound echoing off the surrounding trees. "You know I can't resist a good challenge."

Demi claps her hands, signaling the start of the hike. "Okay, let's get moving! We've got about four miles to the summit, so pace yourselves."

As we begin walking, I fall into step beside Cato. The trail has dirt paths and rocky terrain, surrounded by towering pines and the faint scent of wildflowers in the air. It's peaceful, yet exhilarating with the chatter of the group.

"So," I say, nudging Cato lightly with my elbow, "what do you think of this whole hiking thing?"

He grins, glancing at me sideways. "It's not exactly my usual scene, but I like the idea of it. Plus, I get to see you try to keep up, which should be very fun."

I pretend to be offended, widening my eyes. "Oh, you think I can't keep up? Just wait till we hit the steep parts."

He chuckles, his gaze easing. "I'm counting on it."

As we continue up the trail, Demi strikes up a conversation with the rest of the group, introducing me to her friends. There's Sam, a lively graphic designer with a love for photography, who's currently deep in a passionate monologue about the pros and cons of vintage lenses. There's also Jamie, an elementary school teacher with a knack for charming kids and adults alike, who seems to float effortlessly over the social terrain, as if the rough patches don't even exist. It's impressive and, also, mildly intimidating.

"So, Alex," Sam begins, catching up to us with his camera in hand. "Demi says you're a designer too?"

I nod, feeling a bit more comfortable as the conversation flows. "Yeah, I work mostly in branding and digital design. It's fun, but it doesn't give me views like this," I say, gesturing toward the scenic landscape around us.

Sam laughs, snapping a picture of the mountains in the distance. "True, but it's all about balance. You've got to get out here and recharge every now and then."

Jamie chimes in, her voice serene. "Nature has a way of centering us. It's like pressing a reset button."

Cato nods in agreement, a wistful smile tugging at his lips. "It really does. I don't get to do this often, but it reminds me of home. We had a mountain basically in our backyard back home at Everest."

Jamie freezes mid-sip of her drink, her eyes snapping to him like a hawk spotting prey. "Wait, you're from Everest? Me too!"

"Michigan?" Cato asks, his excitement bubbling to the surface.

"Yeah!" Jamie exclaims, her voice an octave higher than usual. Her expression shifts from surprise to a delighted grin. "I can't believe this. Nobody ever knows Everest! It's like we're a secret club."

Cato laughs, shaking his head. "I know, right? Half the time, people think I'm talking about the actual mountain. I've had to clarify so many times that it's a town and not some wild expedition."

Jamie snorts, nodding. "Same here! I've had people ask me if I'm some kind of mountaineer. I mean, sure, I hiked up the hill behind my grandma's house once, but that's about as adventurous as I got."

Cato grins, leaning a little closer. "Okay, but did you ever try the giant cinnamon rolls from the café, High Peak? Because that's what Everest is really about."

"Are you kidding me? My brother's best friend owns the place! Those cinnamon rolls were my childhood," Jamie says, practically beaming now.

Cato clinks his glass gently against hers, his smile wide. "Well, Jamie, I guess it's official—we're Everest alumni."

"Everest alumni," Jamie repeats, raising her glass like they've just agreed on a sacred pact. "I think that makes us practically family."

Demi, who's leading the group, turns around and points toward a bend in the trail. "Alright, guys! The next stretch is a bit steeper, so take it slow. And remember, we're not racing to the top."

I shoot a quick glance at Cato, my competitive spirit flaring up. "We might not be racing with everyone else, but I'm beating you to the top."

He laughs, clearly enjoying the banter. "We'll see about that."

The path ahead becomes rockier, and I focus on my footing as we start the climb. The effort is real, but there's something refreshing about it—the physical challenge, the smell of pine in the air, and the occasional bird call breaking the silence.

We reach a small clearing halfway up the mountain, and Demi calls for a break. "Alright, hydration time! Take a few minutes to rest up before we tackle the final stretch."

I plop down on a flat rock, catching my breath. Cato joins me, handing me a water bottle. "Doing okay?" he asks, half-teasing, half-concerned.

I take a swig of water, trying to hide the fact that I feel like I'm going to hyperventilate, then flash him a grin. "Never better. I could do this all day."

He raises an eyebrow, his voice playful. "You sure? Because I saw you wobble back there."

I laugh, shaking my head. "Oh, please. You were the one who almost tripped over that root."

We both burst into laughter, drawing curious looks from the others. It feels good—simple, lighthearted, and free from the heavier conversations we've had recently.

Jamie stretches her legs and looks over at us. "You two make hiking seem like a comedy show."

Cato grins at her. "We try. It's part of our charm."

Sam joins in, wiping sweat from his brow. "I like it. Adds to the vibe."

As we resume the hike, I notice that Cato seems more relaxed, his usual guardedness replaced with a carefree smile. It's a side of him I haven't seen much of, and it makes me feel closer to him.

"So, did you ever do hikes like this as a kid?" I ask, curious about his past.

He shakes his head, his voice tinged with nostalgia. "Not really. I grew up basically in the wilderness, but my family wasn't big on outdoor stuff. My idea of adventure was sneaking into the garage to draw on the old car with that weird chalk you can use on cars."

I laugh, picturing a young Cato covered in chalk dust. "Rebel artist even then, huh?"

He nods, a playful glint in his eyes. "You could say that. What about you? Were you the nature-loving type?"

I hesitate, then let out a laugh. "Honestly? No. I was more of the 'find any excuse to avoid youth group hikes' kind of kid. I remember hiding behind the church once, just to avoid a youth meeting."

Cato's laughter is immediate and genuine. "You didn't!"

"I did," I admit, still laughing. "They looked for me everywhere—at home, around the neighborhood—but they never checked behind the church. I got away with it by saying I'd been 'waiting outside' all along."

He shakes his head, clearly amused. "You're sneakier than I thought, Alex."

I shrug with a grin. "Desperate times call for desperate measures."

As we approach the final stretch of the trail, I feel a renewed burst of energy. The summit is close, and the thought of reaching it with Cato makes me push harder. Demi, a few steps ahead, cheers us on. "Come on, guys! The view up there is worth every step."

When we finally reach the top, the view takes my breath away. The entire city stretches out below us, a patchwork of buildings and greenery, framed by the distant mountains. We all stand there in awe, taking in the beauty and the sense of accomplishment.

"Wow," I whisper, a sense of peace washing over me. "This was worth it."

Cato stands next to me, his hand brushing lightly against mine. "Yeah," he says softly, his voice filled with warmth. "It really was."

* * *

We're heading down from the summit, the hike filled with casual chatter and nice views. I fall behind a bit, distracted by a pretty spot through the trees. When I look around, I realize I've lost sight of the group.

"Huh, where'd everyone go?" I mutter, trying to retrace my steps. The path splits in different directions, and I'm not sure which way to go. I decide to keep moving, hoping I'm on the right track.

As I walk, I hear water nearby. I follow the sound and soon come across a small river. It's a nice spot, and I take a moment to enjoy the view.

"Alex!" I hear Cato call out.

"Over here!" I shout back.

Cato jogs up, looking a bit winded. "There you are. We were wondering where you went."

"Sorry about that," I say. "Got distracted by the scenery and lost track of you guys."

He nods, catching his breath. "No worries. Just try to stick closer next time, alright?"

"Will do," I agree. "This is a pretty nice spot, though."

Cato looks around and shrugs. "Yeah, it's not bad. Ready to head back?"

I nod, and we start walking. "Thanks for coming to find me," I say.

"I mean, come on," he replies. "Like I'd leave you behind."

We make our way back to the trail, chatting about the hike and looking forward to rejoining the group.

* * *

We walk side by side along the winding trail back to the main path, Cato's hand firmly wrapped around mine. The feeling of his touch radiates comfort, making me feel safe despite the fact that I'd just gotten myself lost.

"I told you I'd keep you close," he teases, casting me a mischievous grin.

I roll my eyes playfully. "Oh, I see how it is. You're going to rub it in, aren't you?"

He laughs, his voice echoing in the stillness of the forest. "Oh, you better believe it. I mean, who gets lost on a perfectly marked trail?"

I let out a loud laugh. "Listen! We didn't have the woods where I grew up."

He squeezes my hand a little tighter, his voice dropping to a low, ominous tone. "Well, while we're out here... I might as well tell you the stories of this place."

I raise an eyebrow, intrigued by his sudden change in tone. "Oh? What stories?"

He pauses, leaning closer to add a layer of mystery. "Legend has it that deep in these woods, there's a lost hiker from the 1950s. They say he's still wandering the trails, trying to find his way back... and he carries an old, rusty lantern that flickers at night."

I let out a fake gasp, playing along. "No way! That's so scary! What do I do if he finds me?"

Cato's grin widens, clearly enjoying the moment. "Oh, if he finds you alone, he asks you for directions... but no matter what you tell him, he always gets lost again. And if you don't answer him, he cuts out your tongue because he doesn't like being ignored."

I burst into laughter, unable to keep up the act. "Okay, that's ridiculous. Who comes up with these stories?"

He shrugs, his eyes glinting with mischief. "Hey, you never know. Maybe it's true. You did get lost, after all."

I narrow my eyes at him, smiling. "Are you saying I'm the lost hiker now? Because that's not fair."

He nods sagely, his voice mock-serious. "Well, you did check all the boxes. Distracted by nature, wandered off, got separated from the group... sounds like classic lost hiker behavior to me."

I nudge him with my shoulder, trying to suppress my laughter. "Alright, alright, you win. I'll be sure to hold your hand the entire time on our next trip. Not becoming a ghostly legend for me."

He chuckles, his voice tempering. "Good. I wouldn't want to lose you out here for real."

There's a sincerity in his tone that cuts through the playful banter, making me pause. I glance up at him, feeling compassion spread through my chest. "Thanks for coming to find me, Cato. I mean it."

He looks down at me, his expression relaxes even more. "You don't have to thank me, Alex. I'd do it again in a heartbeat. I'm not letting you get lost—not on my watch."

We continue walking, the forest around us gradually becoming more familiar as we approach the main trail. Cato's grip on my hand never wavers, and I find myself enjoying the simple closeness of it.

He clears his throat, a sly smile returning to his face. "But you know, that's not the scariest story about these woods."

I feign shock, widening my eyes. "No way! There's a scarier one?"

"Oh, absolutely," he says with exaggerated seriousness. "They say there's a mysterious creature that roams these parts, especially after dark. Half-human, half-deer... they call it the Stag Man. He lures hikers off the trail with eerie, echoing calls that sound like laughter and sobbing."

I laugh, shaking my head. "Now I know you're making this up. A half-human, half-deer? That's straight out of a bad horror movie."

He grins wickedly. "Hey, you'd be surprised. Some hikers swear they've heard it at dusk—rustling in the bushes, calling out names."

I pretend to look around, making my voice quiver theatrically. "Cato, what if the Stag Man comes for us right now? We'll never make it back."

He pulls me closer, his voice low and dramatic. "Don't worry, Alex. I'll protect you from the Stag Man."

The sincerity in his words means even more than the humor, and I squeeze his hand gently. "I think I'm good as long as I've got you with me."

He glances down at our intertwined hands, placing a kiss on mine, and a genuine smile spreads across his face. "Same here."

We finally emerge from the wooded area onto the wider part of the trail, the main path visible just ahead. The rest of the group is gathered near a clearing, talking and laughing as they wait for us.

As we approach, Demi catches sight of us, a teasing grin forming on her face. "Well, look who finally decided to join the rest of us! Did you two have a little side adventure?"

Cato laughs, giving me a conspiratorial wink. "You could say that. Just a minor detour to keep things interesting."

Demi raises an eyebrow, clearly amused. "Uh-huh. Well, I hope the Stag Man didn't give you any trouble."

I burst into laughter, shaking my head. "Oh shit! Cato wasn't kidding about that. No Stag Man sightings this time."

Cato gives me a playful nudge, his voice low. "I told you he is real!"

The trees start to thin, the wide-open clearing signaling the camping area at last. I let out a small sigh of relief, not just because we made it safely, but because Cato is still beside me, his hand casually brushing against mine as we walk.

The sight of the camp area is welcoming: a few tents already set up, logs arranged around a central fire pit, and the faint scent of charred wood lingering in the air from previous campers. Demi, always one step ahead, is already pulling out bags of food from her backpack.

"Alright, everyone!" she announces with a clap of her hands. "Time for the grand finale: barbecue time!"

Excitement runs a course through the group. It's the perfect ending to the hike—a mix of exhaustion, hunger, and a sense of camaraderie that only a day spent together in nature can create. I drop my backpack near one of the logs, rubbing my shoulders.

Cato sets his backpack down next to mine, grinning. "You look like you could use a burger, Alex."

I chuckle, patting my stomach. "More like two. I'm starving."

He reaches into a cooler someone has brought and pulls out a couple of raw patties. "Well, you're in luck. I make a mean burger."

Demi, who has taken on the role of grillmaster, hands Cato the spatula with an approving nod. "He's not lying. Cato's got some secret grilling skills. You're in for a treat, Alex."

Cato winks at me, taking the tongs like he was born to do it. "Alright, let's see what I can do."

As the grill starts to sizzle, I settle onto one of the logs, my body still tingling from the day's exertion, but feeling a pleasant sense of fatigue. I watch Cato flip the burgers with surprising ease, his focus on the grill giving him an effortless confidence.

"So," I ask, breaking the silence, "where'd you learn to grill?"

He glances up, smirking. "Believe it or not, my dad taught me. He was big on barbecues—thought they were the best way to bond with the family."

I smile, picturing a younger Cato learning to flip burgers under his dad's watchful eye. "That's a good tradition. I don't think I ever really got into grilling, though. Most of my childhood summers were spent at church picnics."

He raises an eyebrow, teasing. "Church picnics, huh? So, you were the good boy eating sandwiches while everyone else was grilling?"

I laugh, feeling a bit embarrassed. "Hey, sandwiches have their place! Besides, I did have a few barbecue moments... mostly when I snuck away to grab some from the neighbors."

Cato's eyes sparkle with amusement. "Rebel Alex strikes again. First hiding behind the church, now sneaking burgers. You really had a wild streak, didn't you?"

I lean back, shrugging playfully. "What can I say? Sometimes you've got to break the rules to get a decent meal."

He laughs, turning back to the grill as the smell of sizzling meat fills the air. The rest of the group starts gathering around, anticipation evident on their faces. Sam is already setting up a small table with buns, lettuce, tomatoes, and condiments.

"Alright, everyone," Cato announces, sliding a perfectly cooked patty onto a bun. "First burger is up! Who's hungry?"

Jamie eagerly reaches out. "I'll take it! I'm famished."

Cato hands her the burger with a grin. "One Cato-special coming right up. Hope it lives up to the hype."

She takes a big bite, her eyes widening with delight. "Wow! This is really good, Cato."

He beams, clearly pleased with the compliment. "Glad you like it."

Demi hands me a plate, nudging me playfully. "You better try one too, Alex. Can't let Cato show off without tasting his cooking."

I take the plate, eyeing Cato as he prepares my burger. "No pressure, right?"

He gives me a cocky smile, carefully assembling the burger before handing it to me. "Only the best for you, Alex."

I take a bite, the flavors bursting in my mouth. It's juicy, perfectly seasoned, and everything I need after the long hike. "Damn," I mumble through a mouthful, "this is really good."

Cato's face lights up with pride. "Told you you were in for a treat."

I nod, taking another big bite. "You weren't kidding. I might actually be full after this."

As everyone gathers around, the atmosphere grows even more relaxed. There's laughter, light teasing, and the occasional clink of beer bottles. The group shares stories of their own hiking adventures, from funny falls to unexpected animal encounters.

At one point, Demi raises a bottle, her voice loud and clear. "To the hike, to good friends, and to Alex for managing to get lost and found in one piece!"

Everyone laughs, including me. I raise my bottle, feeling a warmth that has nothing to do with the campfire. "To not getting lost again!" I add, earning another round of laughter.

Cato leans closer, his voice low but filled with affection. "I'm just glad we're here, together. This... this means a lot to me."

I turn to him, my smile melting. "Yeah, me too, Cato."

We clink our cans gently, sharing a private toast as the campfire crackles in front of us. It isn't just a barbecue—it's a moment of connection, a sense of belonging I haven't felt in a long time. As the night wears on, filled with laughter and the smoky scent of the bonfire, I know this is a memory I'll hold onto.

Cato glances at me again, his eyes steady. "Think you'll come hiking again?"

I pretend to think about it, a teasing glint in my eyes. "Only if you promise to grill burgers every time."

He chuckles, his voice filled with care. "Deal. As long as you promise not to get lost."

"Deal," I agree, the smile on my face as real as the firelight dancing between us.

twenty-four
CATO

The city's dimly-lit skyline emerges in the distance as we drive back from the hike, the adrenaline of the day still surging in my veins. Alex is in the passenger seat, his hair windblown, cheeks slightly flushed from the exertion. He has this excited energy, like he can't quite sit still.

"You know," he says suddenly, breaking the comfortable silence, "I'm not ready to head home yet."

I shoot him a quick, curious glance. "Oh yeah? What's on your mind?"

He grins, a playful glint in his eyes. "I don't know… maybe we could grab something to eat? I mean, we had those burgers back at camp, but I'm pretty hungry again."

I laugh, nodding in agreement. "I could eat too. I think I saw a food truck park up ahead when we left the city."

Alex's face brightens. "Perfect. I love food trucks."

We make a quick detour, pulling into the lot where a few brightly colored trucks are parked. The delicious aromas of sizzling meats, spices, and fresh tortillas fill the air. I park the car, and we hop out, still wearing our hiking gear.

"Okay," I say, surveying the options. "Tacos, birria, or maybe some spicy noodles? What's calling to you?"

Alex taps his chin theatrically, pretending to ponder the decision. "Hmm… let's go with tacos."

I chuckle, appreciating his logic. "Tacos it is."

We walk up to the taco truck, the menu proudly displaying an array of choices—carnitas, al pastor, barbacoa, and a special 'extra hot' salsa. I glance over at Alex. "Feeling brave enough for the 'extra hot'?"

He grins, his humorous side coming out. "Are you kidding? After the hike we just did? I'm good on the torture today."

I raise an eyebrow, amused. "I guess I can't argue with you there."

I place our order: two carnitas tacos each, loaded with the infamous 'mild' salsa, plus a couple of lime wedges on the side, and a Mexican cola. I pay for our order and the vendor hands us our tacos wrapped in foil, the spicy scent hitting us immediately.

We find a small table nearby and sit down, unwrapping our tacos. "Ready?" I ask, lifting mine.

Alex smirks, lifting his taco as well. "Always."

We take the first bite at the same time, the flavors exploding in our mouths—juicy meat, smoky salsa, and the sharp tang of lime.

"Holy—" I start, my eyes watering.

Alex smiles, "Oh my God," he manages to say between bites. "Fuck, that's so good!"

I laugh, "I honestly didn't peg you for a taco guy?"

He nods, gulping down some water. "Who doesn't like tacos?"

We both burst into laughter, tears streaming from our eyes from the sheer intensity of the heat. "It's so good," I say, my voice a bit hoarse, "but I don't know if I can finish it."

Alex looks at his half-eaten taco, then back at me, determination flashing in his eyes. "I'm finishing it. No way I'm wasting this deliciousness."

We finish our tacos, each of us feeling the burn but also the satisfaction of conquering the challenge together. As we clean up, I look at Alex, still catching his breath but smiling widely. "Ready to head home?" I ask.

He nods, a lingering grin on his face. "Yeah, but we're doing this again sometime. Next time, maybe we'll do the 'extra hot' salsa."

I laugh, patting him on the back. "We'll see about that."

* * *

We step out of the elevator, the doors sliding open to the comfort of my penthouse. As soon as we cross the threshold, I can feel the shift in the air—an undeniable pull that has been growing between us all day. I turn to Alex, and our eyes lock, the tension that has been building since the hike suddenly becomes overwhelming.

Before I can say anything, he closes the distance between us, his lips crashing against mine in a kiss that is urgent and filled with pent-up emotion. I respond immediately, wrapping my arms around his waist, pulling him closer. The intensity of the moment is raw, electric. It feels like all the barriers we've been holding up are finally breaking down.

"Cato," Alex whispers between kisses, his voice breathless, filled with longing.

Hearing my name spoken like that, in that tone, sends a shiver down my spine. "Alex," I manage to murmur back, my voice low and rough with desire. I cup his face, deepening the kiss. It's messy, urgent, and completely consuming.

He presses himself closer, his hands gripping the back of my neck, his touch both desperate and tender. I let my fingers trail down his spine, feeling the way his body responds, the heat rising between us. Every touch, every kiss feels like a confession—an admission of everything we haven't been able to say with words.

We stumble toward the living room, our lips never parting. I barely notice when we knock over a small vase on the side table; all that matters is him—his touch, his presence, the way he fits perfectly against me. "God, I want this," I whisper, my lips brushing against his ear. "I want you."

Alex's breath hitches, his eyes meeting mine with an intensity that makes my heart race. "Me too," he admits, his voice filled with raw honesty. "More than you could possibly know."

His words break something open inside me, a surge of emotion that makes everything feel even more urgent. I run my hands under his shirt, feeling the tingle of his skin against my palms. He lifts his arms, helping me pull the fabric over his head. As soon as it's off, I can't help but pause, taking in the sight of him, the way his chest rises and falls with each breath.

"You're beautiful," I say softly, my voice filled with sincerity.

Alex blushes, a small, bashful smile appearing on his face. "So are you," he replies, his hand reaching out to trace the tattoos on my arm. His fingers are gentle, curious, exploring the ink that tells my story.

I let out a soft sigh, feeling the intimacy of the moment. I lean in, my lips trailing from his jaw to his neck, savoring the way he shivers under my touch. His hands are everywhere—on my back, my shoulders, tugging at my shirt until it, too, is on the floor.

We move slowly toward the bedroom, our kisses growing deeper, more passionate with each step. When we finally reach the edge of the bed, Alex falls backward, pulling me down with him. We land in a tangle of limbs, laughter breaking the tension for a moment before the urgency returns.

His hands trace the lines of my chest, his touch both tender and hungry. "I want to know every part of you, Cato," he whispers, his voice filled with sincerity.

I feel my heart swell at his words, the vulnerability in his voice making the moment even more intimate. "You already do, Alex," I reply, my voice barely a whisper.

We kiss again, slower this time, savoring the taste of each other. My hands explore his body, feeling every curve, every scar, as if mapping him for the first time. There's something incredibly raw about the way we touch, as if we're discovering not just each other's bodies, but something deeper—something unspoken, yet undeniable.

He arches his back slightly, his eyes closing as he loses himself in the moment. "Cato," he breathes, the sound of my name filled with need and trust.

I lean down, pressing a soft kiss to his forehead. "I'm here, Alex," I whisper. "I'm not going anywhere."

"I've never felt this way before," Alex whispers, his voice barely audible.

I squeeze his hand gently. "Me neither. But I don't want to run from it."

Without a word, I lean closer, my lips hovering just inches from his. It's a tentative moment, infused with hesitation and anticipation. I can feel his breath on my skin, warm and inviting. Then, as if by some silent agreement, we close the gap.

The kiss is slow at first, exploratory, like we're both testing the waters of something new. As the seconds pass, it deepens, becoming more desperate. I feel his hands move up to my shoulders, pulling me closer, and I respond by wrapping my arms around him, drawing him against me.

I want to say a lot of things but I'm too wrapped up in him for the words to leave my lips, I begin to feel a rush of blood in my head, so to ground myself, I look into his eyes and only see someone who genuinely cares for me. In this moment nothing else matters; nothing but Alex.

As I roll myself on top of him, our lips part for a moment. I can feel Alex's breath over my lips, and I hover over him planting my hands firmly on either side of his head. I brush two of my fingers over his forehead, moving his hair lightly out of his eyes. His cheeks turn a rosy shade of red, blushing. He's intoxicating beyond imagination. For the first time, I can see small marks on his face. He has a small cut over his right eyelid and a small mole under his lips. I press my lips against the curve of his neck, tasting the heat of his skin as I draw him closer, my mouth lingering in a slow, deliberate pull that leaves his breath hitching.

I pull myself down to him and suck his earlobes. His entire body goes rigid as if a thunderbolt just ran through his spine. His breath turns heavier and heavier by the moment.

I back off a bit. He lays down covering his eyes with his arm trying to control his breath. It makes my desire for him intensify. I kiss on his neck and collarbone, sinking my teeth into him occasionally, causing him to moan softly.

Looking closely, Alex takes care of himself physically. There isn't a strand of hair on his chest. I circle my finger around his nipple, teasing the hardened peak. Suddenly his hand grabs my head, leading my lips to his chest.

I can feel Alex's desire radiating off of him, and I'm more than willing to take control. My lips latch onto his nipple, teasing and sucking as my fingers dance over his other one. His chest heaves beneath me, and I can hear the raggedness in his breath. My hand trails down his stomach, feeling the hardness of his cock through the denim of his jeans. I begin to rub and squeeze it gently, eliciting moans from him as our bodies press closer together.

I can't help but smile at how adorable he looks in this moment, and the thought crosses my mind that I would love to capture it forever by painting it on all the walls of my apartment. For now, I focus on pulling back to his mouth, gently grabbing his neck from behind and brushing my lips against his. The sensation sends shivers down his spine and his body starts to shake.

I reach out and place a hand on Alex's shoulder, feeling the tension in his muscles. "Are you okay?" I ask, knowing how intense a first time can be. He takes a deep breath, his chest rising and falling quickly.

After a moment, he nods and says softly, "Yes." I can see his eyes encompassing both nerves and ecstasy as he prepares for this new found pleasure.

I unbutton his jeans and like a skilled craftsman; remove his clothes one article at a time. I slowly run my tongue along his neck and collarbone to his nipples and then over his abdomen. He holds my head with both his hands trying to slow me down.

As my fingers wrap around his length, he gasps and his eyes open wide. I can feel his body tense up as I lean in closer, our noses almost touching. "Is this the first time anyone has touched you like this?" I ask gently.

"Yes," he whispers quietly.

"Are you sure you're ready?" I ask again, my stomach twisting with guilt. I peer up at Alex and see the desire and determination in his eyes. He cups my face in his hands and leans down to kiss my forehead.

"I want this, with you and only you," he says, a small smile on his lips. "I'm okay, just nervous."

I take a deep breath and squeeze his hand. "You don't have to be nervous. I'll be right here with you. Always."

Pulling my focus back to his pleasure, I hold his cock with one hand and start gently sliding my hand up and down his length. Against how Alex seems, he has a decent cock with a lot of girth. *It's always the quiet guys with the big dicks.*

My lips press softly against the crown of Alex's dick, eliciting a shiver that runs through his entire body. He grasps my hair tightly in his fingers and pulls me closer to him, his knees bending to encase me in a straight jacket of passion.

I trail my tongue down the length of his shaft, my hand stroking the rest of him with precision. Every stroke, every touch sends waves of pleasure through him, and I relish in the power I have over his sensations.

Moving even closer, I take him deeper into my mouth, feeling his legs wrap around me as he holds me in place. His expression is one of pure ecstasy as I suck harder, taking in his reactions and using them to fuel my own desire.

Just as I want to savor this moment even more, Alex reaches his peak and his body goes limp. His release fills my mouth, seemingly endless and overwhelming. With no strength left in his body, he closes his eyes and simply surrenders to the pleasure.

I pull away with a smile, wiping my mouth with the back of my hand. Alex lays there, panting and trying to catch his breath. I lean over and kiss his forehead gently before lying next to him.

"I'm sorry," he says, still trying to get his breathing under control.

"Why are you apologizing?" I ask, genuinely confused.

"That was so quick. I didn't mean to come so quick," he explains, sounding embarrassed.

I cup his face in my hands and make him look at me. "Hey, it's okay. It was your first time and I don't care how long it lasted. It was amazing."

He smiles shyly and turns his head to hide his face in the crook of my neck. We lay there for a few moments in comfortable silence before Alex speaks up again.

"Can I do something for you?" he asks tentatively.

I run my hand through his hair and nod. "Whatever you want."

He sits up slowly and looks down at me with an intensity in his eyes that takes my breath away. He leans down and kisses me again, this time deeper than before. His hands roam freely over my body, exploring every inch as if he's trying to memorize it.

With each lingering kiss, he expertly removes every article of clothing from my body until we are both stripped bare. His hands roam freely over my skin, tracing every curve and dip with delicate precision. His lips follow suit, leaving a trail of fire in their wake as they explore every inch of me. When his attention finally reaches the apex between my legs, I'm overcome with pleasure and can't help but moan loudly.

He takes his time pleasuring me, skillfully using his hands and tongue to bring me to the brink of ecstasy. Each touch, each caress, is deliberate and filled with a tenderness that makes my heart race. He knows exactly where to kiss, where to lick, and where to press, driving me wild with desire. The room is filled with the sounds of our heavy breathing and the occasional moan that escapes my lips.

When I finally reach my peak, he holds onto me tightly, his strong arms providing a safe haven as I ride out the intense waves of pleasure coursing through my body. My release is explosive, and I feel the hot spurts of my climax coating my abs and Alex's hand. The sensation is almost too much to bear, and I cry out, my body trembling with the force of my orgasm.

We collapse onto the bed in a sweaty heap, spent but still entangled in each other's arms. The feeling of being completely vulnerable and intimately connected with Alex is overwhelming and fills me with a sense of euphoria. His body is warm against mine, and I can feel the steady beat of his heart as we lie there, catching our breath.

Alex looks at me, his green eyes soft and filled with love. "You okay?" he asks, his voice a gentle whisper.

I nod, a contented smile spreading across my face. "More than okay," I reply, reaching up to brush a strand of hair from his forehead. "That was incredible."

He grins, leaning in to press a tender kiss to my lips. "You were incredible," he murmurs against my mouth.

This moment will be etched in my memory forever as one of pure bliss and complete surrender to his touch. The world outside ceases to exist, and all that matters is the man lying beside me, what I feel for him, and the unbreakable bond we've forged.

"You're amazing," Alex whispers against my skin, his breath tepid and smooth against my sensitive flesh.

I can feel his body trembling with exertion, a testament to the effort he's put into making this experience as remarkable as possible for me. I reach up, gently cupping the back of his head, and draw him in for another kiss, our bodies still intertwined despite the potential mess we've created.

As our lips part, I can feel him smiling against me. "I want to make sure you know that you're the reason I could do this right now." His voice is thick with emotion, but I catch the undercurrent of sincerity.

I smile and place a kiss on his forehead. "I understand, babe. I'll always be here for you."

When it's over, we lie tangled together, our bodies slick with sweat, but our hearts full. I wrap my arms around Alex, pulling him close. "I meant it," I murmur into his hair, my voice filled with emotion. "I'm not going anywhere."

He nestles closer, his voice soft but filled with certainty. "Neither am I, Cato. Not now. Not ever."

* * *

I wake up next to Alex, feeling a sense of contentment I've rarely experienced. I can't resist kissing his forehead before I slip out to make us coffee. When he wakes, I see the awkwardness in his eyes about our intimate night, but I reassure him, grateful for our connection. As we share coffee - his made just the way he likes it - I feel the tension melt away.

* * *

Alex stands near the door, adjusting his jacket, I feel a small pang of longing, even though he hasn't left yet. We've spent the last couple of hours talking—about the hike, our shared moments, and a few scattered dreams for the future. The morning has been easy and comforting, like the childhood stuffed animal you never want to get rid of.

He turns to face me, a gentle smile on his lips. "Well, I should get going. I've got some work to catch up on, but… this weekend was really special, Cato. I mean it."

I step closer, unable to resist the urge to be near him. "It was special for me too. I'm glad I got to spend it with you."

He nods, his gaze sincere. "We'll see each other soon, right? This isn't just… you know, a one-time thing?"

I reach out, gently touching his cheek. "No, it's not a one-time thing. You know I want more than that."

He leans into my touch for a moment, closing his eyes as if trying to hold onto the moment. "Me too," he whispers.

With a final, lingering kiss, he turns and walks out the door. I stand there for a moment, listening to the faint sound of the elevator descending, the reality of the situation slowly sinking in.

INK & *Intuition*

I walk back into the living room, the penthouse suddenly feeling a bit too big and far too empty. I slump onto the couch, letting out a heavy sigh.

twenty-five
ALEX

Amelia's voice booms through the conference room as she clicks through the final slides of her presentation. I try my best to look attentive, but my mind keeps drifting, especially with Tommy sitting right next to me, nudging me occasionally with not-so-subtle whispers.

"Man, these presentations just keep getting longer," Tommy mutters, pretending to take notes but actually doodling stick figures in the margins instead.

I stifle a laugh, leaning closer to respond. "Seriously. I think we've hit the world record for the longest explanation of quarterly targets."

Tommy smirks, his voice barely above a whisper. "Think she knows we've been chatting back here the whole time?"

I shrug, keeping my eyes fixed on the screen, where Amelia's laser pointer is enthusiastically circling a bar chart. "Nah, she's too focused. We're safe."

Just as I say that, Amelia's voice cuts through the room. "And that's it for today, everyone. Alex, I need to see you in my office."

My stomach drops. "Oh shit," I whisper to Tommy.

Tommy tries to keep a straight face but fails miserably. "Looks like you're up, buddy. Go take one for the team."

I let out a deep breath, trying to muster some confidence. "Wish me luck."

As I approach Amelia's office, a sense of impending doom settles in. Alright, here it comes. She's going to tear into me for chatting during the presentation.

I knock on the door, and Amelia's voice sounds cheerful, almost too cheerful. "Come in!"

I step inside, doing my best to look professional, even though I'm bracing for a verbal smackdown. "You wanted to see me?"

She looks up from her desk, her smile welcoming. "Yes, Alex, have a seat."

I sit down, expecting the worst. Here we go.

To my surprise, Amelia's tone is surprisingly kind. "So, I wanted to follow up about your new role. How are you feeling about the transition?"

I blink, caught off guard. "Oh, uh... I'm exhilarated about it. A bit nervous, but ready for the challenge."

She nods understandingly. "That's great to hear, Alex. I'm really glad you decided to take on this opportunity. I think you'll do fantastic things in this new position."

Her words take me by surprise. I feel pride and responsibility settling in. "Thank you, Amelia. I really appreciate your confidence in me."

Amelia leans forward, her smile genuine. "You've earned it, Alex. Your thoughtfulness and dedication to your work are exactly why you're perfect for this role."

I nod, feeling a sense of determination. "I'll do my best to live up to those expectations."

She smiles, her demeanor still friendly. "I know you will. We'll set up a meeting next week to go over the specifics of your new responsibilities."

I stand up, relieved that the conversation went well. "Sounds great, Amelia. I'm looking forward to it."

Just as I reach for the door handle, Amelia's voice takes on a more playful tone. "Oh, and Alex?"

I turn back, a bit confused. "Yes?"

Her smile widens, but it's not exactly comforting. "If I catch you and Tommy chatting in the back during the next presentation, I'll make sure to deduct 10 percent of your salary. Just a heads-up."

My face goes pale, her words landing like a well-timed punchline. "Wait... what?"

Amelia's smile remains bright, but her eyes have a mischievous glint. "You heard me. So, unless you want to contribute to the company in a very different way, maybe just pay more attention next time."

I try to laugh it off, but the fear is real. "Understood. No more chatting, I promise."

Back at my desk, the words *10 percent salary cut* echo in my head like an unwelcome mantra. I glance over at Amelia's office from the corner of my eye, half-expecting her to be watching me with a sly smile, but she's fully immersed in another call. Still, I'm not about to take any chances. I straighten up and adjust my chair to look as productive as possible.

I pull up my task list on the screen, my focus shifting back to work. "Alright, Alex," I mutter under my breath, "no more slacking off. Poking Amelia is like poking a dragon with a stick."

I imagine Amelia, not as the well-dressed manager she is, but as a fire-breathing dragon perched atop a pile of spreadsheets, ready to unleash hellfire at the slightest sign of rebellion. The mental image makes me smirk.

Just then, Tommy sidles over to my desk, looking curious. "So, how'd it go? Did you get roasted?"

I look up at him, trying to keep a serious expression, but failing miserably. "Oh, it was fine... mostly. Except for the part where she told me that if we chat during another presentation, we're getting a 10 percent salary cut."

Tommy's eyes go wide, and he visibly shudders. "No way! She actually said that?"

I nod, my voice dropping to a dramatic whisper. "Yup. And she said it with that creepy smile of hers, too. I swear, I saw my paycheck flash before my eyes."

Tommy slumps against my desk, clutching his chest theatrically. "Man, I always thought she was strict, but that's next-level villain stuff. I mean, who threatens a 10 percent salary cut with a smile?"

I shrug, feeling both amused and terrified at the same time. "It's like she's got this evil superpower. Smiling and scaring you at the same time."

Tommy crosses himself mockingly. "Lord, give me strength. May I never anger the Great Amelia, Keeper of the Paychecks."

I laugh, shaking my head. "You and I both. I think we need to start treating her like royalty from now on. You know, 'Yes, Your Majesty,' 'No, Your Majesty.' Bow every time she passes by."

Tommy nods solemnly, clearly getting into character. "Absolutely. Maybe we should leave offerings of coffee and cookies on her desk, just to be safe."

I grin, leaning back in my chair. "I think you're onto something. Maybe we'll even get a raise instead of a cut."

He snorts. "Yeah, right. But honestly, Alex, I'm impressed you made it out of there alive. I thought for sure she'd at least give you a verbal lashing."

I nod, still feeling a bit dazed by the encounter. "Me too. I was prepared for a full-on scolding. But she was actually pretty chill about the promotion decision. It's just the chatting thing she's not letting go of."

Tommy shakes his head, sighing. "Well, lesson learned. No more side chats during presentations."

I raise my hand like I'm making a solemn oath. "Agreed. From now on, we are model employees. Eyes on the presentation, mouths shut, and hearts full of fear."

Tommy mimics my gesture. "Amen to that."

We both burst into laughter, our desks shaking slightly with the force of it. It feels good to let out some of the tension, even if the situation is a bit ridiculous. The fear of the 10 percent cut still looms in the back of my mind, but at least I have Tommy to make it bearable.

* * *

I fumble with the grocery bags as I get to my apartment door, trying to balance them while searching for my keys. The plastic handles dig into my fingers, and sweat starts to bead on my forehead.

"Finally," I mutter, unlocking the door and stepping inside. I drop the bags onto the kitchen counter with a sigh of relief.

I start putting things away—bread, eggs, some fruit, and of course, a big container of coffee. As I reach for my phone to check the time, I realize I haven't heard from Cato all day, so I type out a quick text.

Me:

> Hey, just got done doing some grocery shopping. What are you up to?

His reply comes faster than I expect, almost like he's been waiting for my message.

Cato:

> In a session right now, but free in about 3 hours. If you're interested, you can come watch me work.

INK & *Intuition*

Watching Cato work is something I've come to really enjoy—seeing the way his hands move, how focused he gets, and the passion that flows into each tattoo he creates. I text back with a smile:

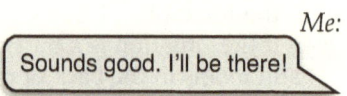

Me:

Sounds good. I'll be there!

With the evening's plan set, I decide to head out a bit earlier than planned. I grab a quick snack, toss on a clean shirt, and make my way to the door.

As I step out onto the landing, I nearly bump into someone. It's the same girl who knocked on my door by mistake a while back. She's holding a takeout box, with a backpack hanging loosely over one shoulder.

"Oh, hey!" she says, looking a bit surprised.

"Hey!" I reply, equally startled but smiling. We stand there for a moment, an awkward silence settling between us.

She shifts the takeout box in her arms, letting out a small chuckle. "Sorry about the confusion a while back. Wrong apartment."

I wave it off, grinning. "No worries at all. Happens to the best of us."

"I'm Eve by the way," she smiles.

"It's nice to finally put a name to the face. I'm Alex."

There's a brief pause as she scans me, maybe trying to figure out if I'm someone worth remembering. I'm about to say something more, when she nods and adds, "Well, hope you're having a good evening."

"Same to you," I reply, giving a friendly nod.

We both walk away in opposite directions, the encounter short and simple. As I head down the stairs, I feel a hint of curiosity. Who is she? A new tenant? A visitor? I shrug it off—there are more important things on my mind. Namely, Cato.

* * *

F. A. SENG

As I enter Eternal Ink, the soothing buzz of the tattoo machine, and *"I Write Sins Not Tragedies" by Panic! at the Disco* fills my ears. There's something comforting about it, like a background melody I now associate with Cato. I push open the door, the little bell above it chiming its usual greeting.

Demi stands behind the counter, a steaming cup of coffee in hand. She flashes me a wide smile as I step in. "Hey, Alex! Good to see you."

I grin, nodding toward the coffee. "For me?"

She holds it out, eyes twinkling with mischief. "Of course. I figured you'd need it after last weekend's hike."

I laugh, taking the warm cup from her. "You know me too well."

Cato is at the back, head bent over a client's arm, deeply focused on the intricate design he's creating. He glances up briefly, locks eyes with me for a moment, and a slow smile spreads across his face—a playful smile that reaches his eyes. A flutter of excitement rises in my chest as I give him a small wave.

The client, a middle-aged man with a buzz cut, seems relaxed, his arm resting on the chair as Cato works. The tattoo looks like it's shaping up to be an elaborate dragon, its scales detailed and intricate, winding around the man's forearm.

"Hey, babe," Cato calls out, his voice low but welcoming. "Come here for a sec."

I walk over, coffee in hand. "What's up?"

Cato pauses for a moment, wiping his hands with a cloth. "I was just thinking... would you be up for making a sketch of my client here while I finish the tattoo?"

I blink, surprised by the sudden request. "You mean, right now?"

The client, looking just as surprised, glances between us with curiosity.

Cato smiles, confident and reassuring. "Would you mind if Alex sketched you? I like to hang unique artwork in the shop, something that represents the people who've been here. A sketch of you would be a great addition."

He turns to me with a nod. "Plus, Alex here is a talented artist."

The client seems intrigued by the idea.

Feeling a blush creep up my cheeks from Cato's words, I manage a small smile. "Well, I'd be honored if it's okay with you," I say to the client.

The man nods, his eyes widening with interest. "Sure, why not? Never thought I'd get sketched while getting inked."

I grab my sketchbook and find a seat nearby, close enough to see the details of the scene but not so close as to get in Cato's way. I flip open to a blank page, feeling a surge of excitement as I begin to outline the shapes—the curve of the man's arm, the determined focus on Cato's face, and the almost meditative stillness that seems to settle over the client.

As I sketch, I get lost in the moment, capturing the interaction between Cato and his client—his careful precision, the client's trust, and the subtle exchange of energy between them. It's more than just a tattoo; it's a shared experience.

"That looks really good," Cato comments as he glances over, a hint of pride in his voice.

My chest swells a little. "Thanks. It's all about catching the vibe, you know?"

He nods, eyes glimmer with understanding. "Exactly."

The client chuckles, watching me from the corner of his eye. "I feel like a celebrity now, getting tattooed and sketched at the same time."

I laugh. "Well, it's not every day you get to be part of a masterpiece."

As I continue working on the sketch, I notice Demi watching from the front, a proud smile on her face. She's clearly enjoying this little collaboration, and I can't help but feel a sense of belonging.

When Cato finally finishes the tattoo, he stands back, admiring his work. "What do you think?" he asks the client.

The man examines his new tattoo, a satisfied grin spreading across his face. "It's perfect. Exactly what I wanted."

I tear the sketch from my book, handing it to Cato. "And here's the sketch you requested, kind sir," I say playfully.

He looks at the sketch, his eyes lighting up. "Wow, this is amazing. Thank you."

I grin. "Glad you like it."

With the session over, Cato, Demi, and I decide to grab a quick dinner before going our separate ways. We find a cozy little diner down the street, one of those hidden gems that serves the best chicken tenders with ranch dressing.

As we sit around a small table, Cato leans back in his chair, eyes filled with satisfaction. "You really brought the client experience to a whole new level today, Alex," he teases, his tone playful.

I laugh, shaking my head. "I aim to impress. Honestly, it was fun—never thought I'd be sketching a tattoo session."

Demi, sipping on her lemon tea, chimes in. "You two make a good team. Maybe we should do this more often. Sketch and ink—Eternal Ink's new service."

Cato nods thoughtfully, considering the idea. "Could be something, you know. Art in all its forms."

I raise my cherry cola. "To art, then. In all its messy, wonderful forms."

We clink our cups together and the conversation shifts to lighter topics—our favorite movies, embarrassing childhood stories, and even a brief debate about whether pineapple belongs on pizza. It feels easy, natural, and full of laughter.

After dinner, we all stand outside the diner, the evening sun setting. "Well, I should probably let you two get back to the shop," I say, glancing at the time. "But this was a lot of fun."

Cato steps closer, his smile soft. "It was. Thanks for coming, Alex. You really made it better."

A smile spreads across my face. "I'm glad I came. See you soon?"

He nods. "Absolutely."

Cato places a swift kiss on my cheek before he turns and leaves, leaving me smiling like a fool.

twenty-six
CATO

August

We're still deep in conversation over the intricate details of Alex's compass tattoo design when the door chime rings. I look up to see Richmond striding into Eternal Ink with his usual confident air, dressed impeccably in a tailored suit that makes him look more like a gallery owner than an artist.

"Well, well, look who's here!" I call out, a wide smile spreading across my face.

Richmond approaches, grinning. "Cato. Alex. How are two of my favorite people doing?"

Alex glances up, surprised by the compliment. "Oh, hey, Richmond! We're good, just brainstorming the design for my tattoo still."

Richmond claps his hands together, his voice filled with energy. "That's what I love to hear—creativity in action. I just wanted to drop by and say the gallery was a huge success."

"That's fantastic news!" I say, my eyes lighting up. "It was such an honor to be there, Richmond. We honestly had a great time."

Alex nods enthusiastically. "Yeah, it was incredible. I've never been to anything like it before. It was inspiring."

Richmond's eyes gleam with amusement. "I'm glad you both enjoyed it. I wanted to make sure it was memorable, and it seems like it was."

"It definitely was," I agree. "The collection was diverse, and the turnout was amazing. So many familiar faces and a lot of new ones too."

Alex jumps in, his voice excited. "And the way you curated the pieces was brilliant, Richmond. It felt like there was a real flow to the gallery."

Richmond looks genuinely pleased. "Thank you, Alex. That's exactly what I was going for—an experience that was cohesive, yet diverse in its artistic expression."

He pauses, as if considering something important. "Actually, that's why I'm here. I'm planning another gallery in a couple of months, and I was thinking... how about a collaborative piece from the two of you?"

I blink, caught off guard. "A collaborative piece? You mean, something we both work on together?"

Richmond nods eagerly. "Exactly. I've seen what both of you can do individually, and I think combining your talents could create something truly exceptional."

I glance at Alex, whose eyes have widened. "I... I don't know," he stammers, looking uncertain. "I'm just a graphic designer. I don't really think I'm gallery material."

Richmond tilts his head, serious. "Alex, I've seen your sketches, and I can tell you honestly that they're more than just design work—they're art. You have a unique perspective, and I think it's something that could be celebrated in a gallery setting."

Alex shifts in his seat, clearly taken aback. "I... I don't know what to say. It's flattering, but I'm not sure if I'm good enough for something like that."

I lean forward, my voice filled with encouragement. "Alex, don't sell yourself short. We've both seen your work, and Richmond's right. You have a real gift, and it's more than just digital art—it's personal, and it's meaningful."

Richmond adds sincerely, "It's about expression, Alex, not fitting into a certain mold. From what I've seen, you have a lot to express."

Alex looks between us, cheeks slightly pink. "I'll have to think about it. It's a big leap, you know?"

I reach out, giving his shoulder a reassuring squeeze. "Of course. Take your time. Just know I'd be honored to collaborate with you on something for the gallery. I think we could create something really special."

He smiles, tension easing from his face. "Thanks, Cato. That means a lot."

Richmond claps his hands together, enthusiastic once again. "That's the spirit! Think about it and let me know. I believe in both of you, and I think the art world deserves to see what you can create together."

He turns to leave, pausing at the door. "Remember, the best art comes from taking risks. Don't be afraid to step out of your comfort zone, Alex."

With a final nod and a wave, he walks out, leaving behind an air of euphoria and possibility. I look over at Alex, who's still processing the unexpected offer.

"So," I say, playful but sincere, "what do you think? Ready to create something together?"

He lets out a nervous laugh, rubbing the back of his neck. "I don't know, Cato. It feels... big. But maybe that's exactly why I should do it."

I smile, feeling a surge of admiration for him. "That's the right mindset. And remember, you're not doing it alone. We're in this together."

Alex nods, a hint of determination in his eyes. "Okay, then. Let's think about what we could create. I'm up for the challenge."

* * *

I lean back in my chair, still absorbing Richmond's suggestion. The idea of creating a collaborative piece with Alex feels exhilarating and a little daunting all at once. I turn to Alex, who seems to be wrestling with his own medley of jubilation and hesitation.

Before either of us can say anything, Demi chimes in from behind the counter, her eyes bright with enthusiasm. "Guys, this is a fantastic idea!" she calls out. "You have to do it."

I laugh, her energy contagious. "You think so, huh?"

Demi nods vigorously, walking over to join us. "Absolutely! It's not every day you get an opportunity like this. Plus, I think the two of you could come up with something truly amazing. It'd be a waste not to try."

I glance over at Alex, hoping her encouragement has sparked something for him too. "What do you think?"

He lets out a small sigh, looking thoughtful. "I think it's exciting, but… I have no idea how we'd pull it off. Sketches are one thing, but how do you incorporate tattoos into a gallery piece? It's not like we can tattoo a canvas."

I chuckle, imagining it. "True. Putting a tattoo on a canvas wouldn't really have the same impact, would it?"

Demi crosses her arms, leaning against the counter as she considers the challenge. "Okay, so we need to think outside the box. How about using photography? You could create a photo series of the tattoos, showing the whole process."

Alex shakes his head thoughtfully. "Good start, but we need something even more direct. Richmond wants us to make a bold statement that captures both of our styles. It has to be more than just pictures."

I lean forward, trying to think from a different angle. "Right. We want it to feel alive, something people experience, not just see."

The three of us fall silent, each of us lost in thought. I can see Alex's mind working, his gaze darting around as if piecing together a puzzle. Suddenly, his eyes light up, and a grin spreads across his face.

"Wait!" he exclaims, his voice urgent. "What if we don't just put the tattoo on a canvas? What if we make the person the canvas?"

I raise an eyebrow, intrigued. "What do you mean?"

His excitement is contagious as he explains. "What if we tattoo someone—a model, maybe—and they become the artwork? They could pose at the gallery, with the tattoo as the centerpiece, making them a living, breathing part of the piece."

Demi's eyes widen, a huge grin spreading across her face. "Oh my God, that's brilliant! The model would literally be the canvas."

A surge of delight rises in me as the idea sinks in. "Alex, that's... actually genius," I say, admiring his vision. "It's the perfect blend—your sketches and my tattoo work, combined into a living piece of art."

Alex's hesitation melts away, his eyes shining with newfound enthusiasm. "It would be risky, and we'd have to find a model who's up for it, but imagine it—the tattoo as part of a person, not just something on display. It's raw, it's personal, and exactly the kind of statement Richmond loves."

Demi claps her hands together, practically bouncing with excitement. "I love it! It's provocative, it's unique, and it's totally unforgettable."

I nod, the pieces coming together. "We could create a design specifically for the model—something that's both abstract and symbolic, incorporating elements from both of our styles."

Alex is already sketching ideas, his pencil moving quickly across the page. "What about a design representing duality—the merging of two art forms into one cohesive piece? We could use elements of nature mixed with abstract shapes."

I lean over, looking at his rough sketch. "Yes! And we could use the model's body as part of the design, letting it flow naturally with their movements."

Demi nods, eyes wide with elation. "The gallery could feature a live reveal, where the model enters and takes center stage. It would be a powerful moment—people would feel the art, not just see it."

Alex looks up with slight unease in his expression. "But do you think Richmond will actually go for it? It's a pretty unconventional idea."

Confidence surges as I answer. "Are you kidding? Richmond thrives on bold concepts. He's always looking for something that challenges the norm. And this… this is exactly that."

Demi adds, her voice filled with certainty, "Trust me, he'll love it, Alex. This is the kind of idea that gets people talking."

Alex takes a deep breath, his face breaking into a wide grin. "Okay, then. Let's do it."

I reach out, and place a passionate kiss on Alex's lips, "Really?"

"Yeah," Alex smiles. "You convinced me."

Demi chimes in, her voice bubbling with enthusiasm. "This is going to be amazing. I can already see the headlines: 'Eternal Ink Breaks Boundaries with Living Art at the Gallery.'"

* * *

The past couple of weeks at Eternal Ink have been a whirlwind. The collaborative project with Alex has taken on a life of its own, and finding the right model has become our top priority. Demi and I sift through profiles, but the search isn't exactly easy. After all, a tattoo isn't just an accessory—it's a lifelong commitment, something someone will carry with them forever.

Sitting in my chair, flipping through profiles, I feel frustration growing. "We've interviewed almost ten people," I say, shaking my head. "But most of them back out when they hear the part about the tattoo being permanent."

Demi leans against the counter, looking equally exasperated. "Can you blame them? It's not everyday someone signs up to be a living piece of art for a gallery. It's a lot to ask."

I nod, understanding the hesitation. "Yeah, I get it. It's not just about the gallery; it's about carrying this art for the rest of their lives. I wouldn't want someone to regret it down the line."

Just as I'm about to suggest taking a break, the door chime rings. I glance up to see a young woman walk in. She looks to be in her mid-twenties, with shoulder-length brown hair and a slightly worn expression, like she's already faced her share of challenges.

"Hi," she says hesitantly, her voice soft but clear. "I heard you're looking for a model?"

Demi straightens, flashing her usual welcoming smile. "Yes, we are. Come on in, have a seat."

The girl walks over to the chair in front of us, eyes shifting between Demi and me. "I, uh, heard about this from a friend. They said it's for some kind of gallery? And it involves a tattoo?"

I lean forward, keeping my tone gentle but direct. "Yes, that's right. We're planning a collaborative art piece where the tattoo itself becomes part of the exhibit. It's a bold idea, but it's also a lifelong decision. We want to make sure you understand exactly what's involved."

Demi nods, adding, "It's about more than the money. This is going to be a permanent mark on your body, something you'll carry with you forever. We'll make sure it's meaningful and beautiful, but you need to be 100 percent sure."

The girl listens intently, her expression a mix of curiosity and determination. "I get it," she says after a moment. "I've actually thought about getting a tattoo before, but I never really had the money for it. So, I guess this would be... killing two birds with one stone, right?"

Demi and I exchange a quick glance, both gauging her sincerity.

"Yes, in a way," I reply cautiously. "But we don't want you to make this decision just for the money. Tattoos are deeply personal, and this one is going to be designed specifically for the gallery, meaning it's likely to be quite prominent."

She looks thoughtful, gazing at the floor for a moment before meeting our eyes with a steady look. "I understand. I won't lie—money is a big factor right now. But I've made worse decisions in my life, and this one feels like something I can own."

Demi leans forward, her tone serious but kind. "Just be certain. Removing a tattoo can be more painful than getting it, and it's not always fully effective. This design will be large, and we don't want you to regret it a year from now—or even ten years from now."

The girl nods, a hint of a smile appearing. "I appreciate the honesty. But I need the money, and honestly, I like the idea of being part of something bigger. I've always been fascinated by art, and this feels… significant, somehow."

I feel a flicker of hope, seeing the spark in her eyes that says she understands what we're trying to achieve. "Alright," I say, nodding slowly. "We'll need to go through a few more steps —concept discussions, design consultations, and the logistics of the gallery itself. But if you're committed, we'd love for you to be our model."

She smiles, and this time it reaches her eyes. "I'm down. Just let me know when and where, and I'll be there."

Demi stands up, offering her hand. "Sounds great! Go ahead and fill out this application and we'll be in touch once we have the designs ready and the schedule sorted."

The girl shakes both our hands, her grip firm. "Thank you. I look forward to it."

As she heads to the door, I call out one last piece of advice. "We'll get the contract drafted by the time you come back in. Please remember, if at any point you change your mind, just let us know. No hard feelings."

She pauses, turning back with a grateful smile. "I appreciate that. But I think I'm ready for this."

With that, she leaves, the door chime ringing behind her. I turn to Demi, feeling relief. "Well, we finally found someone."

INK & *Intuition*

Demi grins, giving me a playful nudge. "And not just anyone—she seems like the real deal. I think she actually understands what this is about."

I nod, a surge of anticipation filling me. "Yeah, I think so too. Now, we just need to make sure we create something that's worthy of all this effort."

Demi leans back against the counter, her smile turning thoughtful. "You know, Cato, this might be one of the most ambitious projects we've ever worked on."

I can't help but smile. "Yeah, it is. And I think we're ready for it. I'm gonna go call Alex and give him the good news"

* * *

We gather around the large design table in the center of the shop, sketchbooks spread out like a canvas of scattered thoughts and unfinished ideas. There's a feeling of tension—this project is ambitious, and each of us has our own vision of how it should take shape. I can see the determination in both Alex and Demi's eyes, and I know my own matches theirs.

Alex is the first to speak, his voice filled with a quiet enthusiasm. "So, I was thinking… what if we go for a tattoo that covers the entire back? You know, something massive, like a full-back mural. It would be bold, dramatic, and impossible to ignore."

He flips open his sketchbook, revealing an early draft—an intricate blend of swirling patterns, mythical creatures, and abstract shapes. "The back is like a canvas, right? We could tell an entire story with one design."

Demi, leaning over the table with her arms crossed, nods thoughtfully but doesn't seem entirely convinced. "I see where you're coming from, Alex. But what if we approached it differently? Instead of one massive piece, we could create different tattoos on various parts of the body—like a series of interconnected stories. It could be more dynamic that way."

She flips open her own sketchbook, pointing to concepts for arms, legs, and even a subtle design near the collarbone. "Imagine it—an arm representing one part of the theme, a leg symbolizing another, and maybe even a design near the collarbone to tie it all together."

I listen intently, ideas swirling in my mind. Both approaches have merit, but they're radically different. Alex's concept aims to make a singular impact, while Demi's focuses on a diverse, fragmented expression.

"Those are both strong ideas," I say, feeling the weight of the decision settle on me. "But this gallery isn't just about making a statement—it's about changing perceptions."

Alex tilts his head, a curious look crossing his face. "What do you mean?"

I lean back in my chair, searching for the right words. "This project is our chance to create something visually striking and challenge the stigma around tattoos. A lot of people still see tattoos as rebellious, unprofessional, or even dangerous. I want this piece to show that tattoos are art—not just ink, but a form of self-expression that's deeply meaningful."

Demi's eyes light up. "You want the design to be more than just beautiful—you want it to have a purpose."

"Exactly," I agree, nodding. "It has to draw people in, even those who might not normally appreciate tattoo art. It has to be something that breaks barriers."

Both Alex and Demi seem on board, but we still haven't found the right idea.

"So, how do we make that happen?" Alex asks, his voice filled with curiosity.

I rub my chin, feeling the pressure to come up with something that satisfies everyone's vision. The stakes feel higher than ever, and the project's potential is exhilarating, yet daunting. My mind sifts through countless possibilities—traditional styles, abstract designs, modern concepts—but nothing feels quite right.

Then, suddenly, it clicks. Inspiration flashes through my mind like a spark catching fire. I straighten up, feeling a surge of confidence. "Wait... I think I've got it."

Alex and Demi both lean in, their eyes wide with anticipation.

"What is it?" Alex asks, excitement bubbling in his voice.

I take a deep breath, organizing the idea in my head before sharing. "I can't reveal all the details just yet, but what if we create something that's not just seen, but felt? Something that starts as a mystery and unfolds as you move closer to it?"

Demi raises an eyebrow, intrigued. "You mean a design that's multi-layered? Like a hidden message within the art?"

"Sort of," I say, my voice low but full of giddiness. "Think of it like a story—one that only becomes clear as you take in different parts of the body, but still flows together as one cohesive piece. It would be like a riddle in ink, a design that's both simple and complex."

Alex looks amazed, as if the idea is slowly taking shape in his mind. "So, it would draw people in—literally. They'd have to move around to understand it fully."

"Exactly," I say, my voice gaining certainty. "It would be like peeling back layers, revealing the deeper meaning of the piece step by step. It's a metaphor for how people see tattoos too —at first, they might just see ink on skin, but when they look closer, they find the story, the depth, the emotion."

Demi is grinning now, her energy matching mine. "I love it. It's symbolic, it's clever, and it has that mystery factor. But Cato… what's the actual design?"

I can't help but chuckle. "That's the part I want to keep a secret for now. Not even you two are going to know everything until the final stages. Trust me on this—it'll be worth it."

Alex and Demi exchange a glance, both intrigued and slightly frustrated by my cryptic response.

"Alright, Cato," Alex says, a playful smile forming on his lips. "We'll play along. But you better deliver something spectacular."

I grin back, feeling a renewed sense of purpose. "Don't worry. This is going to be something we will never forget."

Demi leans back, letting out a sigh of relief. "Okay then, let's do this. We've got a concept and we've got a team. What more could we ask for?"

"Nothing," I reply, my voice steady with determination. "Let's get to work."

The three of us dive into sketching, the energy in the room bursting with passion. I can't reveal the whole plan yet, but I know one thing for sure—this will be the most challenging and fulfilling project of my career.

twenty-seven
ALEX

September

I pull up a few reference files on my laptop, scrolling through designs that have elements we're considering—swirling abstract patterns, intricate line work, and bursts of color that practically pop off the screen. "Look at this one," I say, turning the screen toward Cato. "The shading here is incredible. It's almost like it's alive."

Cato leans in, his eyes narrowing as he studies the image closely. "Yeah, that's impressive. I like how the lines aren't too rigid. It feels organic."

I nod, feeling a surge of inspiration. "Exactly. I think that's the vibe we're going for, right? Something that feels natural, like it's a part of the skin rather than just ink on it."

He grins, his eyes lighting up with vibrancy. "You're catching on quick."

A heat spreads through my chest at his words, and I can't help but smile. "Well, I've got a pretty good teacher."

We both laugh, the kind of easy, shared laughter that makes the work feel less like work and more like a shared passion. We return to our sketches, pencils scratching across paper as we bring our vision to life. I'm working on a section with abstract shapes, trying to figure out how to make them flow seamlessly into the main design without disrupting its harmony.

Cato is focused on a different part of the design—an intricate pattern that forms the core of the piece. "I think this part needs more depth," he murmurs, adding shadows to the lines. "We want it to feel like it's emerging from the skin, not just sitting on it."

I lean over to peer at his sketch. "It looks amazing so far. I think adding some color gradients here could really make it pop."

He nods thoughtfully. "Good idea. We can blend in shades of blue and green, maybe even a bit of gold to give it a luminous effect."

We pause, staring at our sketches. The designs are evolving, each line and curve bringing us closer to the final piece. After a while, the intensity of the work starts to take a toll.

I stretch my arms over my head, feeling the tension in my shoulders. "Ugh, I need a break."

Cato looks up, his own hand cramping from hours of drawing. "I could use a break too."

Without warning, I grab a pencil and gently poke Cato's arm. "Tag, you're it."

He blinks in surprise, then laughs. "Oh, it's like that, is it?"

Before I know it, we're swatting at each other with our sketch pencils, dodging playful jabs. It's childish, but it feels good to release some tension. We're laughing so hard that I nearly fall off my chair.

"Alright, alright!" I gasp, holding up my hands in surrender. "You win this round."

Cato grins, wiping away a tear of laughter. "I always win, Mitchell."

We both look at each other and slowly lean in for a kiss, and just before our lips meet, Demi appears in the doorway, hands on her hips and a stern look on her face. "You two are supposed to be working, not having a sword fight with your pencils."

Cato straightens up, trying to look serious but failing miserably. "We're just taking a quick break, Demi."

"Uh-huh," she says, arching an eyebrow. "Well, your break is over. Get back to work, or I'll put you both on cleanup duty after the shop closes."

I shoot a mock salute. "Yes, ma'am!"

She shakes her head, a small smile tugging at her lips. "I swear, you two are like school kids sometimes. But keep at it. The design is looking really promising."

With Demi's scolding behind us, we dive back into the work, the playful energy replaced by a renewed focus. We know the design has to be perfect—more than just a tattoo; it's the centerpiece of the exhibition, a representation of our combined creativity.

* * *

The next few days are a blur of sketches, revisions, and discussions on everything from color theory to line thickness. We spend hours fine-tuning the design, making sure every detail is exactly right. Some days, the ideas flow effortlessly, and other times, we hit roadblocks that leave us both frustrated.

"Why isn't this working?" I mutter one evening, staring at a section that doesn't seem to blend with the rest.

Sensing my frustration, Cato leans over to take a closer look. "It's okay, Alex. This is all part of the process. Sometimes, you have to break something down before you can build it back up again."

His words are comforting, and I take a deep breath, feeling the pressure ease. "You're right. Let's try a different approach here. Maybe if we soften the lines and add a bit of texture…"

He nods, his pencil moving in sync with mine as we make adjustments. "Now that's looking better," he says after a while, satisfaction clear in his voice.

Finally, after days of intense work, we step back to look at the finished sketch. It's a masterpiece—bold, intricate, and filled with layers of meaning. The lines flow seamlessly, the colors are perfectly blended, and the design tells a story as much about us as it does about the model who will wear it.

"We did it," I say quietly, a sense of pride swelling in my chest.

Cato smiles, his eyes reflecting the same sense of accomplishment. "Yeah, we did."

We stand there for a moment, just admiring our creation, before Demi walks in and gasps. "Holy shit, you guys… that's stunning."

* * *

About 30 minutes later, the door to Eternal Ink swings open, and in walks the girl. As soon as I see her, a jolt of recognition hits me. Eve Taylor—the girl I met in the apartment building, the one who'd knocked on my door by mistake a few months ago.

"Hi," she says, her voice tinged with nervousness, but I also hear some relief. "Thank you for calling me back."

"Of course," I reply, trying to keep my voice steady despite the surprise I feel. "I didn't expect to see you here, Eve."

She blinks, clearly taken aback that I remember her name. "Oh… it's you. I didn't realize you were part of this."

I nod, managing a small smile. "Yeah, it's a small world, I guess."

"How do you know Cato?" Eve asks.

I laugh shyly and scratch the back of my neck. "Oh… he's my… um…"

"He's my boyfriend." Cato, sensing the awkwardness I feel, never having figured out what we were, steps forward with his usual calm demeanor. "It's good to see you again, Eve. We wanted to talk to you about the exhibition and confirm your participation."

Boyfriend. My heart flutters at the title.

Eve nods quickly, her expression caught between delight and trepidation. "I'm ready. I mean, I hope I am. What do you need from me?"

Cato gestures for her to sit down at the table, his voice gentle but serious. "First, let's talk about the terms and have you sign the contract. You'll be the main feature of this exhibition, and your role is significant. For your participation, you'll receive $50,000."

Eve's eyes widen instantly, her mouth dropping open in shock. "Fifty... thousand?" she repeats, as if trying to confirm she heard correctly.

Cato nods, his tone firm but kind. "Yes, that's correct."

Her eyes well up, and she quickly wipes away a tear that threatens to fall. "I... I can't believe this," she stammers. "This is more money than I ever imagined getting for something like this. I'm truly grateful."

Watching her reaction, I feel a pang of emotion. It's clear that this money means more to her than just financial support—it's a lifeline.

Then she looks back at Cato, a hint of confusion on her face. "Why didn't you mention this amount earlier? I mean, when I first came here, I had no idea it would be this much."

Cato leans back slightly, folding his arms thoughtfully. "I didn't want the amount to be the deciding factor, Eve. This project is deeply personal to both me and Alex, and we wanted to make sure that whoever became part of it did so out of genuine interest. We wanted someone who walked into this shop on their own volition, not just because of a financial incentive."

Eve nods slowly, a faint smile spreading across her face. "That makes sense. Honestly, I would have done it for less. But I'm grateful for your integrity, Cato. It's rare."

Cato gives her a warm, genuine smile. "Thank you, Eve. That means a lot."

I take that moment to pull out the final sketch of the design—the masterpiece we've been working so hard on. "Now," I say, carefully sliding the sketch across the table to her, "this is the design we've created for the exhibition."

Eve's eyes sparkle with curiosity as she reaches for the paper, her fingers trembling slightly. She leans forward, studying the intricate lines and patterns intently. I watch her closely, trying to read her reaction.

A wide smile slowly spreads across her face, her eyes lighting up like fireworks. "This is... this is incredible," she breathes. "I don't know exactly what it is, but it feels... powerful."

I can't help but smile back, pride swelling in my chest. "It's meant to be mysterious," I explain. "The design tells a story, but the story is unique to each person who sees it. That's the beauty of it."

She nods eagerly, her enthusiasm palpable. "I love it. I don't know how to describe it, but I feel connected to it already. I'd be honored to wear this as part of the exhibition."

Cato's eyes lighten as he speaks, his voice sincere. "We're glad to hear that, Eve. This design is about transformation, freedom, and personal expression. We wanted it to mean something to you as much as it does to us."

Eve's gaze shifts between the two of us, her voice filled with gratitude. "Thank you, both of you, for giving me this opportunity."

I feel a warmth settle in my chest, a sense of fulfillment that words can't quite capture. "No, thank you, Eve," I say earnestly. "This project wouldn't be the same without you."

She wipes away a few tears, her smile full of hope. "I promise I won't let you down."

Cato nods, his voice gentle but determined. "We know you won't. This is just the beginning."

* * *

Working on Eve's tattoo is an intense experience, one that goes beyond mere ink and needles. Each session reveals more of her story, and with every line etched onto her skin, we

251

learn about her journey—a journey marked by financial struggles, immigration hurdles, and a relentless determination to create a better life for herself.

"Sometimes," she tells us one afternoon as Cato works on the intricate design spreading across her back, "it feels like the world keeps asking for more and more, even when you have nothing left to give."

Her words strike a chord with me. I've never truly understood the sacrifices someone in her position has to make, but seeing the weight of her struggles in her eyes makes it all too real.

Cato pauses for a moment, his tattoo machine humming softly in the background. "It's hard," he says gently. "But the fact that you're here, doing this, shows strength. You're turning your scars into something beautiful."

Eve smiles at that, her face tempering. "I hope so. I want this tattoo to be more than just ink. I want it to symbolize everything I've survived."

I nod, feeling admiration and empathy. "It will. This design is as much about your past as it is about your future. It's about transformation."

As the final days before the exhibition approach, anticipation grows more palpable. We've poured everything we have into this piece, and now it's time to reveal it to the world.

twenty-eight
ALEX

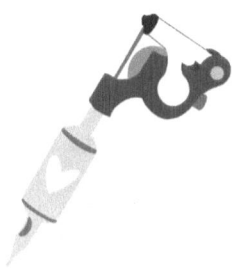

The day of the gallery is finally here. Cato, Demi, Eve, and I get to the venue a solid two hours before the doors officially open. Amelia solidified the venue for Richmond with the help of her bosses.

I look over and notice the nervousness on Eve's face, though she tries her best to keep a brave front.

"Are you okay?" I ask as we step out of the car, the crisp morning air biting at our skin.

Eve adjusts her overcoat, draped over her tattoo like a protective shield. "Yeah," she replies, her voice a little shaky. "Just a bit nervous. I've never done anything like this before."

Cato walks up beside her, placing a reassuring hand on her shoulder. "You're going to be amazing. Just remember, this is your story, your transformation. Own it."

She nods, her eyes filling with determination. "I will. Thank you both—for everything."

Inside the gallery hall, the staff hustles around making last-minute adjustments while other artists set up their displays. The large auditorium at the center is reserved for our showcase, a circular space with dimmed lights that add to the sense of mystery and anticipation.

"You ready for this, babe?" Cato asks, his voice a hybrid of elation and earnestness.

I take a deep breath, feeling a rush of adrenaline. "As ready as I'll ever be."

The three of us move toward the center of the auditorium. Even with her tattoo hidden, Eve's presence feels magnetic. She exudes a quiet power that speaks volumes about her journey.

As the clock ticks closer to opening time, I hear the murmurs of arriving guests growing louder outside. Eve shifts nervously, glancing around the room.

"You're going to be okay," I whisper to her, my voice full of encouragement. "Just remember why you're here. This is your moment."

She nods, taking a deep breath. "Thank you, Alex. I just… I never thought I'd be here, standing in a room like this, with people waiting to see me."

Cato steps in, his voice filled with reassurance. "It's not just about seeing you—it's about seeing your story, your strength. Trust me, people will be moved by it."

Finally, the doors swing open, and I hear the eager chatter of the crowd as they start to enter. The sound washes into the auditorium like a wave, full of curiosity and eagerness.

"Showtime," Cato says quietly, glancing at me with a small, confident smile.

Eve takes a deep breath, closes her eyes for a brief moment, then nods. "I'm ready."

As guests filter in, they walk around admiring various artworks—paintings, sculptures, photographs—but the center stage, marked with a bold sign that reads "Cato Sinclair and Alex Mitchell," remains empty. Curious murmurs ripple through the audience.

"Where's the art piece?" someone whispers.

"Is this by *the* Cato Sinclair? The tattoo artist?" another guest speculates.

Cato watches with unwavering calmness, eyes focused on the empty stage. Eve, with her coat wrapped around her, steps forward, looking nervous but determined. She takes her place under the soft spotlight, and a hush falls over the crowd.

Slowly, she begins to remove her coat. Every second seems to stretch out as she unveils the artwork we spent weeks creating. My heart pounds, caught between anticipation and pride.

The coat falls to the floor, and an audible gasp ripples through the audience. Eve stands tall in a long, midnight-blue, backless dress, her back to the crowd, revealing the massive tattoo that spreads across her entire back—a bird breaking free from a rusted cage, its wings outstretched as it soars upward, defying gravity itself.

The bird is breathtaking, its feathers meticulously detailed, each stroke symbolizing resilience, freedom, and breaking free from chains. Dark shades bleed into lighter hues, giving the impression of movement and transition, while the shattered cage, with bars falling apart, is rendered with stark realism.

The audience stands in awe, their reactions almost immediate. Murmurs of admiration ripple through the crowd.

"Oh my God... it's stunning," someone whispers.

"This is more than a tattoo—it's a statement," a woman in a sleek black dress exclaims, her eyes wide with astonishment.

Eve stands motionless, her shoulders squared, her head held high. I can see the glint of determination in her eyes, bearing not just the tattoo, but the journey it represents.

Cato leans in, his voice low but filled with emotion. "This is it, Alex. This is what we wanted—to break barriers, to make people see beyond the ink."

I nod, unable to look away from Eve. "It's incredible, Cato. More than I ever imagined."

Guests draw closer to the stage, their expressions a blend of curiosity, awe, and respect. A man in a tailored suit approaches, his eyes locked on the tattoo. "What inspired this piece?" he asks, his voice filled with genuine interest.

Cato steps forward, addressing the crowd. "This tattoo is about transformation. It's a story of breaking free from the chains that hold us back—whether they're societal expectations, personal struggles, or the weight of the past. It's about finding freedom, no matter how difficult the journey."

The crowd absorbs his words, nodding thoughtfully. Eve turns her head slightly, a small, proud smile on her lips. "I wanted this to represent my own journey," she says, her voice strong and clear. "I've faced many challenges, but I've never stopped fighting for my freedom. This tattoo is a reminder of that."

Some guests even begin clapping, and a few wipe away tears. One woman, with streaks of gray in her hair, approaches Eve with a soft smile. "It's beautiful, dear. And so are you—for sharing this with all of us."

Eve's smile widens, her eyes glistening. "Thank you," she says, her voice filled with gratitude.

Applause grows, filling the hall with a sense of unity and appreciation. I feel a lump rise in my throat, fighting to keep my emotions in check. This is more than a gallery; it's a triumph of the human spirit, captured through art.

Turning to Cato, I whisper, "You did it, Cato. You really fuckin' did it."

He looks at me, his eyes reflecting the same sense of fulfillment. "No, Alex... we did it. This was a team effort, through and through."

I smile, the satisfaction in my chest undeniable. "Yeah. And it's only the beginning."

* * *

The gallery is winding down, but the energy in the room remains electric. Guests mill about, some chatting animatedly about the pieces they have seen, while others gather near the auction platform, eagerly waiting for the final event of the night.

F. A. SENG

I stand beside Cato, feeling a mix of exhaustion and exhilaration. The gallery is a huge success, with people chirping over Eve's tattoo and the story behind it. As the auction begins, I watch as various artworks are presented, one after another. The bids start modestly, with pieces going for $1,000 or $2,000. Then, a stunning sculpture is auctioned for $213,600, drawing gasps and applause from the crowd.

As the applause dies down, Cato steps forward, motioning for Eve to join him. She looks uncertain at first, but I give her a reassuring nod, and she slowly makes her way to the stage. The guests grow quiet, curious to see what Cato has to say.

Cato's voice booms over the microphone, confident yet sincere. "Ladies and gentlemen, thank you for your incredible generosity tonight. It's a privilege to share this art with you, and I'm grateful for the support you've shown."

He pauses for a moment, then gestures toward Eve, who stands by his side, her hands clasped nervously. "I want to take a moment to talk about Eve," Cato continues, his voice filled with emotion. "Her story is a profound inspiration for both Alex and I. The tattoo you've seen tonight isn't just ink on skin—it's a representation of her resilience, her journey, and her courage."

The crowd is silent, captivated by Cato's words. I can see tears forming in Eve's eyes, but she keeps her gaze steady, her chin lifted with a sense of pride.

Cato takes a deep breath before continuing, "Now, as you know, we can't exactly auction off a tattoo. It's a part of Eve, something she carries with her always. But what we can do is pool together our appreciation for her bravery, for sharing such an intimate part of herself tonight."

The guests seem intrigued, a ripple of curiosity passing through the crowd.

"I'd like to invite all of you," Cato says, his voice resonating with sincerity, "to contribute whatever you feel this moment has meant to you. Every dollar donated tonight will go directly to Eve. This isn't about buying art—it's about showing support for someone who has given so much of herself, not just to us, but to the spirit of this gallery."

Eve's eyes widen, her hand flying to her mouth in shock. "I… I didn't know about this," she whispers, looking up at Cato, her voice trembling. "I can't believe this."

Cato leans closer to her, his voice gentle. "You deserve this, Eve. You've shared something incredibly personal with everyone here tonight. Let them share a bit of their gratitude with you."

Richmond takes over the microphone, a warm smile on his face. "Alright, folks, let's open this up. Remember, every contribution, big or small, counts. Let's show some love."

The bidding starts modestly, with guests raising their paddles to pledge $500, then $1,000. The numbers rise quickly, with more and more people contributing.

"$3,000," one man calls out.

"$5,000," a woman adds from the back.

The excitement builds, the crowd growing more animated with each bid. Eve struggles to hold back her tears, her eyes darting between the generous guests and Cato, who stands beside her, offering silent support.

Then, a middle-aged man in a sharp suit raises his paddle. "$13,000," he announces confidently, drawing a collective gasp from the audience.

Eve's hand flies to her chest, her breath hitching. "Oh my God," she whispers, her voice barely audible. "This is… this is unbelievable."

I feel a lump in my throat as I watch the bids continue to climb. The amount quickly reaches $50,000, then $80,000, and by the time it passes $100,000, the room is buzzing with excitement.

"$183,000," someone calls out, pushing the total to a staggering amount. The crowd erupts in applause, some people wiping away tears, others clapping enthusiastically.

Eve is now openly sobbing, unable to contain the flood of emotions. I rush to her side, placing a comforting arm around her shoulders. "It's okay," I whisper. "You deserve this, every bit of it."

She turns to me, her eyes brimming with gratitude. "I… I don't know how to thank you, Alex. This will cover all of my debts and then some. I'll be debt-free for the first time in 12 years."

Her words hit me like a punch to the gut, and I feel tears welling up in my own eyes. "Eve, you've earned this. Your story, your strength—it inspired everyone here tonight."

Cato steps closer, his eyes filled with pride. "This is more than just an auction, Eve. This is a celebration of you—your resilience, your bravery. You're not alone anymore."

She nods, wiping her eyes with the back of her hand. "I… I can't believe this is real. Thank you. Thank you so much."

As the final amount of $210,000 is announced, the crowd rises to their feet, giving Eve a standing ovation. The sound is overwhelming, a combination of clapping, cheers, and shouts of encouragement. Eve stands there, her hands pressed to her chest, tears streaming down her face as she tries to absorb the love and support that surrounds her.

As the crowd begins to disperse, Richmond turns to face Cato and I. His face is beaming with pride and excitement.

"You two seriously are the best," he smiles. "I can't thank you enough for being here tonight. Your contribution to this gallery has been nothing short of extraordinary."

Cato shakes his hand firmly. "Richmond, we should be thanking you. This opportunity means the world to us."

I nod in agreement. "Yeah, we couldn't have done this without your support. Thank you for believing in us."

Richmond's eyes sparkle with genuine appreciation. "The pleasure was all mine. What you've done here tonight, with Eve's piece... it's revolutionary. You've changed lives today, gentlemen. I hope you realize that."

We exchange a few more words of gratitude before Richmond is pulled away by other guests eager to speak with him.

As the last of the attendees filter out of the gallery, Cato, Demi, Eve, and I find ourselves alone in the now-quiet space. The energy of the night still hums in the air around us.

"I can't believe it's over," Demi says, breaking the silence. "It feels like we've been working towards this forever."

Eve, still looking a bit shell-shocked from the auction, nods in agreement. "I... I don't even know how to process everything that's happened."

Cato grins, throwing an arm around my shoulders. "I say we process it with a celebration. Who's up for some late-night pancakes?"

I laugh, feeling the tension of the evening start to melt away. "Pancakes? Really?"

"Hey, don't knock it till you've tried it," Cato defends. "There's this great 24-hour diner just a few blocks from here. Best pancakes in the city."

Demi's eyes light up. "Oh, I know the place! Count me in."

We all turn to Eve, who still seems a bit overwhelmed. "What do you say, Eve?" I ask gently. "Feel like joining us for a very unconventional celebration?"

A slow smile spreads across her face. "You know what? After tonight, pancakes sound perfect."

As we make our way out of the gallery, the weight of our accomplishment settles in. We've done something incredible tonight, something that will have a lasting impact. Now, we're going to celebrate it in the most wonderfully ordinary way possible.

F. A. SENG

twenty-nine
CATO

October

I'm hiking through the mountain forest with Alex, surrounded by the peaceful sounds of nature. It's refreshing to see his awe at the scenery, especially when he mentions he's never explored these trails before, despite living in Metro Heights for six months. I share with him how I often come here alone to find peace and clear my head.

Our conversation takes a playful turn when I tease Alex about the possibility of encountering mountain lions. His initial nervousness is amusing, but it quickly gives way to laughter as he realizes I'm just messing with him. We pause by a river to watch cranes hunting, and I'm pleased to see Alex appreciating the natural rhythm of the wilderness.

INK & *Intuition*

It's heartwarming to hear Alex reflect on the unexpected joy of hiking with a tattoo artist. I can't help but joke about his caution regarding wildlife. As we continue our hike, I'm struck by how much I'm enjoying this day with Alex, and how this place seems to bring out the best in both of us. There's a growing connection between us in this serene setting, and I find myself looking forward to more moments like this.

I lead Alex through the winding path that veers off from the main trail. It's a narrow, slightly overgrown track, and I can see the curiosity on his face as he tries to guess where I'm taking him. The thick canopy above us creates a dappled effect, the sunlight breaking through in patches.

"Where exactly are we going, Cato?" Alex asks, his voice filled with anticipation.

"You'll see," I reply, a grin tugging at my lips. "It's a bit of a surprise."

Alex's eyes narrow playfully. "Should I be worried? Or is this your way of trying to get me eaten by that mountain lion we talked about?"

I chuckle at his paranoia. "Don't worry, you're safe. It's just a little detour to a place that's close to my heart."

After a few hundred meters, the trees clear, and we step into a small clearing. In the middle of it stands a medium-sized cottage, surrounded by the dense forest and a small stream that flows gently nearby. The sound of birds chirping fills the air, blending perfectly with the soft gurgle of the stream.

Alex's eyes widen as he takes in the sight. "Wow… this is incredible, Cato."

I smile, feeling elated as we approach the cottage. "Here we are," I say, gesturing towards the rustic structure nestled among the trees. "My little hideaway from the world. Found this place a while back when I was looking for somewhere to recharge. It's become my favorite spot to disconnect and just… be."

Alex looks genuinely impressed, his eyes roaming over the rustic exterior of the cottage. "I had no idea you had a place like this. It's like something out of a fairytale."

I nod, leading him closer to the front door. "It's not fancy, but it's got everything I need. Come on in—I'll give you the grand tour."

We step inside, and I watch as Alex's eyes light up, taking in the interior. The cottage is cozy yet elegant, draped with white and blue curtains that sway gently in the breeze from the open windows. The furniture is Victorian style, each piece carefully chosen to match the vibe of the place—a little bit of vintage charm and modern comfort.

"Whoa," Alex says, his voice low with awe. "This is… beautiful, Cato. I never imagined you'd be into Victorian décor."

I laugh, closing the door behind us. "Surprised? I like to keep people guessing."

He walks over to one of the plush armchairs, running his hand over the fabric. "It's like stepping back in time. You've got a real eye for design."

I shrug modestly. "I guess my artistic side extends beyond tattoos. I wanted this place to feel different, like a completely separate world from the city."

He nods, taking it all in. "You succeeded. It's so peaceful here."

I lead him to the center of the cottage, where a wooden ladder leads up to a small loft area about seven feet above the ground. The loft of the structure is designed as a bedroom, with a large, plush bed covered in soft linens. Above the bed is a glass ceiling, offering a perfect view of the blue sky.

"This is my favorite part," I say, gesturing to the loft. "On clear nights, you can see the stars right from the bed. It's pretty magical."

Alex climbs up the ladder, his movements slow and curious. He reaches the loft and lies down on the bed, staring up at the glass ceiling. "This is amazing," he says, his voice filled with wonder. "I can't believe you get to wake up to this view."

I climb up after him, sitting on the edge of the bed. "It's my little piece of heaven," I admit. "Sometimes, when everything gets too overwhelming, I come here, lie down, and just watch the sky. It's like all the stress just melts away."

Alex turns to face me, his eyes softening. "I can see why. It's got a certain magic to it, like it was made for moments like this."

I feel a sudden urge to open up, the intimacy of the setting making me feel comfortable enough to share more of my past. "You know, when I first bought this place, I wasn't sure if it was the right decision. It felt like I was running away from something, trying to escape. Over time, I realized it was about finding peace—real, deep peace."

He nods, his gaze thoughtful. "I get that. I think we all need a place like this, where we can just be ourselves, away from everything."

I look into his eyes, feeling a surge of emotion. "I'm glad you're here, Alex. I've never really shared this place with anyone else before."

His expression relaxes further, a small smile tugging at the corners of his lips. "Really? I'm honored, Cato."

I laugh lightly, trying to lighten the mood. "Well, don't get too comfortable. You still owe me a cooking session. There's a tiny kitchen downstairs, and I've got some ingredients stored away. Up for making lunch?"

He grins, a mischievous glint in his eyes. "Absolutely. Only if you help me chop the veggies."

"Deal," I agree, feeling a sense of joy that is both simple and profound.

We climb back down from the loft and make our way to the kitchen area, which is small but functional. We set about preparing lunch, our movements synchronized as we chop vegetables, stir sauces, and share stories. The cottage fills with the smell of freshly cooked food and the sound of our laughter.

As we sit down to eat by the window, with the forest stretching out beyond us, I realize that this is one of those moments I'll remember for a long time. It's more than just a hike, more than just a cottage—it's a chance to share a part of my world with someone who is becoming the most important person to me.

F. A. SENG

The air inside the cottage is comforting, carrying a sense of intimacy that feels almost tangible. As the evening sun dips below the treetops, its golden light filters through the glass ceiling above, casting shadows across the loft. Alex and I lie side by side on the bed, our bodies close enough that I can feel the heat radiating from his skin.

For a long moment, we simply lay there in comfortable silence, our hands resting between us, fingers lightly brushing. I turn my head to look at him, his profile soft in the fading light. There's a certain vulnerability in his expression, a quiet openness that makes my heart ache in a way I didn't expect.

I reach over, my fingers finding his, and gently intertwine our hands. Alex turns his head toward me, his emerald eyes meeting mine with a mixture of uncertainty and unmistakable desire. There's a palpable electricity in the air, a sense that something profound has shifted between us.

"You want this?" I whisper, my voice husky with anticipation.

Alex's lips curve into a subtle smile. "Yeah. I've never been more certain of anything," he murmurs as he begins removing his clothes.

I lean in, my lips brushing against the sensitive skin of his neck. A shiver runs through him, and I feel it reverberate through my own body. My hands move to his shoulders, kneading the taut muscles there.

"God, that feels amazing," Alex sighs, his eyes fluttering closed.

He rolls onto his stomach, and I trail kisses down his spine, my tongue tracing each vertebra, eliciting quiet gasps from Alex. As I reach the small of his back, I pause, admiring the two dimples just above the swell of his buttocks.

"You're gorgeous," I breathe, my hands cupping the firm globes of his ass.

Alex lets out a breathy chuckle. "Says the gorgeous one."

I grin against his skin, then continue my journey downward. I push his legs apart gently, my fingers skimming through the cleft of his ass. The moment I brush against his

265

entrance, Alex lets out a low, guttural moan that sends a jolt of electricity straight to my cock.

"Oh god," he gasps, his hips lifting slightly off the bed.

I replace my fingers with my mouth, my tongue swirling patterns around his sensitive flesh. Alex writhes beneath me, his fingers clutching at the sheets.

"Cato," he pants, "I want to see you."

I give him a questioning look, and almost as if he can read my mind, he begins undoing the button on my jeans and pulling them down.

I look down and see Alex mapping my body with his eyes, pausing briefly to study each area of skin. The sight sends a jolt of desire through my veins.

I grab hold of Alex's waist and guide him onto his back. I get on my knees and position myself at his entrance. The anticipation is almost unbearable, but I force myself to pause.

"Are you ready?" I ask, needing to be absolutely certain.

Alex nods, then seems to think better of it. "Yes," he says firmly. "Just… go slow? I've heard this can hurt."

I lean down, pressing a tender kiss to his shoulder. "I promise you, Alex, I won't hurt you. Ever."

I reach for the lube, coating myself generously. Then, with utmost care, I begin to push inside. His tight heat envelops me, and I have to grit my teeth to maintain control.

"Fuck, you feel so good" I whisper as I sink deeper.

When I'm fully seated, Alex turns his head, his face flushed and eyes wide with wonder. "I thought this would hurt a lot more," he admits.

I smile, brushing a lock of hair from his forehead. "I told you, I'm not going to hurt you. I'll always be gentle with you, Alex."

Slowly, I begin to move. The sensation is indescribable, and judging by the sounds Alex is making, he feels the same way.

"Cato," he moans, "it's… you feel… fuck you're so big."

"I know," I pant, picking up the pace slightly. "You're incredible, Alex. So tight, so perfect."

Our bodies move together in a rhythm as old as time itself. Alex's legs wrap around mine, pulling me closer. Our hands find each other again, fingers interlacing as I brace myself above him.

The room fills with the sound of our labored breathing, punctuated by moans and whispered endearments. I can feel the tension building, coiling tighter and tighter in my lower abdomen.

"Alex," I groan, "I'm close. So close."

"Me too," he gasps. "Don't stop. Please, don't stop."

I thrust harder, deeper, and Alex cries out in ecstasy. His body clenches around me, and it's my undoing. With a final, powerful thrust, I topple over the edge, Alex following right behind me.

As we come down from our high, I carefully withdraw and roll to the side. Alex immediately turns to face me, his expression one of awe and contentment.

"That was…" he starts, then shakes his head, seemingly at a loss for words.

I chuckle softly. "Yeah, it was."

We lay in comfortable silence for a few moments before Alex speaks again. "You know, I didn't think it was possible, but…" He glances down, and I follow his gaze to see that he's already half-hard again.

I raise an eyebrow, a smirk playing on my lips. "Round two?"

Alex grins, a mischievous glint in his eye. "Give me a minute."

In response, I roll him onto his stomach, eliciting a surprised laugh that quickly turns into a moan as I begin to worship his body all over again.

* * *

The cottage is silent, except for the soft sound of our breathing and the faint rustle of the sheets. The radiance of our bodies, still damp with sweat, lingers in the air. Alex and I lie side by side, the tangled sheets covering us, our legs entwined beneath them.

The world outside feels distant, as if it exists on another planet altogether. Here, in this small loft with the glass ceiling above, everything feels still. Peaceful. Real.

I shift slightly, reaching out to pull Alex closer, feeling the rise and fall of his chest against mine. His skin is warm, his body relaxed, but there is a vulnerability in the way he lays on me—a sense that he is baring more than just his body.

"You okay?" I whisper softly, my hand gently rubbing his back.

He nods, but there is a hesitation in his eyes. "Yeah, I'm okay… it's just… I've never felt this way before."

I smile, pressing a light kiss on his forehead. "Me neither, Alex."

We lie in silence for a while, my hand tracing gentle patterns on his arm. It's Alex who breaks the silence, his voice low and filled with a mixture of pain and relief.

"You know, Cato, growing up wasn't easy for me."

I feel a sudden swell in my chest, sensing where this conversation might be headed. I don't want to push him, but I also want him to know he can share whatever he needs to.

"What do you mean?" I ask gently, my eyes searching his.

He swallows hard, his voice cracking slightly. "I grew up in a very conservative household. My parents were devoted Christians, and there were strict views on… everything, really. But especially on being gay."

I tighten my grip around him, feeling a protective urge rise within me. "I'm so sorry you had to go through that."

Alex's eyes grow distant, as if he is reliving the memories. "It was tough. I remember when I was around twelve, I started feeling different. I didn't really understand it then, but I knew I wasn't like the other boys in my church group."

He pauses, his voice thick with emotion. "My cousins noticed too. They'd tease me, call me names, make jokes about how I'd never have a 'real' family. It hurt, but I kept it all inside because I was too afraid to say anything."

My heart aches for him, imagining a young Alex feeling so isolated in his own home. I reach out, gently wiping away a tear that has escaped his eye. "I can't imagine how hard that must have been. You didn't deserve any of that."

He nods slowly, his eyes brimming with more tears. "The worst part was the pastor," he continues, his voice trembling. "When my parents found out about me, they took me to him. He tried to… 'purify' me, to drive out the so-called 'evil spirits.' It was terrifying, Cato. I felt like I was drowning."

The rawness in his voice is palpable, and I can feel my own eyes stinging. I pull him closer, wrapping my arms tightly around him. "Fuck, Alex… I'm so sorry," I whisper, my voice filled with anger and compassion. "You should have been loved for who you are, not made to feel like you needed fixing."

Alex buries his face in my chest, his body shaking with silent sobs. I feel his grip on me tighten, as if he is holding on for dear life. I respond by holding him even closer, trying to pour all my love and reassurance into that embrace.

"I'm here," I murmur into his hair, my lips brushing against his temple. "You don't have to carry that pain alone anymore. You're safe with me, Alex. You're perfect just the way you are."

He lifts his head, his eyes searching mine. There is so much emotion there—pain, relief, and a desperate longing for acceptance. "I've never felt this free before," he admits, tears streaming down his cheeks. "For the first time in my life, I feel like I can just be me."

I feel my own tears spill over as I hold his gaze. "You don't have to hide here, Alex. Not with me. I want you to be exactly who you are."

He lets out a shaky laugh, his tears mixing with a hesitant smile. "I didn't think I'd ever hear someone say that to me."

I lean in, pressing a tender kiss on his lips, tasting the salt of his tears. "I'll keep saying it, every single day if you need to hear it."

We lie there, our foreheads touching, our breaths mingling in the quiet stillness of the loft. The weight of his past feels heavy, but I can also feel a sense of lightness in the air—a release, a healing that has begun.

"Thank you, Cato," Alex whispers, his voice raw with emotion. "Thank you for seeing me, for accepting me."

I smile, brushing a strand of hair away from his forehead. "It's not hard to see you, Alex. You're pretty amazing."

He blushes, the faintest hint of color creeping into his cheeks. "You know, I always thought this feeling was something that happened to other people. I never imagined I'd find it... here, like this."

I feel my heart swell at his words, joy and gratitude filling me. "Well, you've got it now. And I'm not going anywhere."

He smiles then, a real, genuine smile that lights up his face. "Good," he says simply. "Because I'm not letting you go."

We lie in silence for a while longer, our bodies pressed close, the pain of the past slowly giving way to the brightness of the present. There is something profoundly healing in that moment—a sense of belonging, of acceptance, and of a love that is as raw as it is real.

thirty
CATO

The engine of my Range Rover hums steadily as we merge onto the highway. Beside me, Alex sits with a mix of excitement and nerves, his hands fiddling with the strap of his bag. As we drive towards Alex's childhood home in Minnesota, I can sense his growing anxiety. We still have an eight-hour journey , which gives us plenty of time to talk about what to expect.

"So, tell me more about your mom," I prompt, trying to prepare myself.

Alex sighs, running a hand through his hair. "She's... very religious. Bakes cookies, volunteers at the church, you know the type. She's also pretty set in her ways, especially when it comes to... well, this kind of thing."

I nod, understanding the underlying tension. "You mean bringing a guy home?"

"Exactly," Alex confirms. "It's not something she's used to. Her faith is a big part of her life, and I'm not sure how she'll react to us."

* * *

As we near Priarstone, Alex's hometown, the landscape shifts to reflect a more traditional, religious community. Church steeples rise in the distance, and modest homes dot the quiet streets.

We pull up to a neat two-story house with a white picket fence. Before we even reach the porch, the front door opens. Alex's mother stands there, a tight, expectant smile on her face. Her eyes darting between us, lingering on me with some confusion and concern that speaks volumes about the challenge we're about to face.

"Alex!" she calls, her voice a little too high-pitched.

"Hi, Mom," Alex replies, trying to keep his tone steady as he leans in for a quick hug.

She barely reciprocates, her gaze quickly shifting back to me. "And you must be… Cato?"

I step forward with my warmest smile. "Yes, ma'am. It's nice to finally meet you."

"Nice to meet you too," she says, her voice holding a hint of uncertainty as she shakes my hand briefly.

Her eyes are searching, as if she is trying to fit a piece of a puzzle that simply doesn't belong. She looks back at Alex, her expression unreadable. "Why don't you both come in? Dinner's almost ready."

We follow her into the living room, which is filled with religious memorabilia—crosses on the walls, framed Bible verses, and a large family Bible prominently displayed on the coffee table. I can feel Alex's tension radiating off him, and I try to keep my own nerves in check.

His father emerges from the kitchen, wiping his hands on a towel. He is a tall, broad-shouldered man with a more open expression than his wife. "Welcome, Cato," he says, offering a firm handshake.

"Thank you, sir," I reply, acknowledging the faint trace of hospitality.

As we all gather around the dining table, Alex's mother sets down a platter of roast chicken, the aroma filling the room. It is a homey setting, but the atmosphere feels anything but comfortable. We all sit down, and there is an awkward silence as the meal is served.

Trying to ease the tension, I say, "The food smells amazing, Mrs. Mitchell."

She gives me a brief smile, her eyes flickering to Alex. "Thank you, Cato. It's one of our family's favorites. And please, call me Helen."

As we start eating, Alex's mother suddenly turns to him, her tone more inquisitive than before. "So, Alex, when is... the girl arriving? I thought you were bringing someone special."

Alex's fork clatters against his plate, and I feel a jolt of unease pass between us. His face turns pale, but he clears his throat and says, "Mom... Dad... I want to introduce you to Cato properly."

I can see his mother's confusion deepen, her brows furrowing. "Yes, we know Cato is here, but when is the girl coming?"

I can feel the knot in Alex's stomach from the way his shoulders tense. He takes a deep breath, his voice slightly shaky but determined. "Mom, there is no girl. Cato... Cato is the one I wanted you to meet."

The air seems to freeze, and his mother's expression shifts from confusion to shock. She sets her fork down slowly, her mouth slightly open. "What do you mean, Alex?" she asks, her voice full of disbelief and rising anger.

Alex's voice grows firmer. "Mom, Cato is... my boyfriend. We're together."

The room falls silent, the only sound is the faint ticking of the wall clock. His mother's face turns an alarming shade of red, and her eyes widen with fury. "What do you mean, 'together'? Alex, this is absurd!"

I keep my eyes on Alex, trying to offer silent support. He meets my gaze briefly before turning back to his mother. "Mom, I know this isn't what you expected, but this is who I am. I'm in a relationship with Cato."

Her hand shakes as she points toward me. "But he's... he's a man! And a... tattoo artist? How could you do this to us, Alex? To our family?"

Alex's father tries to intervene, his tone calm but firm. "Now, let's not jump to conclusions, honey. We should at least try to understand—"

"Understand what?" she snaps, her voice breaking. "That our son is living in sin? That he's chosen this lifestyle?"

I feel a deep sense of guilt, like I'm intruding in a family drama that has been building for years. I want to say something, to try to ease the situation, but I'm not sure what words could possibly make things better.

Alex leans forward, his voice low but steady. "Mom, it's not a 'lifestyle.' It's who I am. It's always been who I am. And I want you to meet Cato, not as a stranger, but as someone I care for deeply."

His mother's face is a mask of hurt and anger, her eyes welling up with unshed tears. "I raised you to be a good Christian, Alex. I never thought I'd see this day. I never thought I'd have to face this shame."

Tears spring to Alex's eyes, and his voice cracks. "I'm still the same person, Mom. I'm still your son."

The room seems to spin with tension, the weight of old beliefs clashing against a reality that is impossible to ignore. His mother stands up abruptly, her chair scraping loudly against the floor. "I... I can't do this right now," she says, her voice trembling. "I need to be alone."

Without another word, she walks out of the room, leaving an unbearable silence in her wake.

Alex's father rubs his temples, clearly struggling to find the right words. "Give her some time," he says quietly. "This is a lot for her to take in."

Alex nods, wiping his eyes. "I know, Dad. I just… I just wish she could try to understand."

His father places a hand on his shoulder, his voice heavy with emotion. "I know, son. I'll do my best to help her see that."

I reach out, placing a comforting hand on Alex's arm. He looks at me, his tear-filled eyes filled with pain and gratitude.

* * *

The front door closes behind us with a heavy thud, and the cool evening air hits me like a shock after the suffocating tension inside the house. Alex and I stand on the porch for a moment, the silence stretching between us, the weight of the confrontation still pressing down on our shoulders. I turn to look at him, his face flushed and his eyes filled with hurt.

He forces a small, weak smile. "Hey, that wasn't so bad, right? At least Dad didn't throw a Bible at us."

I can't help letting out a small laugh, but it is one tinged with sadness. "You don't have to make jokes, Alex. I know that wasn't easy."

He sighs, his shoulders slumping. "I just wanted it to go differently, you know? I thought maybe… maybe she'd try to understand, even just a little."

I reach out, placing a hand on his shoulder. "I know you did. You were brave in there, Alex. It's not easy to face that kind of rejection, especially from family."

He looks away, blinking rapidly as if trying to stop the tears from spilling over. "I just feel like I disappointed them… like I've always been a disappointment."

I feel a surge of anger at the injustice of it all, the way he is made to feel guilty for simply being himself. "No, Alex. You didn't disappoint anyone. You were honest, and that takes a lot of courage. They're the ones who need time to see that."

He turns back to me, his eyes filled with a mix of gratitude and vulnerability. "Thank you, Cato. I don't know what I'd do without you right now."

I pull him into a tight embrace, feeling his body tremble against mine. "You're not alone in this, okay? We'll face whatever comes, together."

He nods into my shoulder, taking a few deep breaths to steady himself. "I know, but it still hurts. It hurts more than I thought it would."

I hold him for a moment longer, then gently pull back, looking into his eyes. "Come on," I say softly. "Let's get out of here for a bit. I can get us a hotel for the night."

We walk silently to my Range Rover, and I drive a short distance down the road until we reach a small clearing by the edge of a field. It is quiet here, the only sound is the faint rustling of leaves in the evening breeze. I park the car, and we get out, both of us instinctively seeking a place that feels safe and away from prying eyes.

We find a large oak tree that stands alone in the open field, its branches stretching wide like a protective canopy. I lean against the trunk, watching as Alex paces back and forth in front of me, his frustration evident in every step.

"I don't know why I thought it would be different," he says suddenly, his voice breaking. "I've been dealing with this my whole life—trying to be someone I'm not, just to make them happy."

I step closer, my eyes never leaving his. "You don't have to be anyone but yourself, Alex. Not for them, not for anyone."

His eyes meet mine, a flicker of hope with lingering pain. "I know, but it's hard, Cato. It's so damn hard."

Without thinking, I close the gap between us, reaching up to cup his face with both hands. "You've been stronger than anyone I know. You faced them, even when you knew it might go badly. You're brave, Alex. So damn brave."

The vulnerability in his gaze is overwhelming, and I feel a deep, primal need to protect him, to show him that he is loved despite everything. I lean in slowly, giving him the chance to pull away if he wants to. But he doesn't.

Our lips meet, tentatively at first, the kiss soft and filled with unspoken words—of comfort, of reassurance, of love. But then, something shifts. The kiss deepens, growing more urgent, more passionate, as if we are both trying to pour all the pent-up emotions into that one moment.

I feel his arms wrap around me, pulling me closer, his fingers digging into my back as if he is afraid to let go. I respond in kind, my hands tangled in his hair, holding him as close as possible. It is a kiss filled with raw need, the kind that blurs the line between comfort and desire.

I break the kiss for a brief second, my breath coming in ragged gasps. "I love you, Alex," I whisper, the words slipping out without hesitation.

His eyes widen, shimmering with unshed tears that catch the light like tiny, fragile stars. A tremble runs through his chest as he draws in a shaky breath, the weight of the moment pressing against the air between us. "I love you too, Cato," he says, his voice breaking with raw sincerity. The words spill out, not rushed, but deliberate, as though they've been waiting for the right moment to escape. His gaze locks with mine, an unspoken promise reflected in the depth of his expression, vulnerable yet resolute, as though speaking those words has simultaneously set him free and tethered us closer together.

The words hang in the air, as real and tangible as the stars beginning to appear in the darkening sky above. We kiss again, this time slower, savoring the moment, the sweetness of it, the promise it holds.

thirty-one

CATO

The sun shines brightly the next morning, casting an inviting glow over Alex's hometown. The tension from yesterday has eased, and I can see a glimmer of relief in Alex's eyes as we stroll through the familiar streets. He seems lighter, more relaxed.

As we walk past an old red-brick building, he stops suddenly and gestures with a wide grin. "This is my school," he says, his voice filled with nostalgia.

I look up at the modest building with faded paint and a large playground in front. It's charming in a small-town kind of way. "Did you cause trouble here, or were you a good student?" I ask with a playful nudge.

He shakes his head, chuckling. "I wasn't that bad. Just a little mischievous. I got caught sneaking into the teacher's lounge once, trying to grab some extra snacks."

I raise an eyebrow, impressed. "Stealing snacks from the teachers? Now that's bold."

"Well, when you're twelve and hungry, you'll do anything for an extra bag of chips," he replies, grinning.

We continue walking, the old buildings giving way to open fields, and eventually, we find ourselves at the entrance of a sprawling apple orchard on the edge of town. The sign above the entrance is a little worn, but it's colorful and cheerful, with painted apples and trees decorating it.

"I used to come here all the time as a kid," Alex says, his eyes lighting up. "It's a bit silly, but it's fun."

"Hey, I'm always up for silly," I reply with a grin. "Lead the way."

We buy our tickets and walk in, greeted by rows upon rows of apple trees, their branches heavy with ripe fruit. The sweet scent of apples fills the air, mingling with the earthy smell of the orchard.

"Ah, to be young and surrounded by apples," I say with mock wistfulness, making Alex laugh.

We grab baskets and start wandering through the rows of trees. Alex reaches up to pluck a particularly red apple from a nearby branch. "These Honeycrisps are my favorite," he says, offering it to me.

I take a bite, savoring the crisp sweetness. "Mmm, I can see why. It's delicious."

We spend the next hour picking apples, competing to see who can find the biggest or most perfectly shaped ones. At one point, I playfully toss an apple to Alex, who catches it with surprising dexterity.

"Nice catch!" I exclaim. "You've got some hidden talents there."

He grins, tossing it back. "Years of practice. We used to have apple-throwing contests here when we were kids."

As we continue through the orchard, we come across an old tractor set up as a photo opportunity. "Oh, we have to take a picture here," I insist, pulling out my phone.

Alex laughs but obliges, climbing up onto the tractor seat. I snap a few photos, then join him for a selfie, both of us grinning widely with our baskets of apples.

"You know," I say as we hop down, "I think we should make apple picking an annual tradition. It'd be fun to come back here every fall."

"Yeah?" Alex asks, his expression softening. "I'd like that."

We make our way to the orchard's small cider press, where we can watch apples being turned into fresh cider. The rich, sweet smell is intoxicating.

"Want to try some?" I ask, nodding towards the samples they're offering.

"Definitely," Alex replies, his eyes bright with anticipation.

We each take a cup of the fresh cider, clinking them together in a little toast before taking a sip. The flavor is incredible – sweet and tart and unmistakably apple.

"This is amazing," I say, savoring the taste. "We should get some to take home."

Alex nods enthusiastically. "Absolutely. It'll be a nice reminder of today."

As we finish our cider and prepare to leave with our bounty of apples and a jug of cider, I can't help but feel a balminess that has nothing to do with the autumn sun. This simple day at the orchard, seeing Alex so relaxed and happy in his hometown, has been perfect.

"You know," I say, wrapping an arm around his shoulders as we walk back to the car, "I think I'm starting to see the charm of small-town life."

Alex leans into me, a contented smile on his face. "Yeah? Even with all the quiet and the lack of tattoo shops?"

I laugh, giving him a gentle squeeze. "Even with that. As long as there are apple orchards and you, I think I could get used to it."

* * *

The sun begins to set over Alex's hometown, casting an orange glow over the small diner where we've decided to stop for dinner. The neon sign flickers in the window, the faint hum of old country songs playing from the jukebox in the corner. Alex seems distant, his eyes occasionally drifting toward the window, as if he's seeing something far beyond the quiet street outside.

"Are you okay?" I ask softly, reaching across the table to touch his hand.

He looks up at me, his eyes clouded with sadness. "I just… I'm not ready to go back there right now, Cato. I can't face that house tonight."

I nod, squeezing his hand gently. "We don't have to. We can stay another night at the hotel, take your time. No pressure. Besides, I booked it for the whole weekend just in case."

His shoulders seem to relax slightly, the weight of the day easing off a bit. "Thank you," he says, his voice barely above a whisper.

We finish our meal in silence, each bite of food a small reprieve from the heavier situation that has been going on at Alex's parent's house. I can sense the conflict still swirling within him, the pain of the confrontation with his parents clinging to the edges of every word he speaks. But I also sense the relief that comes with being away from that house, even if just for another night.

When we get back to the hotel, I can feel Alex's tension returning. He sits on the edge of the bed, his head in his hands, the exhaustion of the day finally catching up to him.

"I just keep thinking about how disappointed they were," he says, his voice filled with raw emotion. "I know they're hurting, but it's so hard to feel like I'm the cause of their pain."

I sit down beside him, my hand finding its way to his back, rubbing comforting circles. "You didn't cause this, Alex," I say gently. "You were just being honest, being yourself. That's not something to apologize for."

He looks up, his eyes glassy with unshed tears. "It's just… it hurts, you know? I want them to accept me, but I also know that might never happen."

I lean closer, pressing my forehead against his. "I know it hurts, and I know it's not fair. But you're not alone, Alex. I'm here, and I love you for exactly who you are."

281

INK & *Intuition*

The words seem to break something within him, and he lets out a small, shaky breath. "I love you too, Cato," he whispers, his voice filled with vulnerability.

I cup his face in my hands, wiping away a stray tear with my thumb. "We'll get through this," I murmur, my voice filled with conviction. "Together."

I can feel the warmth of his skin beneath my fingertips as my hands slide down to his waist, pulling him closer. He responds eagerly, his arms wrapping around my neck, drawing me in as if he is afraid to let go.

The air in the room seems to thicken, the glow of the lamp casting shadows that dance around us. We kiss, and it becomes deeper very quickly, filled with love, desire, and the need for closeness that only this moment can bring.

"Cato," Alex growls softly.

I pull back slightly, my forehead resting against his, both of us breathing heavily. "Yeah?" I ask, my voice low and filled with both tenderness and desire.

He nods, his eyes dark with emotion. "I need you."

I feel a surge of heat at his words, a deep, aching love that I can barely contain. I lean in again, capturing his lips with mine, the kiss filled with a passion that speaks of everything we feel but can't quite say.

We move slowly, almost reverently, as if savoring each moment, each touch. The bed creaks softly beneath us as we fall back onto the sheets, our bodies pressed close, skin against skin. There is a sense of urgency, but also a deep, underlying tenderness—a desire to show each other that this is more than just physical, that it is about trust, love, and acceptance.

The feel of Alex's skin, the heat of his breath against my neck—it is intoxicating, overwhelming in the best way possible. Every touch, every kiss feels like a promise, a reassurance that we are exactly where we need to be.

The passion between us grows, each movement filled with love and desire, the kind that comes from truly knowing someone and wanting to be closer than ever before. The sheets tangle around us, the room filled with soft gasps and whispered words of love.

As we move together, our hands begin to explore, fingers tracing the contours of each other's bodies.

My hands find the hem of Alex's shirt, and with a gentle tug, I begin to lift it over his head. The fabric slides away, leaving his skin bare to my touch. My eyes roam over him, filled with a mix of admiration and desire. He reaches for my shirt, pulling it off with the same careful movements, revealing the toned muscles beneath.

We take our time, undressing each other with a sense of desperation. Each piece of clothing that falls away brings us closer, both physically and emotionally. The room is filled with the rustling of fabric, the soft sounds of our breathing, and the occasional murmur of affection.

When we are finally free of our clothing, we come together once more, our bodies pressed close, skin against skin. The sensation is electric, every nerve ending alive with the intensity of our connection. We move together, our movements synchronized, each touch and kiss a testament to the depth of our feelings for one another.

My hands slide down Alex's back, my fingers tracing the curve of his spine. "I want you so much," I whisper, my voice husky with desire.

"Then take me," he replies, his breath hitching as my lips find the sensitive spot just below his ear.

I shift, positioning myself above him, my eyes locked onto his. "You're so beautiful," I murmur, my voice filled with awe. "I can't get enough of you."

He reaches up, his hands tangling in my hair as he pulls me down for a deep, passionate kiss. "Show me," he whispers against my lips. "Show me how much you want me."

My response is immediate, my movements becoming more urgent, more intense. My hands roam over his body, exploring every inch of skin, leaving a trail of fire in their wake. "God, you feel so good," I groan, my voice thick with need.

INK & Intuition

He arches into my touch, his own hands moving to explore my body, feeling the hard muscles beneath my skin. "Cato," he gasps, his voice trembling with desire. "I need you."

I don't hesitate, my body moving against his. Each thrust, each movement is a testament to the depth of our connection.

"You're mine," I whisper, my voice rough with emotion. "All mine."

"Yes," he breathes, his own voice filled with the same intensity. "Always."

The night stretches on, filled with moments of passion and tenderness, each one a reminder of the love and trust that we share. As we finally come to rest, tangled in the sheets, our bodies entwined, there is a sense of completeness, a feeling that we are exactly where we are meant to be.

As we lie entwined in the aftermath, our breaths still ragged and our bodies warm, I turn to him, my fingers gently tracing patterns on his chest. "I mean it, Alex. No matter what happens, you're not alone."

He looks at me, his eyes filled with gratitude and a quiet, exhausted happiness. "I know, Cato. And I finally feel like I can be myself… because of you."

I pull him closer, holding him tightly as if I can shield him from all the pain and uncertainty that lay ahead. "I'm not going anywhere," I promise.

* * *

Alex's phone buzzes on the coffee table. He glances at it, then freezes as he reads the caller ID: Dad.

He hesitates, his thumb hovering over the screen. I can see the conflict in his eyes, dancing with hope and fear that always comes up when his parents reach out unexpectedly.

"Go ahead," I say gently, nodding toward the phone. "Answer it."

He takes a deep breath, then picks up the call and puts it on speaker. "Hey, Dad," he says, trying to keep his voice steady.

"Alex," his father's voice comes through, firm but calm. "Your mother and I... we want to talk to you. Both of you, actually."

Alex shoots me a questioning look, and I nod encouragingly. "We'll head over," he replies, his voice more resolute than I've heard in a while.

When he hangs up, he looks at me, uncertainty evident in his eyes. "What if it's just another argument, Cato? I don't know if I can go through that again."

I reach out, placing a hand on his. "It might be difficult, but if they're willing to talk, it's worth a try. The best way to live up to your parents' expectations is to confront them, honestly and openly."

He lets out a sigh, his shoulders slumping slightly. "You're right. I know you're right. It's just... scary."

I squeeze his hand, giving him a reassuring smile. "I'll be right there with you."

* * *

The drive to Alex's parents' house feels longer than usual, even though the road is recognizable. We pull up to the same white picket fence, the same neat little yard that now feels like a battlefield of emotions. The only difference this time is the small, hopeful glimmer that maybe, just maybe, this confrontation could be different.

I reach out and take Alex's hand, my grip firm. "Ready?"

"As ready as I'll ever be," he replies.

We walk up to the front door together, side by side. Alex knocks, and after a few moments, his mother opens the door. There is a different air about her—still cautious, but less strained. She steps aside, letting us both in.

When we enter the dining room, I notice the table is set for four, an unexpected sight that immediately fills me with trepidation.

"Come sit," his father says, gesturing to the two empty chairs across from them. His tone is neither warm nor cold, but it carries a seriousness that sets the tone for what is clearly a planned discussion.

We sit down, the room quiet except for the soft clink of silverware as they adjust their places at the table. His mother clears her throat, her voice wavering slightly. "Alex, we asked you here because we would like to understand."

"Understand what?" Alex asks, his voice guarded but open.

His father leans forward, his eyes steady. "We would like to understand... this relationship. You and Cato."

There is a moment of heavy silence as if everyone is waiting for someone else to speak. I can feel Alex's hand shaking slightly next to mine under the table. I place my other hand over his, a silent show of support.

"Mom, Dad," Alex starts, his voice soft but filled with determination, "Cato is someone I love. I know this isn't what you expected, but it's real. It's not going away."

His mother's eyes are watery, but she holds back her tears. "We're not saying we understand, Alex. But we don't want to lose you. And if Cato is important to you, then... we need to try."

I feel a surge of emotion at her words, both surprise and cautious optimism. "I appreciate that," I say sincerely. "I know this is hard, but I want you to know that I care about Alex deeply. He means everything to me."

His father looks at me, his eyes showing scrutiny and curiosity. "How long have you two been... together?"

Alex takes a deep breath, then replies honestly. "For a while now. We've been taking it slow, but it's serious."

His mother wipes away a tear, her voice shaky but genuine. "It's just... it's so different from what we imagined for you, Alex. We always thought you'd have a wife, children, the kind of life we had."

Alex's grip tightens around my hand. "I understand that, Mom. I really do. But I need to live my life as myself, not as the version of me that others expect."

His father nods slowly as if he is trying to digest the words. "And you're happy? With him?"

Alex turns to me, his eyes filled with a love that is undeniable. "Yes, Dad. Happier than I've ever been."

I feel my throat tighten, the sincerity of his words hitting me like a wave. "And I promise you both," I add, my voice steady but filled with emotion, "I'll do everything I can to make sure Alex stays happy."

There is a long pause, the kind that feels like it could break either way—toward acceptance or rejection. Finally, his mother speaks again, her voice muted but clear. "We don't know how to be okay with this, Alex. But we want to try. If you love him… then we'll try to love him too."

Alex's eyes fill with tears, and he quickly wipes them away. "That's all I've ever wanted," he says, his voice cracking with emotion. "Just a chance."

His father reaches across the table, placing a hand over both of ours. "We're not perfect, but we're willing to learn."

The tension in the room seems to lift, replaced by a tentative, fragile hope. It isn't full acceptance—not yet—but it is a step in the right direction, a step toward understanding.

Alex turns to me, his face painted with relief. "I didn't think they'd ever say that."

I smile, my own eyes misty. "Sometimes people surprise you."

His mother manages a small, hesitant smile of her own. "Stay for dinner, both of you. We can talk more. It's not much, but it's a start."

thirty-two

CATO

The day-and-a-half-long drive back to the city feels like a heaviness has been lifted off our shoulders. It wasn't a perfect visit, but it was one filled with unexpected moments of connection and a willingness to understand. Alex is more relaxed, his face reflecting relief and hope. We don't talk much on the way back—sometimes, silence is its own form of comfort.

When we reach Alex's apartment around 2 p.m., he turns to me, a gentle smile on his face. "Thank you for everything, Cato. You being there… it made all the difference."

I nod, my voice low but intimate. "I'd do it all over again, Alex. You're worth it."

He leans over, giving me a quick kiss. "I'll see you tomorrow?"

"Definitely," I say, watching him disappear into his building, missing him as soon as he's gone.

I pull up in front of Eternal Ink, and the neon sign glows faintly in the dusk, a familiar sight that feels comforting. I step inside, expecting to see Demi working on a client or sketching at her station.

Instead, I'm met by an unsettling sight. Derek is sitting in one of the waiting chairs, his posture casual but his eyes coldly focused on me. The moment I step inside, he stands up, a sly smile spreading across his face.

"Cato," he says with a venomous tone. "Been a while."

My guard goes up immediately, memories of our tumultuous past flooding back. I keep my voice steady, trying to maintain control. "Derek, what are you doing here?"

He steps closer, his expression shifting from smug to something almost desperate. "I came to see you. I've been thinking about you, about us."

"There is no 'us' anymore, Derek," I say firmly, crossing my arms. "We've been over this."

He doesn't seem to hear me, or maybe he just chooses to ignore it. His eyes are locked on mine, a strange mix of anger and longing in them. "You don't really mean that, do you? We had something, Cato. You can't just throw that away."

I feel a flare of frustration, but I force myself to stay calm. "Derek, we ended for a reason. You need to respect that."

He moves closer, closing the distance between us with quick, aggressive steps. Before I can react, his hand grabs my wrist, pulling me roughly toward him. "Don't act like you didn't miss me," he says, his voice low and dangerously close.

I try to pull away, but his grip is tight, his eyes burning with an intensity that is both unsettling and familiar. "Let go, Derek," I say, my voice sharp.

But he doesn't let go. Instead, he leans in, his face inches from mine, and before I know what's happening, he tries to force a kiss on me.

"Cato, what the hell?" comes a sharp voice from behind us.

It's Demi, standing at the entrance to the back room, her eyes blazing with fury. "Derek, get off him right now!"

Derek jerks back, momentarily startled by her sudden appearance. I take the opportunity to pull away, my chest heaving with anger and disgust.

"Don't you ever do that again," I spit, my voice cold and filled with finality.

Derek's face twists into a sneer, but there's a hint of defeat in his eyes. "You think you're safe with him?" he asks, his tone mocking. "I'll be back, Cato. This isn't over."

Demi steps forward, placing herself between me and Derek. "Yes, it is over. And if you don't leave right now, I'll call the cops."

Derek stares at me for a moment longer, his eyes filled with a dark, lingering intensity. "Fine," he says finally, backing toward the door. "But this isn't the last you'll see of me."

He turns and walks out, the door slamming behind him with a jarring finality.

I let out a shaky breath, my shoulders slumping as the adrenaline slowly fades. Demi turns to me, her expression shifting from anger to concern. "Are you okay?"

I nod, though my voice is rough with lingering emotion. "Yeah, I'm okay. Just… caught off guard."

She sighs, crossing her arms. "That guy is toxic, Cato. You need to make sure he stays away."

"I know," I say, rubbing my wrist where Derek had grabbed me. "I thought I was done with him."

Demi's eyes soften, and she places a hand on my shoulder. "You are done with him, Cato. Don't let him drag you back into that mess."

I manage a small, tired smile. "Thanks, Demi. I think I'm gonna head home."

"Call Alex and tell him, please," Demi says. "He should know."

I nod solemnly. "Yeah, I will."

* * *

I close the door behind me, the lock clicking into place, feeling louder than usual. My chest is still tight, the echoes of Derek's voice replaying over and over in my head. I lean back

290

against the door, sliding down until I'm sitting on the floor, knees pulled up.

What the hell just happened?

My wrist still aches where he grabbed me, the memory of his touch like a stain I can't scrub off. I rub at it absentmindedly, my fingers trembling. The penthouse is silent, too silent, and the stillness feels suffocating. My keys are still in my hand, biting into my palm. I toss them onto the counter, the metallic clatter echoing through the silence.

I should call Alex. I know I should. But even thinking about it feels impossible right now, like my body is weighed down by something heavy and unrelenting. I push myself up and drag my feet toward the couch. Collapsing onto it, I grab a pillow and hug it to my chest, staring blankly at the ceiling.

The thoughts come rushing in.

What if he comes back? What if Demi hadn't walked in? What if I hadn't been strong enough to push him away?

The what-ifs swirl around in my head until I feel like I'm drowning in them. My breath catches in my throat, and I force myself to sit up, trying to shake it off. But the room feels too small, the walls closing in on me. My chest tightens even more.

I need to get out of my head.

I reach for my phone, scrolling mindlessly through my contacts until I see Alex's name. My thumb hovers over it, but I can't bring myself to press it. What would I even say? "Hey, Alex, guess what? Derek showed up and tried to force himself on me. Oh, and by the way, I'm falling apart."

I toss the phone onto the coffee table and bury my face in my hands.

Bailey walks over, his nails clattering on the hardwood floor, nudging my hand with his slimy, squeaky ball.

I don't look up, just keep my face buried in the pillow. "Not now, Bailey."

He lets out a low moan and plops down on the floor.

I shake my head. "I'm fine, buddy. I'm just not in the mood to play."

Bailey exhales heavily, clearly depressed.

INK & *Intuition*

I want to call him. God, I want to call him. But I can't. Not like this.

F. A. SENG

thirty-three

ALEX

I lean back on the couch, my phone resting on my chest, still no word from Cato since he dropped me off earlier this afternoon. It isn't like him to ignore my calls or texts, and that tiny seed of anxiety that planted itself in my mind earlier is starting to grow. I stare at the screen, waiting for it to light up, hoping for a message or a missed call notification, but nothing.

"Come on, Cato…" I mutter under my breath, dialing his number again. This time, it goes straight to voicemail.

With a frustrated sigh, I toss the phone aside and lean my head back against the couch, staring up at the ceiling. It's been a long day, and all I want is to hear his voice, to know that everything is fine. But now? Silence. It isn't helping my nerves.

The door to the apartment creaks open, and Tommy walks in, dropping his bag by the door with a dramatic groan.

"Man, today was rough," he announces, kicking off his shoes with exaggerated movements. "You wouldn't believe the kind of hell I just went through."

I sit up slightly, raising an eyebrow. "What happened?"

Tommy walks over to the kitchen counter, grabbing a beer from the fridge, and pops it open with a sigh of relief before plopping down next to me. "Amelia," he says, pausing for effect, "completely roasted me. Like, full-on 'Dragon of the Spreadsheets' mode."

I blink, not quite sure if I heard that right. "Dragon of the Spreadsheets?"

He takes a long swig of his drink, nodding. "Yep. I don't know what got into her today, but apparently I submitted some numbers wrong last week, and she went nuclear."

I can't help but laugh. "What did she say?"

"Oh, she gave me the full Amelia treatment. 'Tommy, this is unacceptable,'" he mimics her voice with over-the-top seriousness, "'You've got to pay attention to the details. How do you expect us to run a smooth operation if you can't even get basic figures right?' I mean, come on, it was one decimal point off! One!"

I snort, shaking my head. "So you poked the dragon, huh?"

"I didn't just poke it," Tommy groans, "I woke it up, dumped cold water on its head, and handed it a stack of flaming spreadsheets."

I can't help laughing at that. "Dude, that sounds intense."

"You're telling me!" Tommy throws his hands up dramatically. "I was literally sweating under her glare. I thought I was going to be demoted to, I don't know, Spreadsheet Janitor or something."

"Spreadsheet Janitor?" I raise an eyebrow. "Is that even a thing?"

"It might be after today," he deadpans, taking another sip. "You missed the show, man. If you were there, I'm sure she'd have cut you some slack. She's always nicer when you're around."

I chuckle. "Oh, so I'm your dragon slayer now?"

"Basically," Tommy grins. "You've got that 'calm the beast' vibe. Me? I'm just dragon bait."

I laugh again, feeling a bit of the tension ease off as we joke around. It's good to laugh after the weekend I had, even if I still have that nagging worry about Cato sitting in the back of my mind.

"So, what about you?" Tommy asks, kicking back on the couch. "What's going on? Why do you look like you're waiting for a disaster to happen?"

I sigh, picking up my phone and holding it out. "I've been trying to reach Cato all afternoon. He hasn't answered my calls."

Tommy frowns, sitting up. "That's weird. Is everything okay with him?"

"I don't know," I say, my voice tinged with frustration. "I'm sure this weekend wasn't easy for him either, but he usually picks up. Now, it's just… silence."

"Maybe his phone died?" Tommy suggests, though I can tell even he doesn't fully believe that explanation.

"Yeah, maybe," I mutter, though it doesn't make me feel any better. I stare at my phone again, willing it to light up with a notification, but still nothing.

Tommy gives me a sympathetic look. "I'm sure he's fine. Cato's tough, right? He can handle whatever's going on."

"I know," I say softly, leaning back against the couch again. "It's just… sometimes I can't help but worry, you know?"

He nods, taking another sip of his soda. "Hey, if it makes you feel any better, if he doesn't call you back by tonight, I'll personally hunt him down and drag him here for you."

I smirk, appreciating the effort. "Thanks, Tommy. I might just take you up on that."

Tommy grins, giving me a playful nudge. "Anything for my best bud. Plus, I need some entertainment after the whole

295

Dragon of the Spreadsheets incident. The day has been way too serious."

I laugh again, the sound a little lighter this time. "Alright, deal. But let's hope it doesn't come to that."

"Fingers crossed," he says, holding up his hands in mock prayer.

* * *

It's just getting dark out and I still haven't heard from Cato, and my gut is telling me something is off. The walk to the shop feels longer than usual, every step causes my anxiety to increase. I keep trying to push the uneasy feeling aside, hoping to find Cato busy working on a design or finishing up with a client. But as I approach, my heart sinks.

The neon sign above the door is off, and the shop is dark inside. The "Closed" sign hangs crookedly in the window. I pull at the door, but it's locked.

"Damn it," I mutter to myself, feeling a rush of panic.

I pull out my phone and dial Demi's number, pacing back and forth in front of the shop as I wait for her to pick up. After a few rings, her voice crackles through the line, sounding hurried.

"Alex? What's up?" she asks.

"Demi, why is the shop closed?" I ask, trying to keep the worry out of my voice. "And where's Cato?"

There's a pause on her end, and I can feel the tension build as I wait for her to respond. "Alex, it's… it's a long story. Wait, didn't Cato call you?" she says hesitantly.

"No?," I choke, my voice tight. "What happened?"

She lets out a sigh, her tone softening. "Derek showed up again, Alex. Things got bad—he tried to force himself on Cato. I had to step in and threaten to call the cops again."

My heart drops, my mind reeling with the sudden rush of anger and fear. "What the hell? Is Cato okay?"

"He's shaken up," she admits, her voice filled with concern. "He went home; he said he was going to call you."

I clench my jaw, my grip tightening around the phone. "I'm going to his apartment right now."

"Please do," she says urgently. "He needs you."

I end the call and take off in a sprint toward Cato's penthouse, the world around me becoming a blur. I can barely think, my mind racing with the thought of Cato facing Derek alone, the trauma of the past resurfacing in such a brutal way.

By the time I reach his building, my lungs are burning and my legs feel like they're on fire. I don't even wait for the elevator, bounding up the stairs two at a time until I reach Cato's floor. I stop in front of his door, trying to catch my breath before knocking rapidly.

"Cato! It's me, Alex," I call out, my voice rough from the run and the panic that is building inside me.

There's no response at first, and I feel a surge of desperation. I knock again, louder this time. "Cato, please open the door!"

A few seconds later, I hear the sound of footsteps, and the door creaks open slowly. Cato stands there, looking exhausted and broken, his eyes red and his face pale. His shoulders are slumped, as if the weight of the world is pressing down on him.

"Alex…" he says weakly, his voice barely audible.

I step forward, not waiting for an invitation, and pull him into a tight hug. "I'm here," I whisper, holding him as close as I can. "I'm here, and I'm not going anywhere."

He lets out a shaky breath, his arms wrapping around me slowly. "It was… it was horrible, Alex," he murmurs into my shoulder. "He just showed up, and I couldn't stop him."

I tighten my hold, my heart aching at the raw vulnerability in his voice. "It's okay, Cato. You're safe now. I've got you."

We stand there in the doorway for what feels like an eternity, the silence filled only by his uneven breathing and the distant hum of the city outside. I can feel him shaking slightly, and it makes me want to protect him even more fiercely.

"Let's get inside," I say gently, guiding him toward the couch.

He nods, letting me lead him to the living room. As we sit down, I keep my hand on his back, rubbing slow, soothing circles. He closes his eyes for a moment, trying to steady himself.

"Tell me what happened," I urge quietly, wanting to help him release whatever burden he's carrying.

He hesitates, his eyes filled with a mix of anger and shame. "He came to the shop. At first, it was just words, but then he tried to force a kiss on me. He was just waiting there for me."

My jaw tightens, a burst of anger coursing through me. "Fucking asshole," I mutter under my breath. "Did he hurt you?"

Cato shakes his head slowly. "No, Demi got there and stepped in before it got worse. It just… it brought back all the memories, you know? Of everything he did, everything I tried to bury."

I reach for his hand, holding it firmly. "I can't even begin to understand what that was like for you, but I'm here now. You're not alone in this, Cato."

I can still feel the tension lingering in the room, a heavy reminder of what Cato has just been through. He is slumped against me on the couch, his head resting on my shoulder, his breathing slow but steady. He feels fragile, like he is fighting to stay strong even though his past has tried to break him again.

I glance down at Cato's phone lying on the coffee table. It's still on, the screen glowing faintly, as if waiting for something—perhaps a confrontation, perhaps closure. I have a sudden need to do something bold, something that will stake my claim and make a point, not just to Derek but to the world.

An idea strikes me, and without thinking too much, I grab the phone.

"Hey," Cato says, his voice tired but curious, "what are you doing?"

I turn to him with a mischievous smile. "I'm making sure Derek knows where you stand. And where I stand, too."

He raises an eyebrow, confused. "Alex, what are you up to?"

Instead of replying, I lean in and press a deep, affectionate kiss on his lips. I feel his surprise melt as he kisses me back, a small smile tugging at the corners of his mouth.

I quickly hold up his phone, and snap a selfie of us mid-kiss. As we break the kiss, I immediately open Derek's contact to send him a quick text.

"Wait, what are you—" Cato starts, but I'm already typing.

I send the photo along with a simple message.

Cato:

> Stay the fuck away from Cato, or we'll be pressing charges.

I hit 'send' and drop the phone back on the table, grinning from ear to ear.

Cato stares at me, stunned, before he bursts out laughing —a genuine, hearty laugh that fills the room and seems to lift the lingering weight off both our shoulders.

"You did not just do that," he says, still laughing, his eyes wide with disbelief.

"Oh, I definitely did," I say, feeling proud of myself. "Derek needs to know that you're off-limits. And that you're mine now."

Cato shakes his head. "You're crazy, you know that?"

"Crazy for you," I retort, playfully bumping his shoulder.

He laughs again, this time quieter, the sound filled with both relief and affection. "I can't believe you actually sent that to him. Don't you think that was a little childish?"

I shrug, my grin only growing wider. "Sometimes the only thing that works against a childish person, is a childish action. Besides, it's not just about him knowing. It's about you knowing, too."

His smile falters for a moment, a hint of vulnerability flashing in his eyes. "You really mean that, don't you?"

I reach out, taking his hand in mine and squeezing it gently. "I do, Cato. I want you to know that you're safe with me. I'm here, and I'm not going anywhere."

He looks at me, his eyes becoming tender, and for the first time since I'd arrived, I see a spark of relief there. "You really have a way of making me feel better, even when everything feels like a mess," he admits.

"Good," I say, giving his hand another squeeze. "That's the plan."

He smiles, a grateful smile that makes my heart swell. "I never thought I'd find someone who would do something like that. Showing me off," he says with a chuckle. "But I guess I'm lucky to have you."

"Damn right, you are," I tease, nudging him playfully. "And just so you know, if Derek tries anything else, I've got more selfies where that came from."

Cato shakes his head, still laughing. "You're impossible, Alex."

"Impossible to resist," I shoot back with a wink, making him laugh even more.

F. A. SENG

thirty-four
ALEX

november

The morning sun pours through my apartment window, casting a glow over the sketches strewn across my desk. I stare at them, feeling a rush of excitement with a tinge of nervousness. The last gallery was a success—better than I'd imagined—but the creative fire within me isn't quite ready to be extinguished. I need more. I want more.

I can't shake off the idea that has been forming in my mind for the past few days, a new concept that feels both ambitious and thrilling. I grab my phone and dial Cato's number, eager to share my thoughts.

"Hey, good morning!" he answers, his voice slightly groggy.

"Morning, sleepyhead," I tease. "Listen, I've got an idea. How about we do our own gallery?"

I can almost hear the smile in his voice. "Already? You don't waste any time, do you?"

I chuckle. "Nope. But hear me out. What if this time, we focus on digital art?"

There's a pause on the other end as Cato considers the suggestion. "Digital art, huh? That's a really cool concept. It's a different medium, but it's got so much potential. I'm in."

His quick agreement sends a jolt of exuberance through me. "You're serious?"

"Of course," he replies with a hint of amusement. "You know I love trying new things. Plus, your digital work is incredible, Alex. It deserves to be showcased."

His words feel like a loving embrace, filling me with confidence. "Thanks, babe. I was thinking we could have a mix of digital art, animations, and interactive pieces—stuff that people can engage with."

"That sounds amazing," he says, with genuine enthusiasm in his voice. "Let's do it."

I grin, feeling the thrill of a new project taking shape. "Alright. I'll get started on the planning. First, I need to talk to Amelia and get her approval."

"Good luck with that," Cato says with a laugh. "And tell her I said hi."

"Will do," I reply, already grabbing my bag and preparing to head out.

* * *

When I reach the office, the familiar noise of work fills the air, with colleagues chatting, phones ringing, and the faint hum of printers in the background. I make my way straight to Amelia's office, knocking on the door and waiting for her to call me in.

"Come in," her voice sounds from the other side.

I open the door to find her seated behind her desk, surrounded by stacks of papers and a large coffee mug that reads, "Spreadsheet Queen."

"Good morning, Amelia," I greet, trying to sound as confident as possible.

"Morning, Alex," she replies, giving me a curious look. "What brings you here so early?"

I take a deep breath, diving right into it. "I've got an idea for another gallery."

She raises an eyebrow, intrigued but cautious. "Another one? Didn't we just have one a couple of months ago?"

"Yes, but this one's different," I say quickly, trying to keep the excitement in my voice steady. "I want to do a digital art gallery this time—animations, interactive pieces, the works. It'll be something fresh and engaging."

Amelia leans back in her chair, tapping her pen thoughtfully against her notepad. "Digital art, huh? That's a big shift from the last one. Are you sure this will work?"

"I believe it will," I insist. "Digital art is growing, and it has a huge audience. We can attract a different crowd, one that's more tech-savvy and looking for something immersive."

She nods slowly, still appearing unconvinced. "It's a good idea, Alex, but I need to run it by my boss, Ron. You know how these things go."

I lean forward, feeling a sudden burst of boldness. "Tell Ron that it's my idea but Cato Sinclair will be a co-organizer."

Her eyebrows shoot up, surprised by my statement. "Cato's involved in this?"

"Yeah," I confirm, a hint of pride in my voice. "Cato loves the idea and wants to be a part of it. And if you mention his name to Ron, I'm pretty sure he'll approve."

Amelia smirks, clearly amused by my confidence. "You're really pulling out all the stops, huh? Using Cato's name to get what you want?"

I laugh. "Hey, whatever works, right? I just have a feeling that if Ron hears it's Cato's project, he'll be more inclined to say yes."

She pauses, considering my words. "You know, you've got a point. Cato's reputation in the art world is solid, and having his name attached could really boost this project's chances."

"So, will you bring it up to him?" I ask, my voice a medley of eagerness and hope.

Amelia nods slowly, a small smile forming on her lips. "Alright, Alex. I'll pitch it to him."

"Thank you, Amelia!" I say, sincerely grateful.

"Don't thank me yet," she warns, though there's a hint of tenderness in her tone. "Let's see what he says. I'll do my best."

I leave her office feeling a rush of adrenaline. The possibility of another gallery, this time centered around digital art, is within reach. I can't wait to get back to Cato and start planning. I pull out my phone, quickly type a quick text to him.

Me:

> Amelia's going to pitch the digital art gallery to her boss. Fingers crossed!

Within seconds, I get a reply from Cato.

Cato:

> You've got this, baby. I'm proud of you.

* * *

I'm sitting at my desk, mindlessly scrolling through emails, when a notification pops up. I click it, and my eyes widen as I read Amelia's email:

F. A. SENG

From: Amelia Noor

To: Alex Mitchell

Subject: Exhibition Proposal

Alex,

Good news!
My boss has approved your digital art exhibition proposal. Let's make it happen.

Amelia

I jump out of my chair, a huge grin spreading across my face. "Yes!" I exclaim, unable to contain my excitement. A few heads turn in my direction, and Tommy, sitting at the neighboring desk, gives me a curious look.

"What's got you all hyped up?" he asks, leaning over the divider.

I hold up my phone, unable to hide my smile. "I pitched another exhibition that Cato and I had come up with to Amelia, and we got approval! It's happening!"

He raises his hand for a high-five, grinning. "Nice, man! You and Cato are gonna kill it."

"Thanks!" I say, slapping his hand enthusiastically. "It's going to be something completely new."

I quickly text Cato.

Me:

> We got approval for the exhibition!
> Let's do this!

His response is immediate.

Cato:

INK & *Intuition*

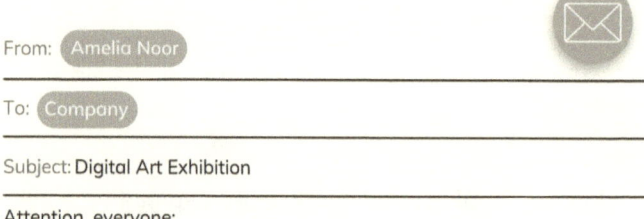

> Amazing! Can't wait to get started.
> Proud of you, my love!

I feel a jitter in my chest, knowing that Cato is just as excited about this as I am. My phone buzzes again, and it's an email from Amelia, sent to the whole office:

From: Amelia Noor

To: Company

Subject: Digital Art Exhibition

Attention, everyone:

A digital art exhibition has been approved. If anyone wants to participate, please submit your work by the end of the month to myself or Alex Mitchell. Let's make this a big success!

Thanks, Amelia

It's official. I can almost feel the anticipation in the air, a sense of creativity starting to build. I waste no time and head straight to Amelia's office. I knock lightly, and she waves me in, looking busy but pleased.

"Hey, Amelia," I say, unable to suppress my grin. "Thank you for helping to push this through."

She looks up, her eyes twinkling with amusement and satisfaction. "You really believed in this project, Alex. I could see that. Apparently, so did my boss—especially when I mentioned Cato Sinclair."

I laugh, scratching the back of my head. "Yeah, I figured that might help sway the decision."

"It definitely did," she replies, smirking. "Now, let's get moving. We'll need everything from planning the layout to marketing strategies, and of course, gathering their submissions. Are you ready for that?"

"Absolutely," I say, feeling a flare of determination. "Cato and I will start working on the layouts tonight."

"Good," she says, giving me an approving nod. "Let's make this gallery a real success. I'll handle the logistics and marketing, but I'll need regular updates from you."

"You'll have them," I promise.

* * *

Later that evening, I rush over to Eternal Ink, feeling a surge of energy with each step. The shop is as lively as ever, with the soft hum of the tattoo machines and the scent of fresh ink in the air. I spot Cato at his station, focused on a client's design. Demi is chatting with a customer near the front desk, but as soon as she sees me, she raises an eyebrow.

"Someone's looking extra happy today," she teases.

I grin. "We got the approval for the digital art gallery, Demi! It's official."

She beams. "I heard! Cato filled me in this morning plus I already saw the ad that your boss posted on social media. That's amazing, Alex! I knew you guys could pull it off. Now, we just need to make sure everything runs smoothly."

"Thanks for keeping things in order, Demi," I say sincerely.

She waves it off with a smile. "Anything for you two."

I walk over to Cato, who has just finished up with his client. He turns to me, a broad smile spreading across his face. "So, it's really happening?"

"It is," I confirm, unable to contain my exhilaration. "Amelia's already sent out a call for submissions. We're going to get so much talent coming our way."

"Perfect," he says, his eyes shining with enthusiasm. "We should get started on our pieces as soon as possible."

I nod. "Agreed. I was thinking of creating a series that blends traditional tattoo art with digital elements—something that bridges our two worlds."

Cato's eyes light up. "I love that idea, Alex. It's exactly the kind of thing that'll set this gallery apart."

We sit down at the large worktable in the back of the shop, pulling out sketchbooks and laptops. As we start brainstorming, Cato is filled with ideas. He sketches a rough outline of a tattoo-inspired digital mural while I open up my software to work on the digital elements.

"What if we added animation to some of the designs?" I suggest. "Imagine the tattoo shifting and moving, like the wings of a dragon or waves rippling across an ocean."

Cato's eyes widen. "That's genius. It'll bring the designs to life in a way that's never been done before."

We both lean in, sketching and discussing different concepts, lost in the creative flow. It's one of those moments where everything seems to click—the ideas, the passion, and the energy between us.

Suddenly, Demi pops her head in, looking amused. "You two are like a couple of kids in a candy store. I swear, the way you're geeking out over this gallery is adorable."

We both laugh. "Can you blame us?" I say. "This is a dream project."

Demi nods. "I can see that. By the way, you're already getting requests for interviews. Journalists want to know about the concept, the collaboration, and how you plan to merge tattoo art with digital art."

"Really?" I ask, surprised by the quick response.

"Yep," she confirms. "Looks like this gallery is going to be even bigger than the one we did with Richmond."

thirty-five
ALEX

The morning of the interview arrived sooner than I'd expected. Cato and I sit side by side in the small lobby of the local newspaper office, waiting for our turn. The room is bustling with journalists typing away, phones ringing, and the faint smell of fresh coffee lingering in the air. I can feel the anticipation between us.

"You ready for this?" Cato asks, leaning in with a smile.

"As ready as I'll ever be," I reply, giving him a small nudge. "It's kind of surreal, isn't it? Us, being interviewed for a digital art gallery?"

"It is," he agrees, nodding thoughtfully. "But it's a chance to tell our story, Alex. To show people why this matters."

I take a deep breath, feeling both the weight and elation of the moment. A young woman with glasses and a notepad finally approaches us.

"Alex Mitchell and Cato Sinclair?" she asks, her voice friendly but professional.

"That's us," I reply, standing up with a smile.

"I'm Leah, and I'll be doing your interview today," she says, shaking our hands. "Thank you both for coming in."

"Thank you for having us," Cato replies warmly.

We follow Leah into a small conference room, with walls adorned with framed headlines from the past decades. A recorder and a notebook are already set up on the table. We take our seats, and Leah wastes no time getting started.

"So," she begins, adjusting her glasses, "I've read about your upcoming digital arts gallery. It's quite an intriguing shift from the last event, which focused on more traditional forms of art, including tattoos. Why the move to digital arts this time?"

I exchange a quick glance with Cato, then lean forward, eager to answer. "That's a great question," I start, choosing my words carefully. "You're right—digital arts are widely available, but that's precisely the point. While paintings and traditional forms of art are often celebrated and well respected, I feel that graphic designers don't get the same level of recognition."

Leah seems intrigued, nodding thoughtfully as I continue. "Think about it: digital art is everywhere—advertisements, websites, branding, even the apps we use daily. But how often do we recognize the artist behind it? Digital creators are the ones who shape much of the modern visual landscape, yet their work is often seen as purely functional, not artistic."

Cato chimes in, his voice steady and passionate. "That's exactly why we wanted to bring this gallery to life. We're not just showing digital art; we're celebrating it. We want people to see the creativity, the skill, and the passion that goes into these works, just like any traditional painting."

Leah raises an eyebrow, clearly captivated. "That's an interesting perspective. Some people might argue that digital art isn't 'real' art in the traditional sense. What would you say to that?"

I feel a ripple of determination. "I'd say that art isn't defined by the medium, but by the message and the creativity behind it. Whether it's a painting on canvas or a design created with pixels, the heart of the artist is still present. It's still storytelling, just in a different form."

Cato nods, backing me up. "Exactly. The digital realm offers endless possibilities—animation, interaction, and even immersion. These are things traditional mediums can't always achieve. It's not about replacing traditional art but adding to the diversity of the artistic experience."

Leah scribbles some notes, clearly impressed. "I like that perspective. So, you're not just bringing digital art to the forefront; you're advocating for a shift in how we perceive it."

"Absolutely," I reply, feeling more confident with each word. "We want people to understand that graphic designers and digital artists are just as creative, just as innovative, and just as deserving of recognition as any painter or sculptor."

"And what kind of response are you hoping for from the public?" Leah asks, leaning forward with genuine curiosity.

Cato answers this one. "We're hoping for excitement, of course, but more than that, we want to spark a conversation. We want people to walk away with a newfound respect for digital art and to see it as something worthy of admiration—not just a tool, but a true form of expression."

Leah nods thoughtfully, her pen moving swiftly across the page. "It's clear that this gallery means a lot to both of you. What do you think is the most significant piece in the collection?"

I hesitate for a moment, exchanging a glance with Cato. "We have a few standout pieces," I begin, "but there's one that's particularly special to me. It's called Breakthrough, and it's a blend of digital sketches overlaid with animation. It's meant to represent breaking free from stereotypes, both in art and in life."

Cato adds with a smile, "It's one of my favorites too. It combines traditional tattoo themes with digital innovation, and it really captures the spirit of what we're trying to achieve."

Leah leans back, a smile spreading across her face. "It sounds like you're not just hosting a gallery; you're starting a movement."

I feel a swell of pride at her words. "That's the goal," I say simply. "To change how people see art—digital or otherwise."

After a few more questions about the logistics, the audience, and our vision for the future, Leah closes her notebook. "Thank you both for your time. I'm really looking forward to seeing this gallery."

"Thank you, Leah," Cato replies warmly. "We appreciate the opportunity to share our story."

* * *

The day of the gallery has finally arrived, and the space is electrified. I stand near the entrance with Cato, watching as guests stream in, their faces lit up with wonderment. The gallery is a spectacle of digital innovation, filled with vibrant displays, animated projections, and interactive installations that showcase the true potential of digital art.

As we take in the scene, Richmond approaches us, his eyes gleaming with pride. He's dressed impeccably in a sleek suit that seems to complement the futuristic vibe of the gallery.

"Alex, Cato," he reaches out and shakes our hands. "This is absolutely phenomenal. You've truly outdone yourselves."

I feel a rush of gratitude and accomplishment. "Thanks, Richmond. We're glad you could make it!"

Richmond nods, his gaze sweeping across the bustling gallery. "The turnout is incredible. I've already spotted several influential critics and collectors. This could be a game-changer for digital art in our city."

"That's what we wanted," Cato replies.

"Well, I won't hold you kids up. Enjoy this moment, you both deserve it." Richmond laughs, clapping us on the back before fading into the crowd.

"Can you believe this?" I say, nudging Cato gently. "Look at this crowd!"

Cato grins, his eyes twinkling. "It's incredible, Alex. You really pulled it off."

"No," I correct him, smiling wide. "We pulled it off."

He chuckles, wrapping an arm around my shoulder. "Fair enough."

As we move through the crowd, I notice some familiar faces—artists, journalists, and even a few well-known names in the advertising world. It's surreal to see them here, mingling with young digital artists and exploring their work.

"Hey, look over there," Cato whispers, nodding discreetly toward a small group. "Isn't that David Cooper, the CEO of BlueWave Advertising?"

I follow his gaze, spotting the tall man in a sleek suit who is inspecting one of the animated pieces. My heart skips a beat. "It is! He's one of the biggest names in advertising. If he's here, that means we've got serious attention."

Cato's expression turns serious. "Let's go introduce ourselves. This could be a huge opportunity."

We make our way through the crowd, carefully navigating the groups of guests and the occasional clumsy bump. As we approach David Cooper, he turns to us with a polite smile.

"Mr. Cooper, I'm Alex Mitchell, one of the organizers of this gallery," I say, extending my hand.

"Nice to meet you, Alex. And this is?" He gestures toward Cato.

"I'm Cato Sinclair, co-organizer and artist," Cato says, shaking his hand as well.

David nods approvingly. "I've heard of you, Cato. You've made quite a name for yourself in the tattoo world. And now digital art too? Impressive."

"Thank you," Cato replies, smiling humbly. "We wanted to show that digital art deserves as much recognition as any other medium."

David glances around the room, his eyes scanning the various artworks. "You've done an excellent job here. I can see a lot of potential—especially for advertising campaigns that need a creative edge."

I can't hide my excitement. "That's exactly what we were hoping for. Digital art isn't just about pixels on a screen; it's about creating experiences and telling stories."

David nods, clearly impressed. "I can see that. I'll be keeping an eye on some of the artists here tonight. Who knows? Maybe I'll commission a piece or two."

"Please do," Cato says with a kind smile. "These artists have put their heart and soul into their work. Any recognition would mean the world to them."

With a final nod and a polite "Enjoy the rest of the evening," David moves on to the next display.

I turn to Cato, feeling a rush of adrenaline. "We did it, Cato. We really fucking did it."

"Yeah, we did," he agrees, his voice filled with pride.

* * *

As we continue making rounds, we stumble upon Tommy, who is standing in front of one of his animated designs with a beaming smile.

"Tommy!" I call out, making my way over to him.

"Alex!" he shouts back, practically bouncing on his feet. "You won't believe what just happened."

I raise an eyebrow, intrigued. "What happened?"

"I sold one of my pieces!" he exclaims, his excitement bubbling over. "For $300!"

My jaw drops. "Are you serious? That's amazing, Tommy!"

"Right?" he says, his eyes wide with disbelief. "I never thought anyone would actually buy my work, let alone for that much!"

Cato joins in, giving Tommy a playful nudge. "Congratulations, man. Looks like you're officially in the art world now."

Tommy laughs, still in a daze. "I know, right? I mean, $300! I feel like I just hit the jackpot."

I can't help but laugh along with him. "Well, don't spend it all at once."

"Oh, trust me, I won't," Tommy says with a grin. "This is going straight into my 'Buy Amelia Some Better Coffee' fund. Maybe if she has better coffee, she'll stop being the Dragon of the Spreadsheets."

We all burst into laughter, drawing a few curious glances from the crowd. But I don't care. This moment is worth every bit of hard work we've put in over the past months.

The rest of the evening flies by in a whirlwind of conversations, handshakes, and even more sales. Several of the digital artists manage to sell their pieces, and I can see the gleam in their eyes—a thrill that is both new and transformative.

As the night comes to a close, Amelia approaches us, looking unusually pleased. "Well, Alex, I have to hand it to you. This was a success beyond what we anticipated."

I smile, feeling a sense of accomplishment wash over me. "Thank you, Amelia. We couldn't have done it without the support of the company."

"And you," she adds, her expression softening a bit. "You really showed us what digital art can do."

Cato wraps an arm around my shoulders, squeezing gently. "He's pretty good at that, isn't he?"

Amelia nods, a rare smile on her face. "Yes, he is."

As the crowd begins to thin, I find myself standing next to Cato, watching the last few guests leave the gallery.

"You know," I say quietly, "this gallery wasn't just about digital art. It was about proving that people like us—people who create in different ways—can make a difference."

Cato turns to me, his eyes filled with kindness. "You've always known that, Alex. Now, everyone else knows it too."

I smile, leaning my head on his shoulder. "Yeah, I guess they do."

thirty-six
ALEX

After the incredible success of the gallery, Cato, Demi, and I decide we deserve a drink—something to let off steam and celebrate a night that has gone better than we could've imagined. The pub is filled with energy, the music loud, and the laughter even louder. We find a cozy booth near the bar and order a round of drinks.

"To the best damn gallery this city has ever seen!" Demi declares, lifting her glass.

"To digital art finally getting the recognition it deserves!" I add, grinning from ear to ear.

"To us," Cato says, his voice low. "We did this together."

We clink our glasses, taking big sips of our drinks. Everything feels perfect, like the culmination of months of hard work and late nights. I feel a sense of pride, not just in the work but in us—our bond, our journey, and the obstacles we've overcome to get here.

F. A. SENG

As the night progresses, our conversation drifts to various topics. At one point, Cato's expression turns serious, and he leans in closer to us.

"You know," he begins, his voice layered with both relief and determination, "I've been meaning to tell you both something. I finally did it—I filed a restraining order against Derek."

Demi and I exchange surprised glances before turning our attention back to Cato.

"That's huge, Cato," I say, reaching out to squeeze his hand supportively.

Demi nods emphatically. "It's about time. How do you feel about it?"

Cato takes a deep breath, a small smile playing on his lips. "Honestly? I feel… free. Like I can finally breathe without constantly looking over my shoulder. It wasn't an easy decision, but I knew it was necessary."

"We're proud of you," I tell him, my voice filled with sincerity. "That must have taken a lot of courage."

"It did," Cato admits. "But I realized I couldn't let him control my life anymore. This gallery, this night—it's a new chapter for all of us. I wanted to start it without any shadows from the past hanging over me."

Demi raises her glass again. "Well, then here's to new beginnings and standing up for yourself. You're stronger than you know, Cato."

We toast again, the atmosphere now charged with a different kind of energy—one of hope and newfound strength.

As the night winds down, Demi leaves to grab us one last round of drinks, leaving Cato and me standing quietly at an empty pool table. The faint hum of music and chatter fills the bar, but in this moment, it feels like we're in our own little bubble.

"Hey," Cato says softly, breaking the silence. His voice carries a certain nervous energy. "I've been meaning to give you something… and, uh, ask you something at the same time."

I raise an eyebrow, caught off guard by his tone. "Should I be nervous?" I ask, half-teasing but also curious.

"No, baby," he replies, his voice steady now as he reaches into his pocket. When he pulls out a small box, my stomach flips. "I just—well, I wanted to give you this."

He hands me the box, and I glance at him before carefully opening it. Inside is a small brass key shaped like a heart. I pick it up, feeling the cool metal in my fingers. "What's this?" I ask, looking up at him in surprise.

Cato shifts his weight, rubbing the back of his neck with a shy smile. "So, uh, I had this made a couple of months ago," he starts, the words tumbling out. "It's a key. To my place. Well, our place, if you want it to be."

I blink at him, his words catching me off guard. "Wait, what?" I ask, my heart pounding.

He steps closer, taking my free hand in his. His eyes search mine, full of hope and something else—something deeper. "Baby," he says, his voice tender but sure, "I'm asking if you'd move in with me."

For a moment, I can only stare at him, the weight of his question sinking in. My fingers tighten around the key as my chest fills with elation and disbelief.

"Cato," I finally say, my voice cracking slightly. "Are you serious?"

"Dead serious," he says with a nervous laugh. "I want us to wake up together, go to sleep together, and have somewhere that's just ours. No more nights apart unless we have to. I'm ready for this—if you are."

I look at the key again, feeling its significance in every ridge and curve. Then I look back at Cato, his expression open, his heart in his hands.

"Yes," I say, a smile spreading across my face. "I want that too."

Before I can say anything else, Cato's lips crash into mine. The cheers and clinking glasses from the bar fade into the background as his arms wrap around me, pulling me close.

When we break apart, his forehead rests against mine, and I can feel his grin against my skin.

"I love you," he says, his voice filled with happiness.

"I love you too," I whisper, holding the key tightly in my hand. "Now, let's go find Demi and tell her she's got a new moving buddy."

Cato laughs, pulling me in for another quick kiss. "Deal. But first, I'm going to win this next game of pool—for us."

"We'll see about that," I tease, nudging him toward the table. The future feels wide open, full of possibilities, and for the first time in a long time, I can't wait to step into it. With him. Together.

INK & *Intuition*

thirty-seven
CATO

December

I stand at my station, quietly going through some sketches, when Demi approaches, her face serious. It's rare to see her this focused, so I know something is up.

"Cato," she says in a low tone, trying to keep her voice between us, "we need to discuss the logistics for tonight."

I nod, feeling the weight of her words. "Yeah, is Tommy coming? I'm sure he'd want him there."

She laughs lightly, but there's a hint of exhaustion in it. "Yeah he'll be there, along with Richmond and some other friends of yours."

As we continue discussing the plan, I feel a strange mix of exhilarating pressure. The gallery has been a massive success, and it feels like things are finally falling into place.

Suddenly, the familiar creak of the shop door breaks our conversation, and I look up to see Alex walking in, his face bright and cheerful.

"Hey, you two!" he calls out, waving as he steps inside.

"Hey, baby," I reply, my voice sounding a bit flat even to my own ears.

He approaches us, his smile faltering slightly. "What's going on? Everything alright?"

Demi quickly jumps in, her tone casual but with an edge of urgency. "Nothing big, just some boring logistics stuff for the shop. You don't need to worry about it."

Alex glances between us, clearly sensing the awkwardness. "Are you sure? I can help if there's something you need."

Demi shakes her head, giving him a wide smile that doesn't quite reach her eyes. "No, really, Alex. It's fine. Cato and I have got it covered."

Alex looks at me, his brows furrowed with concern. "Cato, is everything okay?"

I force a smile, trying to sound reassuring. "Yeah, just dealing with some scheduling headaches. Nothing major."

Even as I say the words, I can see that Alex isn't convinced. He steps a bit closer, his voice lower and filled with genuine worry. "You seem... off. Did something happen?"

Before I can respond, Demi intervenes, her voice light but firm. "Alex, seriously, it's fine. Cato and I just need to finish this discussion, okay? Maybe you can head home for a little bit and I can come by later?"

I can see the confusion in Alex's eyes, but he nods slowly, clearly unsure of what's going on. "Okay... I'll just, uh, see you at home then. Love you"

"Thanks, baby. I love you too," I say quietly, feeling a pang of guilt as he turns and walks back toward the door. I hate being distant with him, but right now, there are things I need to sort out, and Demi knows it too.

ALEX

I hang up the phone feeling worried. Cato has been evasive, and it's not like him to keep things from me. I want to believe his story about the important guest, but something still feels off. I try to shake it off and focus on work, but my mind keeps drifting back to the call.

Later that afternoon, I receive a text from Cato that catches me off guard.

Cato:

> Hey Babe, there's a party at 4th Avenue tonight. It's kind of a big deal, and I'd really like you to be there. Formal dress code. I've got a suit ready for you and a little surprise too.

A party? Now, this is unexpected.

* * *

I arrive at the shop a couple of hours later to pick up the suit. Demi is waiting with a garment bag draped over her arm and a wide grin on her face.

"Here's your suit, Alex," she says, handing it to me. "And there's something special inside."

I unzip the bag to reveal a sleek black suit, perfectly tailored. Nestled in the pocket is a small brooch in the shape of a butterfly. I pick it up, examining its delicate design.

"A butterfly?" I ask, a bit puzzled. "What's this about?"

Demi's grin grows even wider. "It's Cato's idea. He thought it'd suit you—symbolizing transformation and freedom, you know?"

My heart warms at the thought. "He's got a way of surprising me, doesn't he?"

Demi nods, her eyes twinkling. "You better get ready. It's going to be a memorable night."

* * *

322

F. A. SENG

I arrive at 4th Avenue around 7 p.m, my heart pounding slightly as I adjust my suit jacket and pin the brooch to my lapel. The venue is elegantly decorated, with comforting lighting, soft music, and the hum of conversations filling the air. As I walk in, I'm surprised to see familiar faces everywhere.

"Tommy!" I exclaim, spotting my friend from work near the entrance.

"Alex! You made it!" Tommy shouts back, clearly delighted.

I walk over to him, feeling slightly confused. "I didn't expect to see you here."

"Well, your guy Cato knows how to throw a party," Tommy says, winking. "He's got half of the advertising industry here. Amelia's even around somewhere."

"What?" I'm shocked. "Amelia's here too?"

Tommy laughs. "Oh yeah, she's making rounds like a politician."

I scan the crowd, trying to make sense of it all. There are at least two dozen guests—colleagues from the office, artists I've met at the gallery, even some of Cato's old clients from the tattoo shop.

"This is wild," I mutter to myself. "I thought it was just going to be a business thing."

"Cato's full of surprises, isn't he?" Tommy adds with a chuckle. "So, where is the man of the hour, anyway?"

"That's what I'd like to know," I say, glancing around again but still not spotting him.

I make my way through the crowd, greeting recognizable faces as I go. I finally spot Demi near the bar, chatting animatedly with a group of guests. I walk over, eager to get some answers.

"Demi!" I call out as I approach.

"Hey, Alex!" she says brightly, giving me a hug. "Looking sharp."

"Thanks," I reply, unable to keep the confusion out of my voice. "Where's Cato? I've been looking for him since I got here."

Demi smirks, her eyes filled with mischief. "You'll just have to wait a little longer. He's got something planned."

I frown, feeling a mix of curiosity and impatience. "What's he up to? You know I don't like surprises."

"Trust me, you're going to love this one," she says, her grin widening. "Just be patient, Alex."

My heart races as I stand near the center of the room, a hundred questions swirling in my head. I keep glancing around, hoping to spot Cato in the sea of faces. The guests are busy chatting, laughing, and enjoying the drinks, but all I can think about is where Cato is and what he has planned.

Suddenly, I feel a slight tap on my shoulder. I turn around, and there he is—Cato, looking breathtaking in a sleek, tailored navy-blue suit. His brown hair is neatly styled, his eyes are full of emotion, and there's a kindness in his gaze that seems to make the entire room fade away.

"Hey," he says softly, a small smile playing on his lips.

"Cato!" I exclaim, feeling a rush of relief. "Where have you been? I've been looking everywhere for you."

He takes a deep breath, his eyes never leaving mine. "I've been getting ready for something important," he replies, his voice calm but with an undercurrent of nerves.

Before I can ask anything else, he reaches out and takes my hand, holding it tightly. "Come with me," he says, his tone leaving no room for questions.

He starts to lead me through the crowd, and a cocktail of intrigue, anticipation, and puzzlement. "What's going on, Cato?" I ask, trying to keep up with his quick steps.

"You'll see," he says, glancing back at me with a smile that is equal parts mysterious and sincere.

We reach the center of the room, where the guests seem to instinctively part to make way for us. I notice that a small spotlight has been set up, illuminating a little stage area that I hadn't noticed before. The room falls silent, and all eyes are suddenly on us.

"Cato, what's happening?" I whisper, feeling my nerves start to kick in.

F. A. SENG

Cato turns to face me, still holding my hand, his expression serious but filled with love, and it makes my heart flutter. "Alex," he begins, his voice carrying clearly across the room. "I know this might be a surprise, but there's something I've been wanting to say for a while now."

I feel a lump in my throat, my pulse pounding in my ears. "Cato…"

He takes a deep breath, his eyes locked onto mine with an intensity I've never seen before. "From the moment we met, you've brought color into my life in ways I never thought possible. You've challenged me, inspired me, and made me want to be a better man."

I can feel tears welling up, my emotions overwhelming me as he continues.

"We've faced so much together—good, bad, and everything in between. But through it all, there's one thing I've always been sure of: my love for you," he says, his voice trembling slightly with emotion.

I cover my mouth with my hand, trying to hold back the tears. "Cato…"

He suddenly gets down on one knee, his free hand reaching into his pocket to pull out a small velvet box. My heart stops for a moment, and I can't believe what's happening.

"Alex Mitchell," he says, opening the box to reveal a simple yet stunning silver ring with a small diamond in the center. "Will you marry me?"

The room seems to blur around me, my vision swimming with tears as I try to process the moment. Everything feels surreal, like a dream I'd never dared to have. The warmth of his hand, the sincerity in his eyes, and the ring that sparkles in the light—it's all too much.

I feel a wave of disbelief crash over me. "Cato… Are you serious? This is really happening?"

Cato's eyes are filled with love and hope, his voice soft but firm. "Yes, Alex. I'm serious. I want to spend the rest of my life with you."

325

The weight of his words hits me like a tidal wave, and I realize that this is exactly what I want too—more than anything. I wipe away my tears, nodding frantically. "Yes… Yes, of course, Cato. Yes!"

The crowd erupts into applause and cheers as Cato slips the ring onto my finger. He stands up, his face breaking into the biggest smile I've ever seen. Without thinking, I throw my arms around him, holding him as tightly as I can.

"I can't believe this," I whisper in his ear, my voice still shaky from the tears. "This is the happiest moment of my life."

"Mine too," he murmurs back, his arms wrapping around me in a comforting embrace.

I pull back just enough to look at him, my heart swelling as I take in the sheer joy on his face. Then, unable to hold back any longer, I cup his face in my hands and press my lips to his. The kiss is deep and full of everything I can't put into words—love, gratitude, and the overwhelming certainty that this is exactly where I'm meant to be.

The crowd cheers louder, but their voices fade into the background as the world narrows to just us. When we finally break apart, his forehead rests against mine, and his eyes shimmer with tears of his own.

"I love you, Alex," he says, his voice steady despite the emotion in it. "I always have, and I always will."

"I love you too, Cato," I reply, my voice barely more than a whisper. "Forever."

As the cheers begin to die down, Cato squeezes my hand and grins. "There's one more thing," he says, his voice warm with excitement.

"One more thing?" I ask, tilting my head in curiosity.

Cato nods toward the door, and suddenly a little ball of golden fluff bounds into the room, tail wagging furiously. My jaw drops as the puppy skids to a halt in front of us, barking happily.

"Meet Burt," Cato says with a laugh. "I thought Bailey could use a friend—and maybe you could too. Consider it an engagement gift."

Tears spill over again as I crouch down to pet the puppy, who immediately licks my hand and wiggles closer. "Oh my God, Cato. He's perfect," I whisper, scooping the little guy into my arms. Burt's warmth and softness seem to mirror the love radiating from Cato.

"He's ours," Cato says, crouching beside me to scratch Burt behind the ears. "Just like you and me. A family."

Looking between Cato, the ring on my finger, and the wriggling puppy in my arms, I feel like my heart might burst. This is love. This is everything.

INK & *Intuition*

epilogue
CATO

March

The glow of the setting sun filters through the large windows of Eternal Ink, painting the room in hues of gold and amber. The shop smells faintly of ink and antiseptic—a scent I've grown to love, one that feels like home now. My hand hovers over the tattoo machine, my heart pounding harder than it ever has before.

Alex sits in the chair, his back to me, shirt lifted just enough to reveal the curve of his shoulder blade. He glances over at me with that half-smile I've fallen for a million times.

"You sure about this?" he asks, his tone teasing.

"I should be asking you that," I reply, grinning. "You're the one letting me mark you forever."

"Forever sounds about right," he says quietly, and my chest tightens.

Demi leans against the counter near the register, her arms crossed as she watches us with an amused smile. "You're being dramatic, Cato. It's not like you haven't done this a million times before."

"This is different," I say, shooting her a look. She shrugs and goes back to sorting supplies, though I catch her smirking.

"Don't let her rattle you," Alex says, laughter in his voice. "I trust you."

I pause, letting those words settle over me. Alex trusts me—with his skin, his body, his heart. My hands are steady as I dip the needle into the ink, the deep black glistening like liquid velvet. The design we worked on for months is taped to the desk in front of me: a globe wrapped in intricate lines, with a compass piercing through its center. Every detail tells our story—the places we've dreamed of, the direction we've found in each other.

I take a breath and press the machine to Alex's skin, the soft buzz breaking the quiet of the shop. He doesn't flinch, and I can't help but smile. He's braver than I am sometimes.

The first few lines come easily, my focus narrowing until it's just me, Alex, and the design. I've done thousands of tattoos, but this one feels different. Every stroke is a promise, every curve and angle a reflection of us.

"You're doing great," I murmur, my voice low.

"You always say that," Alex replies, his voice muffled as he rests his head on his arms.

"Because it's always true."

Time passes in a blur. Demi brings us coffee at some point, and a few customers come and go, but none of it touches the quiet bubble around us. My hands move instinctively, the design taking shape, and when I finally pull back, I can't help but feel a rush of pride.

"All done," I say quietly.

Alex sits up slowly, careful not to twist his shoulder. Demi hands him a mirror with a flourish, her grin wide. "Let's see the masterpiece."

Alex holds up the mirror, angling it to catch the reflection of the intricate world map with a golden compass in the center. For a moment, he's silent, his eyes tracing the lines. Then he turns to me, his gaze bright and full of something I can't quite put into words.

"It's perfect," he says, and I feel my chest swell.

I reach out, running a light finger along the edge of his shoulder, careful not to touch the fresh ink. "You're perfect," I reply, my voice barely above a whisper.

Demi groans from across the room. "Okay, lovebirds, wrap it up. Some of us have to lock up and go home, you know."

Alex laughs, the sound soft and warm. As Demi flicks the lights off one by one, plunging the shop into dusk, he turns to me, a glint of mischief in his eyes.

"Well?" he says, stepping closer. "Aren't you going to seal it with a kiss?"

I grin, pulling him into me without hesitation. My hand cups his jaw as I kiss him, slow and deep, the world around us fading into nothing. When we finally pull apart, his forehead rests against mine, his breath mingling with mine in the quiet.

"Forever," I whisper, my voice steady and sure.

"Forever," he echoes, and I know in that moment, there's nothing truer.

As we step out into the cool evening air, his hand in mine and the fresh tattoo between us, I know this is just the beginning of our next adventure—together.

ALEX

"Alex, please," Cato whispers, his voice trembling as he lies back on the bed, his body taut with anticipation. His cobalt eyes locked onto me, searching for reassurance. "I want this. I want *you*."

I hesitate, my heart pounding in my chest. I can't tear my gaze away from Cato, who looks so vulnerable yet so beautiful lying there. The faint scent of antiseptic still lingered in the air from my tattoo session earlier, a reminder of the intimacy we had already shared. But this—this is different. Cato hasn't been touched like this since Derek and the weight of that knowledge presses heavily on my shoulders.

"Are you sure?" I finally ask, my voice soft but laced with concern. I reach out, brushing a hand gently along Cato's side, feeling the warmth of his skin beneath my fingertips. "We don't have to do anything you're not ready for."

Cato exhales sharply, his lips curving into a small, determined smile. "I'm sure. It's been long enough. I want it to be you, Alex. Only you."

Hours earlier, we had been in Cato's shop, the buzzing of the tattoo machine filling the air as I sat patiently, letting Cato work his magic.

Now, back at our penthouse, the energy between us has shifted. The air is charged with something unspoken, an undercurrent of desire that neither of us can ignore. As we settle onto the bed, Cato takes the lead, guiding me closer until our bodies are pressed together, and heat radiates between us.

But now, as I hover over him, uncertainty gnaws at the edges of my confidence. I want this—want Cato—more than anything, but the fear of hurting him, of bringing up old wounds, holds me back.

"Alex," Cato says again, softer this time. He reaches up, cupping my face in his hands, his thumbs brushing over my cheekbones. "Look at me."

I do, my breath catching as I see the raw emotion in Cato's eyes. "I'm scared," I admit, my voice barely above a whisper. "What if I'm not what you need? What if—"

"Stop," Cato interrupts, his tone firm but gentle. "You're exactly what I need. You've always been. Derek… that was a long time ago. This is about us. About right now."

Those words break through the wall of doubt in my mind. I exhale slowly, nodding, and lean down to press a soft kiss to Cato's lips. It's slow and deliberate, a silent promise that I'm here, that I will be careful, that I will cherish every moment.

Cato responds eagerly, his hands sliding down to grip my shoulders, pulling me closer. Our kisses deepen, becoming more urgent, more desperate. I can feel the tension building in Cato's body, the way he arches into every touch, every caress.

When I finally pull back, breaking the kiss, Cato's chest heaves, his eyes dark with need. "Alex," he breathes, his voice ragged. "Please."

That single word shatters any remaining hesitation. I nod, my hands trembling slightly as I reach for the bottle of lube on the nightstand. I take my time, making sure Cato is comfortable, easing him into it with gentle touches and whispered reassurances.

As I enter Cato, the world seems to narrow down to just the two of us. Every gasp, every moan, every shiver is seared into my memory. I move slowly, carefully, watching Cato's face for any sign of discomfort. But there's none—only pleasure, raw and unfiltered.

Cato's hands grip the sheets tightly, his body arching as waves of sensation crash over him. "Fuck baby," he gasps, his voice cracking. "God, yes…"

The sound of my name on Cato's lips sends a jolt of electricity through me. I lean down, capturing Cato's mouth in another heated kiss as our movements become more synchronized, more frantic. The room is filled with the sounds of our breathing, the rhythmic creak of the bed, and the occasional gasp or moan that escapes our lips.

It isn't just physical—it's emotional, a culmination of all the love and trust we've built together. And as we reach our peak, Cato's eyes well with tears, though his lips curve into a smile.

"Alex," he whispers again, his voice thick with emotion. "Thank you…"

I kiss him again, swallowing the rest of his words, pouring every ounce of my feelings into this one gesture.

F. A. SENG

Because, at this moment, nothing else matters—just the two of us.

THE END...

MAYBE...

CATO & ALEX WILL RETURN.

Acknowledgements

To anyone who has ever had to come out, thought about coming out, or still carries that truth quietly within themselves—I see you. I know the weight of unspoken truths, the fear that creeps in when you imagine what might happen if you finally say those words out loud. I know how it feels to wrestle with the voices of love, expectation, and doubt, and to wonder whether the people you care about will see you differently—or whether they'll see you at all. I know, because I've lived it too.

As a gay man raised in a religious household, I understand the deep, complex pain of trying to reconcile who you are with what you were told to be. It can feel like an impossible balancing act—faith and identity pulling you in opposite directions, love and fear competing for space in your heart. It's a journey filled with moments of courage, moments of hesitation, and moments when it feels easier to hide. But please know this: no matter where you are on your journey, you are not alone. Whether you've come out to the world, only to a trusted few, or only to yourself, your truth is valid. You are valid.

This book is for you, the ones who have walked this path before me, the ones who are walking it now, and the ones who will walk it someday. I hope it reminds you that your story matters, your voice matters, and you are worthy of love and acceptance exactly as you are. There is no timeline for living your truth. You can take your time. The most important thing is to be gentle with yourself and to know that your identity is a gift, not a burden.

Thank you for existing in a world that can sometimes feel too small for all the complexities of who we are. Your courage, whether quiet or loud, whether internal or shared, is an inspiration. You are part of a legacy of love and resilience that stretches far beyond this moment. You are seen, you are loved, and you are enough.

With all my love and appreciation,
F. A. Seng

MORE BY F. A. SENG

The 'Greylith' Series
Greylith

Interconnected Stand-Alone Romances
Love & Frost
Ink & Intuition (Metro Heights Duology)

F. A. Seng is an accomplished author known for weaving intricate tales of romance, mystery, and self-discovery. With acclaimed novels like "Love & Frost," a heartwarming winter romance, and "Greylith," a gripping fantasy filled with a unique magic system and emotional journey, F. A. Seng has captivated readers with vivid imagery and heartfelt storytelling. In his latest work, "Ink & Intuition," F. A. Seng explores the transformative power of creativity and intuition in an aspiring artist's journey. F. A. Seng brings a wealth of experience and insight to their writing.